THE
WITHERING

"*The Withering* is a compelling story set against a stark dystopian landscape. Patton has put together a gripping scenario that combines suspense, intrigue, and a truly likable cast of characters to cheer on. This smartly written, tautly paced, and carefully plotted tale will linger with you long after you turn the last page."

SHANA DOW
Author of *The Keepers of the Balance* series

"I stayed up into the wee hours and read the whole thing. Superb storytelling . . . Compelling and thought-provoking. It will be a great witnessing tool for the sci-fi/fantasy community!"

DAPHNE SELF
Author of *When Legends Rise*
Contributor in *Into the Unknown: Seven Short Stories of Faith and Bravery*

"I really felt those Perelandra vibes throughout, and the mix of tension with (superbly done) supernatural elements made me feel like I was reading a peer of Peretti or Dekker."

KATE STEIN
Author of the *Earthbound* series

THE
WITHERING

P.S. PATTON

AMBASSADOR INTERNATIONAL
GREENVILLE, SOUTH CAROLINA & BELFAST, NORTHERN IRELAND

www.ambassador-international.com

THE WITHERING

ISBN: 978-1-64960-213-8
eISBN: 978-1-64960-321-0
Library of Congress Control Number: 2022938704

Cover artwork by Louis Strologo of Muhju Art
Cover design by Andrea Patton
Interior typesetting by Dentelle Design

AMBASSADOR INTERNATIONAL
Emerald House
411 University Ridge, Suite B14
Greenville, SC 29601
United States
www.ambassador-international.com

AMBASSADOR BOOKS
The Mount
2 Woodstock Link
Belfast, BT6 8DD
Northern Ireland, United Kingdom
www.ambassadormedia.co.uk

The colophon is a trademark of Ambassador, a Christian publishing company.

For my family

ACKNOWLEDGMENTS

To Judith Anne,

who taught me the importance of freedom and fun, who was always there for me, and who has always been my biggest fan.

To John Michael, Tyler Wade, and Samuel Conner,

I love you more than you know, and more than I care to let show. No one quite understands me like you, and the opposite too, as we were the only four cubs from our litter. I am incredibly proud of the great lions you've become. Geography aside, we are always one pride.

To Lisa Louise,

who taught me how to read, how to write, how to think, how to pray, how to ask the right questions, how to carry myself with dignity, how to respect myself, and how to properly bite my tongue, among a great many other things. I am still learning from you, and you've never let me fall. You are my wisdom.

To Patrick Stephen,

my namesake, who showed me what it takes to be a father, that there is an easy way and that there is a hard way, and that they are rarely

7

ever the same, how to take care of others, how to work hard, how to love ferociously, and how and when to spit, curse, and fight, among a great many other things; and who is still who I hope to be someday. You are my strength.

To Andrea Elyse,

who introduced me to a vast and wonderful world outside of my own narrow scope, who worked my heart, mind, and soul into things far more noble than they ever could have been otherwise, who has known the torment of me at my very worst, and the disappointment of me at my very best, and who every day has chosen to love me anyway. You are my dearest friend, my love, my inspiration, my immovable anchor, my most dependable muse, responsible for countless songs and poems, the beautiful soul to which I'm boastfully bound, above or 'neath ground, or til trumpet doth sound.

To Sophia Pepper and Thomas Phinehas.

You have taught me deep and sacred things which words cannot begin to explain and conscious minds cannot begin to comprehend, things which only our very souls can fathom. You are my hope, my joy, and my purpose. You are the best thing I've ever done, and ever will have done. May God grant you each a stronger faith, a greater mind, and a braver soul than mine.

AUTHOR'S NOTE

The first time I visited another world was my initial trip into Narnia as a boy. I'm not entirely certain, but I believe it was my Great "Grumpa" Don and my late Great Grandma June who gifted me the complete box set of C. S. Lewis's *Chronicles of Narnia* around twenty years ago or more, a gift which I continue to treasure to this day. It was read through several times during my early years, and I am currently four-sevenths of the way through reading it to my children.

Once I'd grown a little older, I found new worlds to visit, most notably Middle-Earth, Malacandra, and Perelandra. In each of these worlds, I discovered something hidden and true beneath the text, yet I didn't understand fully what I was detecting viscerally until my high school years, at which point I dove headlong into the Bible and began to absorb eternal truths that felt familiar, albeit much more real.

One thing became clear to me as I read God's Word. God is the first and best author. The most intricate plot conceived by man is but a dim reflection of God's shining example, which we are blessed to have standing ever before us. J. D. Salinger's use of symbolism and metaphor seemed to me profound until I saw how the Holy Spirit did things—using real human lives, legendary dynasties, and the rise and fall of empires as living types, symbols, and metaphors; with His people and their enemies alike, recording it all for every generation to wonder at.

There was never a time in my life as far as I can recall in which I did not believe whole-heartedly in the one true living God, but there is a time in every thinking person's life when they must decide whether or not they believe, and more importantly why they do or do not. It is not an unhealthy thing to question one's faith, so long as you are honest with yourself in diligently seeking satisfactory answers to those questions. If you are, you will find that Jesus is faithful to His promise that if you seek Him, you will find Him.

You may find Him in ways you wouldn't expect—on YouTube, on the silver screen, in the pages of a fantasy novel. You may find Him in your study of quantum mechanics, in the behavior of photons, in the "Big Bang," in the gravity which tethers us to this Earth, or in the aerospace technology which propels us beyond its atmosphere. You may discover Him in the writing of a song, in the painting of a mural, in the construction of a building, in the taking of a photograph, or in the reparation of a faulty appliance. You may encounter Him in holography, in the coding of software or video games or apps, in the studies of biology, chemistry, physiology, archaeology, or in the process of winemaking. You might see Him in the beauty of a sunset, in the vastness of the ocean, in the solitude of the forest, in the fortitude of a mountain, in the mystery of a dream, in the brilliance of a starlit sky, or in the perfect still of the darkest night.

Whatever your place in life, whatever your passion, whatever your profession, whatever inspires you, whatever you love; one truth unifies all these things: God did it first, and He did it better. We are made to create, to build, to organize, to curate, to inspire, to perform, to teach, to serve, to heal, and to love because that is Who God is; and whether one believes it or not, we have all been made in His image.

One final note. I feel I must mention that the timeline represented in this story is not intended to be taken as a Biblically, historically, or astronomically accurate account. It is meant to be a setting for a fictional story, and nothing more. I want to make that clear up front, because there will undoubtedly be some well-meaning and well-read readers who will point out that my account of events is not consistent with either the Biblical account or the current scientific theory regarding the chronology of our universe. That sort of scrutiny would make Aslan and Uyarsa out to be false idols, and would have the *Chronicles of Narnia* and the *Space Trilogy* (yes, I said the *Space Trilogy* and I won't apologize for it) burned for their blasphemy.

If, however, we can recognize fiction and fantasy for what they are, alight our heads of our cynic's caps, and allow ourselves to be swept away by God's incredible gift of storytelling; then we just might find something hidden and true beneath the text, something eternal and very real calling to us from the fantastic realms of our imaginations.

THE EMPYREAN VALLEY

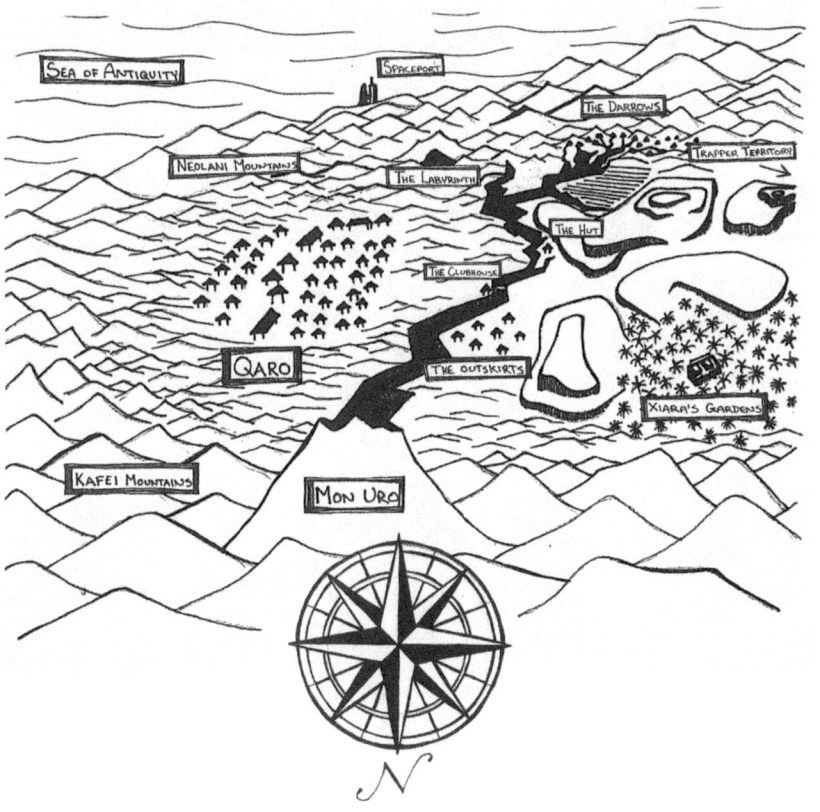

SEA OF ANTIQUITY · SPACEPORT · THE DARROWS · NEOLANI MOUNTAINS · THE LABYRINTH · TRAPPER TERRITORY · THE HUT · THE CLUBHOUSE · QARO · THE OUTSKIRTS · XIARA'S GARDENS · KAFEI MOUNTAINS · MON URO

N

PART I:

THE TRAPS WE FALL INTO

THE SPITTING IMAGE

CHAPTER ONE

There is nothing ahead but death and dying . . .

The words—*her* words—haunted Rho as he peered out at the bleak scene before him. He tried to imagine what he'd find beyond it, what he was now headed toward, and what would await him once he arrived.

The cries grew louder with each step. He paused and tilted his head with a grimace. "It might be a clay fox."

Nod looked to his older brother with puzzled eyes. "Is that really what they sound like?"

"I could be wrong, but I can't imagine what else it could be. I think it's injured."

Nod's lips curled into a mixture of worry and disgust. "It sounds like something being murdered."

"It's a clay fox," Rho nodded as he began to walk again. After the day's long trek, it felt as if his boots had been carved from stone and adhered to his aching feet, and he knew his little brother must be in worse shape.

Wooden poles studded the horizon, equidistant, with wires stretched from one to the next. The poles he saw now were as tall as he was, though only one shadowmark ago—these poles made it easy for him to gauge the passage of time accurately—they had been at least five times taller. They had gradually descended in height as if a great sandstorm had all but buried those he saw now. Some of the poles had fallen over, and one was leaning at an extreme angle, suspended by the wires which held fast for the time being.

Still other wires had long since become detached and laid raveled together along the desert floor. All the poles were covered in foul language, immature doodles, and indiscernible scrawling.

In the distance, steel structures protruded out of the hard-packed dirt at random, remnants of a world that once was. They were all rectangular in shape, often with large antennae, ladders leading up to higher levels, and boarded up doors leading to a forbidden world below. These were the "Access Doors," and they were rumored to be portals to the underworld. They were kept sealed, lest demons crawl up out of the depths and enter the world of man.

They first heard the cry about a half-shadow prior, and it grew louder and increasingly distressed as they drew closer to the poor creature. The road wound its way through a sad little shun-town. There were remnants of stone farmhouses, small sections of fencing, and a few rusted and worn tools lying together on the hardpack; the ruins of a community of survivors that had attempted to rebuild here after the Days To Come. Most of these small communities would never find a way to survive—they either gave up and headed for the nearby city of Qaro or held out until starvation or thirst took them. What remained were scattered monuments to futility and hopelessness known as shun-towns. No one had lived in this one for ages.

The sound came from behind one of the remaining walls. They made their way around the ruined stone structure and found the creature there. It was a small clay fox, just a baby. Its front leg was caught in a steel trap. Seeing it bent and mangled made Rho's stomach queasy.

"He's going to make a nice meal for someone," Nod suggested with a hint of regret masked by a forced optimism.

Rho glared at him, but refrained from calling him an idiot. It was almost a reflex, a dirty habit, and one he was trying hard to quit. They'd buried their mother only three days prior, and he hadn't been able to escape the dark fog he'd been stumbling through ever since. He knew it wasn't fair to his little brother, who had endured the same loss, but maintaining any measure of patience felt a lot like carrying around a fistful of sand.

The final verse of a song his father wrote came to mind.

A greater love no one has other
Than giving your life for another.
Take care of your mother,
Look out for your brother,
When all you have left is each other.

The words were sharper now after their mother's passing. All the more reason to ease up on his younger brother. Nod had already been through enough in his twelve sun-cycles, and Rho was certain things would not get easier for him. That's not how things worked on Noloro.

There is nothing ahead but death and dying.

Rho's glare softened. "He's too small. Probably won't be worth the trouble of skinning and deboning."

"Yeah, you're right," Nod agreed. "Besides, he's just a baby."

Rho threw his pack down and crouched, slowly maneuvering closer. The fox paid no mind to the boys as it thrashed all around the trap. Its injured leg was nearly amputated at this point. After a moment, it began gnawing feverishly at the leg where it met the trap.

Rho sighed and met his little brother's gaze. He reached for the trap, carefully grabbing the spring levers on each side.

"What are you doing?" Nod protested.

"What do you think I'm doing? I'm freeing it."

The frightened creature bared its teeth and frantically pulled away.

"You can't! That's poaching!"

"I'm not poaching it. I'm freeing it."

"It *is* poaching. It's worse than stealing! And it's probably a Trapper's."

"Don't tell me you think it's wrong to free a baby fox from a steel trap. It's the only compassionate thing to do."

Nod sighed. "I didn't make the law. I just respect it, and you should, too."

Rho ignored his brother and pushed down hard on the steel trap levers, but his hand slipped. The fox leapt wildly with an ear-piercing shriek.

"It's not worth it, Rho. It's gonna die no matter what you do. Look at that leg!"

"What then? Do you really think we should just leave it here like this?"

"That would be the smart thing. If the Trappers catch us or track us down, they won't ask questions. They'll just kill us. You know that. Don't be dumb."

"Maybe it's not the Trappers'," Rho said, but he knew better. Either way, his brother was right.

He looked at the little fox with its disfigured leg dangling beneath the steel jaws, an avulsed clump of skin and dark fur matted with thick blood. It was just a baby, such a beautiful young life, something he'd rarely seen in his seventeen sun-cycles. This dead and dying valley did nothing but take, and he hated it. This little creature should have its whole life ahead of it. Instead, here it was thrashing itself to death, doomed to die before its life had even begun.

Not if he had anything to do with it.

He secured his grip on the levers again and pushed down to release the springs. As soon as there was a slight relief of pressure, the fox ripped itself out from between the steel jaws, causing more damage to it nearly amputated leg in the process. The little thing scampered off on three legs, yelping and stumbling. Its injured leg dangled and dragged limp behind it, until it stopped a few yards away and turned to look at the boys cautiously.

"You think we can do anything about that leg?" Rho asked, already knowing the answer.

"I don't know why you did that." Nod shook his head with a mix of disapproval and pity.

"Clay foxes are protective of their young," Rho said with as much certainty as he could fake. "Its mother will find it and watch out for it."

Nod closed his eyes and lowered his head.

"We'd better hope someone's watching out for us."

CHAPTER TWO

Jeema called on the spirits, asking them to provide a protective shield of light as she shuffled the deck in hand. Two of her dorm mates sat cross-legged before her on the wooden floorboards of their dormitory. The third was peering out the window at the enormous moon, its morbid glow illuminating the room with a dim red light.

"What's it like when Lady Virion comes?"

Jeema stopped shuffling and stared at the deck. Then she shrugged and shook her head.

"I don't know how to describe it. It's like another side of me sort of . . . takes over, I guess. It's like it's me, but at the same time, it's not. I know that doesn't make sense. She's like the part of me that knows things I don't and can do things I can't."

"Have you always been able to do it?"

"Really, Martol." Emi slammed her hands on the windowsill. "We're gonna miss it if you don't shut up."

Jeema shared a look with Martol. "Not always." Then looking to Emi she asked, "What time is it?"

"Nearly full shadow."

Jeema took a deep breath and closed her eyes, resumed shuffling the deck, and concentrated on reaching out to the spirits for their guidance. She cleared her mind and felt Lady Virion filling the void, gently yet confidently coming forth from the back of her consciousness, assuming control of her limbs. Jeema allowed it to happen and opened her mind to Lady Virion.

"Hello, girls."

"Lady Virion?"

"Hi, Martol. How'd the exam go?"

"Not well. I couldn't sleep last night and—"

"Shut up, Martol. It's almost time."

"Relax, Emi," Virion showed a cool smile. "We're just getting to know each other a little better. The spirits won't be scared off by a little chit chat."

"I know . . . " Emi said. "I just don't want to bore them to death talking about Martol's stupid—"

"We care, Emi." Beranthia's hand clasped Martol's and Martol smiled back, rolling her eyes and bobbing her head, mocking Emi and mouthing 'no one cares.' Beranthia concealed a laugh behind her other hand.

"I can feel their presence." Virion closed her eyes and continued to shuffle.

"Are they more powerful spirits than you?" Martol asked.

Virion smiled and nodded.

"So if there's different levels, are you higher up, or more toward the bottom?" Martol asked.

"I've been learning for years under the careful watch of a mentor. I was what you might call an apprentice, but I've finally been permitted to go out on my own."

"Go out?"

"That's what we call it when we manifest in a Nolorian body. I usually only go out like this on a full moon, but now that I'm allowed, I'll probably start going out a lot more often."

Martol's eyes grew wide, and everyone could see a multitude of new questions forming behind them. "Where do you go when you're not with us? And where does Jeema go when you're using her body?"

Virion simply smiled. "It's full shadow. It's time." Emi scurried to the floor beside Martol.

"I can feel them. They are here. The spirits are with us now. Whose turn is it tonight?"

"Beranthia went last month," Emi whispered.

"It's your turn, Lady Virion."

"Is it?" After a moment, she stopped shuffling and burned the top card to the bottom of the deck, then she laid out seven cards in a horseshoe pattern face-up between them. She opened her eyes and stared at each of the girls with a calm intensity. She took a deep breath and inspected the cards before her, making her way from left to right.

"This is who I was in the past."

"The Fool?" Martol chimed in with a laugh.

"Shut up, Martol!" Emi punched her hard in the shoulder.

"Owww! Why do you always do that?"

"Because you never shut up."

"All I did was say the name of the card. She drew the Fool, for goodness' sake."

"You're a fool."

Lady Virion waited for silence. The girls turned their attention back, Emi still shaking her head and Martol rubbing her shoulder.

Lady Virion continued. "This is who I was in the past. The Fool: innocence, beginnings, a free spirit." Virion's hand moved to the second card. "This is who I am in the present. The High Priestess: the subconscious mind, sacred knowledge, intuition."

Her hand hovered up to the third card. "This is who I will be in the future. The Mother: beauty, nature, abundance."

"On Noloro? I don't think so."

Emi backhanded Martol's leg.

"What? I'm just saying! Beauty? Abundance? On Noloro? That's the past, not the future."

"No, but remember," Beranthia interjected. "She's not reading Noloro's future. This is Lady Virion's future."

"Wait," Emi put a hand out. "It could also be a literal interpretation, right? What if it actually refers to the Mother herself?"

"Lady Xiara, you mean," Martol corrected.

Emi rolled her eyes.

"Yeah, like I said—the Mother."

"Lady Xiara is the Mother," Beranthia chimed in. "She has a lot of different names."

"Right!" Emi leaned forward. "What if it means you're going to meet her? Isn't she, like, the Queen of all magic?"

"Something like that," Lady Virion shrugged. "I don't know. I suppose it could mean that."

Martol's eyes lit up. "Who knows? Maybe Lady Virion will be a famous sorceress one day. Maybe you'll be famous enough to meet Lady Xiara. Maybe you'll become her apprentice and take her place when she retires or dies."

"You are so dumb." Emi shook her head.

"Lady Xiara can't die," Beranthia said. "She's immortal."

"Shall we?" Lady Virion moved her hand up to the fourth card, at the apex of the horseshoe pattern.

"This is my best course of action. The World: travel, a journey, change."

"What, are you going to run away again?"

Emi refrained from smacking Martol this time and instead closed her eyes, dropped her head to her chest, and huffed loudly.

"Maybe. It depends."

"Well, if you do—I mean, if you really do, for real, this time—I'm coming with you."

"No, Martol." Beranthia grabbed Martol's arm. "They'll put you in the slow room."

"Not if we don't come back." Martol smiled at Lady Virion. Virion smiled back.

"Jeema will never make it across the chasm—I'm sorry, Lady Virion, but you know it's true—and you'll all end up back here, and they'll put all of you in the slow room."

"No, we won't." Every eye shot over to Emi. "Jeema will make it across. We'll be there to help her."

Martol's smile grew into a grin and she threw her arms around Emi, but Emi slapped them away.

"Get off me, you idiot!"

"All right, all right! I'm just glad you're coming with us."

"Me, too." Lady Virion smiled. "What about you, Beranthia? You in?"

Beranthia's mouth moved, but she didn't speak.

"She's not going anywhere," Emi said. "She wouldn't leave this dump if it caught fire."

"I just . . . " Beranthia started. "I like it here. I do. I know you guys don't, but I do. I'm sorry."

"It's all right." Martol took Beranthia's hand and patted it. "Ignore her. I'm glad you found a home here."

"Thanks, Martol." It grew silent again, and Lady Virion placed her hand over the fifth card.

"This is where I'll find my help. The Sorcerer: knowledge, action, power."

"Dartaun!"

Everyone looked at Martol, and even Emi was intrigued.

"Dartaun the Great! He'll be here tomorrow. He's a sorcerer. That can't be a coincidence."

The girls exchanged glances, then Emi laughed.

"So what, Dartaun the Great is going to help three random orphans escape?"

"Hey, I didn't draw the cards," Martol said.

"Let's just finish the reading, shall we?" Lady Virion moved her hand down to the sixth card. "This is where I'll run into obstacles. The Hanged Man: selflessness, sacrifice, surrender."

"How is that an obstacle? Those all sound like good things."

"I really don't know," Lady Virion pondered. "This one's a little lost on me. Sometimes it's a mystery you have to figure out as you go."

Lady Virion's hand moved down over the seventh and final card. "This is where my journey will take me." She paused.

"That's good right?" Martol asked.

"Well," Lady Virion tilted her head and winced. "Normally the Star means hope, purpose, renewal, which *is* good . . . " She paused again.

"It's upside down," Emi pointed out.

Lady Virion nodded. "When it's inverted, the Star means pretty much the opposite: despair, futility, destruction."

"Not necessarily," Emi said. All eyes were on her again. "It could also be the literal interpretation, just like with the Mother."

Again, the girls exchanged glances, trying to grasp any way such an interpretation could be possible.

"I guess it could just mean a star, couldn't it?" Martol asked.

"I don't see how that would mean much of anything, but yeah, in theory, you could read it as the literal interpretation."

Lady Virion collected the cards up and looked at the girls.

"I think Martol's right about Dartaun. The fact that he's coming here tomorrow, the night after the full moon—the night after this reading—doesn't feel like a coincidence to me. It feels purposeful. Spirits don't just go out for no good reason."

CHAPTER THREE

They heard the approaching engines growling long before they saw them, and motospeeders meant only one thing: Trappers.

Not only did the Trappers lay claim to exclusive trapping rights on Noloro, but they also owned every single remaining motospeeder on Noloro, and even if that wasn't entirely true, who would dare to start up an engine and risk a Trapper hearing it? Either way, engines meant Trappers, and Trappers meant death—doubly so if they caught you messing with their food supply.

"They tracked us." Nod urgently spun to his older brother in hopes that he would know what to do, but Rho had no idea. There was no way to hide their tracks out in the open.

"There." Rho pointed toward a series of caves at the base of a tall butte. They ran for the entrance to the largest cave as a storm of dust brewed on the horizon and headed their way.

"They'll just follow our tracks in here! We can't hide."

"We'll go in until it's dark, and then we'll backtrack."

The two boys entered the dark of the cave. Rho kept one hand dragging against the wall and the other out in front, proceeding as quickly and carefully as he could. Nod followed close behind. Once deep enough into the cave, Rho found a foothold and climbed onto the wall. Nod followed suit, and the two made their way back to the cave entrance, back toward the ever-growing roar of engines.

Rho peeked his head out first and spotted the entrance to the next cave over. Their position concealed them from the view of the approaching motospeeders, but for how long? If the Trappers were to round the corner and spot them out in the open, their scalps would be nailed to a Trapper's wall come tomorrow. The engines thundered toward them. Rho's foot slipped, but he managed to keep it from touching the dirt. Trappers would notice even a small scuff in the dirt and track them down. He collected himself, took a deep breath, and transferred his sweaty grip from one jutting rock to another until he arrived at the entrance to the next cavern. He turned the corner, waiting there with his head poking out to keep his eye on Nod, who was moving at a slower pace, not even halfway from one cave to the other.

"Come on! They're almost here!"

Nod shot Rho a panicked look, frozen.

"That section's tricky. I almost slipped, but you've done this a million times! You can make it!"

Nod's eyes moved from Rho down to the rocks near his feet, planning his next move. He lunged sideways, but his foot slipped. His hand lost its grip and he fell to his knees in the dirt. Nod's frightened eyes shot up to meet Rho's. There was no hiding that.

"It's okay, just run! They're coming!" Rho now shouted over the storm of engines. It was too late. "They're here!"

"No!" Nod shouted back. "I'd lead them right to you! I'll try to find a way around to you! There's got to be a passage."

At that, Nod ran back the other way toward the first cave entrance.

"No! Nod! Come back!" Rho watched him disappear into the cave. He knew he should go after him, but what if they came around the corner just at that moment? They would find the tracks either way. He knew he had to go . . . but what if there was no other way out? They'd be trapped. There had to be a better way.

A motospeeder came whipping around the corner. Rho quickly pulled his head out of view and made his way along the wall into the dark of the cave. He cursed himself for not running after Nod. Maybe they could have found another way out, maybe not—but at least they would have been together. Why didn't he go with him? Why couldn't he move?

"Coward," he told himself through gritted teeth.

One after another the engines shut off, five of them total. Rho didn't dare peek his head out to look, but he could hear the kicking of kickstands, followed by the scraping of hurried boots in the dirt and the jangling of heavy chains as the Trappers dismounted and moved toward the entrance of Nod's cave.

"Yooo-hooo!" a deep voice called out. "Knock, knock, knock!"

Other voices then spoke over each other.

"Stay with the horses, Claudio."

"Copy that, Boss Man."

"The footprints match. Two sets. Kids."

"Or women."

"Kids or women."

"You got the torches?"

"Right here."

"Give me that thing."

"Why do I get stuck with this one?"

"'Cause you're an idiot."

"So?"

"So shut up and find 'em, huh?"

"You're both idiots."

The voices faded as the Trappers trekked deeper into the cave. Rho lowered himself to the dirt and stood still, listening intently. Nothing.

How could he have let this happen? He should have run after Nod. Who cared if they saw him? At least his brother wouldn't be all alone in that cave with five Trappers after him. He racked his brain for something, anything he could do to help Nod. He thought he might have a chance at stealing one of the motospeeders. There was only one guard, and though he probably wouldn't stand a chance in a fight, coward that he was, he was fast. If he could hop on a motospeeder, he could draw them away, but then what? He'd never been on anything with a motor before and had no idea how to work the thing. Would he even be able to start it? Even if he could, they'd catch him before he got far. No. It was a terrible idea. Still, he had to do *something*.

There was a faint shout from deep within the cave, but he couldn't make out any words. So the two passages *were* connected. Perhaps he could find Nod before the Trappers did. He wasn't sure how. He had no lamp to see by, and he'd be useless in the dark. Besides, if Nod was back there somewhere, he would head for the light, trying to find Rho's passage. He was better off waiting here and keeping hidden. Or was he? Was it better to stay here, or was he just too frightened to move? He already knew the answer. Nod was brave—brave enough to make the selfless decision to run headlong into certain danger to lead the Trappers away from his brother.

Rho wasn't sure if he admired or hated Nod for that, but he hated himself for his own inaction. He'd let his little brother become bait, while he hid in the shadows.

Another shout, but this time from outside the cave entrance. Then another. They grew louder as the men emerged from the cave. Rho tiptoed toward the entrance of the cave. He saw the motospeeders, kept hidden in the shadows.

The guard—"Claudio," they'd called him—was a thin and scrappy-looking man with long, greasy black hair. He wore a torn and faded black denim vest, baring his tanned and tattooed arms. He methodically sharpened a large knife on a whetstone, and looked up as the voices grew louder, though he didn't move or stop sharpening. Slowly, the voices became discernible.

"Where is he?" This voice was low and gruff.

"We're not stupid, kid!" This voice was higher. "There's another set of footprints, so it does you no good to keep hiding."

Then Rho's heart sank as he heard Nod's voice.

"He's gone. He ran away."

"Some friend you got there," the gruff voice said.

"Guess he don't care about you none, so why you trying to protect him?" the higher voice asked.

"I'm not protecting him. I told you where he went. Besides, he's not the one that let your fox go free. I did. He told me not to, so there's no reason to go looking for him. I'm the one who did it."

Rho was stunned. Nod was taking all the blame on himself. Every part of him wanted to run out and save Nod. Everything in him was urging his body to run out of the shadows to his brother's side, live or die. Something deep in his soul was pushing him out of the shadows and into the daylight, but his body wouldn't budge.

There was another part of him that understood it was no use just walking out there and surrendering himself as well. As long as he remained hidden, there was still a chance he could rescue Nod. He'd have to wait for the right opportunity to present itself.

Still another part of him couldn't help but wonder if he was deceiving himself. Was hiding really his best course of action or was he finding a way to justify hiding instead of helping his brother? He didn't have an answer.

"Tiny fox by the looks of his prints."

"It *was* tiny," Nod replied. "It wouldn't have been worth the work. No meat on its bones."

"That's not for you to decide," the gruff voice said.

"You'd better shut up if you know what's good for you, kid," the higher voice said. "Boss Man knows when someone's lying to him."

The two men came into view, one of them with his hand firmly gripping the back of Nod's dusty blue cloak, shoving him toward the circle of motospeeders. A moment later, two more men emerged.

Rho gathered every ounce of courage to will his feet toward the entrance of the cave, out of the shadows, but they didn't move. He was paralyzed.

The man with his hand on Nod shoved him forward, and the four men surrounded the stumbling boy.

One of the men carried himself with a natural authority and was clearly in charge. That must be "Boss Man," Rho thought. He wore a dark, dusty brown leather jacket and pants with heavy chains hanging about his waist. Deep lines cracked across a wise face with a fierce expression, though Rho figured he couldn't have been older than fifty sun-cycles. As he approached Nod, he reached for his hip and unhooked one end of the chain. The rest of the chain fell to his side and hit the dirt with a thud.

"Where's your buddy?"

"He's gone, and he didn't do anything anyway. He told me not to, but I didn't listen to him."

"Well that's unfortunate, but I guarantee you'll never make that mistake again."

Rho had to do something. *Now.* Trappers were notoriously ruthless and known to kill those who crossed them without an afterthought. But what could he do? If he walked out there, they'd both be captured and whipped, and he'd give up any potential chance he might get to rescue Nod.

The man raised his arm and brought the chain down onto his brother, who turned and covered his head, his back taking the brunt of the chain. Nod cried out—a sound Rho would never forget—and collapsed to the dirt. Tears rolled down Rho's face as he cowered in the dark of the cave. He fell to his knees and buried his face in his dirty palms. Behind him, he heard footsteps approaching. He turned to see two beams of light emitting from within a separate passageway. The other two men headed his way and would certainly find him if he stayed. There was nowhere to hide, no escape into the depth of the cavern, no way past the lights without being seen.

Rho jumped to his feet and searched for any form of escape, but there was none. The approaching light lit up the passageway. There was nowhere for him to go but out. His instinct was to run, but where?

To Nod.

His body obeyed this time, and he put one foot in front of the other to do what he knew had to be done. He emerged from the cave, waving his hands at Boss Man, who had lifted his chain over his head for another lashing.

"Stop! Leave him alone!"

The three men turned, and Boss Man smiled.

CHAPTER FOUR

The mess hall blazed with excitement over the arrival of Dartaun the Great, the infamous sorcerer. Dartaun was scheduled to perform later that afternoon, at seventh shadow. Jeema scooted to make room for Martol. Emi, Beranthia, and two other girls shared a table with them.

"Someone's got loose lips," Emi said under her breath.

"What do you mean?" Martol asked.

"Someone's been spillin' things they swore to keep secret."

"What happened?" Jeema asked.

Emi nodded to the two girls at the end of the table and spoke in a hushed tone loud enough for only their table to hear.

"These two both asked me if Lady Virion could do their reading at the next full moon. Seems the word is getting out about the Mysterious Lady Virion."

Jeema glanced over at the girls, both with flushed cheeks and darting eyes.

"Is that so?" Jeema's eyes went to Martol.

"What?" Martol protested. "You think I've been blabbing?"

"I know you've been blabbing," Emi sneered.

"I just . . . " Martol stammered. "Don't you want to be famous someday, Jeems? I mean, you could be the next Lady Xiara!"

"That's not the point!" Emi slammed her hands down on the table as boys and girls from the surrounding tables turned their heads toward the commotion.

Jeema shook her head. "It doesn't matter," she whispered. "Last night was Lady Virion's last reading at Miss Tilly's School for Orphans."

Beranthia leaned forward with an urgent whisper.

"Oh, don't tell me you were serious about . . . about *leaving* again!"

Jeema looked insulted. "Dead serious."

"Dead as grass." Martol smiled, then shrugged toward the two girls at the end. "Sorry girls, not gonna happen. Lady Virion's taking her show on the road."

The girls gave disappointed nods, stood, and took their trays to another table.

"What is wrong with you, Martol?" Emi's face scrunched up. "Goodness' sake! You keep a secret like a bird keeps grounded."

"Like you keep your cool, is more like it," Martol shot back.

"You'd better learn to shut that big mouth of yours!"

"It's okay." Beranthia held out a timid hand in hopes of calming the situation.

Jeema opened her mouth to speak, but nothing came out. Something across the room caught her attention. Elder Yru was looking at her. He hated Jeema, and she hated him even more. He was pompous, mean, and had a habit of making her life miserable. It was a sport to him, and it troubled her that his eyes were fixed on her now. What troubled her even more was that one of the girls who had been sitting at their table just moments ago was now whispering in his ear. He stood and furiously wove through tables across the mess toward her. Her first instinct was to bolt, but she knew from experience that would only make matters worse. She cleared her throat and caught no one's attention.

"Hey!" she snapped, eyes fixed on the trouble that was nearly upon them.

The other girls followed her gaze and stiffened up at the elder's fiery eyes that now burned through Jeema. Soon the chatter died and the only sound heard in the mess was the clapping of Elder Yru's shoes on the wooden floor. His whiny voice broke the silence with one shrill word.

"Witchcraft?" He grabbed a handful of Jeema's cloak and jerked her up out of her seat. Jeema clenched her jaws and resolved not to cry.

"What's this I hear about summonings and full moons?"

Elder Yru pulled Jeema clean off the bench. The ties at the collar of her tunic cut into her neck as she scrambled to find her footing.

"Anything you'd like to confess in the light of day, Jeema? Or is it Lady Virion?"

"Are you upset that we didn't invite you to girls' night, Elder?"

"Save it!" He shoved her forward and she tumbled to the floor, knocking the back of her head hard against the bench on the way down.

"You can run your filthy mouth all you want in the slow room."

Not today, she thought. *Of all days, not today.* She rubbed the back of her head and did her best to act confused—whatever she could do to garner every last drop of sympathy Elder Yru might have stored away in his rotten heart. It was an unusual strategy for her, but it was an unusual day. Whatever she could do to avoid missing Dartaun's performance.

"Oh, give me a break." Elder Yru rolled his eyes.

"I'm sorry, Elder," she said, looking off into space as if teetering on the brink of consciousness. She couldn't tell if he was buying it, and she dared not look at him for fear of breaking the act.

"We were just telling stories. We weren't really . . . "

"I said save it." He grabbed her again by the back of the cloak, and this time, he grabbed a good amount of hair with it—no doubt intentionally. If there was any sympathy stored up in him, he was saving it for another orphan. He hoisted her up to her feet and prodded her toward the hall.

She had another idea.

"I'll go, I'll go! Just please give me the afternoon. Don't make me wait till night! It's just cruel to put a girl in the slow room at night."

Yru laughed a shrill and heartless laugh, and Jeema knew it was over.

"You think I'm an idiot then? I know exactly what you're doing, you dirty little witch. You will not be watching Dartaun the Great this afternoon, you will not be running away with him, and you definitely will not be seeing any moonlight tonight. It'll just be Lady Virion and the darkness."

CHAPTER FIVE

"Well, now. What have we here?"

"He didn't do anything. It was me. I let the fox go."

"You let this little guy take a beating for you?"

Claudio and Boss Man stood still while the third Trapper ran at Rho, grabbing his green cloak at the neck. Rho reached up behind him and grabbed the Trapper's wrist and was met with a hard knock on the head. He got the message and allowed the man to shove him on toward Boss Man.

Boss Man took a close look at Rho, and his demeanor seemed to change. It was subtle, but Rho could feel the ruthlessness melt into something like curiosity.

"You two brothers?" he cocked his head and squinted. Rho nodded. Boss Man looked at Nod, who had risen back to his knees.

"Some poor excuse for an older brother you've got there, kid. I would never let anyone lay a finger on my little brother. Of course, my little brother's dead. Died in the Days To Come with everyone else." Boss Man spat, then looked back at Rho, studying him. "Then again, you did finally get the courage to come face me like a man."

Courage? Rho knew better. He knew it wasn't courage that drove him out of his hiding spot in the cave. He couldn't leave the safety of the cave to help his own brother, but he could certainly do it to save his own skin. He turned and looked at the entrance to the cave. Apparently, the men had never seen him. They were probably still in there searching for him.

"What's your name, boy?"

"Rho."

"Rho." Boss Man contorted his mouth, as if the name tasted strange on his tongue.

"Why do I know you, Rho? Have we crossed paths before?"

Rho had never seen the man in his life, and he was sure they'd never met. He shook his head, stood up straight, then spit on the ground between himself and Boss Man. It was something his father had done whenever he felt disrespected and wanted to show that the feeling was mutual. The Trapper behind him smacked his head with an open palm, but Boss Man just laughed.

"I think I do know you, boy! What's your last name?"

Rho looked to Nod, unsure if he should answer. Nod stared back, his eyes overflowing with worry and void of any answers, his face smeared with dirt and tears. He looked broken, and it made Rho sick. He realized that it was up to him to find a way out of this for both of their sakes. Seeing his brother beaten for his own foolish mistake sparked something in him. He felt an anger rising in him, and he felt he might finally be ready to do something about it. His dad's song ran through his mind once again.

Look out for your brother,

When all you have left is each other.

Rho stood tall, looking Boss Man dead in the eyes. "It's Perish."

"Rho *Perish*." Boss Man laughed again. "Of course you are! Would you look at that, fellas? This here is Grier's boy. I knew I recognized that face as soon as I saw it, and the way you spit at me like that, just like I seen your pa do a million times. You really are the spitting image of Grier."

Rho looked to Nod, who still hadn't moved. His lips were sealed tight, his head hung low, but his eyes moved back and forth between Boss Man and Rho.

"You knew our dad?" Rho asked. He felt confused, but something told him if he played this the right way, there might be a chance to talk his way out of this situation.

"Knew him? He and your mother saved my life! They took me and Claudio in during the Days To Come. Good people, your mom and dad. Your mom was nothing short of a saint. A holy woman, if ever there was one. That's how we met the rest of these guys, back in the Darrows before Ortero kicked us out of town, but that's a different story. We were just kids ourselves back then, scared and trying to survive. That was when the world started changing—before Noloro hardened us. That was before either of you were born. How old are you now, son?"

There was a definite shift in Boss Man's tone, as if he'd slipped into another time, when he had been someone else entirely. Rho wasn't sure if he should be ready to fight, run, or shake hands. He wasn't surprised that these men had known his parents. The Empyrean Valley had a very small population, and there were only a handful of communities left. As far as he knew, the Empyrean Valley was the only place on all of Noloro where life hadn't been wiped out entirely. For a band of rovers, there weren't many places left to rove.

His mother had brought hope to so many. Her immovable faith laid the foundation for the community of survivors that gathered and built a new life in the Darrows. Rho no longer shared her faith, but he understood the importance of hope. He understood that the Darrows had needed her. They needed something to believe in and hope for when there appeared to be nothing ahead but death and dying. He could respect that, even if he didn't share that hope. Perhaps he and Boss Man had that in common. It was clear that Boss Man and his band of Trappers had no regard for the morality of his mother's religion, but he got the feeling they did hold a certain reverence for her.

It crossed his mind that Boss Man might be simply playing with him, but there was a sincerity in those wild eyes that told him otherwise. Boss Man's entire demeanor had changed as soon as he realized who their parents were. It seemed the only thing he could do now was to answer the man's question and be grateful for their good fortune. "I'm seventeen."

"You believe that Claudio? Seventeen sun-cycles!"

"I don't know. Seems like longer to me, Boss Man. Ain't been an easy road since the Darrows."

"Tiev tells it, but easy or not, I think you and I got *old* somewhere along the way."

"Tiev tells it," Claudio agreed. "Older'n anyone deserves to be these days."

"So how are ol' Grier and Lady Lejin?"

Rho paused, unsure how to answer. His tongue stuck to the roof of his mouth, and it hurt to even think about. He didn't feel present. It was almost as if he was standing outside of his body, watching himself struggle to speak. Somehow he managed to answer.

"Our mother passed away just this week. She'd been fighting illness these past seven sun-cycles, and it finally took her. My dad used to take the mule cart to Qaro every month to fetch her medicine, but he disappeared nearly a year ago. We're on our way to Qaro to look for him."

Now Boss Man's harsh demeanor left him entirely, replaced with a solemn sympathy. Rho was embarrassed by the Trapper's pity and his eyes fell to the dirt.

"You won't find him in Qaro, son."

Rho's eyes shot back up.

"Why's that?"

"I can't say for sure, but I suspect he wasn't going to Qaro to fetch your ma's medicine. I suspect he was going to . . . *her.*"

Rho's face flushed red. How did he know about *her*? He caught a knowing gleam in Boss Man's eye. His eyes narrowed and he cocked his head.

"You know exactly who I'm talking about, don't you?"

Rho's breath caught in his chest. He nearly panicked, but he wasn't sure why. He felt as if he'd been caught in a lie. He glanced down at Nod, who looked perplexed, but Rho got a hold of himself and silently nodded.

"I'd heard he was going to see her. According to rumor anyway. I don't know for a fact, and I never ventured near that cursed hut myself. I've seen too many men lay themselves down in her web, and I've seen what she does to them. Little by little, she sucks the soul right out of them till there's nothing left but a lifeless shell of a man. At some point they just disappear. Never seen one come back once she hooks her fangs in 'em."

Rho's stomach turned and his head began to spin. He felt like his legs might give out. He clenched his jaw and looked back to Nod, whose face was pale and beyond confused. He didn't want to talk about what happened to his father, but if what Boss Man said was true, they had to find her.

"Where is the hut?" Rho asked. He was flat and to the point. He didn't want to talk about it any more than he had to.

"Due west, not far from here—just before you hit the chasm. You'll make it before sundown, only . . . " He shook his head. His voice dropped lower and his tone grew deadly serious. "I don't think you'll find her there."

A surge of adrenaline shot through his body. His hands tingled and his legs felt weak. It was as if Boss Man had just stolen something precious from him.

"Why not?" he asked. He had to nearly gasp for breath as the world began to spin faster.

"I've heard reports she up and left the hut. Don't know where she went off to, but she ain't there no more. Even so, I would avoid that place at all costs."

Rho steadied his breathing. It would do him no good to panic in front of these men. He closed his eyes until the world slowed down again, then opened them and nodded.

"We'll do that. Thank you."

Boss Man eyed him with amusement, clearly not believing him for an instant. It didn't seem to matter to him much in the end, as he eventually nodded. He walked over to Nod and held out a hand and helped him to his feet.

"I'm gonna let you go with only a whippin'. That's on account of your ma and pa. After the Days To Come, wasn't many good people left in this world. They were maybe the last of 'em. I should skin you both for stealing my game, but I have too much respect for your parents."

Boss Man's wild eyes shot back at Rho, and he got the feeling Boss Man meant it literally. How a man could go from beating his brother with a chain to giving them friendly advice was beyond him. It made his skin crawl. The only thing he could come up with is that these were men who had been hardened, corrupted by the harsh world around them. Like Mother Noloro, these men had been stripped of anything nurturing or life-giving, and all that remained was a cutthroat instinct to live at any cost, regardless of those it hurt.

"Thing is, your ma and pa saved our lives, and that's worth more than any fox. You'd better be thankful your parents took pity on us lowly sinners, boys. Do it again, though . . . " His voice rose into a growl as he pointed a finger at Rho.

"We won't," Rho said.

Boss Man nodded and mounted his motospeeder. He started up the engine, revving it several times. A moment later the two missing Trappers emerged from the caves, running toward the group, hands in the air trying to figure out what exactly was happening.

"You're just gonna let 'em go?" one of them yelled when he was finally close enough to be heard.

"Shut up and mount your horse," Boss Man ordered them.

A moment later, the Trappers rode their motospeeders north, leaving Rho and Nod standing alone in a thick cloud of dust.

CHAPTER SIX

The slow room . . .

Jeema had spent far too much time in there over the years. She ran away from the orphanage several times, and each time she received an even longer sentence. She'd come to appreciate the silence and the peace of the small, cold metal locker, and in the darkness she could clear her mind—expand her energy out into the universe. It was here in the darkness, when she first discovered that other part of herself—that secret part of herself. Lady Virion had grown out of her fear, out of her shame, out of her desperation. She had called out to the universe, and the universe had answered. It was there where she had come to embrace the darkness without and within. She could handle an all-nighter in the slow room, but what really rankled Jeema this time was that she would miss Dartaun's magick show.

Curled up with her knees to her chest, Jeema allowed herself to fall into a state of welcoming, and her mind began to search for Lady Virion. If there was any hope for getting out of here, it lay with her mysterious and magickal friend. She summoned her and felt her presence almost immediately. It felt like swallowing hot Rommi Stu on a cold night, and it warmed her body from the inside out, except there was an electricity about it which had been quite painful at first. Jeema didn't know whether Lady Virion's arrival had become less painful over the years, or if she'd simply grown accustomed to the pain, but either way it was a pain she now welcomed. It spread and consumed her until she became a spectator in her own body, and then Lady Virion was in control.

Are we . . . ? Of all the days, Jeema! Of all the days, you chose today to get yourself locked up in box! Do you ever think about how your actions will affect me?

Lady Virion was never particularly kind to her, but today Jeema could tell—she could feel—an unusual hostility within her.

I'm sorry, Lady Virion. It wasn't my fault, honestly. It was one of the—

You are useless! Absolutely useless! How am I supposed to meet Dartaun the Great when I'm stuck in here? My legs are falling asleep from sitting like this. There's no way I can stay in here.

My legs haven't fallen asleep.

Well they're going to!

Jeema shifted her body around to find a more comfortable position. Then silence . . .

I really am sorry, Lady Virion.

Drop it, Jeema. I'm not in the mood.

Jeema let out a sigh. Silence.

I'm sorry, Jeema. I'm just in a bad mood. I have to get out of here. I have to see Dartaun before he leaves.

Jeema knew how important this was to Lady Virion, though she didn't quite understand why. Every time she asked about it, Lady Virion brushed her off. She seemed determined to keep Jeema in the dark. That was fine with Jeema. She knew that if she was ever going to learn how to use magick, she'd have to be patient and learn from watching and listening closely.

Do you think he'll teach me?

Teach you?

Yeah, you know . . . teach me to do magick like him? Like you?

At this, Lady Virion burst out laughing, and it became obvious to Jeema in that moment that Lady Virion had never intended to help her. Something felt different about Lady Virion, as if a veil had been lifted, and she understood that everything up until now had been a ruse. The promise of becoming a great sorceress, the power she'd attain by learning to use magick, it was all a lie. Lady Virion hadn't said it with words, but Jeema understood it in the mind she had foolishly opened up to the spirit. She could feel it in her heart. She felt manipulated and used. Her cheeks grew hot, and she knew there was no way of hiding her embarrassment from Lady Virion. She'd never felt so vulnerable, and all she wanted to do in that moment was to crawl further into the back of her mind and hide herself from Lady Virion.

Oh, you mortals are so slow to understand. Mortals can't do magick, Jeema. Only spirits can do magick. Do you still think I'm here to teach you?

Lady Virion had never spoken to her like this before. While it was becoming increasingly clear that she'd been fooled, she still didn't understand why. Virion had promised to teach her to use magick, to make her powerful so she could protect herself from bullies like Elder Yru, so she could protect herself from ever having to face the same terrible fate as her parents. Why would Lady Virion turn on her? Why would she suddenly refuse to teach her? She could feel Lady Virion's animosity growing inside of her, but she couldn't grasp the reason for it. Whatever it was, she didn't like it, and she pressed her consciousness toward the forefront of her mind, pushing against Lady Virion, wrestling for control of her own body.

But Dartaun can summon a spirit within him, like I do with you, right?

Again, laughter. This time, even more hideous and hateful. It frightened Jeema. She reached out to fill each corner of her mind with her own consciousness, to leave no empty room, to force Lady Virion out. It didn't seem to be working. As much as she expanded her consciousness, the darkness around her seemed to grow blacker and thicker.

How do you not get it yet? Dartaun is a spirit like me. The first, and most powerful of us. He is our king.

But you don't have a body, and he does.

Laughter filled the darkness once again, and this time it was accompanied by intense electric pain through every part of her body.

I don't have a body? You really are stupid, aren't you, Jeema? Dartaun acquired his body the same way I acquired mine! It was offered to him! You invited me in, Jeema! You offered yourself to me!

Jeema panicked at the thought of having given her body over to a spirit. It wasn't like that. That's not what had happened at all, was it? Is that really what she had done? She hadn't meant to do anything of the sort. She pushed back against Lady Virion with every bit of strength in her soul, but the electrical pains increased and shot through every inch of her body. She tried to protest but couldn't find the strength to speak. She sunk deeper and deeper into the darkness of her mind, until she finally surrendered to it and remembered nothing else.

CHAPTER SEVEN

The boys hadn't spoken much since the Trappers left them. Rho inspected Nod's wounds and found several superficial scrapes. There was already bruising up and down his back. Rho felt sick. Nod's wounds were the result of his own stubborn foolishness at the shun-town with the little fox, and of his own cowardice in the cave. If only he'd listened to his brother. If only he'd respected the laws and the powers that be, if only he'd stepped out of that cave sooner and come to his brother's aid before the chain came down. There was no reason they should have been spared, yet the kindness of their parents had secured their freedom long before they had ever found themselves in any danger. He stumbled his way behind a nearby ruin of a pillar and vomited.

When he finished, he sat open-mouthed and sweating, hardly able to think. He heard his Nod approach from behind.

"Thank you for coming back for me."

Rho wished they could avoid the subject.

"I'm sorry, Nod. I'm so sorry I got you into that. You were braver than I would have been. Mom and Dad would have been proud."

"You saved my life."

"I didn't do anything," Rho muttered. "Mom and Dad saved both our lives back there."

Nod simply nodded. There wasn't much else to say about it.

"We're not really going to Qaro to look for Dad, are we?" Nod asked.

"No," Rho said. "Boss Man was right. Dad was never going to Qaro. He was going . . . somewhere else."

"Where?" Nod asked.

"There's a little hut, and a lady that lives there. Some kind of witch, I think. That's where Dad got Mom's medicine."

"Why didn't you just tell me?" Nod said.

"I didn't know how to." Rho sighed and dropped his head. "I'm sorry. I didn't want you to think badly of him."

"Why would I?" Nod asked.

Because he hadn't seen her. He hadn't seen her beauty. He didn't understand. That was a good thing, Rho thought. He didn't need to understand, at least not right now.

"I don't know, Nod. I'm just sorry."

They spent the remainder of the afternoon in a slow and silent drudgery across the twilit Empyrean Valley. They trekked in the long and intermittent shadow of an ancient sky rail, much of which had fallen to the surface. Rho thought of the people who had ridden that sky rail before the Days To Come, flying across the entire valley in less than a shadowmark's time. His feet felt bruised and swollen in his black boots. His thighs were on fire, and his skin rubbed raw where the top of his boots chafed against his calves. He thought of his brother, who had to be worse off than himself, and for a moment, he thought to pray—to cry out to God for help—but he thought better of it and trudged ahead under the shadow of the ruins.

The elders spoke of a time when water ran from the mountains and down to the foothills. When they turned the hard, red earth to a gentle and brilliant green. That was long before his time and beyond his comprehension. Green earth? It was too foreign to envision. As long as Rho had been alive, Noloro was a world of death, nothing short of a lonely and bitter wasteland.

Rho had always enjoyed hearing stories from the elders—stories from before the Days To Come. His mother always read from the Bel Tiev, but he wasn't interested in stories of the afterlife. He had always been more . . . realistic. He wasn't interested in dying. He wanted to live, and to learn about the world he lived in. He found it amusing that the name of the planet Noloro meant "provider" in Tebbel, the old language. The term "noloro" evolved over generations. It was now more often used as an affectionate term for "mother." He found the irony amusing. Given how barren Noloro had become, no longer able to sustain whatever life had survived the Days To Come. As unbelievable as it seemed to him, he knew from the elders that things had not always been this way.

There was a time when Noloro lived up to her name, beginning with her first son, Afir, and her first daughter, Epella. From the first man and woman came countless grand- and exponentially great-grandchildren. As they settled across the planet, the great mother, Noloro, provided for her offspring. Her descendants multiplied and covered the planet, building, conquering, rising, and falling. As a result, they formed what was once known as "The City Between the Poles": an endless concrete sea between the seas, and even over and across seas. The buildings were tall, and their machines were wonderful. According to the elders, those were the golden years of Noloro. Those had been happy times, before Nolorians were all but exterminated by the Days To Come.

The sun now sunk behind the mountains, and Rho knew that they'd soon have to stop and set up camp for the night, but something told him they were close—very close. He wanted to reach the hut by nightfall. He wanted to get to *her*. He *needed* to get to her. He had so many questions, and he knew that she would have the answers.

He'd been keeping an eye open for any sign left by his father's mule cart from the many trips to the hut and back, but he knew it wasn't likely. It didn't matter how many times he'd made the trip all those years ago. By now, the winds would have wiped away any trace of life. This whole valley—the entire world of Noloro—seemed bent on eradicating life itself.

A thought came to his mind. Had he been foolish to trust the man that had beat his brother with a chain? Boss Man had warned him against continuing to the hut, after all. What were the chances he'd pointed them in the wrong direction? Maybe they should have listened to him and made camp in one of those caves, but it was too late now. They'd never make it back to the caves by sundown.

It started to get cold. The mountains were nothing more than dark, purple shapes in the distance. The heavens behind them were bleeding every shade of red, orange, yellow, and violet. From there, the clouds stretched over the sky, extending out from the deep, shadowy range dead ahead of them. Something else eventually appeared out of the shadows, and there it was—exactly as he remembered it.

The hut.

"That's it." Rho's voice sounded unnatural as it broke through the dead air. Nod said nothing.

As he walked toward the little hut on the horizon, her voice echoed through his mind—"There is nothing ahead but death and dying . . ."

The vague shape soon resolved into a small, round hut sitting in the middle of all that emptiness. A little closer and the chimney began to rise out of the roof. Then the door and the window became visible, along with the well beside the hut. The stone fire pit appeared in the front, a large black pot and various cooking utensils scattered on the dirt nearby. A clothesline stretched from the near side of the house to a post in the back of the hut. On the far side of the house, Rho could make out a small stone structure that he could only infer was some sort of altar.

But he did not see her. Not yet. His heart was racing, and he scanned the area for any sign of her. He wondered if she'd remember him, though he wasn't sure if that would be good or bad.

He did not slow down but pushed himself onward until he collapsed against the wooden door. He struggled against the strap of his pack to raise one flaccid arm up to knock on the door.

Nod caught up to Rho and winced as he removed his pack, then slowly sat down on the ground with his shoulder leaning against the rounded wall of the wooden hut. The two boys' mouths hung open, panting at each other. Every inch of Nod's dirty and tattered clothes was blanketed by new layers of dust. After a day of trekking through the badlands, only the faintest hint of muted color could be seen beneath a hopeless gray coat of desert dust that now covered him. Rho realized that he must look much the same.

Rho knocked again and waited, though at this point, he was nearly certain there would not be an answer. His hands clutched at the door's rickety frame to help balance his own. He turned the knob and the door creaked open. The smell of must and mold rose from the blackness and filled his nostrils. He pulled a box of matches from his sack and struck one against the door frame.

Rho entered the dark room and held out the mini orb of light that illuminated very little. His free hand felt along the wall and immediately found a lantern hanging from a hook inside the doorway. He managed to light the lantern before the match's flame reached his fingertips.

The room went from still and black to a dim, dreary dance of red and yellow. Bookshelves stood against every inch of every wall. They were filled with dusty volumes from an ancient time. An antique rocking chair sat off to one side with elaborate scrollwork carved into the wood. Next to the chair was a small side table with a glass vase. In the vase was what looked to Rho like some sort of flower with a long, thorny stem. Perhaps it had been a rose? He didn't think they existed anymore, but he had seen pictures of them. Yes. He was sure that this had been a rose once.

He heard her voice in his mind again. *Don't you hide from me, Rho Perish.*

There was nothing to indicate that anyone had been inside the hut recently. It appeared Boss Man's reports were correct, which didn't surprise him. What did surprise him was that Boss Man had told them the truth—he hadn't pointed them in the wrong direction after all, nor had he been lying about the hut being empty.

In the middle of the room was a large four-poster bed. A folded quilt rested at the foot of the bed, and the images on the quilt caught Rho's eye. It featured religious figures from the Bel Tiev—the Holy Book—and he recognized some of them, though there was something off about these images. They were unlike any depictions he had seen before. They were morbid and even blasphemous, offensive even to his skeptic's eyes. It was such a wild deviation from any religious art he'd ever seen before. Each square section of the quilt portrayed a classic Bel Tiev scene, stories he knew well since childhood, but they were all askew. There was what appeared to be a fire in the background of every scene. Each figure was portrayed as twisted and mangled as if in pain.

Scenes from the creation story caught his attention; of Afir and Epella, the first man and woman of Noloro. Afir fit in with all the others, a writhing black silhouette despairing before a threatening fire. He clutched a piece of fruit in one hand as he melted beneath the tree of knowledge.

Next to him was Epella, but she was different from every other figure. There was no fire behind her. Instead, she posed gracefully before a crescent moon, dressed all in white. A silver snake wrapped itself around her entire body, his head peeking up from behind her golden hair. Rho knew, as did everyone, that the snake represented the devil, or at least a personification of evil, depending on the interpretation of a village's ortero—the appointed religious authority. In the Bel Tiev story, the devil disguised himself as a serpent and tempted Epella. She gave in to her curiosity and ate of the forbidden fruit. She then convinced her husband, Afir, to eat it with her. As the story goes, Afir ate from the tree of knowledge, and immediately knew that he had sinned. He then refused to eat of the tree of everlasting life, but Epella ate from both trees.

He knew the story well. His mother had read it so often that he knew it better than he cared to.

But this picture . . .

There was something about this picture—something so familiar— that crawled up his spine and made everything feel very real. And then it was real.

He could smell the smoke rising up from the images. He could even hear the crackling and snapping of the flames. He could see bright red light casting itself on the walls around him. It danced behind dark silhouettes of the room's surroundings, and he was suddenly very aware that he was not imagining these things. In a panic, he spun around to see the small door of the hut swing open. In the doorway stood a silhouetted figure moving toward him. The figure appeared black against the backdrop of the fire outside the door. Nod's voice emerged from the silhouette, calm and casual.

"I found a stack of dried wood in back, so I built a fire. Gonna put on a pot of rommi beans."

WHISPERS IN THE DARK

CHAPTER EIGHT

Jeema opened her eyes—sort of. She wasn't in control of her eyes, and they had already been open when she woke up. It was an awful feeling, and she felt helpless and trapped. She'd been locked in the slow room many times before, and it occurred to her that surrendering one's body was a far kinder fate than surrendering one's soul. At that moment, she saw nothing. She glared into the blackness before her and wondered how long she'd been asleep. It didn't matter. She could feel Lady Virion reaching out to the spirits. It was a sensation she'd felt many times before but had never truly feared until now.

She could feel Lady Virion close her eyes and focus, sensing the various energies that surrounded her. Her arms crossed her chest and her head was thrown back, raising itself to the universe. She had no control, and she hated the feeling. One arm extended as high as the tiny box of a room permitted, her elbow flicked and her wrist twirled in a circular motion. Lady Virion was casting a circle which extended all around the Slow Room and encompassed the surrounding energy.

Then Lady Virion's voice escaped from Jeema's mouth. "Kind spirits of the South, you have stayed faithful to our cause! The renewing water spirits of the West have left us. The Northern spirits of eternal light have faded from our view. Only you and your sisters in the East have remained our watchtowers—ever present throughout our plight. Great fire spirits, I invite you into this circle which I, and I alone, have cast for you. I hope that we can commune in peace and friendship.

"Oh, mighty angels of fire! I am punished for the folly of another—this mortal to whom I am bound! I ask the spirits of fire to sympathize with my unjust imprisonment! Free me from this undeserved fate! Will you come to the circle, spirits? Ah, yes! I can feel you with me now. Welcome, fire guardians. You are friends here in the circle."

When she finished, Jeema felt Lady Virion close her eyes in meditation, presumably waiting for a sign that the spirits were at work. This was not the first time Lady Virion had summoned another spirit, and Jeema had felt the spirits before, but this time was a little different. She could feel a certain presence around her—and even within her—that did not belong. It felt much stronger than anything she'd ever experienced in the circle. She felt something else as well, something . . . corrupt? Malevolent? She teetered on the edge of a full panic, and the only thing that kept her from screaming was the terrifying thought of being discovered by an evil spirit. Something told her it was imperative that she remain silent and hidden in the back of her own mind.

That feeling of wrongness slithered up her spine and caused every hair on her body to stand on end. Her muscles tensed and she began to sweat. Was it really a spirit she felt? She had always believed that the spirits were there to guide her—that the universe had something good planned for her. Then why did this feel so very wrong? Why did it feel so . . . evil? She didn't know what to believe anymore.

The silence was pierced by a soft voice that spoke—no, *hissed*—directly into her ear.

The Sssouthern fire sssspiritsss are sssso grateful to have been sssummoned to your circle . . .

Jeema's eyes opened, but there was only darkness in every direction. Her heart pumped adrenaline to all four quarters of her body, making her limbs jiggly. She could feel all of it and control none of it. In all her years of practicing divination, she had never actually heard another spirit speak to her—besides Lady Virion, of course. She had always been able to sense their presence, or at least she thought she had. Never had a spirit manifested physically, if indeed it was a spirit that spoke to her now. She felt as if she couldn't breathe. Again, she felt the urge rising up to scream, though she thought better of it. She imagined Elder Yru waiting on the other side of the door and the great pleasure he would get out of hearing her scream from inside the slow room, but she could not imagine a scenario where her scream would compel him to open the door and let her out. No. She'd be stuck in here either way. It would be better to stay invisible and ride it out.

She felt Lady Virion swallow the lump that had lodged itself in her esophagus. She could tell now that Lady Virion was aware of her own presence, and she could feel a tension rising between them, an unspoken warning to keep quiet. Jeema's initial reaction was one of anger, and a part of her wanted to fight back against Lady Virion, to take back control of her own body. Still, there was a larger part of her which insisted on hiding herself away from the spirits, from whatever evil had now come upon her. In the end, she did nothing, and Lady Virion spoke again.

"Spirit, I hear you. You are welcome here. Have you come to free me?"

Yesssssssss...

Again, Jeema's spine shivered, and her limbs went from jelly to lead. She deeply regretted ever having anything to do with these spirits, but what could she do about that now? Now that the evil spirit was here, she didn't want to anger it. If she could just muster the courage to remain calm and avoid angering Lady Virion until it left them alone . . .

"Thank you, Spirit. I am honored by your presence."

The fire ssspiritsss sssympathissse with your ssstrugglesss . . .

I will help you esscape your prisson, but you mussst firssst lisssten to the wisssdom of the fire guardiansss . . .

Do not ssstay here in Qaro any longer . . .

You were not meant to sssit ssstagnant in thisss asssylum . . .

You ssshow sssuch promissse . . .

Now lisssten closssely, Sssisssster ssspirit . . .

There isss a sssorcerer who isssss vissssssiting thisss very ssschool asss we ssspeak . . .

When he leavesss thisss place, you mussst follow him into the dessssssert . . .

He knowsssss the way to the Mother . . .

You mussst ssseek and find the Mother . . .

Do you undersssssstand?

"I understand."

Remember thisss . . .

When you find yoursssssself down and lost and all alone, all you have to do is look up . . .

That issss when you will sssssee your path clearly . . .

The ssspiritsss will be walking with you . . .

"Thank you, kind spirit of the South."

Jeema remained as still and invisible as possible while Lady Virion sat in silence for a moment. The mysterious fire spirit offered no response. Jeema felt her arm reach up again to break the circle and then it grasped the door latch. It released and the small door swung open into a world of blinding white.

CHAPTER NINE

Nod shoveled a spoonful of warm rommi beans into his mouth and huddled close to the fire. The temperature had dropped with the sun, and by now it was cold outside of the fire's warmth. Rho dropped a pinch of brown tobacco leaf into a square of paper and rolled it into a grit. He picked up a nearby stick and placed the end of it into the fire. He used the stick to light the end of the grit and then breathed it in slowly. He then raised his head and parted his lips, and the red smoke escaped like a departing spirit and floated up to the heavens. He tossed the stick back into the flame.

Nod rolled his eyes. He hated that Rho had formed a habit of smoking the brown leaf, but he had already made it clear how he felt about it, and he saw no point in beating a dead horse. He turned his attention to the stars and wondered at how small he was; life was so short and precious.

"Do you remember what Mom was like? I mean, before she got sick," Nod asked.

The question seemed to plunge into Rho's chest like a dagger, and he coughed a pillar of red smoke from out his mouth. Before she got sick? He'd had a million fractured memories all jumbled together, overwhelming his thoughts ever since her passing. Sure, many of his memories were of the poor, helpless thing she'd become. She'd been unable to perform even the simplest tasks, and though the nurse had often been there to help, the vast majority of the responsibility rested on Rho and Nod.

He didn't want to admit it, but a part of him resented her for getting sick, and for leaving them. An even bigger part of him resented his father for abandoning them there with a sick mother. None of it was pretty. None of it was fair. He loved them and he hated them, but he hated himself for hating them. He missed his mother, and he felt free of her, and he hated himself for that, too. There were too many conflicting emotions for him to even comprehend.

Still, there were sweet memories from before his mother had become sick. They were buried beneath a mound of grief, but if he cleared his mind, he could hold onto one for a moment, but no longer. He closed his eyes and breathed in slowly. He saw his mother and father dancing in the rommi field as the sun rose behind them. He saw his father kiss his mother in the kitchen. He saw his mother lifting a young, crying Nod into her arms. He saw his mother and father in the entryway to his room, his mother blowing him a kiss and his father simply smiling before they both disappeared into blackness. Even the sweet memories hurt too much, and he snapped himself out of his recollections, eyes wide and breath short. He noticed there were tears on his cheeks, and he quickly wiped them away, turning from Nod. He drew in another long drag from his grit, held it there for a moment, then exhaled quickly, realizing he had not yet answered his brother..

"Of course, I remember. Don't you?"

"Not really. I guess I was too young to pay attention when she was still well."

Rho looked down into the fire.

"I guess maybe you were," he said. "She started getting sick in my tenth sun-cycle. You were in your fifth. That's when dad started going to Qaro to get her medicine, only . . . "

"Only he wasn't going to Qaro?"

"Exactly."

Rho's voice was muffled by the grit which hung loosely from between his lips. His hands were busy at the moment as he dropped a pinch of tobacco into a new square of paper, then began to roll it. Nod glared skeptically. He didn't want to bother responding to such a preposterous statement, but his curiosity eventually got the better of him.

"Let's say we believed the Trapper," Nod said, "and Dad wasn't getting Mom's medicine in Qaro. Where was he getting it, then?"

"Right here," Rho said. "In that hut."

Nod squinted his eyes, trying to figure out what kind of game Rho was trying to play. He put his empty bowl down and looked around at the ground, searching for something. He reached down and picked up a small stick. Then he pulled his knife from his hip and began to sharpen the wooden stick to a point. It was a habit that annoyed Rho. If you're going to whittle something, then actually whittle something, he'd told Nod a hundred times. Don't just sharpen a stick to a point every time like a dolt.

Rho was tempted to tell him again but thought better of it and kept his mouth shut.

After a moment, the creases of Nod's face softened up, and Rho could see his eyes begin to fill with questions that he couldn't figure out how to ask. They blinked absently for a moment, then they began to scan the little hut, apparently in search of the answers.

"I heard the Trapper say the same thing, but it doesn't make any sense to me. I can't tell if you're trying to be funny or not. I don't know what this is."

"It's the truth," Rho said.

Nod said nothing. His hands continued to work at the stick with his knife.

"Listen," Rho said. "I came with him one time. He was always off to fetch medicine for Mom—supposedly in Qaro—and I had never seen another town before. I wanted to see what the people were like. I wanted to try some different food. I wanted to see a girl, one that was my own age for once in my life. I wanted to get out of the village and see something new. So one morning, I hid inside of the tack box on the mule cart.

"He left at sunrise and traveled till about noon. Just past midday we arrived here, to this little hut. Only, when we pulled up, there was someone here to greet him. Her name was Xiara, but I didn't know her name until later."

"Xiara? Lady Xiara?" Nod's eyes widened.

"What, you've heard of her?"

"It's a name from the Bel Tiev. Lady Xiara. She was an evil sorceress, to say the least."

Rho decided to move past this quickly. He didn't want to get derailed with a Bel Tiev study.

"So we pulled up . . . right there." Rho pointed toward the well. "She was round back, hanging her clothes from the line—the most beautiful thing I've seen in all my sun-cycles."

Nod's face grew red, and Rho wasn't sure if it was due to embarrassment or anger. He pressed on anyway.

"Dad stopped the cart and hopped down. He tied the mule to the hitching post and filled its sack with grain. He seemed so sad. I could tell he didn't want to be here. It seemed like he was almost being forced to go in. They both walked into the hut and I didn't see either of them for a long time after that. I was devastated. It really didn't seem like Dad was there for selfish reasons, but it didn't matter. I was still heartbroken seeing him with *her*. A part of me was so angry with him, but another part of me trusted him and believed in him. It seemed like whatever he was doing was for Mom. It was for all of us."

Nod's face went from one shade of red to an angrier shade.

"See, this is why I didn't tell you," Rho said.

"You should have told me, Rho." Nod was no longer sharpening the stick. He sat, red-faced and white-knuckled, clenching his knife tightly.

"You're right. I should have told you about this a long time ago. I should have told you where we were going, too. I just didn't know how to tell you. I didn't want you to think badly of him. I just thought it made more sense to keep it simple. Besides, I really *was* planning on going to Qaro after we finished here."

Nod stared into the fire and shook his head slowly.

"Anyway, it grew dark, and the lantern burned in the window for another shadowmark or so before it finally went out. I had no idea what to do. I knew I couldn't let them find me, so I just waited in the wagon. Dad never returned until the following evening, so I figured he wouldn't be coming back out to the wagon until morning, so I crawled out of the box and stretched. I was a lot more comfortable, but I was bored out of my mind, and I had all night ahead of me. Dad had an open bottle of fire gut tucked away in there, and a pack of the brown leaf, too. I'd never tried either before that night, and I was young, and stupid, and upset. I tried them both. I didn't know how much was good for you and how much was bad for you."

"It's all bad for you. Doesn't matter how much," Nod cut in.

Rho ignored him.

"I drank and smoked more than one ought to in his thirteenth sun-cycle. I started getting sick, but I held it together. Night fell and I started feeling drowsy, but as I was about to knock out, I saw her walk out of the hut.

"She came out in a long, white gown that shimmered like magick in the moonlight. She walked straight toward me. I hid, but it didn't matter. She could see me right through the closed door of the box. I could feel her eyes on me, or maybe it was just her presence. It was like she was in my mind. She knew my name and she called me by it. I still remember her voice calling to me, saying, 'Don't you hide from me, Rho Perish.'

"So I opened the door, and there she was, right in front of me. When I saw her close up, she was even more beautiful than I could ever describe. When I looked at her—it's strange, but I remember thinking that there had to be a God. In that moment, I knew He was real, and that He was an artist—the first and best of all artists."

Nod gave a skeptical sneer.

"That's the fire gut playing tricks on you. Everybody knows that stuff makes even ugly girls look pretty. You just found out what it does for pretty girls."

"Maybe so, but she also . . . she knew things."

"What things?"

"Bad things. Things she said would happen. She told me that dad would leave one day soon and never come back home. She was right about that, obviously."

Rho looked up at Nod, who concentrated his gaze into the fire.

"She told me about Mom, too."

The pain was so fresh it was hard to even speak about. True, he had contemplated his mother's death to no end, but he wasn't sure how to speak about it out loud. He stared into the fire until he felt that heaviness dissipate.

"She also said the Days To Come were coming to an end and the Withering was now upon us."

Nod's eyes widened at this, and he locked eyes with Rho. There was surprise and a hint of fear in his expression, and Rho could see he had made some connection with the Bel Tiev. Rho desperately wanted to avoid the topic, but he could see that might be inevitable now. He left no room for interjection and hoped his brother would simply listen.

"She said a lot of things that I never would have believed at the time, but now . . . "

"What did she say about the Withering?"

Rho sighed. There really was no avoiding it. He might as well just get it over with.

"She said the sun was growing hotter, and that the moon's orbit was moving closer and closer to Noloro, and that soon it was going to crash into Noloro so hard that the planet would actually reverse its axis. She said when that happened, every living thing on Noloro would be dead within a month. She said, 'there is nothing ahead but death and dying . . . unless . . . '"

Rho's mouth contorted as if he'd just swallowed something bitter. He grabbed the back of his neck and massaged it as his eyes fixed themselves on the crackling fire.

"Unless what?" Nod narrowed his eyes at Rho.

"Unless we escape."

His eyes shot up to gauge Nod's reaction, but Nod didn't react. His expression was unchanged and clearly waiting for Rho to elaborate.

"It's some really off the wall stuff, Nod. She said there's no one left in the South, and that it's completely unlivable because the planet is dying. She said there's an ocean just beyond the Neolani Mountains to the north. It's called the Sea of Antiquity, and she told me I would get to swim in it someday. She spoke of a space shuttle, the kind Dad used to build before the Days To Come. I mean, I remember some of it, but it doesn't always seem right, and it seems to change, like remembering a dream. I might be remembering it all wrong. It doesn't really make sense to me anymore. I just remember her saying, 'When one world ends, another begins.'"

Nod's gaze focused back on the fire, and Rho continued.

"After that, she went back into the hut and at some point I conked out, all drunk and stupid. Dad walked out of the hut the next morning with Mom's medicine in hand and we started back. I hid in the tack box as we set off. I was so sick off the fire gut and the brown leaf, and the cart was bumping all around on the road making it worse. It was awful. I ended up having to open the door to throw up over the side. I tried, but there was no way to keep it quiet and the cart slowed to a stop. I thought Dad would kill me, but for some reason he wasn't even mad. He said he was glad to see me. I think he was too tired to yell at me. He looked like he'd just died and come back from the grave.

"I asked him if he was okay. I'll never forget what he said, and how he said it. He said, 'As long as you, your brother, and your mom are okay, then I'm okay.' I never felt more dishonorable and ashamed of myself than at that moment. There I was, hiding in his cart, reeking of the brown leaf I stole from him, and sick off the fire gut I also stole—but he wasn't even mad at me. He was just glad that I was there with him.

"He never told me to keep it a secret, but it just seemed to be the right thing to do. Partly because I wasn't entirely sure it hadn't been a dream. I think I slept for the better part of three days after that, and everything seemed like a blur. Maybe I was wrong to keep it a secret, at least from you. I just didn't want anyone to think any less of Dad. I can still see his eyes. They were so kind as he looked down at me and said, 'Remember, Rho . . . *'A greater love no one has other than giving your life for another.'*"

"That's a passage from the Bel Tiev," Nod said, not bothering to conceal his irritation as he continued shaving his stick to a sharp point.

"You're right," Rho said, "but I remember it in the form of a song he wrote and used to sing when I was working with him in the fields. He'd sing it often, but only when no one else was around. He made me promise never to let Mom hear me sing it. I was younger at the time and I didn't really understand its meaning, but I remembered it all the same. I guess that was the point. It went like this . . ."

Rho swallowed and began to sing.

I'm taking the wagon out riding,

To visit a lady in hiding,

No mistress, no lover,

I want nothing of her,

Except for the life she's providing.

A darkness is hidden inside her.

She's more venomous than a spider,

She supplies what I need,

By her set price, I bleed.

The lady is truly a biter.

A greater love no one has other

Than giving your life for another.

Take care of your mother,

Look out for your brother,

When all you have left is each other.

"I think he wanted us to know the truth, but we were too young to understand what was happening at the time. He knew he wouldn't be with us by the time we were old enough to comprehend, so he put it into a song. It worked. I memorized it, though I didn't know what it meant. At some point, much later, I did finally realize the meaning of it, and . . . "

"I don't understand the meaning! I don't understand any of this," Nod shouted as he glared up at Rho. His jaw was clenched and tears began to form in his eyes.

"It just meant that Dad was never going to Qaro for Mom's medicine. He came here, to this hut, to the witch. Lady Xiara. I don't know if you were old enough to realize it at the time, but he looked sicker each time he came back with Mom's medicine. I don't know what sort of dark magick she was doing to him, but I'm pretty sure that's what was keeping Mom alive, and slowly killing Dad."

Nod shot to his feet.

"You really think Dad's dead?" His sharpened stick pointed out of one hand and his knife blade glimmered in the other.

Guilt fell over Rho, and he didn't really know why. Wasn't it obvious that Dad had died? Sure, finding Dad was the agreed upon reason for leaving the Darrows, but that was more to placate the disapproving villagers. He figured that Nod at the very least suspected they might not find him. Rho knew the truth in his heart. He'd accepted it long ago. He realized now that Nod was still in denial.

"If you think Dad's dead, then what are we even doing here?" Nod demanded.

Rho responded calmly, "There's nothing left for us in the Darrows. Once we find Lady Xiara, she can tell us how to . . . "

"Maybe I don't want to go anywhere! Maybe I liked it in the Darrows, Rho! Did you even think about asking me? Maybe I had a life there."

"What reason could you possibly have to stay there now? Mom and Dad are gone. It's my job to look after you."

"I don't need looking after, and even if I did, who ever said that would be your job?"

"Dad did!"

Silence. Rho broke his glare and his eyes dropped to his side.

"Dad said it was my job to look after you.

"Take care of your mother . . .

"Look out for your brother . . .

"When all you . . . have left . . . "

His voice cracked to a sharp halt.

Nod's eyes still had a faint flicker of fight left in them, but his expression softened into some mixture of annoyance and understanding.

"Listen, I get it," Nod said in a calm but firm voice. "You're my older brother, and you feel like you have to take care of me, but you don't. I'm gonna be okay. Honestly, I'm more worried about you. You smoke all the time. You tell me that we're going to Qaro to find Dad and now you tell me he was killed . . . by a witch. So which is it? Are we looking for him, or is he dead? Are you lying about why we're going to Qaro, or are you lying about Dad dying?"

"I'm not lying about anything, Nod."

"Well, it wouldn't make sense for you to go looking for him if you really thought he was dead, so I am choosing to believe he's still alive, and that we should keep looking for him."

Rho felt awful. He feared he had just placed far too great a burden on a boy who had already endured too much pain. Of course he was in denial. He just lost his mother. He shouldn't have to accept that his father was dead, too.

"Anyway," Nod shrugged. "You want the bed?" He gestured toward the hut.

"No." Rho shook his head. "I'm good here by the fire."

"All right," Nod nodded as if everything had been reluctantly settled. "Guess I'll take the bed then." He turned coldly and walked toward the hut.

"'Night," Rho offered, but was met only with the crunching of Nod's footsteps in the dirt. Then the creaking and slamming of the door.

Rho felt terrible. He pulled out one of his pre-rolled grits and lit another twig in the fire. Lifting it up to light the end of the grit, he took a drag and held it there for a moment as if to give it time to work, to burn away all his anxiety. Then he let it out.

The hut door opened, and out came Nod, holding the creepy Bel Tiev quilt. He took a couple steps, threw the quilt into the dirt, and hurried back inside, slamming the door behind him.

CHAPTER TEN

"Thank you! What a fantastic audience!"

Jeema crouched behind a table in the back of the hall as Dartaun the Great soaked up the applause from the assembly hall stage. His face was concealed in shadow under a black hooded cloak. The orphans stared back at him from rows of navy blue uniform shirts and white pants.

"You know, I too am an orphan, just like each of you. I came into this world without a father or a mother. Instead of parents, I had a master. I was his slave and I did his bidding. He never loved me, nor I him.

"One day, I resolved to tell my master that I would no longer be treated like a slave. After that day, I was no longer welcome in his house. I was alone, afraid, and very angry, but I am grateful for that now, because it made me strong. There's a lesson here that I think each of you can draw from. I want to tell you that if you ever feel alone or unloved, just remember: parents are overrated. You're not as bad off as some would have you believe.

"Love is overrated. Not only can you make it on your own, but you will be stronger and better off because of it. Don't ever let anyone tell you differently.

"Now, on with the show! Would any of the elders like to volunteer for my first act?"

He pointed to an overweight, middle-aged instructor who brandished his chubby hand with enthusiasm.

Oh great! Another one of Elder Dulner's amazingly fantastic, never-ending stories in the making . . .

I like Elder Dulner. He's nice.

I know. That's what drives me nuts. Every time you start a conversation with him, I have to sit there and listen to him go on forever. Always about the most uninteresting possible thing.

Just because he's not into witchcraft doesn't mean he's uninteresting. He's one of the only instructors here that actually reads the Bel Tiev. I'm glad he got picked.

He may know his history, but he's not on our side, I can tell you that much.

You believe in the Bel Tiev?

Of course I do. Everyone does.

Not in my experience.

Your experience is limited to arrogant mortals. Their vain opinions are of interest to exactly no one. You won't find a spirit who doesn't believe every word of the Bel Tiev. It's not a matter of what you believe, it's a matter of which side you're on.

As Elder Dulner approached, Dartaun the Great beamed at him and shook his hand with vigor.

"What's your name, sir?"

"Dulner," answered the elder.

"Well, Dulner, you look like you've got a good head on your shoulders. Let's see if we can't fix that!"

In one theatrical maneuver, Dartaun the Great flapped an enormous black curtain in the air to reveal a large wooden upright frame. Suspended from the top of the contraption was a blade about three feet wide by two feet high. Next to the apparatus was a wooden rocking chair. A wave of wondrous awe-filled gasps and shrieks swelled up from the crowd. Elder Dulner's eyes twinkled and his dopey smile spread as he turned toward the audience of anxious students and peers.

"Now, if you'll be so kind as to stand right here, against this support." He positioned the Elder behind the structure facing the audience. "Now rest your neck right here in this groove. There. Perfect. Now relax."

Dartaun the Great fastened a wooden board over the topside of the Elder's neck, securing it in place. Elder Dulner was now bent over with his large neck resting directly under the large blade. His bald head extended out toward the audience from the hole in the wooden boards. He smiled, wagging both hands at the orphans and sticking his tongue out at them. The room erupted with laughter and cheers.

Look at that stupid grin. He's so pleased with himself. He's going to be telling this amazing story to everyone he meets for the rest of his life.

Hush. I want to hear this.

"Now, Dulner?" Dartaun spoke now as if he were the prosecution questioning a witness at the town courthouse. "Would you please tell the audience whether or not you believe in the Bel Tiev?"

The sorcerer's words cut off whatever noise remained in the room. Elder Dulner's face became stern and disapproving.

"Now hold on just a tick," Dulner rebuked. "Maybe you find this picture amusing, but given our town's history, this brand of theater is deeply insensitive, to put it mildly. Truth be told, it's quite cruel—and hurtful, even—to every single person in this room."

Dartaun's eyes seemed to light up with a half-hearted attempt to hold back a smile, and his tongue made a quick sweep across his upper lip. He knelt down to Dulner's level and brought his pasty face within an inch of Dulner's sweaty, bald head.

"Who said this was theater, Elder Dulner?" The magician's voice was supernatural and haunting. He whispered, but somehow—even at the far end of the hall—she could hear every word as clearly as if he'd whispered into her ear. It dripped with malice and a sick pleasure that made Jeema's skin crawl. It was the sensation she experienced when she encountered the slithering spirit in the slow room.

Lady Virion snorted a chuckle that reminded Jeema of a hog. She reached her hand up to brush her white hair from falling in her eyes, and it was the first time she'd been able to control her body. Lady Virion was distracted with the show, it seemed. Jeema took note of this, but remained still. She wanted to see the show as well. She just hoped that Lady Virion would leave her alone once the show was over. In any case, she was starting to suspect that this really wasn't a show at all.

She noticed Dulner's eyes growing desperate as he searched the room for anyone who might come forward and help him. No one moved. The elders sat frozen. The students were paralyzed. There was only a ruthless silence. In the end, Elder Dulner resigned himself to the situation. Whatever hope was left vanished from his eyes and in its place was resignation.

"I do believe in the Bel Tiev," Dulner declared. "I believe in it with all my heart."

Dartaun squinted his eyes and pursed his lips in a comedic fashion, as if he'd just licked a lemon.

"Oooh. Wrong answer!" he exclaimed.

He rose to his feet and once again addressed the audience.

"Now I want to hear everyone in the audience say, 'Goodbye, Elder Dulner' on three. Is everybody ready? Here we go! One. Two. Three!"

"Goodbye, Elder Dulner . . . " the crowd of uncertain orphans mumbled. Most of them knew something was off but didn't quite grasp the gravity of the matter.

The sorcerer let out a giddy shriek and yanked on a handle, causing the giant blade to free-fall down its track. The blade sunk into Elder Dulner's thick neck, cleaving muscle and tissue, crushing bone, and completely separating head from body. There was a sharp shriek from one of the elders closest to the stage. Her hand shot out as if to erase the brutal scene before her. Bright red blood spurted into the audience as the elder's head was sent spinning away from his body like a top. It eventually came to rest off to one side of the stage, and once again the crowd burst out. This time it was with a unified gasp accented by horrified screams. They lasted but a few seconds before succumbing to an uneasy silence.

Behind the blood-spattered blade, Elder Dulner's lifeless body rested upon the wooden supports. His arms, which had only seconds before waved playfully at the students, now hung limp and swung sickeningly from side to side. The blood had stopped squirting from his severed neck and now it simply spilled out onto the stage, forming a gruesome puddle.

It's a trick right? An illusion! He's okay, isn't he?

That was no trick, Jeema . . .

Oh, please be okay, Elder Dulner! Please let it be a trick!

He's dead, Jeema.

Dartaun the Great lifted Dulner's body from where it rested and dragged it to the rocking chair. A stream of crimson trickled down to the floor and the audience gasped once more. Many people hid their faces behind trembling hands, unable to watch.

Dartaun propped the decapitated body up in the rocking chair so that it sat facing the audience. As he let go of the body, the chair began to rock back and forth with an ear-splitting groan. The sorcerer sauntered toward the elder's head and bent down to inspect it. Then he picked it up and walked back toward Dulner's body with the decapitated head in hand. Standing behind the rocking bag of flesh, Dartaun the Great lifted Dulner's head above his own and held it there. After a short pause, he plunged it down with brutal force onto the elder's neck, shouting "Live, Dulner! Live!"

Blood ran down from the raw edges of the dead man's neck and down the body, leaving dark red, brown, and black stains on his jovial yellow shirt.

I'm getting sick.

I've never seen anything like it.

Jeema felt nauseous and dizzy. She leaned up against the wall for support but was instantly lifted by someone. It was Lady Virion. She had taken control once again. She stood straight up and Jeema could feel a psychotic smile forming on her own face. How terrible it would look if anyone were to see her. She could sense a nearly uncontainable excitement rising in Lady Virion, and it infuriated her.

With one hand, Dartaun the Great pulled a long, black scarf out of seemingly nowhere and wrapped it around the elder's butchered neck. He began vigorously massaging and kneading the neck through the scarf. His eyes appeared to have sunk into the sockets, and he worked his hands in a furious rhythm, as if in some sort of trance. This went on for about thirty seconds until a whimper was heard and the dead man's eyelids began to flutter. Whispers reverberated throughout the hall and eventually condensed into a steady, anxious hum. The elder scanned the room, releasing an enormous yawn. Elder Dulner was alive.

That was too much for me. I don't care if it was an illusion.

I told you already—that was no illusion.

What are you saying, exactly?

That was magick, Jeema. Real, dark magick.

"Now then," Dartaun the Great began again. "Welcome back, Elder Dulner. Everyone say hi to Elder Dulner!"

The audience mumbled something, but it was muddled by the sobbing of children and the harsh whispers of enraged elders. Elder Dulner began to unwrap the scarf from around his neck as Elder Brii hurried up to the stage. As she approached the center of the stage, her right foot slipped in the pool of blood, and she went reeling. She let out a sharp yelp but managed to catch her balance. She collected herself and continued to center stage with a frightened yet determined look on her pale face. It had become apparent to everyone that the show was over.

Time to go.

With all eyes on the stage, Jeema once again became a passenger in her own body. Lady Virion was able to slip out the back without being noticed. As Jeema was carried down the hall to her own bedroom, she could hear Elder Brii's voice trailing behind her.

"Students and faculty—That will be all for today. I'm afraid this is not the type of entertainment we'd hoped to provide for you. Elder Siggie, if you'll begin dismissing the children, I'm going to see our guest out . . . "

She had a sinking feeling they were about to be caught. With nothing to do but watch, she found herself scanning the halls in her periphery, certain that Elder Yru would be waiting around each corner they rounded. Finally, they entered her bedroom and Lady Virion locked the door behind them. She grabbed Jeema's runaway bag—her sleeping bag strapped to its underside—from under the bed and then knelt in front of a white dresser. She pulled open the bottom drawer and retrieved a clean and neatly folded cloak. She threw it around her and quickly fastened the ties. It was a beautiful teal color, with gold trim along the edges. Jeema embraced the warmth of it. It wasn't the cloak itself, but the memories which her past had woven into the cloak which warmed her soul.

Down on her knees again, Lady Virion pulled the bottom drawer out—all the way out. She placed the drawer off to the side and reached into the opening where it had been. She pulled up a floorboard and fished out a deck of cards held together by a brass clip, then threw it into her bag.

Next, she pulled out a thick book bound in black leather. Inscribed on its face in gold letters were the words "Bel Tiev." Lady Virion didn't put this in the bag but left it lying on the floorboards next to it. Jeema didn't read the Bel Tiev as much as she should, but she was suddenly terrified at the thought of not taking it with her. Next, Lady Virion pulled out a small, chimiwood jewelry box. She threw this on the ground next to the Bel Tiev.

Please.

They're just dead weight.

Please.

Her plea was desperate. The thought of parting with her father's book and her mother's jewelry box broke an emotional dam that could not be held back, and she hammered Virion with the full force of it. Jeema was certain that Virion understood the importance these items held. Whether she would take them with her or not remained to be seen. Would she really be so cruel as to leave them? Perhaps if Jeema continued pushing back hard enough, Lady Virion would simply take the path of least resistance. Before Jeema finished the thought, she saw her hands reach down and place both items into her bag. She could breathe again and realized just how tense her body had become in that moment. Perhaps she had more control of the situation than she'd first thought.

Thank you.

Can we go now?

Yes, please.

I won't miss this place. Not at all.

She sprung to her feet and headed out the door. She didn't bother to replace the floorboard or the drawer.

Neither will I.

CHAPTER ELEVEN

The clay fox wouldn't die. Its blood-curdling cry had been carrying through the thin night air for some time now, robbing Rho of any hope of sleep. When it first started, it broke the dead silence, nearly stopping his heart. He judged it to be nearly three spans away, which meant it was likely right there near the shun-town where they left it. Nod had run out of the little hut and scanned the darkness beyond the campfire. It only took a moment before they both realized what it was, and when they did, Nod glared angrily at Rho. He said nothing, but Rho knew exactly what he meant. After he'd made his point, Nod retreated into the hut.

The cries grew louder and more insufferable the longer it went on. It was unbearable. Visions of Boss Man whipping Nod flashed in his mind. Closing his eyes did nothing. He should have listened to Nod. He imagined the little fox out there all alone in the dark searching for its mother. Lost, alone, broken. Like him. The fact that it was still close by the shun-town all these shadowmarks later told him that the poor thing couldn't even walk.

There was no question that Nod had been right. He should have put the poor creature out of its misery. It would have been much easier for the little clay fox, and much less painful. Given that there was no fixing the leg, it would have been the merciful thing to do. Rho lay awake, haunted by a foolish decision.

It wasn't the lack of sleep that bothered him. It was the guilt. With every tortured cry, Rho's heart wrenched itself tighter until he could hardly stand it. He'd had enough of pain and suffering. He'd had enough of death following him—taunting him. He hoped the Trappers were near enough to hear the cries and relieve it swiftly of its pain.

He wanted to believe that the fox would be okay. That it had its whole life ahead of it—that things would get better for it. It was only wishful thinking. Why couldn't he just accept the inevitable? If he'd had his eyes open, he would have seen that the little clay fox never had a chance at survival. It simply had no way of escaping its fate. It was destined to die before its life had really even started. He fixed his gaze on the falling moon and wondered if he and his brother would face a similar fate. He shook his head and refused to think about such things.

Rho didn't know much about the night sky, but he could at least find the twelve guardians. The group of stars directly above him formed Mabo, the serpent. Mabo's tail pointed toward A'uhsei, the king who had conquered death and chased the serpent Mabo across the heavens, according to lore.

Rho's eyes tracked the path from A'uhsei to Mabo and continued across the sky to Aragyn, who was usually depicted as half-woman and half-spider. Rho couldn't remember the lore surrounding Aragyn. He had known these tales as a child, but whether because of the passing of years or because he was now half in a dream, the story of Aragyn eluded him. Instead, he saw Lady Xiara standing before him, shimmering like a field of stars. Her voice was a whisper, and her eyes glowed red as the falling moon.

"There is nothing ahead but death and dying . . . "

Sometime before sunrise sleep took hold of Rho, and the animal's cries grew thinner until they faded into a callous silence.

CHAPTER TWELVE

From the outskirts of town, Jeema remained silent as Lady Virion scanned the empty stretch of road leading out of Qaro from their vantage point in an old buso tree. With Virion in control, Jeema was reduced to a mere voice inside her own head, though she was afraid to even think too loudly. Virion chewed on a buso leaf and Jeema felt an expected and welcome calmness begin to spread through her. The minty leaf made her tongue tingle and left a smoky aftertaste.

From her seat on the lowest branch of the big buso, she was shaded from the wrath of Sol, the Nolorian Sun. She spotted a small bird's nest wedged between a branch and the tree's trunk just above her. She had seen this once before as a little girl, and her father lifted her up to see the little pink eggs. It was rare to see new life in such a world as this.

That might be useful. If we're going out into the desert, I mean.

Jeema could feel Lady Virion's impatience, but only for a second. She seemed to relax and relent. Was it the buso leaf that had caused Virion to ease up? She didn't know.

Go ahead, then.

Jeema found herself in full control of her body again. It felt surreal and strange, like crawling out into the harsh light after a long night curled up in dark of the slow room. She brought herself to her knees and grabbed onto the nest-bearing branch for balance. The nest was small, with enough room for one little egg. It was bright orange with white spots and a shattered, jagged top. The little baby had made a real nice meal for some pokey mouse, or a black joran—the renowned "cannibal of the sky." The top of the shell lay up against its base.

She opened her bag and pulled out her mother's chimiwood jewelry box. It was one of the few possessions she was able to retain after her parents' deaths. In the old days, there had been laws that would have allowed Jeema to inherit her parents' belongings. She might have even lived in their home after their passing, or so she'd been told. When the Days To Come changed the face of Noloro, it changed the way things were done everywhere.

"No such love for an orphaned child," Elder Dulner had once commiserated.

Inside of the jewelry box were matches, bandages, a small sewing kit, cloth strips, shears, wire, a compact mirror, candles, lip balm, and other such useful items. She wrapped the nest carefully in a strip of cloth. She would be grateful for the little nest tonight when it was dark and cold. She picked a handful of buso leaves and placed them neatly in a small pouch inside her pack.

She began to close her pack and then paused. She reached her hand back in and pulled out her deck of cards, removing the band from around them. She rifled through and quickly found the card she was after. The illustration on the card showed a beautiful woman clothed in black. She stood entangled in vines, wading in a sparkling blue stream amidst a thriving forest. Her flowing blonde hair was adorned with pink feri flowers. Her right arm was outstretched, her fingers clutching a silver apple. In her left hand, she cradled two yellow birds. Wrapped around her waist and peeking up over her neck was a silver snake with shining black eyes and a forked black tongue.

The Sorceress.

CHAPTER THIRTEEN

Peaceful sleep and pleasant dreams were two things Rho hadn't experienced in the nights since his mother's passing. Instead, each night his subconscious mind forced him to relive moments which his conscious mind had attempted to bury. They haunted him, unwelcome and uncontrollable, clawing at his heart and twisting in his stomach.

Tonight, he was back in the Darrows, enduring the endless droning of the village ortero, Loah. Her words pulsed against his eardrums until he could no longer decipher any meaning. He tried to listen when the service began, but it was no use. The swirling storm of emotional debris overwhelmed him. It gained momentum as the ortero went on and on—as if it were feeding on her words—and so he abandoned his efforts.

The mid-morning sun unleashed an infinite array of blinding beams. They ricocheted off the desert sand like a boundless mirror. Rho kept his eyes shut.

Though he could not seem to focus on the otero's words, he knew well enough what she would say. He'd been to nine, maybe ten funerals—he'd lost count—in his seventeen sun-cycles. Loah had officiated them all, and Rho had caught on to her game.

Loah had a formula for the program of her funeral services. There was always a small section tailored specifically to the respective individual. Aside from that, every service was exactly the same. Even so, he had a pretty good idea of how the personalized part of this service would sound as well.

She would go on about what an incredible impact his mother had made on the village. How hard she worked to bring hope to a small group of terrified survivors stranded in the middle of a desert. How she established a small community where they could start to rebuild after the Days To Come.

The rest of the service would consist of the same old relevant and moving passages out of the Bel Tiev.

For a brief moment, the ortero's formulaic eulogy anchored him. True, it was predictable and juvenile, but it was familiar. The calm would not last, however, and soon his mind tossed about once again with feelings of guilt, fear, and regret.

Then there was only chaos. Cohesive thoughts which once formed concrete structures in his mind were now gone. He couldn't even remember the places where they had once stood. Ideas, facts, and opinions—they were all gone from his mind. The cerebral storm had obliterated everything, leaving hopeless jigsaw flotsam in its wake.

"You're home now, Lejin."

The ortero's final words stretched out across his mind like an elegant rainbow. It was as if a fierce ribbon of light had driven away the subdural storm that had raged only moments ago.

You're home now, Lejin . . . Throughout her life, his mother had made it known that the Darrows was not her home. Noloro was not her home. Lejin did not consider herself lucky that she had survived the Days To Come. No, it was not luck, but something else. Something bigger. She spoke of it like a sort of commission.

She would often say, "I don't know why God left us here, but I am very certain that he had a reason for it." It was something to that effect. "We must have a purpose yet," she'd opine with a smile. She spent the rest of her life trying to fulfill that purpose.

Purpose. It had to be the most frequently used word in his mother's vocabulary. Rho heard the word so many times that he had forgotten the meaning. His mother tried to instill a sense of purpose into her boys, but it was a struggle with Rho. He had always been too afraid that slaving away in the rommi fields was his true purpose. He watched nine or ten of his fellow villagers waste the final years of their lives working those fields. He pitied them—how they slaved day in and day out until they became too old or sick to keep it up. The saddest part was that once they could no longer work, it was not long before they gave up completely. They stopped caring, convincing themselves that their purpose in life was to work the rommi fields. Then once they could no longer work, it was gone—no more purpose—and that was it for them. No other reason to live.

His mother's purpose was a little bit different. Hers was much more noble, Rho thought. Lejin would tell them that her purpose was to bring her people back to the Lord. To teach them to live fruitful lives. To teach them to serve the Lord, even in these times. To make sure that when He calls them back home, they will be welcomed into the Lord's Kingdom. That is how Lejin saw her purpose.

Rho saw his mother's purpose from a different—more enlightened—perspective. He didn't believe in magickal kingdoms in the sky. He did once. But now his faith rested in what his eyes could see and what his mind could deduce.

He'd seen so much death in his short life, and there was no hope to be found—no escape from the Withering of Noloro. She was right.

His eyes and his mind had edified his faith in the one thing he truly believed in.

There is nothing ahead but death and dying.

Rho thought his mother's faith was both naïve and foolish, but he also knew it was what the Darrows needed. The people of their village needed something to hold on to. Most of these people had actually been around during the Days To Come. They suffered a fate of watching the world they knew vanish around them. Rho got the sense that even though the old world was gone, many of the older villagers' minds were still tied to it. Everything they'd ever known existed within the context of the Noloro they belonged to. And now it was gone. The Days To Come had come and gone, and taken everything from them.

Almost everything. His mother Lejin was able to protect the most important thing from disappearing. Hope. Even if Rho thought it was a false hope, he knew that these people had needed it to survive. He no longer shared it with them, but he was glad they had that hope. He was glad they had her.

That was Lejin's purpose.

The last of the mourners knelt to place a bouquet of fresh white palentines at the foot of a wooden cross. He offered a silent prayer, and then shot to his feet, hastening toward the rommi fields. Rho's eyes followed the man. His skin was leathery, and his wrinkles were deep. His eyes revealed a quiet desperation that his cracked lips would never utter. He shoved his calloused hands into a pair of work gloves, threw a lopsided bag over his shoulder, and headed out. Beyond him, the other men were already back to work.

"I'm sorry for your loss, boys." It was the voice of the ortero. She had the voice of a woolen shirt—warm and comforting in theory, but it sometimes rubbed Rho the wrong way. Rho turned his attention to her.

"Your mother was an inspiration to this village, and she will be terribly missed. Still the sun never ceases in stealing our crops, even in our time of grieving."

Nod's teary eyes looked up at her. "Ortero Loah, may I have just a moment to pray for my mother before I go back to the fields?"

The ortero offered a gentle smile. "Certainly, Nod. You go and pray for your mother, but not for too long, mind you. When you're finished, you hurry back to work like a good boy."

"I will. Thank you, Ortero Loah." Nod trotted back toward his mother's grave and plopped down on his knees. Rho watched him fold his hands, close his eyes, and bow his head. He could see the boy's mouth begin to move, but heard nothing.

"And you, my child." The ortero directed her sugary voice to Rho. "What about this example you're setting for your little brother? While the sweat runs down the backs of the men in the field, the tears run down his face as he rests here with the women."

A storm began to brew in Rho's mind. Thoughts collided and scattered. He hated her. He hated the rommi fields. He hated the Darrows. He fought a strong impulse to yell at the cruel woman, but all he could manage was to lower his eyes and nod his head in shameful agreement.

She put her hand on his shoulder. "I suppose it's not entirely your fault, Rho. After all, you are the spitting image of your father."

It was in that moment that Rho mustered enough courage to leave the Darrows.

CHAPTER FOURTEEN

It was at least half a shadow before she saw Dartaun the Great approaching. Jeema felt Lady Virion tense up and lower herself from her branch as she dropped to the ground. She brushed the remnants of tree bark and twigs off the front of her tunic, and by then the sorcerer was drawing near.

As he approached, Jeema fought the urge to run. Was running even an option, or would Virion use those electrical pains and cause her to pass out again, like she did in the slow room? Where would she even go if she tried? She certainly couldn't go back to Miss Tilly's now. She thought it best to stay on Lady Virion's good side as much as possible. She remained quiet as Lady Virion stood up straight and cleared her throat. She could sense Virion trying to evoke a confidence from within herself. Interesting. Lady Virion was nervous to speak to Dartaun the Great. Was that what the buso leaf was for—to calm her down before she spoke to Dartaun?

If the sorcerer noticed her, he didn't show it. He never even looked at her, walking right on past her as though she were just another buso tree along the way. Lady Virion hurried after the sorcerer and easily caught up, slowing her pace to match his. As she opened her mouth to introduce herself, Dartaun beat her to the punch.

"Am I speaking to the lady or the orphan?" he asked.

We've never met him before. How does he know?

Don't think another word, Jeema.

"My name is Lady Virion."

"Ah, Virion! It's a pleasure to meet you, Little Moon."

"Little Moon?"

Dartaun smiled.

"Two spirits coexisting, and yet, the world only ever sees one of them at a time. One bathes the world in a warm and cheery light, while the other surrounds itself in darkness. That would be you, Little Moon!"

Jeema felt her body began to clench up. Virion drew in a sharp breath and once again addressed the sorcerer.

"A Southern spirit commanded me to follow you."

A faint smile appeared on Dartaun's face.

"That's funny." He smiled. "A spirit told me that two beautiful young ladies would accompany me on my journey."

"Are you going to see the Mother?"

His excited smile spread into a stone lipped grin, and he leaned in toward Jeema to whisper, "She goes by many names, but yes. I am going to see her. Most people know her as Lady Xiara. She's a very beautiful and very powerful sorceress. You'd like her, Jeema."

Jeema's heart jolted when he spoke her name.

How did he know my name?

How would I know? I told you to stay quiet!

Jeema was overwhelmed with a need to get away. She felt something dark around Dartaun. Without thinking, her hands pulled the deck of cards out of her bag and untied its cords. She began to shuffle them nervously, a habit she had picked up to ease her anxiety. For some reason, Lady Virion hadn't stopped her. Perhaps she was too nervous and distracted to even notice? Perhaps it was the buso leaf dulling Virion's senses, letting her guard down?

"Let me see those cards, Little Sun." Dartaun smiled.

He's talking to me.

Virion's disgust burned through her mind like a wildfire.

Well, go on, then.

The sorcerer held his hand out and received the deck from her without question. He began shuffling the deck. After a moment, he held the deck still in his hands.

Dartaun cut the deck and then flipped the top card over. The illustration on the card appeared upside down, so he flipped it to view it properly. He studied it for a moment with an amused smirk. He then handed the card to Jeema. The central figure of the card was a young man in a white robe. The man stood before what appeared to be a stone altar, over which his arms were outstretched. Hovering about him were four objects; a water drop to his right, a leaf to his left, a cloud and lightning bolt above his head, and a flame below him. Around the man's waist, where a sash might belong, there was a serpent who appeared to be eating its own tail.

You know what that means, don't you?

Of course I know what this means. The Mage. It's no surprise that Dartaun drew this card. He's a sorcerer, after all. The Mage represents transformation and change, especially in eternal affairs. It's a new beginning. He represents finding truth through the power of your own intuition.

I've lived with you long enough to know what the Mage card represents, but he didn't draw the Mage, did he?

You saw him draw it.

No. It was inverted when he drew it. I know you saw that and I know you know what that means.

Lady Virion was silent. Jeema could feel her resentment burning hot, but only for a second. It died down quickly and Jeema could feel Virion recognizing and letting go of her denial.

Yeah . . . I know what it means.

The interpretation of the card is still valid, but it is to be viewed not as a gift, but as a warning. At the very least, he is not to be trusted. Should we really be following him? It could be dangerous.

Dangerous for you, perhaps. Not for me.

"Tell me, Little Sun, are you familiar with the prophecy of the egg?"

Answer him.

"No." Jeema's voice quaked.

"I'm not surprised. The prophecy of the egg has never been told before, only witnessed by an orphaned girl who climbed a buso tree on the side of the road. In the tree, she found a nest; in the nest, she found an egg; in the egg, she found nothing. The egg was cracked. Split in two."

Jeema stopped in her tracks.

What are you doing?

How did he know about that?

He's a sorcerer! He knows everything! Start walking, you fool!

"How can that be a prophecy if it's something that has already happened?"

"Has it, though?"

"If you're referring to me finding that egg, then yes."

"That may be, but mark my words, the egg will crack. And when it does, there's no putting it back together. When it cracks, nothing will ever be right again."

The egg will crack? The egg . . . did crack . . . it already cracked. What is he talking about?

It's a prophecy. He's speaking of something that is going to happen. It involves you and me, don't you see? When it happens, it's going to be like that egg we found.

I don't understand. What does that mean?

I'm not surprised. Don't worry about it. I'll know it when I see it, even if you don't.

Jeema felt nauseous. Was it the thought of Dartaun watching her, or was it the buso leaf? She didn't know. She took a deep breath and put on the bravest face she could muster.

"How did you know about the egg?" Jeema demanded.

"A sorcerer never reveals his secrets."

"Are you really a sorcerer?"

"Follow me and find out for yourself."

"Why are you going to see Lady Xiara?"

At that, Dartaun's face grew somber. His eyes focused straight ahead and he clenched his teeth. Jeema immediately regretted asking the question.

Finally, Dartaun spoke, and his hollow voice chilled Jeema to the bone.

"To say goodbye."

CHAPTER FIFTEEN

Sleep fled from Nod, even in the warmth of the soft sheets and on the comfortable mattress. He convinced himself to stop thinking about Rho's tale of his dad and the witch, and of the idea that his dad could be dead. He may have refused to entertain the thought, but the thought was far from done with him. It echoed through the most secret, innermost parts of his mind. Through the deep chambers in which the most basic foundations of truth had been established long, long ago. It wove between the monuments of faith and hope and all that he believed in. It made him nervous to let new ideas enter these sacred places. He couldn't help but think that any sudden shift in weight might cause everything to come crumbling down.

With a focused effort, he finally managed to block out the unwanted thoughts. He wanted to believe his father was alive. He had to be. Though, what did that say about his father? If he was still alive, he'd left them for a better life in Qaro. It didn't seem like something his father would do, but then again, how well did he really know him?

Well enough, he thought. He may not have known everything about him, but he knew that his father was an honest man. He could feel it. He could see it in his eyes.

A memory popped into his mind. He was young—about five, perhaps—staring up into his father's kind eyes. His rough beard brushed against Nod's cheek as his father hugged him. His father had just come in from the rommi fields and smelled of beans and dust and sweat. Nod had carved the end of a stick into a point with a sharp rock and raised it up to show his father.

"Very good, son! It looks like a rocket ship to me."

"What's a rocket ship?" Nod asked.

"Before the Days To Come, teams of scientists would fly into space in special vehicles called rocket ships. They were sort of like a little house that could fly up to the stars. The scientists who flew inside the rocket ships were called *astronauts*. They would explore other planets and live in the many space stations that orbited Noloro. I helped design some of the rocket ships the astronauts used to fly in. I was called an engineer." He laughed and looked upward. "That seems so long ago now."

"Are rocket ships real?" Nod asked.

"You bet they're real!" His dad laughed. "We used to launch them from right up there in the Neolani Mountains. I don't know if there's anything left up there these days, and even if there was, I don't know if they would fly."

"I hope they can fly. I want to see a rocket ship someday."

"I bet you will see a rocket ship, son. Someday."

He often tried to imagine what it was like, flying up into the sky and getting so close to the stars. He had a theory that the stars were actually angels, and that they burned so brightly with God's magnificent light that they were impossible to see beyond the brilliant halo of light around them. All one could ever really see was their radiance.

He imagined walking on the surface of another planet. The red planet Nuyaro had always been the only one he could imagine. In his mind, it looked just like Noloro, except that the surface was made up of a chalky red dust.

That's where I'd go. If I could escape from Noloro before it finishes dying, I would go live on Nuyaro. Except it's impossible. Noloro is the only planet capable of sustaining life, according to Dad. He would know if there was somewhere else to go, wouldn't he?

If anyone would know how to escape, it would be him . . .

He knew how to run away . . .

He remembered his father taking his weekly trips to Qaro to get Mom's medicine. Nod waited with Rho at the entrance to the cave for the silhouette of their father's horse and cart to rise up against the sky, riding north along the ridge. He remembered watching intently so he could be the first to spot him, and he recalled the pride he felt each time he was the first to shout, "Dad's home!" He remembered the excitement of waiting for that small black silhouette to draw closer. He thought his father was heroic, coming back with the medicine his mom needed. Coming back to save her.

He remembered that bright promise of a morning and that unsettling afternoon that had slowly waned into a broken evening, in which he and Rho continued to scan the ridge until the last ray of sunlight dissolved into a black and bitter night. Still, they watched, but they never would see that silhouette along the ridge. The next morning, they were up before dawn, and even their mother was outside watching the ridgeline. There would be no silhouette that day either.

On the third day, two young men from the village set off to search for their missing father. They traveled all the way to Qaro and found no trace of him. They asked around town, but no one was able or willing to remember anything about a man by the name of Grier Perish. They reasoned that perhaps he was going by another name in

Qaro, or perhaps he really had never been to Qaro. Nod understood now that the latter was probably true. In any case, the two men returned to the village with no answers.

Gossip soon spread about a woman in Qaro that Grier may have been visiting, and another story surfaced of a witch and a curse. Concern gave way to rumors. Soon, the only people willing to continue looking were Grier's bed-ridden wife and his two young children. Thus ended the search for Grier Perish.

CHAPTER SIXTEEN

Jeema knew she had to face it someday, but her stomach wrenched at the idea of what was ahead. So many times, she had run away, and she really meant to leave, but she could never make it beyond the chasm. She had never been able to go down into that place again. Not after the Blood Rain.

She could see the edge of the chasm ahead. She knew the River of the Dead was churning down below. Once there had been a great, red river made of lava that flowed from the *Mon Uro*, the once-active volcano that stood far above the rest of the southern range. The river that flowed from the mountains carved The Great Chasm, or so said Elder Dulner. It was the same river which had emptied into the Darrows, forming the northern cave villages that she had learned of in school, but had never seen for herself. Now a different kind of river moved through the depths, one that consisted of bodies—bodies that walked aimlessly and endlessly. There was no life in any of them. No mind. No soul. Just bodies. They still appeared to her in nightmares and carried Dari—her one true love—away from her, forever.

They were close now, but it was already dark. Dartaun would have to stop soon and make camp. Wouldn't he? It was too dark and too late to cross the chasm, she knew that much for sure, but he *was* a sorcerer, after all, and he didn't seem to be slowing down in the least. Even walking through the desert, wearing layers of black from head to toe, Jeema hadn't seen a bead of sweat form on his skin.

The sun had long since dropped below the eastern mountains. The moon covered the entire western sky. As expected, it appeared even larger tonight than she had ever seen it. It was getting closer— no ... it was falling. Jeema was certain it was destined to keep falling until it smashed into the surface of Noloro, and the thought terrified her. She couldn't afford to think about it at that moment.

She tried hard not to look to her right, but she knew what was standing there, and in the end, she couldn't help it. She glanced up and saw it, just as it had been on that day. The little red hut with the yellow door and blue roof. It looked so happy, it made her sick. Her true love had brought her there to hide her. To protect her. To pay for her life with his own.

Jeema felt a sickness rising in her stomach. Why did she look? If only Lady Virion had seized control of her body and made it impossible for her to turn her head to the side, she would have welcomed it.

She forced her mind away from the little hut and back to the situation in front of her. They were almost to the edge of the chasm. Only twenty more steps, perhaps.

Virion?

Yes?

Is he planning on stopping?

I don't know.

We aren't crossing the chasm tonight, are we?

If he crosses, we cross.

In the dark?

What does that matter?

Does he know what's down there?

I suspect he does.

I can't go down there again. I can't do it!

Will you stop thinking so loudly?

He'll stop, won't he? He has to.

Goodness' sake, Jeema! No more thinking. Just walking . . . and pick up the pace, will you?

Jeema caught up with the sorcerer and matched her pace to his. They were so close to the edge now, and Dartaun was not slowing down. Her hands sweated and tears ran down her cheeks. She stopped herself about three steps away from the edge, expecting the mage to do the same, but he didn't stop. Without a word, he kept walking, right up to the edge—and then over it. He kept walking, as if on solid ground. Jeema watched in awe, though not entirely surprised. Dartaun the Great was simply walking across the chasm.

What am I supposed to do now?

I . . . I don't know.

She cupped her clammy hands and shouted across the chasm to the sorcerer. "What am I supposed to do?"

He turned around and tittered. "Whatever you please, my dear! Do whatever it is you please!"

Then he disappeared into the darkness.

CHAPTER SEVENTEEN

In that old, abandoned hut, Nod dreamed a dream so vivid and so realistic that it grabbed hold of him and shook his soul. It was swirling and strange, but it felt like more than a dream—a vision, perhaps.

There before him stood a man wearing a black hood, cloaked entirely in shadow. His skin gleamed red in the moonlight. From out of the shadow appeared a beautiful girl with white hair, maybe a few sun-cycles older than himself. She looked desperate and afraid. She reached her arms out to him, and he knew she needed his help. She spoke no words, but her eyes begged him to rescue her. From what, he did not know, but he reached his hands out and stepped toward her.

Before his foot could touch the ground, the shadow before him exploded, and the blast knocked him off his feet. His body slammed into the ground, and he blinked hard. He could see nothing now but darkness, though he felt something moving around him. Little by little, the red glow of moonlight shone through. It was enough to make out shapes in the darkness, and he recognized the pair of blue eyes before him now. Rho.

Nod stretched his arm out but could not reach his brother. The darkness guarded him, claiming him. Beside Rho, the white-haired girl stood staring back at him as well, both hopeless and defeated. The darkness grew thicker around them and wrapped them in its tendrils.

Then there was a faint glow, but it wasn't moonlight. It was a golden warmth that radiated from behind him. Nod turned and saw nothing. He turned back, and the golden light intensified. He looked down and discovered that the light was emanating from within him.

The dark tendrils, which were wrapped around his brother and the white-haired girl, began to flail. The light was powerful, and it burned up the darkness. There was a hideous shriek as the darkness burst into flame, and Nod felt an overwhelming sense that everything was made right by that perfect, golden light.

Even so, he began to panic. What of Rho and the white-haired girl? Had they been freed from the darkness, or had they been burned up with it?

"Rho?" Nod called out into the blinding light. "Are you okay?"

Nod spun around and saw a man standing before him. The light was burning like a fire all around him but did not appear to hurt him. The man looked both kind and fierce. Fear gripped Nod, and he fell to his knees, unable to speak.

"Be at peace and fear not." The man smiled. "For death has no authority over you."

Nod's eyes flew open. The sheets were damp and cool from his own sweat. He laid completely still, wrestling with what he'd just seen. His body was shaking, his breaths shallow and rapid. He twisted in the sheets and turned from his left side to his right, and he was once again frozen with fear. Just beyond the tip of his nose danced a large silver snake, coiled up, fangs bared, ready to strike.

CHAPTER EIGHTEEN

Jeema froze, peering over the edge of the great chasm into the blackness below. At the edge, the wind blustered and kicked up at her in strong gusts, while the caverns below almost seemed to be warning her with their sickly thrumming. She listened intently and convinced herself that she could hear a chorus of unholy groans carried up from the deep. There was no way Jeema was going down there.

Carefully, she stepped back, away from the chasm. Another step, and then another. Then she was frozen again, and the tingling intensified. That uncomfortable sensation had not let up since Lady Virion's advent in the slow room, but the longer she lived with it, the easier it became to ignore, and she realized that, until now, she'd forgotten about it entirely. Now it was impossible to ignore, like needles stabbing every nerve ending. Against her will, her right foot moved back toward the ledge.

We can't go down there, Virion!

You'd rather go back to the slow room, then?

There aren't any Lurkers in the slow room!

We're not going back, Jeema. The Southern spirit gave me a task, and we're not stopping until it's complete. We must seek the Mother.

I'm not going down there!

You are mine now, Jeema. You'll go where I make you go.

She stepped again, and her loss of control made her certain she would fall over the ledge—down into the River of the Dead. She tried to scream, but nothing came out. A jolt of pain emanated from her throat and made her head throb.

Stop! Don't make me go in there, Virion! Please!

Another step, and she was at the edge. Virion crouched at the edge to survey the face of the chasm, and Jeema's eyes involuntarily scanned for a way down.

With everything she had, she pushed through the pain and spun around. She was shocked to find that she was successful. She actually managed to take back control, and instantly regretted it. Her body burned as if it were being incinerated, and she immediately collapsed to the ground. Everything was black, and she didn't have strength enough to keep her mind awake. The last thing she heard was the cruel and insurmountable voice of Lady Virion booming throughout her head. The sound was like a boot pounding her skull.

I told *you*, Mortal. *You are* mine.

CHAPTER NINETEEN

The snake slithered its head toward Nod's. Its ominous hood fanned out from his neck, its black tongue flicking against the yellow light from the flame on the wall. Nod's instinct told him to keep still, but he began to regret listening to his instincts as the snake's tongue drew closer and began to flutter against his ear. Then a soft whisper.

Sssssstay away, sssssstay away.

Sssssstay away from the garden.

Listen clossssssely and obey.

Rho'sssss heart hasssss been hardened.

I will sssssend you a sssssign

Sssssso you'll know I sssssspeak true.

White hair once entwined,

Ssssshe isssss now sssssplit in two.

Sssssneak away in the night,

Ssssswiftly back to your cave,

Lessssst you sssssuffer a bite,

And a premature grave.

Nod thought his heart would explode in his chest. He was not sure whether he'd imagined the voice or not. Either way, he abandoned playing dead. All in one motion, he smacked the snake away with his hand and shot to his feet. He bolted from the hut and screamed at his brother, who sprang up to a sitting position.

"There's a giant snake in there and it talked! It was licking my ear and it . . . it was talking!"

Rho's eyes were as wide as they could possibly get at such a shadowmark.

"What? You having a bad dream?"

As he finished his question, he saw the snake's head bobbing out from behind the door, followed by the rest of his winding body. It slithered off to the East toward Qaro, the glint of the blood red moon reflected in its silver scales, and the boys silently watched it go.

As their eyes followed the talking snake, they noticed a faint orange glow on the horizon.

Nod frowned and squinted his eyes.

"Is it morning already?"

"That's not the sunrise," Rho said. "That's a campfire."

CHAPTER TWENTY

Jeema heard heavy breathing, but she saw nothing. It only took her a moment to realize that the sound she heard was her own breathing. Her entire body hurt. Her tailbone was sore, her right ankle throbbed and screamed at her, and of course, she tingled everywhere.

She could now make out dark shapes around her, but she had no idea which part of the chasm she was in. They weren't climbing up or down, but hopping from rock to rock through a relatively level terrain. They must either be nearing the bridge, or they had just finished crossing it.

It was clear to her that Virion sensed her presence, but she dared not make a sound for fear of waking the horrors that lurked below. She wanted to ask Virion how she'd acquired these new bruises, but she was too afraid to even think out loud. If the creatures below were sleeping, she wanted to keep it that way. She wasn't sure if they slept at all. She thought it more likely they wandered the chasm floor, just waiting for some wild animal or poor ignorant soul to come wandering into the River of the Dead and become their next meal.

Her eyes continued to adjust, and she made out the path ahead, which meandered along the chasm wall and passed a series of caves near the bottom of the trail. She knew now that she was in fact nearing the bridge, and several times, she heard what she thought were growls, which she hoped belonged to a wolf or a desert cat. She would prefer an encounter with either of those over an encounter with a lurker.

All her hoping did not help. More growls rose from the depths, and she became aware of another sound, as well. It was a faint, constant moaning. It made her gut wrench. That awful moaning that had haunted her nightmares! The mindless moaning of a hungry lurker . . . It was real now, and it was just as horrific as she remembered it— more so. Her knees weakened and she began to sweat, her dress now clinging to her chest and back. All her strength left her, and she could feel Virion's anger rising as her body began to fail them. The Chasm walls began to spin around her. She reached out to grasp for the wall, or anything to steady her balance, to keep her from careening off the ledge and into the River of the Dead. The tingle lashed out at her with a violent shock, and she recoiled.

Knock it off!

I'm sorry. I didn't mean to, it just happened.

Don't let it happen again . . . mortal.

Jeema couldn't believe she just apologized to the evil spirit that had completely taken control of her life. Could she really continue to allow Lady Virion to carry her down into the darkness? Into the horror below? Did she even have a choice?

Jeema could make out the bridge from where she stood. It was close. She picked out individual voices, each with its own frightening characteristics. One was low and angry. Another sounded hungry. This one frustrated and impatient. The next wild and high-pitched. They seemed to have their own personalities, and it made her realize that once, long ago, perhaps, each one of them had been a real, living, breathing person. At some point, they were husbands, wives, kids, friends, students, teachers, orphans . . . At one point, they were just like her, but now . . . They were mindless monsters lurking in the deepest, darkest shadows of the Empyrean Valley, beckoning her with their nauseating moans to wander just a bit further down into the heart of the Great Chasm, into the River of the Dead.

I can't do this! It's too much! I can't do it!

Shut up, you idiot!

I can't keep going! We have to go back.

Goodness' sake, get a hold of yourself!

Virion stopped and Jeema felt her slide the pack from her back and reach inside for something. She rummaged around against her will until she grabbed hold of a buso leaf. She placed it between her teeth and then continued rummaging through the pack for something else. Her hand found it and she instantly recognized its shape that fit perfectly in her palm—her deck.

Here, take these.

And do what?

Shuffle them for me.

Why?

Just do it! I need you to focus on that so I can focus on where I'm going!

The bridge goes straight across.

It's after the bridge I'm worried about. My guide left me, remember?

Jeema extended her fingers and found that she once again had control, though her legs were still moving independently. It was the strangest feeling, but she was relieved to at least have regained control of her hands. She noticed the buso leaf already beginning to calm her nerves, as well.

All right. I'll try.

She closed her eyes, breathed in deeply, and shuffled. After a moment, her head began to clear, if only a little. It really did help. She could feel

Virion's irritation easing up. This had happened earlier, as well, when she had first chewed a buso leaf. Virion seemed more at ease, more willing to let Jeema take control, and less annoyed with her "mortal" host. She'd have to remember that. Jeema stopped shuffling and drew a card.

The card pictured a sea captain standing on the bow of a ship. He held a sextant in one hand and a compass in the other. He looked up at a large star in the sky. At the top of the card was the symbol for air and at the bottom was the symbol for fire. To the right and left were the water and earth symbols, respectively.

The card was known as 'The Guardian,' and if she remembered correctly, it represented peace of mind, tranquility, serenity, and calm. She studied the card until . . .

The Guardian! That's it!

Jeema's free hand flew up and covered her mouth, regretting the thought. The last thing she wanted to do was to help her captor find the evil sorceress she was seeking.

What do you mean?

Nothing, I just . . . I just drew the Guardian.

But it was too late. Virion understood her implication.

The stars! Of course. You can't hide your thoughts from me, Mortal.

Her eyes shot up to the sky. Two steep chasm walls blocked out its entirety, save one starry ribbon. Directly above her was a group of stars known as Mabo the serpent, one of the twelve sky guardians.

When you find yourself down and lost and all alone, all you have to do is look up . . .

Great. She'd given it away. Part of her was mad at herself, but another part of her was proud of herself for connecting the dots before Virion did. As she understood it, Mabo pointed directly toward Aragyn, another of the sky guardians, half woman and half spider. Aragyn went by another name—the Mother—and wasn't that who they were trying to find?

That is when you will see your path clearly . . . The spirits will be walking with you . . .

She'd uncovered the fire spirit's cryptic words, and now she and Virion knew exactly how to find the witch. The only problem was that she no longer wanted to find her.

They reached the top with little difficulty. Adrenaline kept her body moving toward her goal with little thought or need for direction. Virion had relaxed her control over Jeema's body, and Jeema got the impression that Virion didn't even want to be in control. Was it just the buso leaf, or something more? She felt Virion's disgust with her body's limitations. She could sense her disdain for her burning thighs and forearms, exhausted from the arduous climb up the chasm wall. Jeema was amused with Virion's near inability to cope with the throbbing in her bruised tailbone and right ankle. This was all new to Virion, and suddenly, Jeema felt as if she'd gained a little more control over the situation.

As her knee swung up onto solid ground and pushed the rest of her body out of the chasm into the vast desert that awaited her, she realized she was utterly exhausted. Her ankle had held out for this long, but now it began to compensate. It throbbed hard and fast, each pulse releasing a wave of intense pain. She rolled herself onto the desert floor and just laid there, looking up at the Great Guardians.

She knew she couldn't walk any further tonight, and she had a hunch that Virion understood this. The spirit was still present, though she remained quiet and dormant, somewhere in the back of her mind. Perhaps she was sleeping. Did spirits ever sleep? In any case, Jeema was glad for the respite. She wanted to lie there until sunrise, watching the sky guardians slowly glide by, but the adrenaline began to wear off and she began to shiver. It was nearly full-shadow, and the barren desert would only get colder as the night progressed, but she had run away from Miss Tilly's Home for Orphans more than enough times to become a bit of an expert at fire science. All she needed was . . . there—just a little walk to the north, a lone herold tree large enough to draw water from, but small enough that she didn't feel guilty about wasting a perfectly good tree.

Her ankle squeezed tighter with each wave of blood her heart sent to it as she hobbled her way to the tree. The west wind shot through her like icicles. She picked up every large rock she could find along the way and stowed them in her pack. By the time she approached the tree, she had begun to drag her feet, failing under the extra weight of the rocks, but she knew they were necessary. The wind was not strong, but it had that extra bite to it that would necessitate a windbreak.

She was close enough now to drop her pack on the ground and call it camp. She opened her pack and pulled out two tin flagons, each three times larger than the canteen that hung from her hip. Her knife was secured by a small loop she had hand-stitched onto the side of her pack using the small sewing kit that had belonged to her mother. She took it in her right hand and approached the small herold tree.

Please tell me you've got some water.

The tree was not much taller than she was, and small enough for her to wrap her hands around it. Several branches protruded out from the trunk like scarecrow arms with bark as white as ash. She bent down and knocked at the base of the tree with the blade of her knife, first low, then a little higher up, and then a little higher still, until the sound changed. That was the sweet spot. She made a mark here with the knife blade—where the trunk went from suffused with water at the bottom to hollow on top.

She began patiently cutting into the small trunk, roughly a hand above her mark. When she had cut nearly all the way through, the trunk went off like a firecracker, snapping and popping at its weakest point as it lurched toward her. She wrenched the knife handle back and forth until the blade was loose. With a little push, the small tree snapped over onto itself, and gravity did the rest. Next, she carved a little V-shape into one side of the stump.

The stump resembled an empty goblet at the table of a mighty king, and wedged into the bottom of the goblet sat a beautiful cluster of shiny, green pinni pods—more than she'd expected. With her knife, she dislodged one of the pods. Immediately, fresh water began to trickle up from the hole that the pod had been plugging up, and it slowly began to fill the goblet stump.

She cut the tough skin of the pinni pod open and emptied the five green pinni beans into her hand. She popped all five of them into her mouth at once, and the bitter taste immediately made her wish she'd eaten them slower. She chewed, swallowed, and began opening the remaining pods. All the while, the water trickled up from below until it nearly reached the V-shaped notch at the top.

Now, if you could only take away this awful pain in my ankle!

She readied a flagon just below the notch, and a moment later, the water began spilling out of the V-shaped notch. Once she filled both of her flagons and her canteen, she placed the flagons back in her pack and spent the next half-shadow collecting herold needles, dead branches, and decently sized rocks.

Jeema made her way back to where she set her pack and arranged the wood into two piles—the small, knotty branches in one pile and the larger, thicker segments of trunk in another pile. She used the sturdiest of these as a makeshift shovel to carve out a shallow basin in the desert floor. Around the basin, she arranged the rocks she collected. She stacked them higher on the west side to create the windbreak.

She removed her mother's jewelry box from her pack, opened the top drawer and carefully unwrapped the bird nest she'd collected from the buso tree. Twigs, leaves, twine, needles, bark, and who knows what else, were all tangled up in a mess of perfect tinder. There were even some down feathers sitting in a loose little pile where the eggs had been. She placed the nest at the center of the basin and used the small herold needles and twigs to construct a teepee around it, and then a teepee of kindling branches over that.

Out of her pack, she grabbed a book of matches and a few moments later, she had herself a rip-roarin' campfire good enough to sing at. As the kindling branches snapped and fell into the center, feeding the fire, she began introducing the larger lumber for fuel.

Finally, she sat down very gently—using her jewelry box as a seat—and stared into the fire, admiring all her hard work and trying to ignore her throbbing ankle. She used her knife to peel open a few more of the pinni pods she'd gathered and snacked on the bitter green pinni beans they produced. Her body was done for. She looked up at the moon, traveling ever so slowly toward her, taunting her, it seemed. She was too tired to care. Her eyes were heavy now. Her head nodded forward and she gave into sleep . . . and then . . .

What in the world happened?

Jeema nearly jumped out of her skin.

Goodness' sake, Virion! You scared me to death! What is it?

What happened to you?

I fell asleep, what do you think?

I mean the ankle. You're killing me. I was going to have a look around while you slept, but I can't even stand up.

Are you kidding? You did that to my ankle, not me. You knocked me out and when I woke up, everything hurt.

It wasn't this bad. How did it get so much worse?

That's how it works. It's going to hurt like this for days. Maybe more. It's probably going to be worse tomorrow.

I'm not used to this mortal body.

Then leave it alone. It's not yours. Don't try to control something you don't understand.

I may not like the way this body feels, but make no mistake—I am in control of it. Not you. If you don't want me to take control, then you will work with me. Don't fight me. You will not win, I promise. Just take us to Lady Xiara.

I understand, and I will try to work with you, but if you want to find Lady Xiara, you'll have to work with me, too. Even if I try, my body won't be able to take you anywhere right now. It needs rest. If we don't give this ankle a rest, we won't be able to walk anywhere.

Jeema could tell this irritated Lady Virion, but there was no response, and a moment later, she felt the spirit's presence become distant once more. She stared into the fire. Her body needed sleep, but she was hypnotized by the dancing flames.

Snap, snap, pop . . .

The herold branches curled and cracked, and as she watched and listened to the fire, her eyelids became too heavy to keep themselves apart. Her mind was awake, but her poor body was out for the count.

Pop, snap, pop . . .

The red, yellow, orange and white flames began to blur together until they were just a white shape. Her eyelids came together over the dancing shape and her chin dropped to her chest.

Snap, pop, TWIKKK . . .

Her heart jolted. That wasn't the fire. It was behind her. A pokey mouse? A desert cat? She could hope. A wolf? A pack of wolves? She wouldn't survive the night. She remained perfectly still. She felt Virion emerge once again, silent and alert. Jeema moved her eyes toward her knife, back in its place on the side of her pack. She was scared stiff, but it was now or never. Kill or be killed. Don't think; just do. She conjured up whatever willpower she could find, and it took every bit of it to convince her body to move.

She sprung forward, winced as she pushed off her bad ankle, and grabbed for her weapon. Without pause, she limped as fast as she could around behind the fire, putting the flames between her and whatever was hunting her.

Then she saw it. A black figure moving slowly toward her from out of the dark, without shape. It was too big to be a wolf or a desert cat. Whatever it was, it was large—as tall as her, if not taller.

What is it?

I don't know!

The creature was just outside of the fire's light, a formless terror emerging from the dark of the night.

Then . . . a second figure. This one was not quite as tall. Neither creature was the least bit deterred by the fire. She remembered the words of the Southern spirit in the slow room. That awful hissing voice that had caused her skin to crawl.

The ssspiritsss will be walking with you . . .

She didn't want any spirits walking with her. She wanted nothing more to do with them. Especially in the dead of night. The shapes became more defined as they moved out of the darkness and straight for her. Then one of them spoke, and she was relieved to hear a human voice. A rather polite human voice.

"I'm sorry," said the taller of the two figures. "We don't mean to startle you. We saw your fire from our camp, and we were curious to know who else was crazy enough to be sleeping out here. My name is Rho, and this is my brother, Nod."

PART II:

PRETTY THINGS AND
THE COLOR GREEN

AS GRIM AS THE FALLING MOON

CHAPTER TWENTY-ONE

Rho knew many things about the universe, but he did not know why the moon was still closer to Noloro tonight than it had been last night. He had been noticing the difference for years, convinced that he was either imagining things or just growing up, but at some point—about the time his father left, he supposed—he looked up at the moon and realized that this was not just a trick of the mind. The far-off silvery orb he remembered shining brilliantly from up in the night sky when he was a boy in no way resembled this abominable, blood-red, celestial boulder which had become in his mind the messenger of death and destroyer of the world. As he began to explore the reasons for this phenomenon, he had found that most everyone was painfully aware of the occurrence, yet no one cared to discuss how the moon would surely come crashing down onto the planet's surface, finishing what the Days To Come had begun twenty sun-cycles prior. No one cared to discuss how their children would never grow old and never raise families of their own—would never make them grandparents.

Since boyhood, Rho had understood that everything could easily be taken from him in an instant, and it had never seemed fair to him. He wanted a future, a wife, a family of his own; but until now, he'd never seen a girl. There were women in the Darrows, but no girls, so the hope of a wife and children had remained a far-off dream. Until he happened upon this white-haired girl. She was the first girl he'd ever met, and now he feared he had met her too late.

Ever since the day Yru told him that there were others outside of the Darrows, he had imagined himself setting out to find a girl close to his own age. He was sure there was one out there somewhere. When he found her, perhaps they would marry and settle down in some place nice like Qaro, where they could raise their children without the fear of starvation.

He knew better than that now. That great and terrible time-glass in the sky had secured his fate, along with everyone else unfortunate enough to find themselves clinging to life on this dying planet. There was no time to marry and build a home. Even if there were, surely no one in their right mind would bring a child into this dying world, with the messenger of death hanging overhead, patiently awaiting the appointed time. No, the future was no place for a family, nor a wife, nor a child. The future was a funeral, and all of Noloro would be mourned.

Xiara's voice came to him once again.

There is nothing ahead but death and dying.

People cared not to discuss these things, and so life went on in this way—privately counting down, inwardly preparing for the end, and outwardly going on as if it were nothing to speak of. It was the only way one could keep from going mad. Hope was essential to survival, and in this case, denial was essential to hope. Tonight would be no different, he supposed.

The two boys sat cross-legged with palms out in front of them, warming them against the campfire as the girl paced anxiously around it. She was beautiful. He thought that maybe he even loved her, but he knew it was best to ignore those kinds of feelings. He knew it couldn't really be love at all. He figured it more likely that what he really loved was the excitement of having found someone he could love.

Even so, he felt an instant attraction to the girl. Her evenly tanned skin, upon which every warm and intoxicating hue now danced with one another, appeared to him smoother than he had ever seen on any person, save one—but maybe witches don't count. He supposed she'd never spent so much as a single day in a rommi field, and he loved her more for that.

Her hair was delicate and white. Rho remembered the stories of ice and of snow, and of how before the Days To Come it would cover these parts throughout the begging season, dressing the whole land in white, covering the ground well into the giving season. It was because of this that a certain expression could still be heard among the elders—*fair as the fallen snow.* Rho thought that maybe now he could understand what they had meant by that.

Her white hair was pulled back, secured by a red bandana which was tied in a tight knot at the top of her head. Her bangs hung down and cut evenly across her forehead just above her eyebrows. Her emerald eyes came alive in the firelight.

She stirred something entirely new within him, a fire that excited him and made him uneasy at the same time. He instantly knew that he wanted her for himself. Plain and simple. He realized how intensely he was looking at the girl and thought it best to focus his attention toward the sky once again. He gazed up at the approaching moon, that great and terrible time-glass in the sky. That messenger of death. He hated it. More tonight than ever before. He had a brand new reason for hating it, and she was as fair as the fallen snow. For the moment, however, the moon had served the purpose he'd hoped it would. It shot him with a healthy dose of perspective, knocked some sense into him, and made him wise. He was better off for it. He folded his lustful urges away and repeated Xiara's words to himself:

There is nothing ahead but death and dying.

That's all there was to it. There was no time for fantasy, no time for young love, no time to start a family, no time to raise children, no time to grow old.

No time.

No future.

No hope.

Hopeless.

Useless.

Unless . . .

Unless *she* was right.

When one world ends, another begins.

Could there really be an escape? Could there be a future for him someplace else? He had always dreamed of some lovely place where the land is covered in green grass, where snow falls like a blanket of white over the land, where clean blue rivers empty into great and mighty crystal seas, where the sun brings life and not death, where a man could reap and sow any crop he desired, where a man could feed his wife and children from the treasures brought forth by the fertile soil, where a man could grow old and watch his children work the land, where a man could be buried by his children at a proper old age, where a man's body could fertilize that very land that he had worked all his life. Could there really be a place like this?

Even if *she* was right about that, he knew that time was running out. He looked up once more at the moon, a new sense of urgency grabbing hold of him. He knew he needed to find *her* soon. He knew it seemed unlikely—ridiculous, even—but he needed to know. It *was* ridiculous, but it was also the only hope he had left. He had no other hope left. If there was a way off of this dead and dying world, he needed to find it quickly. Otherwise, his future was as grim as the falling moon.

CHAPTER TWENTY-TWO

Jeema was suddenly aware of the vacuum that had replaced Virion in her head. Her unwelcome guest disappeared suddenly and without any reason Jeema could figure on. Was she afraid of these two boys? It seemed that way, but why? What was it about them?

She could tell instantly that Virion hated the younger one. There was something about him that angered Virion the moment she saw him. Is that why she disappeared?

She remembered something Elder Yru had once said: "The enemy of my enemy is my friend." Was she a fool for letting her guard down and allowing them to join her at her fire? Perhaps, but there was something reassuring about them as well, something good that she sensed in them. It was more than intuition; it was something spiritual. She had become more and more sensitive to the spirits, and this felt similar to what she'd felt in the slow room, but somehow very different, too. It was probably the same thing that Virion sensed that caused her to hide. Whatever it was, she was beginning to feel glad they were there. Something about the older one stood out to Jeema. There was something in his eyes that reminded her so much of Dari. They were more than just eyes—they were portals. She looked into them and she was sucked in and shuttled straight back into the past, to that day—the Blood Rain. She felt a dull ache in her heart, but it wasn't altogether bad. That ache was nearly all she had left of her parents, and of Dari. It was a bittersweet, nostalgia-laced ache that she had grown accustomed to—and maybe even cherished.

She forced herself out of her head to address the current situation.

"You say you're searching for some kind of witch," she began, "but you can't tell me anything about her?"

"I don't know for certain if she's a witch or not," Rho replied.

"She doesn't look like any witch I've ever seen," Nod chimed in.

"You've seen her, then?" Jeema asked.

"No, but she's supposed to be beautiful. Witches aren't beautiful," Nod said.

"How many witches have you seen?" Jeema challenged.

Nod looked as if he'd just been knocked on the forehead by a herold branch.

"Well . . . none, I guess. None in real life, anyway. But I've heard about lots of them . . . real ones. From old stories, and from the Bel Tiev."

"Well, I've heard of many witches too, but none like this one," Jeema said, "and we're on our way to see her, too."

"*We?*" Rho squinted his eyes at her.

The girl looked flustered at this.

"I just . . . I didn't know if—I mean, I thought you guys were thinking about maybe . . . coming with me."

"You've heard of her, then?" Nod asked.

"She goes by many names," she whispered, as if someone might overhear. "They call her the Mother, the Serpent's Mistress, the Hungry Spider, Aragyn, Lady Xiara . . ."

She paused. She saw Nod's head jerk up to meet Rho's eyes. The name obviously meant something to them, but Rho just stared into the fire with an eerie serenity. A chilling hint of a smile appeared on his lips.

"Xiara," Rho repeated. "Beautiful Xiara."

Now it was Jeema who reeled in surprise.

"Have *you* seen her before?"

"It was a *long* time ago." His eyes broke away from the fire and met Jeema's.

She saw heaven in those beautiful blue eyes, all far-off and dreaming, and she knew his words were honest. His expression was solemn, like a saint before the gates of Heaven.

"I guess it's almost six sun-cycles past. My mother grew ill and needed medicine. We didn't have anything like the sort she needed back in the Darrows. The best we had was the ortero, who could lay her hands on you when you were ill. Our father went to Xiara and came back with medicine for our mother. I hid in the tack box of his cart once. I saw her there, at the abandoned hut—the one we just came from. She was beautiful and terrifying. She told me things that would come to pass . . . and they have. Well, some of them have."

Rho looked over at Nod, whose eyes were squinted and his lips curled into a very disapproving expression. Rho continued.

"The medicine kept my mother healthy, but at a price. Somehow, going to see her made my father sick. A different kind of sick, you know? She changed him . . . made him into something else. Into less than a man. It was as if she were sucking the life out of him. The last time he came back, he had a whole sack full of medicine with him— enough to last for years. It was like he knew he wasn't coming back, and he wanted to make sure we'd be all right when he was gone. I hid the stash in the tool cavern like he'd instructed me. I wasn't supposed to tell anyone about it. The next week when he left, he had tears in his eyes. It was the first time I'd seen him cry. Ever. I knew that that time was different. I knew that time he wasn't coming back."

She watched Nod, who was concentrating on sharpening the point of a stick with his knife. She couldn't tell for sure, but she thought maybe she had seen a tear fall from his cheek. Rho leaned over and put his arm around Nod's shoulder, pulling him close.

"People thought my father was a coward for leaving us, but the truth is my father loved my mother so much that he gave his life for her. My father was no coward. He was a hero." Rho's eyes strayed upward and rested on the enormous red moon. "I wish I had that kind of courage, you know?" His eyes moved upward and she saw a glint of red moonlight in his eyes. "I just hope I get another chance."

She met Rho's gaze and once again felt an inexplicable sense of trust in him. That in itself made her nervous. Was she inviting them in too quickly, without thinking it through, the way she'd recklessly invited Virion in? No, this was different. She didn't know how exactly. It was the way he looked at her, so deeply into her eyes. When he looked in her eyes, it seemed as if he was swimming in her soul, the way she wanted to swim in his. He was searching for something, and she wanted him to find it, whatever it was he was looking for. It was her first real sense of intimacy with a man, and she wanted to feel more of it.

Nod spoke. "The Bel Tiev says, *'The Serpent's Mistress has many names. She is called Aragyn by some, and Lady Xiara by others. She lures even the righteous to her bed, like an insect in a spider's web. She eats not at the flesh of men, but even at their souls. By her many charms, the best of men are devoured and discarded as men without souls, wandering the depths in darkness until the end of days. They will not escape the fire which pours forth from the serpent's mouth . . . '* There's more, but I don't remember it all."

Nod looked from Jeema to Rho and back again. Rho continued to stare into the fire.

Jeema took a deep breath and cleared her throat. "I've heard she's the most powerful sorceress of all. Why are you looking for her?"

Rho clenched his jaw and his eyes became determined. "She's going to help us escape."

"Escape?" Jeema tilted her head, confused. "Escape what?"

"The Withering."

Jeema's eyes widened.

Nod paused his whittling and looked up at Jeema. "You know about the Withering?"

"I've heard of it," she said.

"From the Bel Tiev?" Nod asked.

Jeema frowned. "No . . . from the Guidestones."

"The Guidestones?" Nod's face curled into a disapproving sneer.

Jeema squinted and cocked her head to one side. "What, you have a problem with that?"

"The Guidestones are a blasphemous mockery of the Bel Tiev."

Jeema shot an incredulous look toward Rho, as if asking him to do something about his brother.

"The Guidestones are precious relics! The amount of ancient history and poetry they contain is incredible."

Nod turned his attention back to his stick and began sharpening furiously.

"Poetry," he scoffed. "Just because something rhymes doesn't make it poetry. It doesn't make it true, either."

"Okay, just take a deep breath, kid. Go ahead and believe in the Bel Tiev. As for me, I *do* consider the Guidestones as poetry, though they are more than that. They are the miraculously preserved myths of the ancients."

"They're distorted mirror-images of the truth, the opposite of the Bel Tiev."

"What, and you're telling me that the Bel Tiev is the one true holy text?" Jeema laughed.

"That's what I'm saying." Nod didn't bother looking up from his whittling.

"Goodness' sake!" Jeema said. "I suppose you also think the Sea of Antiquity is just over those mountains?" Jeema motioned vaguely to the Southwest where the Neolani Mountains would stand, hidden beneath the veil of night.

"You don't?" Rho chimed in.

Jeema said nothing. Her look of disappointment and disbelief said enough.

"Lady Xiara told me I'd swim in the Sea of Antiquity one day," Rho's smile was far off and faint.

Jeema shrugged. "Hey, if there really is an ocean out there, I'll jump right in there with you, boots and all."

"It's worth pointing out," Nod said, "that of all the ancient texts, the Bel Tiev is the only one that enjoys confirmation of its key events from extra-Tievian sources."

"Oh, please . . ." Jeema rolled her eyes. "Different peoples migrated and shared common stories, and mythologies evolved from place to place and from generation to generation. They're all basically the same story with slight variations."

"Slight variations?" Nod said. "The Guidestones are not variations. They are meticulously accurate re-tellings of the Bel Tiev from the enemy's perspective!"

Jeema shook her head. "Not true . . ."

"Take *The Eagle and the Serpent,* for example . . . "

"What about it?"

"It's basically a summary of the entire Bel Tiev from the creation to the Withering, all while painting The Serpent as some great defender and The Eagle as the enemy."

"I haven't heard this one," Rho said in a calm and reasonable tone. "I've actually never read any of the Guidestones."

"What?" Jeema's voice was thick with disappointment. "Nobody *reads* the Guidestones. You *hear* them or you *sing* them. How have you not at least heard *The Eagle and the Serpent?*"

"I don't know." Rho said, without hint of regret in his voice.

"Well, I would recite it for you," she said, "but I wouldn't want to upset our little Tievian any more than I already have."

Nod glared at Jeema. Jeema glared back. He didn't continue the argument.

"Go ahead," Nod submitted. "You should hear it, Rho."

Jeema studied Nod, then Rho. After a moment, she sat up tall and took a deep breath.

"Okay. *The Eagle and the Serpent.* It goes like this . . . "

Jeema sang with a voice that was plain and pure, like a true North wind piping its cheery way through the Darrows.

"Before the world was codified,

The Eagle could not naught abide.

When first breath first man's chest did rise,

The Eagle reigned from regal skies.

He made men tumescent with pride,

And women slight, then later wide.

He made all creatures dim and wise,

Then orchestrated their demise.

The planet shook, the seas were dried,

The bulk of living creatures died.

The Eagle would the world disband,

Except the cunning serpent's stand.

The sole defender of the land,

He slithered north 'cross desert sand.

The tallest mountain did he climb,

Expostulating Eagle's crime.

From out his mouth came forth a flame.

For Eagle's nest did Serpent aim.

He set the northern sky ablaze,

And ushered in the end of days.

Alas, the Eagle, fraught with fear,

Didst flee in form of bombardier.

A flaming egg the Eagle hurled,

Which bore down on the dying world,

The Days To Come didst come and go.

The Withering of Noloro

Deliverest thy final blow,

A fall to fell all life below."

When she had finished, Nod nodded respectfully at her. She returned his nod with a gracious nod of her own.

"Well, now we know you can't sing for rommi." Rho's mischievous smile was sarcastic. Nod chuckled.

Jeema just joined in the laughter, yelling back, "Haha, very funny! I'll bet you'd pay a lot more than rommi beans to hear me sing again!"

"True." Rho nodded. "You're right about that."

They continued laughing.

"Where's your family, Jeema?" Nod asked, suddenly changing the subject. "Are your parents alive?"

Jeema looked down into the fire with a gentle smile across her face.

"No, I've been on my own for a while now. My parents died in my thirteenth sun-cycle."

She grabbed the edges of her cloak and wrapped herself up in its warmth. She closed her eyes and imagined her mother's arms around her. She could almost smell benni cakes and halimar oil. She breathed in and savored the memory for only a moment before it faded. When she opened her eyes again, both boys offered sympathetic smiles.

"It feels weird to say it, but we're orphans, too," Nod said. "Our mom died just six days ago. She was sick practically my whole life, so it wasn't any kind of shock, but it hurts all the same."

"She shared Nod's passion for the Bel Tiev," Rho cut in before Jeema could offer her sympathies. She got the feeling he didn't want to speak about it. "Speaking of which, what else can you tell us about Lady Xiara?"

"Well, my parents were scholars of the Bel Tiev, and they would always emphasize that everything in the Bel Tiev has both a symbolic and a literal meaning. Lady Xiara is symbolic of sin. Sin will eat away at your soul if you let it, until you are nothing but an empty body walking the surface of Noloro with no purpose, no meaning, and no soul. That's the symbolic meaning behind Lady Xiara. But if my parents were right, and there's a literal meaning as well . . . then it seems the literal meaning would be . . . "

"What happened to my father," Rho finished for her. She sensed some bitterness in Rho, as if he knew the truth, but didn't want to hear it from anyone else.

Jeema could understand the feeling. Rho said nothing more. Nod looked up from his overly-sharpened stick. He seemed taken off guard by the sudden and overwhelming silence, but eventually, it began to sink in and sit well enough with all of them.

Jeema looked up at the glowing desert sky and easily found Center Star. It was not a particularly bright star, but it was still one of the most easily identified stars in the sky because it was encircled by a ring of eight brighter stars, which branched out yet again to eight more stars, creating the shape of a spider. A series of three stars which were said to represent a human torso rose up out of the spider's body, and two stars were two arms in either direction. The sky guardian, Aragyn: half-woman and half-spider. Lady Xiara. The Mother.

She hung low in the sky, off to the Southeast, just above a particularly low point in the range that formed a "V" in the series of black shapes that would become mountains again once the sun came back around to light up the Empyrean Valley. She took note of that "V" and studied the shape of it, burning it into her memory, realizing that come morning, that starry map in the sky would erase itself once again.

CHAPTER TWENTY-THREE

Nod crawled into his sleep sack. Rho saw the boy's lips moving, his eyes closed tightly. He left him alone to pray. *So young and foolish,* he thought, *but he's a lovable fool, that's for sure.*

His fingers fumbled with the cords that kept his own sleep sack rolled up tightly, and eventually got them loose by using his teeth. He unrolled it and spread it out over the desert floor near his brother.

He looked over at the girl, Jeema. She had put quite a spell on him. It was going to be an effort not to fall in love with her. She sat there on her jewelry box popping seeds out of a pinni pod, her elegant fingers gently rotating the pod in her hand.

He was grateful for the small part of him that was still reasoning well enough to turn his thoughts away from the beautiful girl in camp. He did his best to keep his eyes looking either downward as he situated his sleeping bag, or upward toward that great and terrible time-glass in the sky; but that part of him was becoming easier and easier to ignore.

He finished his work and sat down against his pack beside the fire. Jeema threw a mischievous smile at him and took a liberal swig of water from her flagon.

"You'd better save some of that," he said with a playful smile, "unless you know where to get more of it."

"Don't worry about me. I've spent far too many nights out here in this desert. There's water all around you; you just need to know where to look for it."

Rho put on his skeptic's face, but softened it with a hint of a smile. "And *you* know where to look for it?"

"Yep." She smiled again and held eye contact as she threw her head back to take an excessively greedy gulp.

He was really starting to like this girl. He smiled at her, but as soon as his eyes met hers, he was surprised to see her smile disappear. She looked . . . stunned. Confused. Afraid. Every drop of her beaming confidence he'd seen only seconds before evaporated, like Noloro's rivers during the Days To Come. It was only there for a second before she turned from him to rummage through her pack. He couldn't be sure, but it seemed as if she were afraid of something. But of what, though?

Rho watched as Jeema drew her arms back out of her pack holding a deck of cards bound together by a brass clip. She removed the clip and slid it onto her belt, and then she began to shuffle the deck, with all the style and ease of a professional *Seven-Sky* dealer. Her eyes studied the stars, scanning the night sky frantically while her hands worked in her lap. Was she avoiding looking at him, the way he had been a few minutes prior? Perhaps that's what she was afraid of—getting too close, and putting herself in a position to lose someone else.

Maybe he was reading too much into it.

Her white hair fell gracefully down along her neck as she gazed off into the heavens. He imagined she would have made a wonderful mother had she not belonged to this final, doomed generation—a child of the Withering. Perhaps there would still be time for such things . . . but there was really no deceiving himself. The moon was bearing down on Noloro so aggressively that he would be surprised if he saw another week pass by.

He knew if he wasn't careful he'd start to feel for this girl, only to have the world end shortly thereafter. But what was he really afraid of? Heartbreak? Pain? Tragedy? It wasn't a relationship he was afraid of, but the false hope that would come from it. That's what he feared. The futile wishes for a happy life together, of marriage and children. But was a false hope really anything to fear? Couldn't he just call it as he saw it from the beginning? Maybe he could just accept that there would be no marriage, no children, no happy life with anyone in his future. The best he could hope for at this point would be a few enchanting days beneath an angry sun, and a handful of bittersweet nights wrapped in another's arms beneath a killing moon.

He snapped out of his trance and realized that Jeema had been speaking to him. What was it that she had said? Her face came into focus, on it an impatient smirk that begged, *please tell me you are joking.*

"Are you gonna play or *what?*" Her arm stretched out toward him, holding the deck out in her left hand, a large stick in the other. On the ground between them, she had drawn seven kimba-limb circles and had made her move. She had taken the center circle, not surprisingly. The first move is *always* the center circle.

Rho had no interest in games right now. He wanted her, and he could see from her changing expression that she understood as much. He was overwhelmed with a sudden urge to lean forward and kiss her, but he couldn't. He was frozen. It would be too weird. The timing had to be right to pull a stunt like that.

Time, he thought . . . *there is no more time. If you want it—if you want anything in this world—you'd better take it right now, before it's too late . . . take it before it's taken from you. Stolen by that great and terrible time-glass in the sky.*

He could sense that she was nervous, but that fear was rivaled by a glinting sparkle of hope. He could see it clear as day, and it suddenly all made sense to him. She was counting on him. He was *her* final chance to love and to be loved, before the Withering lived up to its name.

The only way I can screw this up, it occurred to him, *is to sit here and do nothing.*

He eased himself forward and grabbed her hand, pulling her toward him, her body against his. His clumsy lips came awkwardly together, and miracle of miracles, they found their place on hers. She did not protest, but kissed back with a startling passion that caught him off guard. They kissed desperately, claiming what little pleasure this dying world had left behind for them.

CHAPTER TWENTY-FOUR

Jeema had only kissed one boy before Rho. Dari—her dark-skinned, black-haired, blue-eyed, one true love. Dari had kissed her in the rain outside of a little red hut with a yellow door, near the edge of the Great Chasm. It was just once, and it was quick, passionate, and fully on the lips, from a boy who was destined to die that very hour.

She came to terms with what happened to Dari long ago, and when she had first seen this new boy, she knew almost immediately that she could trust him, partly because he reminded her so much of Dari, but there was something else, too—an intuition. It didn't take long for those feelings of trust and safety to blossom into a reckless longing. She'd only truly loved a boy once before, but she thought maybe—just *maybe*—she was now beginning to feel something— even if it wasn't love, there was still something—for Rho.

The only worry she had was whether Lady Virion would get in the way or not. She had no idea what had happened to her spiritual stowaway, but she had a very strong feeling that Virion was still with her, lying dormant somewhere in the back of her mind. It was so strange the way she had simply disappeared, but she wasn't complaining. Perhaps she was just living up to her end of the bargain. Jeema would take her to Lady Xiara and Virion would let her be. She was thankful for that much. She couldn't imagine how awkward it would be trying to kiss a boy with a spirit swirling around in her head.

This kiss was very different than her first kiss. It was not a sweet schoolboy kiss, but a passionate, hungry, selfish invitation, and she gratefully accepted. She allowed Rho to put his hands on her, first between her shoulder blades and at the nape of her neck, and then at the small of her back along the waist of her blue jeans. It was probably wrong to kiss a boy she'd only just met, but given the current state of her world, she would be pleasantly surprised if there was enough time left for regrets. Jeema sunk into Rho, and for the first time in a long, long time, she felt truly wanted and fully alive.

CHAPTER TWENTY-FIVE

Nod was up first, just as the sun was coming up over the western mountains. He took a few moments to appreciate each magnificent beam of pink, violet, green, yellow, and orange painting its own allotted section of morning sky. The blood-red moon was still taking up the entire southwest corner of the sky, and the sight of it made Nod shiver. He unzipped his sleep-sack and sprung to his bare feet. It was already warm out.

A vision flashed in his mind, and Rho and Jeema were no longer wrapped up in their respective sleeping bags, but tangled up in the dark tendrils of a mysterious hooded man. It was only a flash, then it was gone. He'd completely forgotten the dream—the vision he'd had the night before—but he realized now that Jeema was certainly the white-haired girl he'd seen. He had no idea what it meant. He pondered the vision, but was left confused and frustrated by it.

Nod shook his head and grabbed a stick off the desert floor. He sat down and pulled out his knife. He began whittling away at the end of the stick, sharpening the tip to a point. This only amused him for so long, and he soon grew impatient. He carefully reached out and poked his brother's shoulder with the dull end of the stick, first gently, and then harder, and then harder still.

Rho snapped out of his sleep and scrambled up onto one elbow, his wide eyes trying to find whatever creature was stabbing, or clawing, or biting him. Nod laughed and Rho grabbed the stick, tossing it off to the side. Nod laughed louder. Jeema opened her eyes

as well. Rho looked angrily at Nod, then over at Jeema, then back at
Nod, but this time with a sleepy smile.

"All right." Rho sighed. "Just . . . give me a tick, would ya?"

They walked all morning, snacking on the bitter pods that Jeema
had collected from the herold tree. She shared them with the boys as
they began their trek toward the "V-shape" in the mountains. Along
the way, they found more, and Jeema gave them a lesson on the hidden
treasures of the herold tree. They walked for three shadowmarks
before spotting a little shun-town where they stopped to relieve their
aching legs in the shade of a long-abandoned stone structure and
tend to their weary bodies with water, jerky, and a half-shadow's rest.

Jeema's right ankle throbbed, more swollen today, but she could
still manage to walk without showing it. As the only girl in the group,
she was not about to give off the appearance of weakness. She just
needed something to take her mind off the pain, and she hoped a bit
of interesting conversation might do the trick.

"Last night, when you spoke about Xiara, you said that she told
you things . . . and I was wondering, what kinds of things did she
tell you?"

Nod rolled his eyes.

"Well, she told me that certain things were going to happen." Rho
proceeded cautiously, "Some of those things have happened, like
my father leaving us, and my mother dying. She also told me some
things that haven't happened yet. She told me that Noloro, along with
everything in it, was going to die."

"Because of the moon?" Jeema asked.

"Yeah" Rho said, "but she also said that there is a way to escape it."

"Escape what? Noloro? You mean, like . . . leave the planet?" Jeema asked.

"I don't know. I know it sounds crazy, but . . . I need to find out what she meant. She said, 'When one world ends, another begins.' I've thought a lot about that, and I still don't know exactly what it means, but I do know one thing—if I have the option, I'd rather not be sitting here when the Withering is complete, when the world finally comes to its end."

"Escape Noloro . . . How would that even be possible?"

Rho wasn't sure if she was talking to him or to herself.

"Our father used to design space shuttles before the Days to Come," Nod chimed in, "for an . . . arrow-space company—I think that's how you say it—called Wissler Brothers. He said the scientists never found another planet capable of sustaining life, but space travelers used to go up to the moon and to the space stations in rocket-propelled space shuttles and run experiments. They even had plans to build a colony on Va Eartha, but it never happened. The Days To Come changed everything."

"I remember reading about the elders before the Days to Come, and that they planned to colonize Va Eartha. The book said they were only a few years away, but I think the Days to Come arrived before they were able to."

"Do you read a lot?" Nod smiled.

"Yep! The whole Wallish clan were readers. My mom loved to read old folk tales, and my dad loved history. I used to love reading about outer space and all the stars and planets, but it always seemed more like mythology to me, you know? It's hard to believe it's real. What's that other thing you said? A space station?"

"It's basically a floating science facility, up in space. There might even be some still up there in orbit for all I know."

Jeema's eyes glanced upward. "I've never heard of a space station. You can get there by riding in a space shuttle?" She seemed skeptical.

Rho smiled, and she could tell he was holding back a laugh out of politeness.

"Exactly. Xiara hinted that there may still be a space shuttle up in the Neolani Mountains."

He gestured vaguely to a range of mountains which were far off on the northern end of the valley, and Jeema followed with her eyes.

"Do you really believe there's a space shuttle up there?"

"I have no idea, but it seems everyone from a magickal witch to the Bel Tiev agree that the world is about to end, so I figure I'm willing to find out."

A SPIDER IN THE GARDEN

CHAPTER TWENTY-SIX

When they saw it, they began to sprint. It was the most beautiful thing they had ever seen, and though none of them had ever seen anything like it, each of them knew exactly what it was.

"It's a garden!" shouted Jeema.

"It's amazing!" Nod added with excitement.

"Why is it here?" Rho asked. "*How* is it here?"

"It's *her* garden," a wide-eyed Jeema said. "A garden like that *can't* be grown in the desert. It probably couldn't be grown in all of Noloro, for that matter. This is here only by magick. These are Lady Xiara's gardens."

As they approached, there were no walls, no gates, no hedges, and no fences. There wasn't even a clear edge of the garden. They could see the shrubbery and fruit trees far ahead of them, and below their feet were scraggly patches of yellow grass that grew thicker, greener, and healthier the further in they went. The closer they came to the center, the slower they walked. It was beautiful, but something told Jeema to be on her guard. The others must have sensed it too, as they had all seemed to slow their pace together.

As they entered down a row of fruit trees—it was a pink and shiny fruit she'd never seen or heard of—an unnatural feeling continued to rise in her. There was nothing natural about a thriving garden in the middle of the Empyrean Valley, let alone the most fertile and idyllic paradise that one could have imagined. As they emerged from the orchard, the plants and trees grew larger and the sounds of forest creatures grew louder. All around them were the buzzings and chirpings and flitterings of living things. Tree branches bustled with birds whose songs they'd never heard before, and whose colors they'd never seen. Gorgeous falls of crystal-blue water flowed from enormous stone fountains and emptied into streams which meandered through the greenery, watering tall trees of all varieties which bore luscious fruit of every color. Weathered stone pathways wound themselves through thick shrubbery, sweet-smelling flowers, and elegant vines. Three valley hares hopped lazily across one of the pathways. Unable to contain her excitement, Jeema squealed with joy at the sight of them.

"This is what I always imagined the Garden of Abundance to look like," Jeema said.

"Do you think this could be it?" Rho asked.

"No," Nod chimed in. "Not possible. Mankind was banished from the Garden of Abundance when Afir and Epella sinned, remember?"

"Well, what if this is it?" Rho persisted. "What if that tree right there was the Tree of Knowledge of Good and Evil? And that one there—what if that's the Tree of Everlasting Life?"

Nod looked beyond annoyed. "Then you should leave them alone."

"There's one thing I never understood . . ." Rho continued. "The Bel Tiev says that Afir and Epella both ate from the Tree of The Knowledge of Good and Evil, and Epella ate from the tree of Everlasting Life . . . if that were true, then why wasn't everlasting life passed down to us all from Epella? I mean, why one and not the other, since the knowledge of good and evil was passed down to us?"

"Was it?" Nod shot back.

Rho remained silent and thought on Nod's question for a moment before he wandered off toward some fruit trees. Nod tried to hide his smirk, but Jeema caught it and smiled knowingly back at him.

"You are a clever one." She laughed. Nod blushed.

The three of them spent the afternoon exploring the garden paradise. Still cautious, Jeema found it easier and easier to let her guard down with each new beautiful creature she saw. Jeema imagined it would have taken days to see it all. They picked and sampled every kind of fruit they could find, stuffing their bags full of delicious snacks for the road. They would eat like royalty for the rest of their journey. Their canteens and flagons were filled to the brim with the cleanest water they'd tasted. When they were tired, they removed their boots and rested on the soft grass, watching the canopy above them sway in the breeze. It truly was a paradise.

"Do you *really* think these gardens belong to Lady Xiara?" Rho asked.

"Definitely," Jeema replied. "She's probably watching us right now."

As she said it, a shiver ran down her spine. All three began scanning the greenery for any sign of prying eyes.

"Where do you think she lives?" Jeema asked.

"I didn't see a house—or any kind of building, for that matter," Rho replied.

"Me either. We'd better explore a little more before nightfall," Rho suggested.

Jeema agreed.

"I thought she lived in that hut near the chasm," Nod said, shielding his eyes from the afternoon sun and squinting over from his bed of grass.

"No . . ." Jeema scoffed. "Lady Xiara's gardens are legendary. This is her abode, but she roams throughout the land, moving in the shadows, building webs, and . . ." She paused and realized she was wandering a little too deep into the tall grass. "She stays out of sight, but those who want to find her don't have to try very hard."

Nod nodded his head and the two boys stole a loaded glance at one another.

Way to go, Jeema. That was so very sensitive of you.

"Well," Rho clasped his hands, stretched his arms out in front of him, and cracked his knuckles. "Speaking of trying to find her, what do you say we go explore a little more?"

Jeema couldn't see the sun beyond the canopy, but they'd walked most of the day, and beside that, the diffused light seemed to be a little darker now than it had been when they'd first sat down. She figured they only had maybe one more shadowmark left of daylight.

"It'll be dark within the 'mark. We'd better set up camp pretty soon, don't you think?"

"Should I set up camp while you two search?" Nod asked. "This place has everything we'll need, but we'll still want a fire to keep warm. I'll take care of that and put on a pot of rommi beans. I'll try to have it ready by sundown."

"Good idea." Rho smiled back at his brother.

Rho found it first and called Jeema over. It was a large, steel structure raised up out of the ground, completely covered in large vines that seemed, to him, aware of their presence somehow. They twisted and tangled like large, slimy serpents. Along each of the building's four sides were two rows of balconies with doors of glass, and it appeared that there was at least a third row that had been mostly buried—probably during the Days To Come. Jeema counted twenty balconies per row on each of the shorter sides and forty-four balconies per row on each of the longer sides. One of the longer sides featured an enormous sign which towered high above the roof, which read in the old Tebbel tongue: BAY BELL SUITES.

The letters had been covered in dust and dirt ever since the Days To Come, but segments of it poked through the layers of dust. Jeema knew the color—ultraviolet—from an old textbook that belonged to her father. It was one of her favorites. She often spent shadowmarks just staring at the wonderful colors in that book, studying color charts and gradients, and contemplating how each color had its own personality. Every one gave her an unmistakable feeling that was unique to that color. Ultraviolet was the color of a flower from another time. It felt to her like something she longed for but would never be able to grasp.

"Over here!" Rho shouted from around the corner.

Jeema followed Rho's voice to one of the shorter sides of the building, where an amalgamation of vines had clearly been tamed to form a ramp up to the roof of the building. Rho was already halfway up the ramp. Jeema followed, still in awe of the fantastic setting she somehow found herself in.

At the top was a small garden with more of the same—vines, shrubbery, and rows of fruit trees, with a stone pathway between the rows of trees which led to a small triangular structure with a faded seafoam green door. On the door was a black X.

"Shall we?" Rho proposed.

"Just . . . be careful." Jeema shrugged.

Rho opened the door with caution. On the inside of the door was a small rectangular sign which in the old Tebbel tongue read: ROOF ACCESS. It was dark inside, but the light from outside spilled in to reveal a set of stairs which descended to the right. Jeema looked to Rho for reassurance, but his expression spoke only of uncertainty.

"Down we go, I guess . . . " he said. It seemed like more of a question than anything, but Jeema had no answers.

Step after step, Jeema and Rho descended into the dark underworld below Xiara's gardens. The steps led to a small landing, after which they began to decline to the left. Rho led the way, holding on to the handrail and following the stairs in this new direction. Once this set of stairs came to a landing, a new set would continue down to the left, and the stairs continued this way against each wall of the stairwell. After they had descended a certain distance, the light from the outside world began to fade away to the point that Jeema couldn't see a thing. In the darkness, the front of her boot grabbed the back of Rho's and caused him to stumble forward. He held tight to the rail and regained his balance, avoiding a fall.

"Sorry! I can't see where I'm going," whispered Jeema.

As soon as she spoke it, a flame appeared against the wall from an oil lamp hanging from a gaudy brass sconce. It lit Rho's face, and Jeema could see that he was beyond spooked. Another flame appeared a little further down the stairway, and then another, and then along the next wall, and then the next level down, and then the one below that. Level after level, the stairs were lit up. Rho leaned over the rail and looked straight down. Jeema did the same. Far below, the lamps continued to flicker on until it was too far down to see anymore.

"That's a lot of stairs," Jeema said flatly.

"A lot," Rho agreed. "I've never seen anything like it. Why do you think they built downward instead of building from the ground up?"

"I don't think they did," Jeema mused. "I think it's a remnant from the Elder People, from before the Days To Come. They probably *did* build it from the ground up. I think it's just been buried. Probably during the great floods and quakes of the Days To Come. I read that the Elder People used to build tall buildings that would tower into the sky. They had hundreds of them, all together in big clusters called cities. Not like Qaro. *Real* cities. *Enormous* cities. There are probably a lot more buildings like this one under the gardens—all buried during the Days To Come, I would guess. This is probably the tallest of them all."

"I guess so," Rho replied. "I didn't see any other towers coming up out of the ground. I've seen these sorts of buildings poking out of the ground before. We have some near the Darrows."

Every door they passed was locked, until the third floor down, where they spotted a door propped open. Rho peeked his head in and saw a long hallway with doors on either side. Lamps were lit and hung from sconces all down the long hall. The doors all had numbers next to them. One of the doors had been busted open, with the number 4747 on the wall next to the doorway, and they stopped to peek inside. The room was dimly lit by an oil lamp on a desk which revealed a couch, a coffee table, a long dresser, and two nightstands straddling a bed. On the bed was the skeleton of a man, the sight of which nearly left Jeema unable to stand. She gasped and held onto the doorframe to steady herself.

The skeleton was still dressed in the tattered clothes he must have died in. Out of his stomach protruded a sword with a broad blade. The guard was gold and shaped like a pair of wings. Jeema noted an empty black sheath with intricate moldings made of gold attached to his belt.

"Poor guy," Rho commented. "Looks like he was killed with his own sword. I wonder how that happened."

"Very strange," Jeema said, trying to control the tremor in her voice.

The two exchanged uncertain glances and then quickly continued on down the hall back to the stairwell without speaking of it further.

Down they went, and at each landing they came to, there found a doorway to the right of them, and through each of these doorways was a long hallway with doors on each side, and there were always numbers by the doors. Lamps were lit down the halls, revealing a row of doors on each level, each door with a number on it. It was Jeema who noticed the pattern.

"This level has all thirty-fours. See—3450, 3449, 3448 . . . The next level will have all thirty-threes—3350, 3349, 3348 . . . see what I mean? The first two digits grow smaller each level we go down."

It was true. They began counting down the numbers on the doors as they walked. Somewhere around level fourteen or thirteen, Jeema leaned over the edge and was almost sure that she could make out the floor of the building. The thought of reaching the bottom made her arms and legs feel suddenly very weak and sent a chill through her entire body. She would be very glad to be done walking, but she wasn't sure she wanted to know what was waiting for them at the bottom.

CHAPTER TWENTY-SEVEN

After a long day of trekking through the desert, exploring a mysterious garden paradise, collecting and chopping wood, and building a campfire, Nod was beyond exhausted. Dried wood was difficult to come by in this garden of life, and Nod only found it along the very edge of the garden. As he walked back to camp with the few dried sticks he could find, he had happened upon a large clearing, at the center of which stood an impressive stone fire pit with firewood neatly stacked and five tree stumps arranged around it as seats. Nod's worn-out limbs rejoiced at the miraculous find, which would certainly make his job much quicker and easier. Even after moving their gear to this new camp, he'd still have plenty of time to build a fire and have the rommi beans done before sundown.

The sky above the clearing was open and the sun and moon were both out of sight. As the sunlight disappeared, Nod watched the twilit sky from his sleep sack next to a blazing fire. He expected Rho and Jeema back any moment. A pot of rommi beans sat on the stones next to the flame, keeping warm, and Nod thought about his home in the Darrows. Thinking soon became dreaming, and he found himself standing in the dark. *In a cave, in the Darrows*, he thought—but no. This felt different. The air was still around him, but there was no echo at all—not even the subtle echo of one's own breathing—only a cold, dead silence. Above all, there was an overwhelming feeling of space. Even in the pitch black, the native cave-dweller knew that wherever he was, he was certainly not inside of a cave.

Suddenly before him, the ghost of a glow. A hint of light. A single ray. A burst of color. A chorus of lights. A brilliant orange crest on the horizon. It rose quickly. Faster than the sunrise. A second image flashed in his mind—the silhouette of his father's horse and cart rising up over the ridge as he watched from the Darrows—but he pushed it away, focusing on the spectacle before him. A bright orange sphere was rising quickly against a black backdrop. It illuminated the surface on which Nod stood. It was rocky and dusty and gray and cold—very different from Noloro. The luminous orb continued to ascend until it was floating above him. It got bigger. No, it was getting *closer.* And quickly. It was Noloro, and it was coming closer at an alarming rate.

If he wasn't on Noloro, then where was he? He looked at his feet, and he knew instantly that he was on the moon. It became apparent to him then that it was the moon which was moving rapidly toward Noloro, and not the other way around.

Riding a renegade moon toward his home planet, the glow from Noloro began to emit an intense heat. It grew hotter with each second, and he began to sweat. Suddenly he realized why Noloro was glowing—it was burning. Even as he was hurled through space toward his own dying world, he was not afraid. He knew that impact was inevitable, and somehow in his dream, it seemed right to him.

He was troubled nonetheless. There was something else. Something behind him. He turned around, and there lay Rho and Jeema, flat on their stomachs, clawing at the dusty ground for something they could grip, screaming like mad, and frightened out of their minds.

"It's heartbreaking," a voice said from his left. Nod jumped. There to his left, calm and collected, was a man that he did not recognize, and whose gravity was more powerful and frightening than the burning planet ahead. Frightening as he was, a strong sense of reverence and trust came over Nod.

"The Bel Tiev has prepared you for this. Your brother and Jeema have also been told that this day was coming, but though they have ears, they do not hear. The moon has been falling in the sky for some time, but though they have eyes, they do not see. You've spoken truth to your brother, and to Jeema as well, and though they have minds, they do not understand.

"You are not taken by surprise by these things because your ears have heard the words of the Bel Tiev. Your eyes have seen the Withering all around you. Your mind has understood the truth of what is coming. You stand courageous as you face the fire ahead of you because of your unyielding faith. God has told His people the things which are to come, which even now are coming, and He has prepared your heart for this very day so that it will not fail you. For the ones who have not heard, and have not seen, and have not understood, they now cry out and weep and grind their teeth and tear their clothes while their hearts fail them, overcome with fear."

Nod looked back at his brother and Jeema. Both were laying with their faces buried in the cold dust and their arms covering their heads, while their bodies rolled and squirmed around in the darkness. He looked back up at the fiery, fast-approaching planet Noloro. A drop of sweat fell into his eye and his skin began to burn. There wasn't much time until impact now.

Nod looked back at the man.

"Can we help them?" he asked.

"You may be able to help them," he said, "but it won't be easy. The serpent is going to fight you. He was careful not to move while Rho and Jeema were watching. He needs their trust, and he won't act with them watching. He's been careful and patient to wait until he could get you alone. Now he's got you. He won't let you interfere anymore if he can help it. He has been given authority over Noloro, and all of its inhabitants; but fear not, for the Spirit within you is not from Noloro, but from your Father in heaven. Because you have been sealed with the Spirit, the enemy has no authority over you. What the enemy meant for evil, God will use for good. Therefore, fear not when the enemy strikes you, for I will come to you again at the proper time to restore you, for the grave has no victory over the Spirit within you."

At this, the man turned to look as the moon on which they stood continued to barrel toward Noloro.

"How do I stop him? What do I do?" Nod shouted back at him, but his emotionless face looked on toward the doomed planet. Nod tried shouting again, but this time he could not hear any sound over the roaring blaze of the planet Noloro. He turned away from the blaze and covered his face. He didn't want to see the impact. He simply braced himself to let the inferno swallow him whole.

Then there was nothing. Everything was still, aside from his thumping heart and rapid breathing. Nod opened his eyes. He was back in the garden, safe and sound by the fire. He felt the soft green grass with the palms of his hands and took a deep breath. His racing heart began to settle as he gazed up at the canopy swaying in the gentle breeze. It was dark now, and the garden around him danced with shadows against the light from the campfire.

His brother should have been back by now. He couldn't see very well past the edge of the clearing, so he sat still and slowed his breathing well enough to listen. Nothing.

Then there was something. A rustling to his right. He spun his head to inspect but couldn't make anything out. He listened longer, but there was nothing more after that. This wasn't good. He had no lamp and no way of find one.

Had his note not been clear? It was a straight path from one camp to the other. There's no way they could have gotten lost. Unless his note had blown away, but no. The breeze was gentle, and he'd left a sturdy rock on top of the note just for that reason. Were they lost? In danger? Injured?

Nod bowed low and closed his eyes to pray, letting his head fall to the soft grass, and when he opened his eyes again, what he saw terrified him so completely that his heart nearly stopped.

Nod screamed for help, but there was no one to hear it.

CHAPTER TWENTY-EIGHT

The sign hanging from the ceiling read "Lobby," and an arrow pointed downward as they descended the final flight of stairs into the enormous open space below. There were five large, dusty crystal chandeliers, several ornate spiral staircases leading to various unknown places, and a waterfall that fell out of the darkness above. It emptied into a clear, blue stream which wound through the entire length of the room and disappeared behind an open set of ornate double doors.

There was magnificent flora all around, growing right up out of the inexplicably fertile soil below their feet.

"This reminds me of the gardens in the Darrows," Rho whispered. "It's more beautiful, though."

"You had gardens inside the caves?" Jeema asked. "How is that possible?"

"Some crops actually grow better in diffused light instead of open sun. We used mirrors and sheets to reflect and diffuse sunlight onto the few vegetables and spices that would actually grow in such poor soil. It wasn't nearly as impressive as this, but I feel more at home here than I have anywhere else since I left the Darrows. It's the smell, I think. It kind of smells like home. I wish Nod came with us."

Around the cavernous, indoor paradise were various old-world couches and large, comfy chairs, all with wonderfully intricate moldings that reminded Jeema of her parents' sofa in her childhood home. The thought of her parents made her happy and sad at the same time. She grabbed the edges of her cloak and wrapped herself up in it, closing her eyes to let the moment pass her by. Now was not the time for these feelings.

Ornate picture frames covered the walls, filled with scribblings written in black pen on yellowed parchment. A large bookshelf took up the entire far wall, filled with old dusty leather-bound books. Behind them stood a very large bed with four sturdy trees growing up from the ground at each corner, their gnarled branches twisting together over the center of the bed. A canopy of thick, dark blue and sheer, gold fabric were draped down the bed, and the linens were a shimmering gold.

Near the bed was a vanity, painted white with gold feri flowers and a white marble top. The large mirror was framed with hundreds of small sculpted golden feri flowers, and two gold chandeliers hung down from the ceiling, one on each side of the mirror.

The vines had twisted their way up the sides of each piece of furniture, making them permanent fixtures. Immediately before Jeema was a marble fireplace with golden accents and a fire dancing inside of it. She realized that she should have noticed smoke rising up from a chimney in the garden above, but she hadn't, which led her to believe there must be something magickal happening with the fire. She wondered how many years this magickal fire had been burning. An old copper bathtub that Jeema wanted to crawl inside of was placed very near to the fire. Before the fireplace on either side stood two small trees with a single thin vine pulled taught between and used as a clothesline from which various garments hung, most notably a length of sheer, scarlet fabric suspended by two clothespins before the fire.

Near the fireplace, leaning against the wall, was a ghost from her past. She thought she must be imagining it. She forced her eyes shut, held them closed, and took a deep breath. She expected to open them and realize she was hallucinating, but there it was, just sitting there against a neat stack of firewood. It was a small lumber axe with worn, white tape wrapped around the handle and a single word written in faded black ink: "Wallish."

How could that be? The last time she'd seen that axe, it was disappearing into the River of the Dead, at the bottom of the Great Chasm. She shut her eyes and tried not to think about it anymore.

Somewhere inside her, Jeema sensed Lady Virion stirring with excitement. The faint electric sensation that she'd grown accustomed to increased significantly and made her jump. Virion had been gone so long, Jeema had nearly forgotten about her, but here they were, finally having arrived at their destination, so it made sense she'd reappear now. Virion's electrical shocks continued to increase until it was no longer simply uncomfortable. It was quickly growing more and more painful, with no sign of slowing.

From somewhere behind them, a young and golden voice rang out to pierce the silence. "So, my children, you've come to visit your mother at last!"

CHAPTER TWENTY-NINE

Rho instantly recognized it as *hers*. The sound of Lady Xiara's voice simultaneously warmed his heart and sent a shiver of fear down his spine. Rho spotted her at the top of a nearby spiral staircase. She wore a shimmering white dress, and her long, elegant legs and bare feet carried her down the stairs toward them.

Lady Xiara's long, blonde hair was adorned with pink feri flowers and flowed down to the small of her back. Her arms and legs were covered with thin and graceful vines, which twisted ever so delicately around her wrists and ankles, making their way up her arms and legs and disappearing under her dress. She was the most beautiful thing either of them had ever seen.

"Lady Xiara, I am so delighted to meet you. My name is Lady Virion."

Lady Virion? Rho didn't know what to think about this, but he was suddenly reminded that he didn't really know this girl at all. There was something else as well . . . a feeling. He couldn't explain it, but it was as if Jeema had suddenly become someone else.

"I've always dreamed of meeting you, Lady Xiara. To actually see you in the flesh is . . . to even look at you is—What are you doing? Wait!"

As Jeema spoke, several vines quickly crawled up her legs and wrapped themselves around her torso, pulling her swiftly and firmly against the wall. One thin vine slid itself around her face several times, completely covering her mouth. Rho's first instinct was to run after her, but he stood frozen, fearful of what might happen to him if he dared cross Lady Xiara.

Are you really just going to stand here? Just like you stood there and watched while the Trappers whipped your brother? You're a coward, Rho. Pulled off the ground and pinned to the wall by the vines, the girl struggled. Rho could see that she was trying to scream, but only muffled sounds could be heard.

"Dear child, it goes without saying that a lady does not ramble like an imbecile. Unfortunately, my master has forbidden me from killing either of you, but he certainly didn't say I had to listen to your blathering."

She said this all with an innocent smile and with a grace and elegance that almost made everything that was happening feel perfectly normal. He could see Jeema fighting against the vines, but they seemed to fight back and would not give at all. He remembered the vines he'd seen while searching for the entrance, and how they'd almost seemed alive to him. It didn't seem so far-fetched now. "Try all you want, dear," she advised, "but the harder you struggle, the tighter they'll hold you."

"So if you're not allowed to kill us, does that mean we aren't supposed to die when the moon . . . you know?" Rho asked.

Xiara made a face that seemed to say, *oh, well aren't you just the most precious thing I've ever seen.*

"It's been quite some time, hasn't it, child? You've become a man— and a handsome one at that! If you aren't just the spitting image of your father . . . "

The beautiful lady meandered through the luscious greenery toward him as she spoke sweetly and politely.

"But my, what an arrogant question!" She playfully feigned surprise. "Of course, you're *supposed* to die. The Withering is coming to an end. You were wise to come to me. Had you stayed, you'd be dead in a few days' time. In fact, rumor has it by this time tomorrow, Qaro will be in ashes."

Jeema's body thrashed at this, and she let out a muffled shriek. Then she stopped moving altogether. It wasn't the vines. It was something else. Her eyes lit up as if she'd experienced an intense pain. Her body convulsed and then shut down. Seeing this, Rho ran to her. Whatever fear held him back before was gone. He grasped her hand and placed his fingers on her wrist, searching for a pulse. He took a deep breath and concentrated on keeping his own heartrate down so he could feel hers. Strong and steady. He let out a loud and long sigh. She was still alive, at least.

Maybe the thought of losing her home was too much for her to deal with, causing her to faint. Maybe she was overcome with worry, with fear for those she loves back home. He didn't know much about her, but he knew that Qaro was home to her. If Xiara had said the same thing about the Darrows, he might have had a similar reaction, even if he never cared to return. Then again, could they really even believe Lady Xiara? Why would they take the word of this complete stranger, the one who had attacked Jeema with magickal plant-life immediately upon meeting, like a complete psycho? Perhaps she was just trying to manipulate them . . . but why?

Lady Xiara spoke again without a hint of concern in her voice.

"I think that you and I should go up to the Neolani Mountains together and find your father's space shuttle. If it's an escape you seek, that is the only place I know of that *might* offer a way out. If we did find a shuttle there, we would have your father to thank. He helped to build it before the Days To Come, though I can't promise it will still be there. Even if it is, I can't promise it will still be operational. Even so, if we're very, very lucky, we just might happen upon a way off of this dying world."

She picked a black rose from its stem and held it in front of her, and it instantly withered into a twisted and hideous brown shape right before his eyes.

"You see, everything is *supposed* to die," she explained. "I was *supposed* to die long ago. No one has the right to live forever. Remember, Rho—you must never confuse the *right* to life . . . "

She held the dead rose up and gently breathed over it. Immediately, its petals were restored, injected with new life, and it looked more beautiful and fully alive than it had before.

" . . . with the *gift* of life," she finished.

As she spoke, he saw vines pushing up through the soil at his feet. He backed away, then spun and tried to run, but there were vines rising up behind him, as well. One of them caught his ankle, and he pulled away, to no avail. More vines followed until a full throne of vines slowly formed, rising up from the ground beneath Rho. More vines reached up and pulled him into place upon it, holding him firmly against the seat.

"Is that what you did to my dad? Did you suck the life out of him, like you did with that rose?" Rho blurted.

"Well, well." She looked down at the rose, and then back up at Rho with a playful smile. "It wasn't exactly like the rose, but you're close enough, I suppose. The difference being that your father made a choice, child. He accepted the conditions of our bargain, and he gave his life of his own volition in order to save the woman he loved."

"So, what then? You drain the life out of people, and that's how you stay young?" he shouted. "That's how you've managed to stay alive so long? Isn't it?"

"Ah, but it's also how your mother managed to stay alive so long, isn't it?" She corrected him in a slightly scolding tone. "She was *supposed* to die long before she did, but your father—valiant man that he was—gave up his life little by little, drop by drop, so that your mother could live as long as she did. He gave all that he had and all that he was for her, for as long as he could, one bottle at a time. Of course, I wouldn't be around to help him or anyone else if I didn't take a small share of that life for myself. It was all part of the deal, and your father agreed to the terms. In any case, I thought it such a noble gesture on his part. Most people I deal with come to me with more selfish desires."

Rho's head was swimming with realization.

My dad was no coward, he was a hero. He didn't leave us, he gave himself up for us. The ortero was wrong about him—the whole village was wrong about him.

His dad's song flashed in his mind, and for the first time, he thought he might fully understand the true meaning behind some of the verses that had perplexed and even troubled him as a child . . .

I'm taking the wagon out riding,

To visit a lady in hiding,

No mistress, no lover,

I want nothing of her,

Except for the life she's providing.

A darkness is hidden inside her.

She's more venomous than a spider,

She supplies what I need,

By her set price, I bleed.

The lady is truly a biter.

His mind was swimming. He knew he needed to focus if he was going to get them out alive. Beyond Lady Xiara, Jeema's body hung from a wall of vines. She was depending on him. Nod was depending on him, too. It was up to Rho to look out for them. Rho took a deep breath, then glared up at Lady Xiara.

"I know who you are," he said blankly. "The quilt in the hut . . . the garden . . . the serpent . . . I know your real name."

"I go by many names, child, and all of them are real," she replied.

"I mean your *original* name. Your *real*, real name. You're *her*. The first woman. The one who ate from the tree of everlasting life. The one the serpent first deceived. You are Epella."

"I am she," she conceded with a darkening glare. "Now you answer a question for me. Do you care for her? That one over there—the girl you met only last night?"

That didn't sit well with Rho, though he wasn't surprised that she'd known precisely when they'd met. He looked at Jeema, suspended by a tangle of vines. He wondered if his eyes were deceiving him, or if the vines that held her had loosened their grip on her. He was almost certain she had been higher up a moment ago. He turned his attention back to Xiara.

"I do care for her. I'm not even sure if I know her real name, but it doesn't matter. The world is ending, and we mortals have to look after one another."

"We mortals?" She laughed. She raised an elegant hand to gesture toward Jeema. "I'm going to help you out, so listen to what I say, Rho. That is no mortal. Lady Virion is a spirit—and an evil one at that."

Rho looked at Jeema again in disbelief. Admittedly, something hadn't seemed right when she'd introduced herself to Xiara as "Lady Virion," and he wondered if Lady Xiara spoke the truth. Still, he didn't trust Xiara, and he couldn't help but feel that the girl who had called herself "Lady Virion" was a different person entirely than the girl he'd met in the desert. He couldn't explain it, and he was starting to think he was crazy, yet there was a part of him that insisted he should not believe Xiara.

"The serpent has deceived you, as well," Xiara gloated. "Who do you think arranged your magickal, little meeting in the desert? Why do you think the hut was empty when you came looking for me? It is his greatest desire for the two of you to fall in love and have children for him."

"*What?* Have children for him? For who—the serpent?" Rho scrunched his up face in disgust. He was simultaneously puzzled and disturbed.

"He has a purpose for the two of you, and for your half-breed children after you," she explained with a hint of what Rho thought might be jealousy.

"How does that make any sense? Why would the serpent want anything from two orphans from the middle of nowhere?"

She smiled a poisonous smile that almost made Rho sick. It was the first physical indication of what Rho had begun to suspect shortly after they'd arrived—that Lady Xiara was pure evil, and it had been a mistake to come here.

"Because you are broken things, both of you."

Rho watched her strut around one of the trees, still smiling that same poisonous smile, until she stood before the fire, her silhouette projected through the square of sheer scarlet fabric which hung from the clothesline vine.

"I would prefer if it were my child, to be honest, but he made it very clear that he wants it to be hers, so he's forbidden me from wrapping you up in my web and taking you for myself. Only . . ."

She slid the straps of her dress off her shoulders, and then down to the ground it went, revealing her perfect anatomy in silhouette.

" . . . it's often the forbidden fruit which has the sweetest taste."

She pulled a lacy, black robe from the clothesline and slowly slipped it on. Her perfect silhouette was intoxicating, and Rho felt a variety of conflicting emotions as she slinked out from behind the cut of fabric and back around the tree toward Rho. The robe was very revealing, and Rho was repulsed and aroused all at once. As spirit clashed against nature, he understood just how important it would be for him to resist the temptation before him. The sorceress was conjuring feelings he'd never experienced before, and he was quickly being reduced to a pathetic puddle of a man. He understood that this was another manipulation, one that he could not give in to, but he didn't think he had the willpower to resist her.

CHAPTER THIRTY

Lady Xiara strutted toward Rho. He made every effort to not look the witch in the eyes—not look at her at all. He knew if he gave in to her, even slightly, he would be done for. He struggled to free his arms from his restraints, but the vines tightened around them in response. He was stuck.

"Take me with you, Rho. Leave the girl. I can take you away from this dying world. We can live on, and I can be your wife. I can love you and take care of you and give you children. I'll make you a king, and I'll be your beautiful queen." Her words melted him, tickling behind his ear and sending a warm shiver through his entire body.

He was ready to give into her seduction. It was no use resisting. There was no escaping her magick charms. She was powerful and beautiful. The world was about to end, and she was his only way out. He wanted to go with her. He wanted her to be his queen . . .

Then he saw it. It was just a hint, but it was enough. In her eyes, he saw the darkness his father had sung about. He could see the venom pumping through her veins just beneath her perfect skin. Just a small tear in the veil, and somehow, all was revealed. Did it matter, though? He still wanted her, and she wanted him. There was no other way off of this planet, was there? Maybe she wasn't perfect, but she was beautiful. She would make a wonderful queen. He wanted to be her king. He wanted to live with her forever. He looked into her eyes, ready to give himself to her completely, but there it was again, that little glint of darkness. It was then that a thought popped into his mind. It was a thought he really didn't want to think, but it was there nonetheless, and it was unavoidable. If the serpent was real, and if Epella was real, wouldn't that mean that God was real? Suddenly the thought of a real God up in heaven didn't seem so ridiculous to him. In fact, at the moment, that small part of him that could still manage to reason was crying out for it to be true. A flurry of thoughts filled his mind. Was he a fool for having rejected God? Would God hate him for that? Would God reject him, the way he had rejected God? Without thinking, Rho looked up and shouted, "God, help us! Please!"

He drew a deep breath, opened his eyes, and was shocked to see that Xiara had fallen to the ground. Her pretty jaw hung open in disbelief. He felt an unnatural calm take hold of him. He wasn't sure what had happened, but he felt a deep sense of relief deep in his soul, beyond anything he'd ever felt. It was as if he'd been walking through a desert for years and had only now realized that there had been a river of fresh water flowing right beside him all along. For a moment, Rho felt entirely whole. As Xiara rose to her feet, Rho resolved to himself that no matter what she did—no matter what he saw—he would remain strong for his brother and for Jeema. Strong like his father had been for his mother. Strong like his father had been for him.

"You choose him over me then? Fine. Your father was the same way. Such a fool. Do you really think it's worth it?"

"What do you mean?"

"You're going to die now, Rho. You've made your choice. Is it worth it?"

As Rho tried to process Xiara's question, he looked up at Jeema, still unconscious and suspended against the wall by the same magickal vines that bound him to the chair. She was definitely hanging lower. Her feet were nearly at the ground now. His eyes weren't deceiving him. The vines had become loose around Jeema's motionless body. He noticed that the vines around his own arms had loosened a bit. He tugged his left arm gently against the vines and they squeezed his left arm back with an equal amount of force. They stayed relatively loose against his motionless right arm. He took a deep breath and made his best attempt at relaxing his body, and the vines slowly relaxed their grip, albeit ever so slightly. He tried to remain still as Xiara approached and leaned over him, grasping the nape of his neck in her palm. Her grip was powerful, and he got the impression this was only a taste of her strength. The charade of beauty quickly began to fall away. Xiara's voice became like poison frothing through clenched teeth.

"We would have had the most beautiful, broken children, don't you think, Rho?" She circled behind him and slid her cheek up against his. Her hands moved down his neck to his shoulders, then down his biceps, where she suddenly gripped him with both hands, her nails sinking into his arms like talons. Rho's body tensed, and the vines pulled against his skin in response. "I'm going to make you mine whether you like it or not, boy. There's not much beauty left in this dying world. You might as well enjoy what little is left!"

She released him and streams of blood ran down each arm as she slithered her body around to face him.

"Beauty?" Rho said. "You're not beautiful. You're disgusting and hideous. You're a monster!"

Xiara's face twisted with anger, and she unleashed an intensity Rho would have never thought her capable of.

"Liar!" she shrieked. "I am the first and most beautiful woman of all creation. Every woman after me is a degenerate, mutant *clone*!"

"You don't know the first thing about beauty!" he shouted back at her. "Have you ever actually loved anyone before? What my father did for my mother—*that* is beauty. *You* destroyed my family, and now you want to destroy me too. You think you're the most beautiful thing out of all creation . . . You are the *destroyer* of beauty. You're an abomination!"

"An abomination?" She laughed maniacally. "*I'm* an abomination?"

Rho immediately regretted his outburst as the once-beautiful creature before him began to change into something else—something much darker. Her eyes became large, black mirrors. Her face was still beautiful, but it had become harder, and far more terrifying. Her legs seemed to be . . . shedding. Whatever was beneath the skin was slimy, hairy, and black. Whatever it was made a sickening slurping sound as it sloughed off the dead skin. The vines running along her skin seemed to be drying out and dying, much like the rose had earlier, darkening into an ugly mess of brown rot. Her muscle fibers twisted and expanded, and the vines that graced her legs gnarled themselves into hideous, black protrusions, two on each side. They continued to stretch outward until they pushed their way down to the ground, where they reworked themselves into a pair of gnarled legs. Below her hips, Rho saw the body of an enormous black spider emerging, and he remembered another of the Lady Xiara's many names: Aragyn—half woman, half spider.

Out of pure instinct, he jerked away to the side, and the vines gripped him hard, pulling him firmly back against the twisted throne he sat upon. He was completely helpless, trapped beneath the shadow of the terror before him. He had no choice but to accept that these were going to be the last few moments of his life.

CHAPTER THIRTY-ONE

"I am beauty incarnate!" Aragyn bellowed. "Strength is beauty! Power is beauty! Immortality is beauty!"

The creature's voice sounded the same as it always had, only amplified. It was far louder and far more terrible than any human voice he'd ever heard. When she opened her mouth, Rho could now make out two large fangs dripping with frothy saliva . . . or venom . . . or both. As Aragyn loomed over him, Rho felt as if he'd already been consumed by evil. He could feel the darkness seeping out of the beast and trying to work its way into his soul. It shocked him how tangible—how real it felt—and it dawned on him that he had felt something just as real after he'd cried out to God before. He decided to pray. He didn't really remember how to, and he was afraid God wouldn't hear him, but there was no other hope for him.

God, he prayed. *Please, if you can hear me, save us. If you can't save me and Jeema, then at least take care of my brother, Nod. I'm sorry I didn't believe in you, but I do right now. Please help us.*

Aragyn shrieked, and Rho felt as if his ears had been stabbed with knives.

"You arrogant little brat!" she thundered. "You look at me when I'm talking to you! You show your mother some respect!"

"My mother?" he shouted back. "My mother was an angel! I don't know what kind of devil you are!"

"I am your queen! And do you know how I've managed to stay so young and beautiful for all these millennia, boy? It's the same arrangement every time, just like with your father. It's either some ridiculous sap who's willing to give up his life for the woman he loves, or some pathetic piece of filth begging for someone to love him. You think that love is beautiful? Love is not beautiful. Love is stupid and weak. Love is a death sentence."

"Sounds to me like love is what's kept you alive all this time," Rho said, "even if that love wasn't meant for you."

"Oh, shut up. Love didn't keep me alive. I saw how these pathetic mortals would die for love and I capitalized on it."

"You exploited it, but it was still the source of all your strength, all your power, your immortality!"

Aragyn seethed and let out another terrible shriek. Behind her, Rho caught a glimpse of Jeema's body as it hung completely motionless from a loose tangle of vines against the wall. Her legs were now sprawled out on the ground, and her arms were nearly clear of the sling of vines all around her. Had Jeema been awake, he imagined she would have been screaming, pulling, and writhing. The vines would have gripped her tightly and escape would have been impossible. As things were, her motionless body was slowly slipping through the increasingly relaxed grip of the vines.

"Love is worthless! I'm alive because of my own fiery volition, my own iron will to do what it takes to survive!"

"Yeah?" Rho asked. "And what was that?"

Aragyn's mouth formed a sickly smile as she bent down and whispered into Rho's ear, "How do you think all those beautiful lovers came to be sick in the first place?" Rho's eyes widened in horrific realization. She continued. "You see, I do what I have to do in order to survive, and *that's* the reason I'm still alive. Love had nothing to do with it."

A blind, red hatred covered Rho, and he fought the vines fiercely trying to lunge at the monster before him. He could see that she was enjoying his suffering, but he didn't care. He didn't care about anything at that moment. All he wanted to do was to break free of the vines that bound him so he could kill her.

"You killed my parents! You *are* evil. You're a monster!"

"I am the mother of all! I am Noloro. I am the only reason you're still alive."

"You're just following orders! You're not the one calling the shots! You can't kill me because the serpent won't let you!"

"I'm not *supposed* to kill you, but let me tell you a little secret the serpent taught me a very, very long time ago in the garden where we first met. The rules can mean just about anything if you're clever enough. Besides, I didn't get where I am by playing by the rules."

Aragyn laughed and bared down on Rho. He could feel her hot, sticky breath on his neck. Her ravenous fangs dripped excessively just inches from his throat, and he closed his eyes tight, bracing himself for the strike.

Instead of biting him, she let out the loudest shriek yet, and Rho was certain that his head would explode. He tried to cover his ears, but the vines pulled tighter against his wrists. When he opened his eyes, he saw Aragyn flailing mindlessly through the air as if she were having a seizure.

His eyes followed her beautiful torso downward past her navel, down that hideous spider thorax which contorted and spasmed. There, between the spider's giant legs, was something amazing. He saw Jeema, holding on for dear life to the handle of a lumber axe which she had buried into the spider's underside. There was an incredible determination on her face—an intense focus. She would not be shaken loose from the axe, and the spider's legs finally gave out, collapsing one joint at a time. Jeema yanked on the handle of the axe, and it was dislodged from the spider's belly. A mixture of blood and a sickly yellow pus-like substance spurted out of the wound in regular pulses, splattering on the ground. Jeema ran clear of the dying monster before it swayed and collapsed onto its side, still writhing mindlessly for a few moments. Finally, everything stopped altogether, and the beast was lying dead on the floor.

Jeema stood panting, blood and pus splattered across her boots and pants, leaning on the axe with her right hand. She looked at Rho in silence for a moment until she was able to catch her breath. He looked into her searing eyes and didn't recognize the girl who now growled at him with a disturbing and supernatural hatred that ate clean through his bones and down into his soul.

"She wanted to kill me and escape Noloro in my place. She wanted to keep you all to herself. You're my ticket off of this planet, boy. *Mine*! And *nothing* comes between me and what's mine—*nothing*!"

CHAPTER THIRTY-TWO

A few axe swings later, Rho was freed from his restraints. He was so confused by Jeema's behavior that he didn't even know how to ask her what happened to the girl who had shared her pinni pods with him and taught him to draw water from a herold tree. He finally asked her the first straightforward question that came to his mind.

"Where did you get the axe?"

She looked down at the axe. He could see her mind working out an answer, and he could tell that it wouldn't be a simple one.

"It was just sitting there right next to me. I honestly think Xiara put it there so she would see it."

Something definitely wasn't right with her. He didn't understand what it was, but he could feel it, and it was making his skin crawl.

"So *who* would see it?"

"Jeema."

Rho's stomach turned.

"If you're not Jeema, then . . . who are you?"

The girl sighed, clearly bothered, but she appeared to resign herself to attempting an explanation. She looked into his eyes, and he could sense it—the same darkness he'd seen in Aragyn's. "My name is Lady Virion. I've been living with Jeema for a long time now, since she was very young, even before she lost her parents. I'm a part of her. I know this must be very strange to you, but all three of us want the same thing—to get off of this dying planet before the Withering is complete."

"All three of us?"

"You, me, and Jeema."

"And Nod."

"All right," her jaw jutted out in annoyance, "all four of us, then."

Lady Virion yanked a white linen sheet from the beautiful bed and began wiping the blood and pus from her face. She bent down at the edge of the stream and splashed herself with the clear, flowing water, and cleaned herself as best she could.

"What about Jeema? What happened to her?"

"She passed out. From the pain."

"Pain? From fighting the vines?"

"From fighting me."

Rho's breath caught. Virion was kneeling over the water with her back toward him, and she grew still, as well. He couldn't see her face, but he imagined her expression to be every bit as threatening as her words has sounded.

"She's fine," Virion said finally. "She's just asleep. There was no way we were getting away from those accursed vines with her panicking like that. I had to put her to sleep for her own good. She'll wake up again soon enough."

"So, were you awake that entire time?" Rho asked.

"Yes."

It felt wrong. All of this. Even so, there didn't seem to be anything to do about it except to get back to the garden and Nod as quickly as he could. He couldn't imagine how worried Nod must be. They'd probably been in this building half the night, and they still had a long climb back up the stairs. He turned his attention to the base of that grand staircase leading back to the surface. Only the first several steps were visible, the rest swallowed up in darkness. He took a few steps in the direction of the suitcase, but his footsteps echoed so loudly throughout the empty lobby that he stopped himself again. He began to wonder what other horrors might be lurking in that wicked darkness.

"You said you thought maybe Lady Xiara wanted Jeema to see it . . . " Rho tried to find the right words, but nothing was making sense. "The axe, I mean. Do you know why she wanted Jeema to see that axe?"

"Just to get to her, I suppose."

"To get to her?"

"To get under her skin. To upset her."

"I . . . I feel like I'm missing something."

Virion spun the axe around and held it up for him to read the word written on the handle grip: "Wallish."

Rho's eyes widened as a new wave of questions crashed over him.

"That's Jeema's family name!"

"This axe belonged to her father before he died, but he wasn't the one wielding this axe on the night of the Blood Rain when it fell, down to the bottom, down to the River of the Dead."

Rho opened his mouth to ask . . . something, but he found he had no words. He didn't know what the questions were. He just knew that he had a lot of them.

"It's a long story, and I'd rather not linger down here. There's plenty of time to tell you all about it on the way up and out."

PART III:

NO SHORTAGE OF ORPHANS

THE BLOOD RAIN

CHAPTER THIRTY-THREE

Rho and Lady Virion ascended the dark stairwell. The lamps on the sconces were still lit, but Rho figured whatever magick had kept them burning at Xiara's whim for all these years no longer held any power over them. He imagined they would either die out or burn themselves up eventually.

"She wouldn't want to talk about it," Virion said, "but she *does* want you to know about it."

"How do you know that?" Rho asked.

"Because she likes you, Rho." Virion studied him, clearly trying to gauge his reaction. Rho could feel himself blushing. "Do you like Jeema?"

"I don't know, we've only just met." He tried to hide his face by watching his feet take step after step. It was no use. Her gaze burned in his periphery.

"She wants to know you better, and she wants you to know about her. It's just that she's too shy to tell you herself." Virion didn't sound very convincing.

Everything about this conversation seemed forced and awkward to Rho. "Are you sure about that?"

"I told you," Virion said, "I'm a part of her. I know."

"Have you always been a part of Jeema?" Rho asked.

"No," Virion said. "When I started my training, I was assigned to her. She was just a baby. I wasn't a part of her at all. I studied her, learned everything I could about her—all her vulnerabilities and all her desires. I used those desires to gently coax her into a vulnerable state, then waited patiently for an opening. Eventually, I was able to slip in once she had her guard down. The funny thing is, most of the time, you mortals understand what's happening, but it doesn't matter. If you offer it to them and do it right, it's impossible for them to resist."

Rho's chest became tight and found it hard to form his thoughts. Was he actually speaking to an evil spirit? He didn't want to betray his fear and give her the idea that she had any power over him, so he decided to continue as casually as possible.

"So, you're sort of . . . the opposite of a guardian angel," Rho said.

Virion scrunched up her face. "No. It's not like that at all."

There was silence, and with each step up, the silence seemed to grow more hostile. The only sound was the knocking of their boots on the wooden steps and its echo through the stairwell. Rho needed to think of something else to talk about, and quickly.

"There was something you said before that I didn't understand," he finally said. "You said that the axe belonged to Jeema's dad, but that someone else had it on the . . . blood night?"

"The Blood Rain," Virion said.

"The Blood Rain," Rho repeated. "You said that Jeema would want me to hear that story. Can you tell me?"

Virion studied him. It was hard to make out her expression in the dark, but her eyes seemed void of any emotion. She finally looked away and continued walking in silence. Rho wondered if he'd said something wrong, but eventually, Virion spoke.

"It started with the Red Skull Killers. Bull Jasser was the leader of the Red Skull Killers. He was a fat kid with beady eyes, a scrunched-up snout for a nose, a leathery pair of lips which were always pressed into a painful scowl, and a round face that was apparently only capable of the one expression. He was as mean as a briarhog and maybe as strong, too. Girls steered clear of Bull, and boys made sure they were always on his good side.

"Then there was Dari Lamb, Ortero Tilly's son. He was a handsome boy with dark skin and a kind, caring face. His eyes were the same color as yours. They comforted Jeema. He had black hair that fell over his eyebrows—it had always bugged me. For some reason though, Jeema loved him.

"On rainy days, classes were canceled and the grown-ups were busy working, their attention focused on collecting and purifying as much rainwater as possible, hopefully enough to get the entire town through the killing season without having to resort to rationing. The older kids were expected to work as well, collecting, measuring, and most importantly, watching and learning. One day this younger generation would be responsible for ensuring that the people of Qaro had enough water to survive the killing season.

"It was Jeema's last sun-cycle before she would be expected to help the adults, and it really affected her, just knowing that it was her last one. First Rain was the absolute best day of the year for children in Qaro, and for me, as well. With the adults and older kids all tied up in their work, the children could get away with pretty much anything—and they did. The went on many adventures, played dangerous games, and boys and girls snuck off and spent the day exploring the outskirts with no adults around to correct them. Those were the days when lifelong memories were made, the days that children longed for. What fools they were—waiting all year long for a day with no parents.

"At First Rain, children were jolted awake from their monotonous and burdensome routines, and for one incredible day, the children of Qaro really, truly lived. In a way, your final First Rain marked the final day of childhood.

"On this particular First Rain, Jeema's mother woke her up before sunrise. I heard the rain falling on the roof, and I remember Jeema running to the window to see. It was beautiful. Jeema's mother called to her. She had laid some things out on the bed. One of those things was a cloak—the one I'm wearing now. Next to it was an umbrella—we don't have it anymore, though.

"Jeema's mother told her, 'I still remember my very last First Rain as a child, Jeems, and I know how important it is. You'll have fond memories of this day for the rest of your life, and I wanted to make it a little extra special. Do you like it?'

"She loved it. I remember she couldn't even talk for the lump in her throat, so she just nodded and smiled as the tears formed in her eyes. Her mother smiled and fought back tears herself.

"We tried on our new cloak. We walked back and forth across the room, twirling the cloak and spinning the umbrella. We had no care in the world, just laughed together in that room. She hugged her mother and thanked her and they both cried some more. It was Jeema's last day as a child, and that did not seem right to either of them.

"The final item on the bed was her mother's jewelry box. It's the chimiwood jewelry box in my pack with all the beautiful Tievian designs carved into it—you've seen it. Jeema's father did all the carvings by hand and gave it to her mother on their first wedding anniversary. As a girl, I remember Jeema would just sit on the bed and hold it in her lap, running her hands over the carving, and thinking about the Bel Tiev stories for hours. That box was her faith, her home, both of her parents, and their love for one another, all wrapped into one. It was her favorite, and her mother knew it, so she gave it to her that morning to commemorate her last day of childhood.

"After breakfast that morning, there was a knock at the front door. We peeked from the bedroom as her mother answered the door. It was Dari Lamb. He was standing in the rain, his wet hair stuck against his face under the hood of his oxblood cloak. He asked if he could come in. He had a slingshot in his hand, and he said he had something very serious he needed to talk about. Her mother brought him in and dried him off with a white towel. He spoke with a hushed urgency, and he looked as if he'd just seen a murder. He said that Bull Jasser had told him a dark secret and that our family was in danger."

CHAPTER THIRTY-FOUR

"What most people don't realize is that Bull Jasser wasn't evil by accident—he was carefully molded into a terrible person by his parents and the evil spirits they entertained. Bull's father was the leader of the Brood, a sort of militia that was well-known and feared by the mortals throughout Qaro at that time. They were always promoting radical and violent ideas and masking them with nice words like 'equality' and 'love'—the oldest trick in the book. In the previous weeks, the Brood had been leading a movement to abolish the Bel Tiev because of its 'hateful' rhetoric, threatening the town's orteros and terrorizing Tievian believers.

"The dark secret that Bull had told Dari that morning was that Bull's father Jim was planning to 'cleanse' Qaro of Tievian loyalists that day of the First Rain. In other words, he was going to kill anyone known to own a copy of the Bel Tiev or known to believe in the Bel Tiev. That would be Jeema's and Dari's parents both. Dari's mother was an ortero. Dari said that Bull had been mouthing off about how the First Rain would wash away all the Tievian filth, and how by sunset there would be nothing left of their kind but a pile of rotting corpses.

"He said, 'I told my parents, but they won't leave. They said no ortero could ever leave her flock to face the wolves alone. They told me I had to head across the chasm and stay with my uncle Dulner's family for a while, so that's what I'm going to do. They also told me to stop here and warn your family on my way out of town.'

"When Jeema's father heard this, he threw open the door and scanned the streets, looking for any oncoming trouble. Then he hurried out to the woodshed and returned with his lumber axe. It had white tape around the handle and their family name written on it in black marker—'Wallish.' He handed the axe to Dari and he said, 'You're a good boy, Dari Lamb. Thank you for stopping to warn us, son. Now, you take this axe and do as your parents told you, and you take my daughter with you to Dulner's house. You two leave town, and you don't come back until we send for you. You stay with your Uncle Dulner until this is all over. Whatever happens, you protect my daughter. You keep her safe for me, Dari. You hear me?'

"The boy was obviously frightened. It was actually amusing; he couldn't stop blinking, but he nodded back. Jeema's mother held her close, and her father put his arms around them both and prayed. They hugged each other and cried and kissed one another for far too long, but it's a moment that Jeema goes back to constantly. Finally, her father stood up and put his big, rough hand on our cheek. 'Don't worry, sweetheart. Dulner is a good man, and his wife is an excellent cook. Though, she doesn't compare to your mother, of course. You'll be fine, Jeems. I promise. Now go.'

"Jeema wept, but nodded in agreement. I was eager to see what was happening outside, but Jeema was so scared that she was frozen. Her mother said nothing, but inside Jeema was a deep, painful sorrow that wanted to plead with her mother to stay. Her mother studied Jeema's face frantically with silent and unapologetic despair, then pulled her close and held her tightly for one last hug and kiss as I saw her dad nod to Dari from behind her. Dari reached for Jeema's hand and gently pulled her through the door and out into the rain.

It stung her face like needles, and Jeema struggled to open her brand new umbrella. Only a faint and dull glow of sunlight burned against a thick wall of black clouds on the horizon, like an ominous fire in the heavens. It was black above, black below, and blood red ahead.

"At the far end of the street was yet another red glow. It was hard to tell in the dark and through the rain, but a flash of lightning illuminated a small band of men and women carrying torches through the shadows. It was the Brood, and they were headed our way. It was easy enough to keep hidden in the deep shadows of the houses. Our moves were careful and quick, silent and swift. From the heavens, the ruthless roar of thunder shook the ground beneath us.

"I heard a woman nearby yelling, 'No, Jim! Please!' It sounded like Jeema's teacher, Mrs. Baptiste, only I'd never heard her voice sound like that before. Her house was near, so I turned to see. She was crying, 'Jim! Jim! No, Jim!' and after that, there was only screaming. The door to Mrs. Baptiste's home flew open and shadows danced around a tall, burly ox of a man gripping a long, narrow sword. A glint of moonlight reflected in the steel as he ran in the opposite direction. I knew by his frame that it was Jim Jasser. There was a flash of lightning, and I saw him clearly. He wore a black hooded cloak and the rain dripping from his blade was red with fresh blood.

CHAPTER THIRTY-FIVE

"Jeema tried not to think about what had just occurred. She was terrified to the point where she couldn't move. I wasn't permitted yet to take control of Jeema's body back then, so I was stuck there, paralyzed by her fear. The thunder moved through us like an ancient curse. Dari tugged at her hand, and when Jeema wouldn't move, he put his arm around her waist and gently led her through the shadows and down the road out of town. She was too frightened to run. She was too afraid even to think. As she crossed the street, we spotted another small group of people carrying torches. These were much closer, but they were headed away from her.

"Eventually, Dari got Jeema's legs working somehow, and they ran as fast as they could on the path that leads to the chasm, through the mud and the rain. Her feet felt bruised, they were so cold. Finally, they came to the clubhouse at the edge of the chasm. It was an old, abandoned shack that some of the boys from school had claimed for themselves. They had painted it red with a yellow door and a blue tin roof.

"Dari asked Jeema if she could make it over the chasm, or if she needed a rest. She told him she could use a rest, and to this day she's never forgiven herself for that. They decided to rest in the clubhouse, out of the rain. They slowed to a walk and headed toward the cheery little hut against the pouring rain.

"As they took shelter beneath the awning of the hut, Dari stopped Jeema and asked her if she was okay. She said yes, but she wasn't. It was all rather exciting to me, but to Jeema, everything felt like a terrible dream—so surreal and slanted. She experienced everything and processed nothing, until she looked into Dari's eyes, and I could feel it then that she felt safe. She could focus there. She could hold onto him. We could finally move again. She put her hand on his cheek and they had a moment together. He kissed her, and she kissed him back.

"Then Dari opened the yellow door, and inside sat Bull Jasser, Lud Hopper, and Skid Mackleson—The Red Skull Killers—sitting around a table playing a card game. These were the sons of the Brood who weren't allowed to participate in the day's event. They looked up at us with surprise.

"There was no sound but the thin rhythm of rain on the blue tin roof. Everything was still until Bull suddenly rose to his feet, a machete in his hand. Mackleson reached for a pickaxe, and Lud grabbed a hay hook in each hand. A fell smile spread across Bull's leather lips, and his eyes belonged to a reckless and violent demon—a demon I had known for ages before we took on hosts.

"Jeema looked to Dari, but the boy just stood there with the axe in his hand, ready to protect Jeema. His cold blue eyes glared at the Red Skull Killers. Bull turned his head slightly to the side without breaking eye contact with Dari, and said, 'Looks like the ortero's son and the Wallish girl are trying to skip town . . . and you boys were afraid we wouldn't see any of the action today.'

"Dari raised his axe up over his shoulder, ready to strike. Then he warned them in a soft, yet confident tone, 'Don't even think about it, Bull. We're leaving. You'll never have to see us again.'

"Bull laughed like a choking hog. 'You're right about that, ortero's son. We'll never have to see either of your filthy faces again after today! You know why, Lamby Boy? Because we're going to throw your dead bodies into a real big pit right there in the middle of town. You and your ortero parents and your bigoted Tievian books, and we're going to burn your bodies and your books all together like the trash you are until all your hate and divisive filth is gone and we can finally have our city back. How does that sound, Lamby Boy? Huh? How about you, Wallish? You like the sound of that? Huh?' Bull slammed his fist and the handle of his machete down onto the table with a crash and cards cut across the air, then floated to the ground. Lud started laughing, and Macklson yelled out, 'Yeah, does that sound fun to you, Wallish?' The storm outside lit up the hut and Bull's grinning teeth reminded me of a skeleton. He was wonderfully terrifying.

"Then Bull asked his buddies, 'Shall I do the honors?' and he made a move toward Dari, raising his machete into the air. Dari acted quickly, kicking Bull hard—right in the rommi beans. The boy fell to his side and curled into a big, fat ball, howling in pain. The other two boys stood still, eyes wide in disbelief. I don't think they expected the handsome and respectful ortero's son to put up a fight. I didn't expect it myself, but I'm glad he did because if Jeema died, then everything I'd worked so hard for would be all for nothing. I wasn't able to act for myself back then, and Jeema definitely would not have stood a chance against those boys—against that demon.

"Dari grabbed Jeema's hand and they bolted for the chasm. The Red Skull Killers yelled after them, but the clash of thunder swallowed up all sound. Dari and Jeema made it to the edge before they turned and saw Bull hobble out of the clubhouse, his face red with rage. They started climbing down, but the Red Skull Killers were quick. Bull and Lud started climbing down after them while Mackleson slowed them down by standing at the edge and throwing rocks at them. I thought one had broken Jeema's shoulder blade, but turns out she just ended up with a real bad bruise. Dari got hit in the forehead and started bleeding pretty badly. By the time they got to the bottom, Bull and Lud were right behind them. They ran across the stone bridge, and I heard a horrific noise from down below. The thunder had awakened the Lurkers that walk the depths of the chasm—the so-called River of the Dead. There was a small group of them directly below us, holding their arms up toward us, and there were more emerging from every direction. They were so intriguing—nothing but empty bodies with no soul and no purpose, just wandering and waiting for anything or anyone to fall to the bottom of the chasm for something to tear apart and devour.

A strong gust of wind kicked up and caught Jeema's umbrella, pulling her with it. Jeema lost her balance and fell. She nearly went careening off the edge, but Dari reached back and grabbed onto her by the edge of her brand new cloak. She lost the umbrella, though. It was whipped around by the wind and slammed into the chasm wall before falling down into the depths. It disappeared into a swarm of hungry Lurkers who waited below. I heard them moaning before the thunder clapped and Jeema covered her ears with her hands.

"We reached the other side, but Bull and Lud were already approaching the stone bridge. Dari pulled out his slingshot and told Jeema to start climbing. She did. Mackleson was still on the other side of the chasm chucking rocks, but Jeema and Dari were now safely out of his range. Lud ran across the bridge, and Bull was right behind him. Dari took a marble out of his pocket and aimed. He fired one right past Lud and Bull was pelted in the shoulder. He wailed and cursed at Dari, who fired another marble. This one caught Lud's left eye and the boy fell to his knees, shrieking like a dying goat. Bull ran past Lud and barreled toward Dari, who fired two more marbles at the pig-boy before pocketing the slingshot and picking up his axe. Bull neared the end of the stone bridge and he raised his machete over his head. Dari jabbed his axe straight out in front of him and Bull ran into it with his fat stomach. The air was knocked out of Bull, but the machete came down on Dari's right shoulder, and he cried out in agony, dropping his axe to the ground. A long, jagged bolt of lightning cut across the heavens as Dari grabbed at his wound and fell to his knees.

"By this time, Jeema had reached a ledge that was out of Mackleson's view. For all he knew, Jeema had continued on, but she didn't. I told her she would keep going if she was smart, but she wanted to wait for Dari. She hid out next to a small cave into which she could safely retreat if needed, and she waited and watched the stone bridge from the ledge.

"Jeema looked down just in time to see Bull raise up his machete as he approached Dari, who was still on his knees. Out of instinct, she grabbed the closest stone she could find and hurled it at Bull. She missed, but it hit the ground in front of him. He looked up with surprise, giving Dari enough time to lunge for him. The boys landed on the bridge and Dari pinned Bull's weapon hand to the ground with his free arm. Bull punched with his other hand and slammed his knees upward like a wild animal. At first, Dari held him down and Bull dropped his machete, but eventually Dari was knocked to the hard stone bridge and Bull rolled over on top of him. Dari grabbed for his axe, and both boys rolled onto their sides, kicking each other and wrestling for control of the weapon. They rolled back and forth over the ground, neither boy able to overpower the other.

"Bull spit in Dari's face and laughed. 'I'm gonna kill you, ortero's son! Then I'm gonna kill that Wallish girl!'

"With one swift move, Bull let go of the axe and lunged toward a nearby stone. Dari stumbled backward with the axe in his left hand. Bull grabbed hold of the stone and lunged at Dari, swinging downward at the boy's head. Dari ducked and buried his shoulder into Bull's stomach, and the stone came crashing down on his back. Bull struck again and again, and Jeema started screaming for Dari to stop. Dari plowed into Bull, who held his balance and continued to pummel Dari's back with that stone. Dari collapsed down to one knee. I don't know how he wasn't dead, the way Bull was hitting him like that. Jeema didn't want to look, but I told her she had to. I wanted to see how it all ended. Bull raised the stone up one last time. A bolt of lightning flashed above and there was a ferocious hatred in the demon's eyes. His lips were snarled back to show his teeth and he let out a growl that escalated into a wild scream. As Bull brought the stone down, Dari lunged upward and hammered into Bull with a force that sent both boys flailing to the ground and right over the edge of the stone bridge.

"I remember Jeema screamed, but I couldn't hear the sound of her scream over the roar of thunder. She flew down the ledge, toward the stone bridge. Dari and Bull fell straight to the bottom of the chasm, but the fall didn't kill them. We made it to the bridge and Jeema got down on her stomach, reaching down with both hands as if she could save Dari somehow. Dari looked up at her with fear in his eyes. He still clutched the Wallish axe. Both boys were moving, but very slowly. The Lurkers swarmed around them, grabbing and clawing at them, and I heard both of them screaming. It was the worst thing I've ever seen or heard. I even felt sad for Bull. I could see the panic in his eyes, and they were no longer demon's eyes. They were the eyes of a frightened boy. Then I looked at Dari and . . . "

Virion's voice caught in her throat, and tear drops streamed down her cheeks. There were tears in Rho's eyes, too. He was surprised to hear emotion in Virion's voice. Until now, she had sounded so removed and apathetic. He looked into her eyes and saw that they had changed. Jeema had woken up and taken over telling the story at some point. It was scary to Rho how Jeema and Virion seemed so different from one another, yet so seamlessly merged. In that moment, it was as though Jeema didn't even know he was there. As if she was still shuddering in the maw of a small, dark cave, overlooking the deep evils of the crawling chasm floor. Her eyebrows furrowed in anger and her jaw worked itself mindlessly, as if trying to work out some way of expressing something so painful that it could never truly be understood, not even by her. She opened her mouth to speak again, but she was nearly sobbing—a stark contrast to the detached narration of Lady Virion only a moment before.

"I'm so sorry, Jeema." Rho reached out his hand and Jeema held onto it. Her eyes met his, and Rho's heart nearly broke at the pain he saw inside.

"Dari begged me to help him, but I didn't know what to do. He died to save me, and I just . . . I just watched. He was dying and I laid there and watched him die."

"You can't think like that, Jeema. There was nothing you could have done."

Jeema fell into his arms and wept. He wrapped her up and rocked her there in the darkness for a long time.

"It's okay," Rho reassured her. "It's going to be okay, Jeema. I promise."

Eventually, Jeema grew still and spoke again. "Afterward, I remember Mackleson yelling out at me through the rain. He was calling me names and saying that it should have been me down there instead of Bull. He said the Brood was going to find me and kill me. Lud slowly climbed back up the Qaro side of the chasm, and then they walked toward town and I hid in my cave. I stayed there all night. I couldn't gather the courage to move. It felt like an eternity.

"At some point I fell asleep. I don't know how long I slept, but I knew I had to go back home. I didn't know the way to Dari's uncle's house, and even if I did, I didn't have the heart to tell them what happened to Dari. I started back the way I came, taking my time and staying out of sight as best I could. By the time I got back to town, the morning haze diffused an eerie green light, so I knew that the sun had risen somewhere beyond that thick gray blanket of clouds that now smothered the village. I tiptoed through the alleyways and hid in the shadows until I made my way to the town square. There was a large crowd gathered, but they were somber and quiet. They had wheeled out the gallows and I saw thirteen men and women bound with cords and lined up along the edge of the platform.

"The village butcher and the smith escorted each person up to the gallows to have their names and crimes read aloud to the townspeople by the sheriff before they were hanged. Jim Jasser was charged with the murder of my parents, as well as Dari's parents, Mrs. Baptiste, and others. I watched him hang, along with the rest of the Brood.

"The people of Qaro refer to that year's First Rain as the Blood Rain. As I heard the names of the deceased read over and over again, I remember thinking that this couldn't really be happening. My mother, my father, Dari, Dari's parents . . . nearly every Tievian in Qaro. Gone in one terrible day. Washed off the face of Noloro by the Blood Rain.

"All I have left of my parents is the cloak on my back and the chimiwood jewelry box that my father made for my mother. Those are the two most important things that I own."

"Jeema," Rho whispered, "I'm so sorry that happened to you."

Jeema looked up at him, the tears glimmering in her eyes.

"There was no shortage of orphans in Qaro after that, so the town came together to sell the homes of the deceased and used that money to establish Miss Tilly's School for Orphans, which was named after our deceased ortero, Tilly Lamb—Dari's mother.

Dari's Uncle Dulner purchased his sister's house and moved into town. I stayed with Dulner and his family for six weeks until the school was ready to house us, and Dulner started teaching there. No one knew he was a Tievian except me. Besides some of the orphans, Dulner may have been the only Tievian left in all of Qaro, for all I know. It wasn't something one spoke openly about after that. The Blood Rain changed everything—I know it changed me. I used to believe in the Bel Tiev, but not after that. Not after the Blood Rain. My faith died that day, along with everyone I'd ever loved."

CHAPTER THIRTY-SIX

When they opened the door, the night shone brightly compared to the poorly lit stairwell. The moon was the biggest they'd ever seen it, and it painted the entire garden a shimmering red. They closed the "Roof Access" door behind them and made their way back down the ramp to the garden path.

Jeema held the Wallish axe out in front of her, inspecting it.

"How did your dad's axe end up with the witch?" Rho puzzled.

"That's what I've been asking myself," Jeema pondered, "and I have no idea."

"Obviously, she must have gone down into the chasm," Rho said.

"Down to the bottom—with them." Jeema's eyes were far off, and still red and teary.

Rho wished he could think of something to lift Jeema's spirits, or at least, to take her mind off her painful past.

"I need a good name for this sword," he said. "Any suggestions?"

He unsheathed his new sword and held it out in front of him. On the way down the stairs, taking a dead man's sword hadn't even crossed his mind, but he saw things differently on the way up. They once again stopped into Room 4747 and removed the sword from between the skeleton's ribs. Rho attached the sheath to his belt, and the heavy sword pulled him off balance as he clumsily clanked his way up the stairway. Now out of the darkness, he admired the beautiful weapon. Red moonlight reflected off the sleek blade.

"Do you even know how to use that thing?" Jeema prodded.

There was a hint of playfulness in her voice, and Rho was relieved to hear that she was attempting to snap herself out of her somber mood.

"When you grow up in the Darrows," Rho explained, "there are only two ways teenagers entertain themselves: smoking the brown leaf and fighting. And when it came to fighting, there was wrestling, rock throwing, or dueling. And when it came to dueling, it was either knuckles or wooden swords. I was good at both, but especially with swords."

"Maybe that's entertaining for teenage boys, but what about the teenage girls? What did they do in the Darrows?"

"Girls?" Rho looked at Jeema with puzzlement. "There were none."

"What do you mean?" she asked. "There were no girls at all?"

"It was a small community," Rho said. "There were women, and a handful of boys—all different ages. No girls, though. You're the first girl I've ever met."

"Oh." Jeema pressed her lips together and kept her eyes looking straight ahead as they walked. It seemed to Rho that he had somehow made her uncomfortable.

"Anyway." Rho held his sword up once again. "Every good weapon needs a name. I was thinking about naming it 'Lejin', after my mother. She was a hero. She saved so many lives during the Days To Come. She was brave, and always fought for what she believed was right."

"It's the perfect name," Jeema mused. "I don't know what to name mine." After a pause, she said, "Lady Virion thinks we should name it 'Spider Guts.'"

Rho bursted into laughter. "You win. There is no way to beat that name."

"Well, I guess it only makes sense for her to name it. She's the one that used it to save us down there. Plus the handle's still sticky." Jeema grimaced.

"I wanted to ask you about Lady Virion," Rho said.

"Yeah, I know," Jeema said with a sigh. "I'm sorry, I should have told you about her."

"It's all right, it's just . . . " Rho paused, unsure what to say exactly. Finally he said, "I was just worried about you."

"That makes two of us. I'm a little worried about me, too."

"What do you mean?"

"It's just . . . she's not good, Rho."

"She was nice to me," he said. "We talked the whole way up the stairs. She seemed a little a little . . . detached, but she was nice."

"Because she needs you," Jeema said. "She was nice to me, too—until she grew powerful enough to take over. Only, she couldn't do anything when Nod was there. I don't know why. There's something about him that—"

"Wait, what do you mean 'take over?'"

Jeema stopped. Her eyes lit up like she was experiencing an intense pain. Rho recognized that expression. It was the same face he'd seen her make in the lobby, right before she had passed out. Virion said that she had done that, and that it was painful for her. He'd almost forgotten she said that. He realized he knew very little about what Jeema was dealing with, and if she said that Virion wasn't good, he'd better listen to her.

"I'm sorry, I can't talk about that anymore," Jeema said quietly.

"Lady Xiara told me that Lady Virion was an evil spirit. I don't necessarily believe anything that Xiara said, but if Virion is . . . "

Jeema fell to her knees, and her eyes lit up once again.

"I'm sorry." Rho reached out to steady her. "We can talk about something else."

He helped her to her feet, and her green eyes begged him to help her—that there was much she wanted to say but couldn't. He could see she was in pain, and trapped, and that Virion had some kind of power over her, but he didn't know what he could possibly do to help her. She fell against him and he wrapped his arms around her, resting his cheek against her beautiful white hair.

"She was so beautiful, and you didn't even . . . " Jeema trailed off.

"What?" Rho asked.

"Virion told me what Xiara offered you," Jeema said, "to be your queen, to give you children, to take my place and help you escape, to take you somewhere new—and she was so beautiful. Even with all of that, Virion said that you still wanted to be with me."

She looked up at him with tears in her eyes.

"What else would you expect? I couldn't just leave you down there alone in the dark by yourself."

"Do you know how many times I've been left alone in the dark by myself?"

Rho sighed. "I've never met anyone like you before, Jeema. I care about you, and I would never leave you."

"It's just that . . . everyone I've ever loved has left me. I've been alone for *so* long. I just . . . I can't believe you actually chose me."

Rho studied her. He could feel her heart. It was bruised, but it was brave. He understood that he'd have to be very gentle with it.

"Thank you." She looked up into his eyes, then settled back onto his chest.

CHAPTER THIRTY-SEVEN

By the time they arrived at the campsite where they left Nod, they found only a note weighted down by a rock.

I found a better campsite. Follow the path north.

They followed his instructions and a short time later, they could see a fire in the distance, and Nod asleep in his sleep sack nearby.

They approached the camp quietly so as not to disturb Nod.

"Let's not wake him," Jeema whispered "He was right, this is much better." She sat down on one of the stumps to warm her hands. Rho took a seat on the stump next to her. All was quiet except for the crackle of the fire, and a small, pained whisper.

"Rho." It was Nod. He laid on the other side of the fire, not moving.

"*Rho.*" He heard it again.

Rho and Jeema exchanged a look of alarm and rushed to Nod's side. His eyes were open, but his face was pale and swollen, and he laid perfectly still. Jeema felt his forehead.

"You're burning up, Nod!" she exclaimed. "What happened to you?"

"Snake," he moaned. "Talking snake."

They saw that Nod's forearm had swollen to twice its size.

"Talking snake?" Rho repeated. "Like the one from the hut?"

Nod nodded.

"We've got to get him to a doctor!" shouted Rho.

"There's a good one in Qaro," Jeema said. "Only, if I go back there, I'm not sure I'll be allowed to leave."

"You'll be fine," Rho assured her. "I won't let anything happen to you, I promise."

Jeema believed him.

"Take Spider Guts," he instructed her, "and cut as many of the thickest vines you can find. I'll be right back."

"Where are you going?"

Rho paused for a second and took a deep breath, as if he were asking himself the same question. Then he looked at her, and she could see his frightened, steel blue eyes peering through the mask of bravery he was now wearing.

"Room 4747."

CHAPTER THIRTY-EIGHT

Everything was liquid. The trees bent. The stars melted. The ground beneath him rolled. Nod was being dragged through a sea of searing pain, enduring swell after relentless swell as both time and space rushed past him. To keep his focus off of the venom currently wreaking havoc on his nervous system, he prayed.

God, I don't know why You've brought me out into this desert. I don't know why this snake has been following me, or why it bit me, or why I have to go through this pain now. I don't know why the moon is falling, and I don't know why things are the way they are. I don't know if I will live or die today, but I do know this: that You have a good purpose for all of this, and it's okay that I don't know what that is. You have been with me all of my life, and I know that You will be with me for whatever is left of it. Please, Father, give me the strength to endure this. Whatever You have in store for me, I pray Your will be done, and that I may prove to be honorable and useful to You both in my life and in my death. Thank You for sending my brother to help me. Amen.

Nod continued to distract his mind from the pain by studying the patterns in the movements of the world which swirled around him. Time was nonexistent. One breath might have been a lifetime, and a crackle from the campfire might have been several lifetimes. It soon became difficult to formulate thoughts, and even when he *could*, they were nearly impossible to hold onto. He was sure that his mind was no longer working properly. Soon, all he could do was lie on his side and mindlessly watch the scenery disintegrate around him.

There was a girl. She was using an axe. She used it to cut long things. Green things. Vines. She spoke to him sometimes, but her words were far away. They echoed in the distance with no meaning. Then there was a boy. He knew that boy. It was . . . Rho. He had a mattress. And a sword. Rho stabbed the mattress and made holes in it. They grabbed him and lifted him into the air. He knew the girl . . . Mee . . . Mee . . . Jee? Meejee? Jeemee? Meeja? Something like that. It didn't matter. He was sliding across the night sky. Or maybe he was falling. He reached out to the night. He wanted to hold a star in his hand. His arms would not move. Still, he reached out. He laid on the soft mattress while Rho and Jeemjee dragged him along. He stared up at the night sky, watching the stars smear across the heavens like a million candles melting. He watched the moon fall toward him as it opened its abominable mouth wider to swallow him up. It laughed at him and its eyes glowed with sulfur and hatred.

Then he watched the world grow darker and darker and darker around him.

Then there was nothing.

CHAPTER THIRTY-NINE

The first ray of sunlight shot over the mountains and began Sol's ceremonial ascent over the Empyrean Valley. Rho estimated they still had three shadowmarks to go before they would arrive at the chasm. They had left their camp at the edge of the Great Chasm just after sunrise the day before and had arrived at Xiara's Garden long before sunset. Nod's condition slowed them down, but even so, they should be there by mid-morning.

Rho and Jeema had fastened the vines to the mattress from Room 4747 and had begun dragging it across the desert as quickly as they could manage. Nod was still unconscious, secured to the mattress by three cords of vines.

A faint rumbling sound caught Rho's attention. He froze out of instinct. Jeema stopped beside him, clearly alarmed as well.

Then it hit.

The ground shook and they were both knocked off their feet. Dust filled the air and made it difficult to see or breathe. They scrambled back toward the mattress, reaching out for one another. Rho threw his cloak over his brother's face and he and Jeema buried their faces into the mattress.

They had both felt many quakes in their time, but this was perhaps the most powerful either had ever felt, and it certainly lasted the longest. When the shaking finally stopped, it took some time before the air cleared. When it did, they continued walking. Quickly. Without speaking. It was a solid quarter-shadow before the southern mountains came back into view. When they did, Jeema pointed to the tallest peak in the South.

"That's the Serpent's Mouth," she said ominously.

"In the Darrows, we call it by its Tebbel name," Rho said. *"Mon Uro."*

"The elders at Miss Tilly's use the Tebbel name, too. Ever since the Days To Come, it's been rumbling. I've even seen geysers spring up out of the ground during some of the really big ones. The elders say that the great chasm was actually formed by a river of lava flowing from it long ago."

"We feel the quakes in the Darrows, too. The same lava that formed the Great Chasm formed the caves I grew up in, where the chasm empties into the northern foothills."

"'He set the northern sky ablaze,'" Jeema muttered, "'and ushered in the end of days.'"

"You've said that before. What is that?"

"From the Guidestones. *The Eagle and the Serpent.* I recited it to you the night we met."

Rho looked upon the mountain with reverence.

"It's the story of a great war," she continued, "between the fire spirit of the South and the Northern spirit of light."

"I don't think you're wrong," Rho said. "I think it *is* a war between the spirits. I think it's a war between God and the devil. Do you remember what Nod said? That the Guidestones were just a mirror image of the Bel Tiev?"

"I remember. I've been thinking about it a lot. I'm starting to feel pretty confused about it all, to be honest."

"I know exactly how you feel. I've been skeptical of religion, but meeting Lady Xiara—or Epella—an actual person I've read about in the Bel Tiev—has really been messing with my mind. I actually prayed to God when I was strapped to that chair. I think He saved us, but I don't really know."

He took a deep breath and looked off toward the volcanic peak on the horizon.

"Here's what I *do* know," he continued. "The Bel Tiev prophesies the Withering and the Days To Come, and so do the Guidestones. I think Nod may be right about that much, at least. If God is the eagle, and the devil is the serpent, I think that maybe the Guidestones really are just an inversion of the prophesies from the Bel Tiev, so that in the Guidestones the serpent is the hero."

"'The sole defender of the land,'" Jeema recited.

"Exactly, and Nod always says that every prophecy has both a spiritual and a physical fulfillment. I'm starting to get the spiritual part of it all, but what I'm worried about right now is the physical fulfillment of that prophecy. Especially the part about the serpent's mouth shooting out fire."

"'From out his mouth came forth a flame,'" Jeema said. "'For Eagle's nest did Serpent aim.'"

"Eagle's nest?" Rho's jaw hung open as he thought through the puzzle.

"Heaven, maybe?"

"Maybe." Rho wasn't convinced.

"Well, I guess if God is the eagle," Jeema said, "then His nest is in the North."

"But Mon Uro is on the southern edge of the Empyrean Valley."

"Yes," Jeema agreed, "but this valley is pretty much the northernmost part of Noloro. Elder Dulner said that's the only reason this valley survived the Days To Come, and why explorers have still never found any survivors south of the Kafei Mountains."

"So either way, it's safe to say that the Serpent's Mouth"—he motioned toward the volcanic mountain—"is going to unleash its fire on the northern skies."

Jeema had to remind herself to breathe before reciting, "'He set the northern sky ablaze, and ushered in the end of days.'"

"We need to hurry," Rho said, picking up his pace. "It's gonna blow sometime before this evening."

"*What?*" Jeema struggled to keep up. "How could you *possibly* know that?"

"Xiara! Didn't you hear what she said? 'Rumor has it by this time tomorrow, Qaro will be in ashes.' We need to get there fast! Otherwise, there won't be a doctor there to help Nod." He looked down at his unconscious brother, but Jeema's heart sank as she thought of Dulner, Martol, Beranthia, and Emi.

"If we hurry, we can still warn them." Her eyes met Rho's. He nodded, and they wasted no more energy on talk.

CHAPTER FORTY

The chasm was in sight. The sun was now well above the horizon and Nod had been unconscious for far too long. Rho tried to ease his worry by reminding himself that Qaro was just beyond the chasm.

He had never been to Qaro, but he'd always pictured a quaint little town filled with happy houses. Jeema's story of the Blood Rain made him rethink the "happy" part, but it still had to be better than the Darrows. His eyes fell once again on Mon Uro, the Serpent's Mouth. He imagined a violent explosion, the heavens darkened, the air thick with ash. He imagined Qaro burning, the houses reduced to rubble, the bodies burned beyond recognition. What would that do to Nod? There would be no saving him. And Jeema? If Qaro did burn, she would truly have lost everything and everyone she'd ever known.

"Sometimes I just feel like Hell is walking along beside us." He shook his head in frustration. "Like we're being stalked by death's invisible shadow, as if it were breathing down our necks, deciding exactly how it would like to take us, and how much pain it wants to inflict first. I feel like it's surrounding us. It's laughing at us from the falling moon. It's already claimed this dry and barren land. The only thing that flows down here is a never-ending stream of tears. I don't know if a better life is even possible, but I know what happens if we stay here—I know what happens to us if we don't try."

He saw tears falling down Jeema's cheeks, and he heard the pain in her voice, and he wondered at her strength to push through it.

"I know how you feel, Rho. I really do, though it seems to me there is also so much love here, so much light in all this darkness. It warms my heart to see how Nod looks up to you and the way you care for him, and the way you talk to me the same way—not like I'm a problem you've got to fix, or a burden you've been stuck with. I still can't believe you chose me over Lady Xiara, the most beautiful woman to ever walk the face of Noloro. Our path might be a dark one, but there is a bright and beautiful light in you—even if you don't see it yourself."

Rho blushed. It was a nice thing to say, but if she'd only known him better, she'd know it was a rather ridiculous thing to say. He thought back to how he'd cowered in the shadows unable to move as Boss Man whipped his little brother with a chain right in front of him, and still he didn't act. He remembered when Jeema had been snatched up by Xiara's vines, and how he'd wanted to run to her and set her free, but fear took hold of him, so he simply stood there and let it happen. He didn't feel like anybody's light. He still felt like a coward. He looked down at Nod, that brave soul who had taken all the blame and was beaten for Rho's mistake. Rho felt he didn't deserve a love like that. His father's song rang in his ears once again.

A greater love no one has other

Than giving your life for another.

He had allowed Nod to take the beating in his place—to take his punishment. It was far from living up to his father's instruction—as far as he could possibly get.

Look out for your brother,

When all you have left is each other.

Nod did what Rho couldn't do, and he loved him all the more for it. He felt he needed to repay him somehow. He wished he could be more like Nod, and a part of him believed he could. Another part of him scoffed at the thought. That cynical part of him tittered back and assured him that he'd never be brave, or good, or admirable like Nod. Sure, he was bigger, older, and stronger, but it made no difference. Nod was the brave one, the wise one, the good one. He always had been, and for once Rho felt admiration for that rather than resentment. There was nothing he wouldn't do to save his brother.

When they arrived at the edge of the chasm, the ground shook once again. When the roaring stopped, it was replaced with a different sound, equally as awful. Hundreds of soulless creatures had been stirred from their sleep, waiting for some pitiful soul to fall in and feed them.

Rho and Jeema exchanged nervous glances, then worked quickly to lower Nod down onto the ledge below using the attached vines to maneuver the mattress down the sheer face slowly. After that, they made their way as quickly as possible to the stone bridge.

The ground shook again. It started with a steady rumble and rapidly escalated into violent convulsions. Dust filled the air once again. There was an explosion somewhere nearby, followed by a terrible hissing sound. Rho reached for Jeema's hand, but he could not find it. There was another explosion, much louder this time and directly ahead. He was thrown back against the chasm wall. There were thunderous booms and crashes all around him. The hissing sound that followed was accompanied by scalding hot steam rising up from the ground right in front of him. He could not see it, but he heard it, and he felt its intense heat.

Over the hissing, he heard Jeema screaming from far below, but the shaking hadn't stopped. He tried, but he couldn't get to his feet. With one hand holding tightly to the mattress, he crawled his way to the ledge and peered down into a thick cloud of dust.

"Jeema!" he shouted as he looked straight down. He still couldn't see her, but he could hear her screaming, and her voice was . . . moving. She was running.

"Rho!" Jeema screamed. "Help!"

The terror in her screams grated against his heart. His first instinct was to get to her in any way he could. Then he stopped himself and turned to Nod. He couldn't leave him there alone. Not in this condition. Another violent quake and he might be thrown from the ledge.

"Rho! Please! Help me!"

The shaking let up and the world stilled once again, but Rho had no idea what to do.

OUT OF THE MOUTHS
OF SERPENTS

CHAPTER FORTY-ONE

When the dust began to clear, Rho saw the stone bridge had partially collapsed, and a few supports still stuck up out of the chasm floor, supporting nothing at all. They were surrounded by . . . people? No. They looked like people, but those were definitely not people. They must be the things Jeema called Lurkers. They looked to Rho like they had once been people, but they were now empty, hollowed out.

Jeema let out another terrified scream, and this one came from a little further away. He had to do something, but he was afraid to leave his brother there alone. He was strapped to the mattress, but another violent shake could send the mattress soaring off the ledge into the River of the Dead.

"There are too many of them!" Jeema yelled.

Rho knew he couldn't just sit there with Nod. His eyes scanned the ledge, looking for a possible way down. He looked over the ruins of the collapsed bridge, then an idea came to him. He dragged the mattress up against a massive stone slab and wrapped one vine around it. He wrapped a second vine around a second stone, and tied the vines to secure the mattress in place.

"They're everywhere!" Jeema's cry was getting closer again. Rho leaned over his little brother's swollen face and kissed him on the forehead.

"Don't move," he said. "I'll be right back."

He slid his legs over the edge and started climbing down the face of the chasm as quickly as possible. Jeema's screaming continued and moved closer toward him. From one landing to the next, he found his way down the chasm wall, nearing the River of the Dead.

Finally, he saw her. She was pulling her axe out from one of those lifeless things. She was right—they were everywhere.

"Rho! Hurry! There are too many of them!"

"I'm coming!"

He was close enough to jump now. Rho quickly scanned the floor below for a safe place to land, but the wall started shaking and he lost his grip. He fell to the chasm floor and landed on all fours. There was an explosion, and that horrible hissing noise to Rho's left. A large geyser shot up out of the chasm floor. Another shot up a little further off, and then another. There was an even longer series of deafening explosions, another violent jolt, and then it hit. A fast-moving wall of dust and debris hit them hard from the south. Rho jumped to his feet and spotted Jeema very near to him, slowly getting to her feet as well. He helped her stand.

"Are you okay?" he hollered.

"I think so." She nodded.

"We need to get out of here, now!" Rho said.

Lumbering shapes began to appear in the wall of dust that surrounded them. Rho pulled Lejin from its sheath. Jeema gripped Spider Guts firmly in her right hand as she reached out for Rho's shoulder with her left. Rho tried to search for a place to climb, but the walls here at the bottom were too smooth to grip.

"Follow me, and try to stay quiet," Rho whispered as he led her away from the approaching Lurkers and through the rubble along the chasm's western wall toward the south. The dust was thick, and the floor was riddled with boulders and smaller obstacles, preventing them from moving quickly. Rho kept his left hand on the chasm wall at all times, hoping to find a rough enough section to get a decent purchase and begin climbing out.

Over the hissing, they heard what sounded like moaning. It grew closer on every side, but all Rho and Jeema could see was a gray storm of dust churning around them. They were hit by an overwhelming smell of something burning, and they realized it wasn't entirely dust. Much of what swirled in the air around them was ash. They came upon a section of collapsed wall that seemed more manageable. They climbed up onto a pile of rubble, then jumped from boulder to boulder. Rho landed on a loose stone and twisted his ankle. He lost his balance and tumbled down a small embankment. Jeema cried out after him.

"I'm all right," he reassured her.

A growl erupted from right in front of Jeema, and before she could move, a Lurker grabbed for her and caught a fistful of her hair. Spider Guts slipped from her grip, and her knees and elbows went crazy in an attempt to escape, but the thing was not fazed. It moved slowly, but with superhuman strength, pulling Jeema's long silver hair up into his mouth and biting down with petrified teeth. Jeema screamed and kicked harder. It made no difference. Rho scurried, running his hands along the wall of stone, trying to find a way back up. It was difficult to see anything. He finally came to the end of the stone wall and found a mound of rubble he could climb. One hand over the other, he clawed his way back up the embankment from where Jeema's screams were coming. The dust began to clear, and as he peeked his head over the top of the rubble heap, he could see Jeema struggling with the Lurker, her hair in its mouth.

He lunged himself upward, but a strong hand caught his ankle and pulled him down hard. He landed on top of the creature, knocking the Lurker to the ground. He took a few quick steps out of the Lurker's reach, and quickly realized that he was in trouble. He counted four, then six, then seven Lurkers closing in on him. They moved slowly, but he had nowhere to run with his back against the chasm wall. He was trapped, with no way to help Jeema. She couldn't get free of the creature. She reached out with her right arm, fumbling, grasping, and finally finding the handle of Spider Guts as the Lurker yanked her hair again, pulling her head upward. She held the axe firmly in hand, but hesitated.

What is she waiting for?

She only stood undecided for a moment, then she swung hard and buried the axe into the monster's neck. Rho could hear the sickening plop from where he stood. The Lurker's grip did not let up, but his attention was turned to the short wooden handle which was now protruding from him. He looked almost intrigued by it, and then his attention was turned back to the hair in his hand. Jeema yanked on the hatchet to free it from the Lurker's mass of muscle, and thick black blood began to bubble up like oil. She gave another good hack at its neck, and it could no longer support his large square head. Its face dropped to its chest and its grip loosened up just enough for Jeema to break free.

That's when he realized the Lurkers were closing in on him.

CHAPTER FORTY-TWO

Jeema didn't know a thing about swordplay, but she was shocked to see Rho looked incredibly natural with a sword, at least to her untrained eyes. She'd wondered if he'd been telling tales about his experience acquired from dueling in the Darrows, but now she was inclined to believe him. He weaved in and out of the clumsy beasts, whirling and slamming Lejin's heavy blade about like an aggressive dance exercise.

Jeema made her way down to him. Once by his side, she swung her axe with all her might at each approaching Lurker. She didn't think; she just moved. After a few moments, there were no Lurkers left standing in front of them. There were groans all around them—louder and closer every second—but their immediate path was now free and clear. Rho reached out for Jeema's hand and she took it and followed his lead. They sprinted through the rubble and passed through a small crevice winding back into the chasm wall. They turned and squeezed into a tiny cavity in the wall, hoping to hide for a moment. There was a small landing a little ways up, and this section of wall looked to be rough enough to get a decent grip and climb upward, but their attempts were unsuccessful.

Something grabbed at Rho's cloak and pulled him down off of the wall. He spun and found himself face to face with a Lurker. He was unable to reach across his body with his right hand, so he grabbed the hilt of Lejin with his left, but it was nearly useless in such a small space. Too confined to raise his arm and being yanked nearly off his feet, he could do nothing but keep the thing at a distance by raising his knees. The Lurker ripped at his cloak, the ties of which cut into his neck, until Rho was finally flung to the ground. The Lurker pounced on Rho, bearing down with a hungry mouthful of angry teeth.

Jeema saw an opportunity and didn't hesitate. She lifted Spider Guts overhead and brought it down hard on the back of the Lurker's neck, and it collapsed. Rho kicked himself free of the lifeless corpse and scrambled to his feet.

Through the small entrance to the cavity came the arm and face of a lurker who was attempting to amble straight ahead into the very narrow entrance, apparently incapable of the most basic sort of problem-solving.

Rho raised Lejin over his head and brought it down on the Lurker's upper arm with a *whack*. Thick, black blood bubbled out of the gash and slowly spilled to the ground like putrid syrup. The arm dangled downward. The Lurker stared vacantly and moaned at them. Three more Lurker hands reached through the opening past it. Rho took a deep breath and buried Lejin into the lead Lurker's forehead. Its body collapsed onto the rocks, and slid down to the floor of the opening. A new Lurker took the dead one's place, but this one was more successful at navigating through the tiny opening. Rho struggled to dislodge the sword from the dead Lurker's skull. He was bent over at an awkward angle with only one hand available, but Jeema hacked at the new Lurker's chest until it fell to the ground, landing on top of another dead Lurker.

Rho freed his blade as another Lurker pushed itself up over its fallen brethren and Lejin sunk his sword into its skull, causing it to collapse onto the growing pile of bodies. He felt bones crack beneath his feet, and the smell of rot and death filled his nostrils. He felt nauseous, but he knew this was no time to weaken. He needed to take courage and find a way out of here. He needed to be strong for Jeema and Nod.

One after another, more Lurkers moved into the opening to replace their slain predecessors. Rho and Jeema hacked away, and soon there was a mound of dead Lurkers nearly as tall as Rho, effectively blocking the cavity's narrow entrance entirely. He could see Lurker hands reaching up from the other side, but they were no longer reaching into the cavity. He decided to climb up to the top of the mound to have a better look at their situation.

It was tough to get started from such a tight spot, but he awkwardly made his way up the mound of Lurker bodies. From the top of the mound, he once again pulled Lejin from its sheath and struck at the Lurkers' heads. Each one that fell added additional support to their gruesome barricade. Rho turned and reached his hand out to Jeema.

"Come on!" he said.

She took his hand in hers. He hoisted her up and she joined him at the top. The cavity entrance widened a bit the further up it went, and Jeema could see a large portion of the chasm floor from where they now stood. Before them, an army of Lurkers gathered and blindly bumped into one another as they slowly climbed up the mound in a comical effort to reach Jeema and Rho. Beyond the horde, Lurkers were scattered across the chasm floor, meandering aimlessly. Several geysers shot jets of hot steam up from the chasm floor. As the Lurkers slowly climbed and reached the top of the mound, Rho and Jeema took turns dispatching them, and the Lurker mound continued to grow both taller and wider.

Rho looked down at the group of Lurkers immediately below him, and his heart nearly stopped. There before him stood his father, expressionless, moaning, and arms extended to Rho.

He thought he must be dreaming. It couldn't be, but there was no denying it. It really was him. Grier Perish, in the flesh. Something grabbed at Rho's ankle again, but Rho couldn't bring himself to look away from his father. Somewhere in the distance, he heard the familiar sound of Jeema sinking her axe into a Lurker's body, and the grip on his leg relaxed. It didn't matter. None of it mattered. His father was alive.

There was a distant voice pushing its way through the jumbled mess of thoughts clouding his mind. The voice was an echo at first, but became more and more clear until he recognized it. Jeema. She was near him now, and he could make out words. She was yelling at him, asking him what was wrong. It reminded him of his surroundings, of his situation, and that he couldn't stand there much longer. He couldn't leave his dad there either, surrounded by hungry Lurkers. He turned to Jeema, whose brow furrowed into a vague question he didn't know how to answer.

"He's alive," Rho said.

"What?" Jeema shook her head. "Who's alive?"

"My dad," he said. "He's alive!"

He knelt on the pile of Lurkers and reached out to Grier, who stretched his arms out to Rho.

"Rho!" Jeema screamed. "What are you doing?"

"Dad!" Rho shouted. "Dad, give me your hand!"

Rho reached out, but his hand slipped. He recovered, then started climbing down the wrong side of the Lurker mound toward the horde of approaching monsters.

"Rho! Don't!" she pleaded.

"I have to!" he yelled back to her. "That's my dad! I have to help him!"

"Rho, that's a Lurker!" Jeema shouted. "Your dad isn't down there, Rho!"

The words cut deep. Rho halted and looked again into his father's eyes—or rather, the eyes that used to be his father's—and found nothing looking back at him. He wanted so badly to see his father's kind eyes, to hear his father explain for himself why he'd been gone so long, and how he'd missed Rho and Nod and their mother every day he was gone. He wanted it to be so, but as painful as it was, he knew Jeema was right. There was no doubt that he was looking at the face of his father, but those eyes were completely void of any sign of Grier Perish. The thing mindlessly waved its arms up at Rho, just like the countless other Lurkers that surrounded him. Yes, at one time that thing had been his father, but now it was nothing more than a hollowed-out corpse, aimlessly wandering with no purpose and no soul.

It made Rho sick. His head hurt, and he felt cold and sweaty as his stomach clenched up. He tasted harsh bitterness of pinni pods and stomach acid rising up, and he vomited. When he was finished, he panted for air. He looked down at what used to be his father and began to sob. He felt Jeema's arms under his own, lifting him to his feet, spinning him, and holding him close.

His father really was gone. He had suspected it for some time, had even known it in his heart, but it was different to witness a thing like this—his father's corpse wandering the River of the Dead. No soul, no Grier, just a lifeless, dead body. Perhaps his father was home now, with his mother, with God—all together and happy. Perhaps his father was nowhere, and had just ceased to exist. He didn't know, but he knew his father wasn't here with him now, at the bottom of the Great Chasm.

Rho couldn't help but stare. It had been several sun-cycles since he had seen his father's face. He could almost hear his voice.

Jeema held him close and ran her fingers through the back of his hair.

"I'm so sorry, Rho," she said solemnly.

Rho conjured up a forced smile.

"I never thought I'd see him again." He sat and pondered momentarily, then asked, "How do you think he got down here?"

Jeema's face grew stern. "It's awful to think, but I'm beginning to wonder if this is where she discarded them . . . once she'd taken all the life she could from them and they were of no more use to her. I know she's been down here . . . that's how she ended up with this."

She held Spider Guts up with her right hand.

Rho squinted his eyes with uncertainty.

"The night I met you, you recited a passage from the Bel Tiev. The one about Lady Xiara . . . "

Jeema's eyes narrowed and her head tilted. Then she looked down and nodded, cleared her throat, and recited the passage once again, *"She eats not at the flesh of men, but even at their souls. By her many charms, the best of men are devoured and discarded as men without souls, wandering the depths in darkness until the end of days. They will not escape the fire which pours forth from the serpent's mouth . . . "*

The chasm shook violently and the bodies beneath them shifted. Rho and Jeema lost their footing and grabbed onto anything they could. Rho held on tightly to Lejin. He knew if he lost it, they'd be done for. He used his other hand to grip onto the first thing he could manage and found himself face to face with the bloodied and gnarled face of a Lurker. He couldn't see much else, and he had no control of his movements. There was another explosion—the loudest one yet— and a moment later, a furious blast of wind and a thick cloud of ash. The Lurker mound shifted again, and Rho slid toward the ground as the shaking finally subsided.

Jeema cried out to him from above. There was moaning from just behind him. He whipped his sword around and caught something that made a gurgling sound as it pulled his sword down with it. He dislodged his sword and scrambled back up the lurker mound. The ash swirled upward, and he could make out a few Lurkers approaching the bottom of the mound. He looked up and saw Jeema reaching her hand out for him. He took it and she helped him to his feet.

"We need to find a way out of here, now!"

Jeema's attention was elsewhere. He followed her gaze to see a river of red lava slowly pushing its way into the small cavity toward them. The Lurkers were oblivious to the lava, and one of them walked directly into the rushing red river. As he stepped, his legs were rapidly incinerated. The Lurker's face was eerily void of any pain or human emotion as it slowly sank into the glowing red river. They watched several more do the same thing.

The red river crept its way to the edge of the mound upon which they now stood. As the lava flowed up to the dam of the dead, there came a loud hissing sound, a pillar of black smoke, and the putrid stench of burning, rotted flesh.

Once the lava started working its way under and around the Lurker mound, the hissing grew louder, the smoke rose thicker and darker, and the stench became unbearable. Rho wondered if hell could be much worse than where he now found himself. The lava quickly filled the floor of the small cavity and began to rise up slowly. The mound shifted to one side, and then the other. The lava was rising, but the mound was sinking.

CHAPTER FORTY-THREE

"Rho . . . ?" Jeema questioned anxiously.

"I know, I know!" he responded. "Any ideas?"

"We should have killed more Lurkers!" She almost lost her balance as the mound shifted, sinking further down into the rising lava.

Rho looked up toward the small landing above them, too high to reach, but he might be able to give Jeema a boost. It was the only option he could think of.

"Get up on my shoulders!" Rho shouted over the angry hiss of burning bodies.

Jeema saw the ledge and understood. Rho bent down and she climbed up.

Rho looked down at the horde of Lurkers which were now thigh deep in the lava, slowly sinking while the lava was quickly rising. He watched his father's face carefully for any sign of fear or pain or life. He saw nothing, and that relieved him. Even so, he began weeping uncontrollably as he watched the rising river of lava swallow what was left of his father. He turned away, shut his eyes, and made a promise to himself that he would not look back again.

You're home now, Grier.

Jeema stretched herself up toward the landing, but even on Rho's shoulders, the ledge was too high.

"I can't reach!" she shouted down to him. "I'll have to stand up!"

"Do it!"

Using the chasm wall to steady herself, she slowly and carefully pushed herself up until she was standing on Rho's shoulders. Rho winced as one of Jeema's heavy boots dug into his clavicle. She was able to reach her fingertips to the edge of the landing. She steadied herself to stretch a little further, but the mound shifted again and sank further down into the lava. She looked down at the rising river of death. It was getting close to Rho's feet now. She stretched herself out once again, but this time, she wasn't even close. The mound had sunk too low, and it was still sinking.

"How's it going up there?" Rho questioned impatiently.

"You just do the lifting and let me do the thinking," she shot back.

Rho looked out at the rising river of red lava flowing through the chasm and his heart sank. He looked down at his feet which stood firmly on a dead lurker's dark blue shirt, and he knew he did not have long before it would be him sinking into the river of fire below, though he thought perhaps the heat and the stench would kill him before the lava reached him.

A spark went off in Jeema's brain. She grabbed Spider Guts from her belt and extended the head up over the ledge.

"Brace yourself," she yelled down to Rho.

She pulled down firmly, and then with one foot against the wall and the other on Rho's shoulder, she pushed herself upward and used the axe handle to pull herself the rest of the way up to the ledge. Rho supported her feet and gave her a boost up as far as he could reach. He pushed and she pulled, and a moment later she rolled safely onto the solid and unmoving ledge.

The landing was small, but large enough for the two of them and then some. Most importantly, the landing was void of lava and Lurkers. Jeema spun around and held the axe handle down to Rho, holding onto the axe head.

"Grab on!" Jeema shouted.

Rho looked up at the axe handle through the black cloud of smoke. It was still far above his head. He gave it his all and jumped.

It was not enough—not even close. He landed poorly and nearly tumbled into the rising lava. He regained his footing and stood looking hopelessly up at Jeema. The mound shifted and sank again. He was nearly thrown into the lava. His boots and pant legs began to burn against his skin, and his bare arms and face were pounded with a fierce heat that was meaner than the angriest desert sun.

"It's no good, Jeems," he conceded. "It's too high."

"Wait!" Jeema yelled. "I'll find something else!"

She slid her pack off her shoulders and disappeared for a moment, then reappeared holding her cloak and lowered one end down to Rho.

"Grab on!" she yelled.

Rho held his arms out and stood on his toes, but the cloak was just out of reach.

"I can't!" he yelled.

"Jump! I've got you!"

Jeema braced herself, arms extended downward, gripping the cloak firmly in both hands.

"Okay, here I go . . . "

Rho jumped and stretched his arms upward and snagged the beautiful material with both hands. He gripped the cloak and pulled himself up with all his strength. He awaited the jerk as his bodyweight pulled the cloak downward. He looked at Jeema and saw the terror in her eyes, and in that moment, he knew she could not hold his full weight. His body jerked the material clean out of her hands and he fell straight down, back to the top of the Lurker pile.

"Nooo!" Jeema gasped, bringing her hands to up her mouth. She was horrified at what she'd done. It was over.

CHAPTER FORTY-FOUR

Jeema's cloak whipped downward, landed in the rising pool of lava, and burned up in an instant. Rho looked up. Jeema was looking at him, her eyes filled with tears. Behind them was utter hopelessness. She threw her hands over her eyes and wept.

"I can't lose you! I'm so sorry! I . . . "

"It's okay. It's okay, Jeema," Rho reassured her.

"I'm so sorry, Rho. I'm so sorry . . . " She covered her face and sobbed.

"Quick! Throw me your axe!" Jeema dropped to her stomach and lowered Spider Guts down to him. Then she dropped it, and Rho caught it.

"Now take your pack and wrap the strap around your hand so you can't drop it!"

She did as he said and wrapped the strap around her right hand. She let the pack fall over the edge. She used her left hand to brace herself against the top of the landing so she wouldn't be pulled over the ledge. Rho reached up on his toes with Spider Guts fully extended and found it just shy of reaching the hanging strap. He braced himself as the mound of Lurkers shifted again. The heat from the rising lava was becoming unbearable now.

"I'm gonna jump! You ready?"

"I won't drop you this time! I promise! No matter what!"

Rho jumped. He caught the strap of the pack with the head of the axe and held onto the handle with everything in him. Jeema did the same. She thought her right hand might be crushed by the constricting strap and her right arm felt as if it might be pulled out of its socket. Her muscles had never worked so hard, but she managed to hold onto the pack. There was no room for error.

With one swift motion, he reached with his right arm and grasped the axe handle as high up as he could. Jeema screamed, but held on. His left arm released and grabbed onto the strap of Jeema's pack. He heard a heart-stopping sound—the sound of canvas tearing. He didn't hesitate. He reached up with Spider Guts and caught the ledge with the iron head of the axe. He put all his weight on his right arm, easing the burden on the pack. Still screaming, Jeema scrambled to pull the pack up with everything she had. As it lifted, Rho's left hand caught the ledge. Jeema dropped the pack and reached down to grab the axe handle. Rho shifted all his weight again to his left arm, allowing Jeema to pull him up by the axe. A moment later, his right hand was up on the ledge. With one last bit of effort, he managed to swing his leg up and roll his body onto the small ledge. He laid there on his back, eyes wide and chest heaving.

Jeema dropped to his side, grabbed his face in her hands, and kissed him. He was alive—fully and completely alive. She pulled her lips away from his and stared into his eyes, two precious emeralds submerged in two deep pools of tears. They collapsed and laid there together as they caught their breath. Rho studied the way up and out. It wouldn't be easy, but it was doable. He estimated it would take them a shadowmark or more to reach the top. As he lay there, his eyes wandered off into the great swirl where the sky should have been. He was surprised at a small part of himself that wanted to pray—to thank God, and to ask God to help him, to help Jeema, and to protect Nod. Another part of him wanted to brush the feeling off, and with that came another surprise—a deep and intense guilt at the thought of simply brushing God away. He hadn't felt these sort of feelings since he was a child.

Something fell from the sky and knocked him on the right side of his head. It was a braided vine, and Rho recognized it from the mattress sled. It had been tossed down from the top of the chasm, and now hung just off of the small ledge, whipping wildly from side to side right over the spot where Rho had just been standing.

"Perfect timing, Nod!" Rho yelled up.

This caused Jeema to lose it completely, and she was hardly able to stand. Rho was doubled over, and the two kids laughed and cried like lunatics as the red river consumed everything below them.

CHAPTER FORTY-FIVE

"You didn't think I'd let you die, now did you?" a silhouette shouted down at them. It was a man's voice—definitely not Nod's voice. It was strangely familiar to Jeema, but she couldn't quite place it. Someone from Qaro? One of her teachers? It didn't matter. What mattered was getting out of this chasm.

Rho and Jeema grinned at each other.

"Go ahead." Rho held the vine out to Jeema.

"The perfect gentleman," Jeema replied, grabbing on and wrapping it around her right hand.

Rho reached down and grabbed the end of the vine, then slipped it under her belt and tied a knot. Jeema shot him a flirtatious smile, then tugged at the vine with both hands and held on firmly. Soon, she was being lifted up to safety by the mysterious silhouette.

It didn't take long for her to reach the top, and the stranger reached his hand out to Jeema. She gripped it firmly and was lifted out of the chasm by a backlit silhouette in a dark cloak. The stranger's hand was cold and bony, yet surprisingly strong. She fell to the hard, hot desert floor and was relieved to see Nod resting just a few feet away, still unconscious and lying on the mattress sled.

She quickly pushed herself to her feet and spun to face the mysterious stranger. She was disturbed to see the frighteningly pale face of Dartaun the Great. He sneered and loomed over Nod, who laid unconscious on the mattress at the sorcerer's feet.

"It's so nice to see you again, Little Sun!"

"You!" She gasped. "You abandoned us!"

"*Abandoned* you?" The man sneered. "I just saved your *life!*"

Jeema eyed him with distrust.

"Are you going to stand there and pout or are you going to help me save your boyfriend?" he asked. She shot to her feet and picked up a length of vine.

A short time later, Rho emerged from the chasm. He rolled himself onto solid ground, regained his footing, and immediately ran to his brother's side. Jeema followed, but gave them a respectful amount of space.

"It's a funny thing about venom," the sorcerer said coolly. "The moment it enters your body, death begins."

Rho glared up at the sorcerer. It was obvious to Jeema that he was already beginning to dislike Dartaun.

"Never fear," Dartaun said casually. "I've already given the boy an antivenom. He will not die, though he may sleep for some time yet."

"How did you know he was snakebit?" Rho asked.

"He probably sent the snake," Jeema chimed in.

Dartaun squinted his eyes, studying Jeema.

"I'm sensing a lot of hostility here," Dartaun said, "and I'm wondering if it isn't a bit misplaced, seeing as I just saved all four of you from what were sure to be very painful deaths. Am I missing something?"

"Four of us?" Rho squinted up at the gaunt figure.

"He's counting Virion," Jeema explained.

Rho got to his feet and held out his hand grudgingly. "You're right. Thank you for helping us. I'm Rho."

Dartaun smiled and met Rho's handshake.

"I know who you are, Rho. I've been watching over you since you were but a wee child. I am Dartaun the Great."

Rho pulled his hand away as if sickened by the frigid skin stretched over Dartaun's skeletal hand.

"I know that your whole life, you've felt abandoned. You've found ways to justify your parents leaving you. After all, neither of them really had a choice, did they? But that doesn't change the cold, hard facts, does it? Your world is literally crumbling around you; the surface rumbles and shakes; the depths are bubbling over, covering the surface in hellfire; the moon will soon come crashing down; and you are alone and you are afraid. You feel as if there is no one to protect you, and I want you to know that nothing could be further from the truth, Rho. In fact, that's the very reason I'm here. To watch over you. To protect you. You're not alone anymore. None of you are."

Rho glanced over to Jeema. She wanted to tell Rho not to believe him, but she could feel that electrical pulse growing. Virion wanted to come out, and Jeema didn't want to give her an excuse to shock her into unconsciousness again. Jeema grimaced, and her skeptical eyes met Rho's. He shook his head and then shrugged with an exasperated exhalation.

"So . . . the word is that you've got big plans for us. We're supposed to give you children? Is that right?"

Dartaun squinted and tilted his head slightly, as if trying to study the boy.

"I guess you couldn't make it work with the spider lady, then?" Rho quipped.

Jeema couldn't hold back a giggle. There was a quick and intense shock, and Jeema straightened up. Dartaun looked as if he was working to keep his patience.

"Let me get to the point. The Withering is nearly complete. This world is at its end, but here's the interesting part: when one world ends . . . "

"Another begins," Rho finished.

CHAPTER FORTY-SIX

"Very good, Rho! Very good, indeed!" Dartaun grinned and clapped as he bent down to one knee. Then he grabbed a decent-sized stone and placed it in the dirt in front of him.

"Now! This is Sol, our sun," he said. Then, with one swift swipe of his hand, he scooped up a handful of small rocks and pebbles and held them out for Rho to see. "Are you familiar with the planets in our system?"

"Listen, I appreciate the daring rescue," Rho said, "even if it was just a few ticks too late, but we don't have time for an astronomy lesson."

"Come on, Rho. Let him explain."

Rho was surprised at the amount of annoyance in the girl's voice, but he was even more surprised at the change he saw when he looked up into her eyes. They were darker somehow. Still the same color as before, but Rho thought maybe it was more a *feeling* of being darker than an actual, measurable difference. He realized that he was no longer speaking with Jeema, but Lady Virion.

After a short hesitation, an impatient Virion snatched the rocks from Dartaun's outstretched skeleton hand and dropped to her knees between the other two. She began arranging the rocks and pebbles around Sol.

"All the planets were named in the ancient Tebbel tongue. The planet closest to Sol is Va Folixiero, *the Sprinter*, because of its swift orbit around the sun."

Dartaun nodded in agreement. Virion continued.

"The second planet from Sol is our planet, Va Noloro, *the Provider*, because it is the only planet in the entire system capable of sustaining life."

"That was true at one time, but not anymore," Dartaun's lips spread into a smile and his eyes twinkled, "but we'll circle back to that. Keep going, Little Moon. You're doing fine."

"After Va Noloro, the third planet from Sol is Va Eartha, *the Sister*, because it is so similar to ours. They call it our "sister planet." The old people had plans to colonize Va Eartha, and they probably would have succeeded, if it weren't for the Days To Come."

"You really do know your stuff, Little Moon!" Dartaun applauded. "They *would* have colonized Va Eartha, if it weren't for the Days To Come!"

Virion continued. "The fourth planet is Va Nuyaro, *the Lover*, with its reddish surface, named so because red is the color of passion and romance. Then there's Va Bromera, *the Warrior* because it is the largest and has a big red 'battle scar' on its surface."

Rho had heard the names of other planets before but knew next to nothing of the meanings behind them. He supposed his father would have taught him everything there was to know about the heavens had he been around to do it, and had the Days To Come not made space travel the furthest thing from everyone's mind.

"The next is Va Cantelero, *the Prisoner*, because of the rings that incarcerate it. After that is Va Deseon, *the Fallen*, because of its tilted orbit. Its poles are actually where its equator should be, and it rolls around Sol like a ball. The furthest planet from Sol is called Va Turow, *the Recluse*, because of its remote orbit, all by itself on the outskirts of the sun-system."

"Very good!" Dartaun cheered. He lifted his right hand slowly, and the rock-model of the sun system began to rise up off of the ground. The stone "planets" proceeded to hover in front of them and orbit Sol as a host of new little pebbles rose up off of the desert floor, finding their places as moons orbiting the different planets. There was even a large belt of misshapen rocks which constituted a belt of asteroids between the orbits of Va Nuyaro and Va Bromaro. Dartaun operated the mock sun-system as Rho and Virion looked on in amazement. Dartaun the Great continued with his lesson.

"You've studied the writings of the mortals, and you've learned well, Little Moon! Perhaps you can begin to pick up where they left off. I mentioned before that Noloro is no longer the only planet in the system that could support life. It was once so, but now . . . there is another."

"Va Eartha?" Rho asked.

"Very good, Rho! Your people wanted to migrate there, and they could have done it if it weren't for the Days To Come. They *would* have done it, too. If it weren't for . . . "

It was subtle, but Rho recognized a bitter longing in Dartaun's aimless gaze.

"If it weren't for the Eagle," Virion whispered.

Dartaun's gaze was broken, and his eyes shot to Virion's. He said nothing, and Virion continued.

"'He made all creatures dim and wise, then orchestrated their demise. The planet shook, the seas were dried, the bulk of living creatures died. The Eagle would the world disband . . .'"

"'Except the cunning serpent's stand,'" Dartaun finished with a jagged, yellow grin. "The age of Noloro is over. The age of Eartha is at its dawn."

"You are the serpent, aren't you?" Virion asked. "I mean, the original serpent. You are Va Lucifero?"

Dartaun smiled a vicious smile that squirmed as he spoke. "Somebody's been reading their Bel Tiev! I haven't been called by my slave name for some time now—Va Lucifero. *The Light-bearer.* Yes, I was so called . . . once. Answer me this, Little Moon. What happens when the Withering is complete?"

"Noloro dies," Virion responded coldly.

Rho shivered at the coldness in her voice. He remembered what Jeema had said to him in the dark stairwell.

I'm a little worried about me, too . . . She's not good, Rho . . . She was nice to me, too—until she grew powerful enough to take over . . .

He still didn't understand what was going on with Dartaun and Lady Virion, but all Rho wanted to do at the moment was to get himself and his little brother as far away from these two as possible, but there was no way he was leaving Jeema here, helpless and afraid. Was Jeema under some sort of spell? Was Virion some sort of second personality? Was Virion really an evil spirit living inside of Jeema? Whatever it was, his instincts were telling him not to get any more involved than he had to. Then he remembered something else that Jeema had said in the stairwell, right before Virion had shut her up.

She couldn't do anything when Nod was there. I don't know why. There's something about him . . .

Why couldn't Virion do anything when Nod was around? Rho looked down at his brother and noticed that the swelling was already going down and color was beginning to return to Nod's cheeks. It appeared that the antivenom was beginning to work.

Come on, Nod. Wake up, buddy.

"That's right, Little Moon. When the Withering is complete, Noloro dies. To be a bit more specific, the moon has been orbiting closer and closer to Noloro, as I'm sure you've noticed, and soon it will crash down onto the surface of Noloro, completely changing the landscape of the planet and inverting its rotation on its axis. Even if one were to somehow survive the moon's impact, the surface conditions will be dramatically altered. The resulting atmospheric levels and temperatures will rapidly become incompatible with life. Every*one* and every*thing* on Noloro will die. So much for a loving father . . . "

"What's your point? What do you want with us?" Rho's patience had worn thin.

"That," Dartaun pointed at his solar system model emphatically. The miniature moon crashed into Va Noloro and a fire consumed them both. "*That* is the point. If you stay here, there is nothing ahead but death and dying. This planet *has* no future. If you want a future, your only option is to come with me to the new world." He nearly shouted with excitement and frustration. "As the rightfully reigning King of Va Eartha, I am cordially inviting the two of you to join me in a royal celebration—something truly spectacular—for the birth of my brand new kingdom."

"Thank you, Dartaun," Virion said humbly. "I'm honored."

Rho nearly broke into laughter at the grandeur with which he spoke. The fire from miniature Noloro burned hotter between them.

"There's nothing left for you here, boy! Don't you want to grow old and have a future? Don't you want to be married and have children, to raise a family in a new and perfect world? Of course you do! Don't be stupid."

Rho looked at Virion, who nodded at him, clearly attempting to pressure him into agreement. He couldn't quite fit this enormous proposition into his own reality. It was too big of an idea, too surreal of a conversation to even entertain.

Rho finally managed to blurt out, "How?"

Dartaun took a deep breath and cleared his throat.

"On my ship, of course!" Dartaun extinguished the flaming rocks and gently lowered the floating solar system to the dirt, still in perfect order. "Before the Days To Come, two incredibly brilliant doctors, the brothers Wissler, programmed a privately funded space ship to take a small team to Va Eartha. The mission was abandoned after the Days To Come, but I've had the good Dr. Wissler refurbish the shuttle and prepare it for our journey. All it's missing now is a crew . . ."

Rho scrunched his nose up like he'd just tasted something terrible.

"You want us to . . ." he paused. "I mean, you really think there's a . . ."

Virion helped him out.

"A space shuttle?"

"Come on!" Dartaun protested. "Haven't you been listening to *anything* I've said? What's so unbelievable about a space shuttle, huh? Your father is the one who designed it, for goodness' sake!"

Again, silence from Rho and Virion.

Dartaun sighed. "Listen, that's where we're going—right up there in the Neolani Mountains—on the east side of Soren's Pass, where it winds down to the sea of antiquity. That's where the shuttle is. Are you coming with me or not?"

"Absolutely," Virion said without hesitation.

Rho shot her a skeptical glance.

"All right, Rho," the sorcerer spoke. "Why don't you take a moment to think it over, but in case you haven't noticed, time is not our friend. I suggest you get a grip on yourself, and quickly."

CHAPTER FORTY-SEVEN

Sol had all but disappeared over the western range. The sky bled deep red as slender shadows slithered across the desert floor.

"He's right, you know." Lady Virion tilted her head to catch Rho's eyeline.

"How do you figure?"

"Look. It's not complicated. If we stay here, we die. Let's start there. Is there any question about that?"

Rho could hardly bring himself to look into Virion's eyes. They were dark and detached and lifeless. His eyes fell to the floor. He jutted his jaw out and he gripped the nape of his neck with his right hand.

Virion continued, "I didn't think so. I know you don't like him, but he's our only chance at surviving this, and as far as I can see, there's no real downside for us. If we don't go with him, then it's only a matter of days before the moon comes crashing down on us and we die. If we go with him, the worst case scenario is that we find out he's lying, there is no space shuttle, and the moon comes crashing down on us and we die. Either way, we die when the moon collides with Noloro. On the other hand, if there *is* a space shuttle . . ."

Rho slowly nodded his head. He couldn't argue with that. His fingers gripped the hilt of his sword, Lejin. He could really use his mother's wisdom at the moment. What would she do if faced with this kind of a decision? Would she go against her every instinct and align herself with a suspicious sorcerer and his vaguely dark and mysterious plan to continue the Nolorian race?

Perhaps, if it meant survival, and if it were the only option available. Would she instead keep herself as far away as possible from of any sort of dark sorcery at any cost? Probably, if he was being honest with himself. He knew she would do one thing for certain. She would pray. He considered it, but he didn't even know how to begin. Sure, he'd cried out in a moment of weakness down in Xiara's lobby, when he was certain he was about to die, but that was different. He wasn't even sure if God had heard him then. After all, was it God who saved his life then, or was it Virion? It had been too long since he'd really prayed, and his path had taken him far from God. He knew it would do him no good. If there really was a God, He surely wouldn't be very pleased with Rho. Then it was there again. That guilt he'd felt before. There was a moment—just a flash, really—when Rho allowed himself to be completely honest about it, and he was forced to admit to himself, if only for that fleeting moment, the real reason he refused to speak with God.

He was still angry.

He looked up and wondered at the trillions of stars suspended above him, looking for some sort of sign. He thought of his father, who gave his life over to save the woman he loved. He died, tangled up in a web of evil, giving his life over to darkness for a cause that was good and pure.

He turned and looked off toward the campfire, and toward the sorcerer, and to his little brother, who lay motionless on a tattered mattress, now completely alone and defenseless in this world. Even if he did awaken, it was only a matter of days—maybe less—before his young life would be cut short. The Withering was nearly complete. He could feel it.

The thought of it—the end of everything—didn't trouble him nearly as much as he'd expected. Sure, he felt cheated out of the life he'd imagined for himself. He was still angry that he would never marry, or have children, or grow old. Even so, he found himself slowly coming to grips with his new reality. He'd even managed to find a small bit of solace in the inevitable. His heart longed to see his father and mother again, though he wasn't certain he'd be allowed in heaven, or wherever his parents and brother ended up. That thought terrified him.

Still, there was a small part of him that wouldn't necessarily argue with leaving this dead and dying world—this mirage of empty promises, of delectable imaginations and perpetual bitter denial—and traveling to whatever new realm awaited him on Va Eartha. It was one thing to come to grips with his own mortality, but to see his little brother lying there like that stirred up a fierce urgency to protect him, to deliver him to safety, to live up to his father's expectations. Whether it was fair or not, he was the only one left here to protect his little brother, and he resolved that he would do so, even if it killed him.

"Okay." He looked Virion in the eye. "Let's go find that space shuttle."

CHAPTER FORTY-EIGHT

Next to the campfire, Dartaun stood over Nod's motionless body. He snickered at the boy's lifeless face, but as he looked on, there was a slight twitch in Nod's cheek, then the flutter of an eyelid. Dartaun smirked. There were some signs of life, after all. Dartaun knew he couldn't have been rid of the boy yet. There had never been any antivenom, but he'd played the situation perfectly. If he couldn't be rid of the boy, he could at least use his inevitable return as a means to gain the trust of the other two. What's written was written, and the enemy never failed to deliver on His word. The boy would return. Dartaun had already accomplished his purposes in the boy's absence, and he'd be ready for his awakening. He wouldn't allow the boy to interfere with his plans. He's already had the others on a string. All they needed was a little tug here, and a little tug there. If they believed it was Dartaun who had brought the boy back, all the better.

"I know who you are, boy, even if you don't. I know your role in this story, and it's no use, Little Lamb. It's already in motion. There's no way to stop it now."

Suddenly, the boy's arms extended out and gripped the earth, and his head began to whip back and forth in violent convulsions. His eyes remained closed, and it appeared to Dartaun as if the child was holding his breath. His face grew redder as his head thrashed around wildly. Dartaun took an unsteady step backward and looked on with uncertainty.

After a moment, the boy's body relaxed, and he lay motionless once again.

CHAPTER FORTY-NINE

Nod was awakened by a sudden and desperate need for air. He didn't know how or why he found himself submerged in warm water, but he didn't have time to ponder that now. It was dark, and he couldn't tell which way was up. He swung his head violently in every direction until he noticed a faint beam of golden light piercing the darkness. Once he saw which direction the light was coming from, he was able to orient himself.

Behind him was only darkness, but up ahead, there poured in a heavenly light that carried with it the promise of life. He didn't know how to swim, but he reached toward the light, kicking at the darkness behind him. In that way, he moved slowly toward the light, and the light grew more brilliant with each passing moment. Nod had never been fully submersed in water before, and he certainly didn't know how to swim, but there was no hesitation in him, only instinct. He swam furiously toward that light, never once looking back toward the death and darkness behind him.

Emerging from the mysterious waters, he took in the sweet air, and it filled him with life. He had never breathed air so joyful and lively as this. He floundered toward a nearby rock and pulled himself up onto it. It was as if he were in a different world, and when he gathered himself and peered out at the land surrounding him, he really began to believe that he could not be on Noloro. The vegetation and abundant animal life made Xiara's garden seem like a desert wasteland compared to the scene before him now.

The water was clear, and at its edge, herds of animals lapped at it without the slightest hesitation or fear. The animals were not like any Nolorian animals he'd seen. There were elegant-looking beasts with long necks and tan fur, some with antlers and some without. The small ones were covered in white spots. They grazed off the edge of the water in the greenest patch of land he'd ever seen, a deep and lush shade of green that Nod could never have even imagined before now.

"Grass!" He laughed. "Just like the elders said, only . . . it's so beautiful."

Everywhere he looked, there were all sorts of beasts of every variety. There were large, golden cats, some with regal manes hanging around their faces, and some without. There were large birds soaring overhead with wingspans as long as full-grown men, and when one perched itself on a thick branch of a healthy fruit tree, he was surprised by the size of its long, sharp talons. The most incredible of all the beasts present were the five enormous creatures with leathery gray skin and long noses which moved like arms. They were dipping their noses into the water and raising them back up over their bodies to shower their backs. These creatures looked as if they were actually smiling as they played happily together. There were many other creatures as well, but something else had captured Nod's attention at the moment. Behind the golden cats was what looked like a man, dressed all in white, with skin that was glowing like heated bronze. There seemed to be a fire burning within the man, and it did not hurt him or consume him, but rather emitted powerfully from within him. It was the man he'd seen in his vision the night before. Nod was overcome with a paralyzing fear.

"Do not be afraid," the man said. "For you have found favor in the eyes of your Father. Three things have I for you: a name, a gift, and a task."

"Sir?" Nod asked nervously, "Where am I?"

"This?" The man smiled, raising his arms up in appreciation for the beauty in which he stood. "This is Eden."

"It's so . . . alive," Nod mused. "Are we still on Noloro?" He already knew the answer, but it surprised him to hear it, nonetheless.

"No, this is Va Eartha. It is a new world. Va Noloro has been given over to the destroyer, yet fear not. You have not been left alone. The spirit of God lives in you and guides you in all your ways. Remember, it is appointed to all men to die once. So it was on your world, and so it shall be on this new world. Yet for those who partake of the Lamb, death has no authority, for even though they die, they will live again."

"The Lamb of God . . . " Nod mused.

" . . . who takes away the sin of the world," the man continued. "The Lamb was sacrificed once to take away the sin of the many. All must follow Him to the grave, yet for those who believe, He will lead them into new life."

"In the Darrows," Nod interjected, "we've read the Bel Tiev, and we've waited for the promised Lamb of God. Even after the Days To Come, even as our world ends, we still wait for Him. Has He already come? Did we miss Him?"

"Many have missed Him, but you have not missed Him, Nod. You have found Him, and He is in you. You are being sacrificed along with Him. It is no longer just you who lives, but the Lamb who lives within you. From here forward, the life you will live in the flesh, you will live by faith in the Lamb, who loved you and gave Himself for you at the foundation of the world.

"Time is a mystery to man, but just as a potter throws a vase and does not live inside the vase, even so, your God created time and is not bound by its restraints anymore than He is bound by gravity, which He also created. God decreed such laws for His creation to abide by, but God abides outside of the creation, where such laws are meaningless.

"From your perspective on Noloro, the Lamb has not yet come . . . but when your body breathes its last, and you finally step outside of the constructs of this creation—away from time, space, matter, and energy—and into eternity, then it will become clear that the Lamb *was* and *is* and *is to be* the sacrifice for all. Men who live within the creation are bound by the chains of time, and blinded by the illusion of it, but what happens at any given point in time and space happens everywhen and everywhere for all eternity. There are other worlds than these, Nod, and there are other times than these, yet there is only one door. There is only one way, one truth, and one life . . . "

" . . . and no one comes to the Father except through Him," finished Nod.

"It is as you say," the man affirmed. His expression changed from reflective to purposeful, and he motioned toward a nearby tree. "Now go and take a piece of bark from the palm tree, and find yourself a sharp rock. Use the rock to carve your name deep into the bark."

Nod followed the man's instruction without hesitation. It did not take him long to procure the bark and a sharp rock, and when he did, he carved his name deep into the bark with the rock's jagged edge. After he was finished, he handed the bark over to the man.

"Nod," the man said, examining the hunk of bark in his glowing hands. "Do you know the meaning of your name?"

"It means 'wanderer,'" replied Nod.

The man nodded.

"No longer will you answer to that name. This . . . " He shook the bark in his lifted hand. "This is Nod, the Wanderer."

At this, the man tossed the bark out into the river. The boy watched as the gentle current spun the chunk of bark around and around again, moving it further and further downstream until he could no longer make out his own name.

"Behold your new name," the man held out his hand and opened it, revealing a beautiful stone, smooth and white, with a word—a name—carved into it. The boy reached out his hand and grasped the stone firmly in his own hand. He read his new name, and then he read it again, and then he spoke it out loud.

"Navah."

"Navah," replied the man. "It means 'dwelling.' No longer will you wander as one who is lost. The Lord will make His dwelling in you for so long as you walk the surface of Va Noloro, and once your days on Va Noloro have come to an end, then you will make your dwelling in the House of the Lord forever."

"Navah," the boy repeated.

"Look there." The man pointed across the river, where there was a large clearing in which two trees stood. These were beautiful trees, each different from the other, and both clearly set apart from all the others. Between the two trees, there appeared a man and a woman. They wore no clothes at all, and they walked hand in hand through the clearing.

"Afir," whispered Navah, "and Epella."

"No," the man said. "Afir and Epella were the firstborn of your race, the father and mother of Va Noloro. These are the firstborn of a new race, the father and mother of Va Eartha. Behold, the new creation is perfect in every way, though it cannot remain so."

"Why not?" Navah asked.

"Do not be troubled. This is the decree of the Lord. In the beginning, God created the heavens and the earth. There was darkness, nothingness, emptiness, a void. It was chaos. Yet God is the first and best of all those who build, of all who create, of all the dreamers, the authors, the artists, and the healers. If any living thing ever did any good work under the sun, it was the Lord who did it first and better. Any living thing is only able to do any good thing because it was made in the image of God, Who did it first. Every living thing that has brought life into the world or fed its young was only able to do so because it was made in the image of God who is the giver of life, the provider of all things.

"Out of nothing, God created something good. He filled the darkness with light, and He filled the void with beauty. He created the cosmos, a symphony of spheres. He created time, space, matter, and energy; and He defined them and created laws for them to follow. Laws for time and space, other laws for matter and energy. And so the heavens and the earth obey His laws. There was nothing before Him, and there is nothing after Him because outside of the creation, there is no time—no before and no after. He created time itself, you see. The end of time is as present to God as the beginning, and it's the same for any other specific point in time. So let not your heart be troubled, for your God knows the end from the beginning, and He knows His plans for you, 'plans to prosper you and not harm you, plans to give you hope and a future.'"

"The serpent," Navah interjected. "Is he a part of the creation, or is he something else?"

The man smiled softly. "Indeed, the serpent was created by God. Just like every other created being, the deceiver is bound by the laws of the creation, the laws of heaven and earth, and the material desires that tempt those who dwell within. He is bound by space and time; therefore, he cannot exist in more than one place at any one time, nor can he see the future or the past as God can. From outside of time, God can see the serpent's fall just as presently as he sees the serpent's first rebellion. His fate is inevitable. Sin. Entropy. Death."

"Entropy?" Navah asked.

"Decay, deterioration, destruction. It is the natural way of things. It was introduced to your world long ago, in the days of Afir and Epella, but it has not yet been set into motion here on Va Eartha. This world is still innocent. God does not work according to the natural way of things. He works in the spirit. The spirit creates, makes things new, brings order out of chaos. Creation is the opposite of entropy.

"Each and every act you do results in either creation or entropy. When you walk in the flesh, the natural way of things is decay, deterioration, destruction, and entropy. When you walk in the Spirit, the natural way of things is renewal, healing, redemption, creation. So it is true that every single decision one makes guides the entire world a little bit closer to new life or a little bit closer to destruction."

"Entropy . . . " Navah gazed solemnly toward the couple now sitting on a boulder at the water's edge, the woman nestled in the man's embrace. "It's going to happen here, too?"

"So it is written," the man said grimly, "so it will be; but God will be with them, just as He has been with you. They will be okay. He loves them very much, and He has made a way for them, just as He has made a way for you."

"What about Noloro? Will my brother be okay?" Navah looked up and into the man's kind eyes. The man looked back with a sympathetic smile.

"I don't know, but I am sending him help."

"What kind of help?"

"You." The man smiled. "That is your mission."

Navah thought for a moment, but he wasn't sure what to say to that. Somehow, what the man said made sense to him, but he wasn't sure what to do, or how he could help, or what he was supposed to help Rho with.

"Take this." The man held out his hand. A silver chain hung from his fingers, and at the end was an amulet in the shape of a cross. It appeared to be made up of crystal, and it was completely clear.

"Wear it," the man instructed. Navah obeyed by slipping it over his head so it hung from his neck.

"What is it?"

The man smiled, amused.

"It seems you've become something of a guiding light for two lost souls, but there are forces who would much rather see those souls continue to wander in the dark. To them, you are a threat. To them, you are the enemy. The serpent has attacked you once already, and he will not let up. You will have to be very careful from here on out, and you won't be able to do it alone. Wear this around your neck. It will offer you a strong defense against evil spirits, but only in proportion to your faith. Your faith is strong, Navah, and it will protect you from evil. Don't ever lose it."

Navah inspected the crystal in his hand, assessing the texture with his fingers, turning it over, and peering through it. Then he let it fall back onto his chest and looked back up at the man.

"These forces . . . what do they want with Rho and Jeema?" he asked.

"Death. He wants Death. Not their death, at least not right away. He wants to use them to bring death here, to this new and perfect world. God gives life, but the enemy comes to kill. God provides abundantly for his people, but the enemy comes to steal. God makes everything new, but the enemy comes to destroy. He's already corrupted Va Noloro beyond repair, fulfilling every prophecy written of him in the Bel Tiev. He now knows about this new world, and he plans to corrupt it also. His desire is to plant the seeds of corruption right here on this perfect planet, to infect this new world with his own first man and woman . . . and he's already chosen them."

"Rho and Jeema . . . but why them?" Navah asked.

"He didn't choose them at random, Navah," the man continued. "He carefully selected two broken children from broken families on a broken world, suffering from broken hearts and a broken faith. They have each shut out the light and allowed their hearts to grow dark. The enemy knows this, and that's why he plans to bring them here, to begin the corruption. There will be no happy ending on Va Eartha for Rho and Jeema should they choose to follow the serpent. Their misery will serve his wicked scheme. Once they arrive here, he'll ensure that they remain broken, miserable, and hopeless all the days of their lives."

Navah looked out over the river at the man and woman, and he longed for that kind of purity, goodness, and innocence.

"No, he won't. I won't let him."

CHAPTER FIFTY

Dartaun watched Rho and Virion from a distance. He haphazardly kicked the mock stone solar system that Virion had arranged so carefully, throwing the model into a chaotic mess with a mischievous snicker. The unconscious Little Lamb had been lying peacefully still for some time now.

He was unaware that the boy behind him had opened his eyes and was now rising to his feet. Dartaun spun around to discover the boy standing before him, but something was changed. The boy's presence was somehow a powerful and unshakable thing that caused the great sorcerer's emaciated bones to rattle. This was not the boy he had followed into the dark desert hut, nor was this the boy whose arm he had bitten in the gardens of Lady Xiara. This was a different boy. There was a strength behind his eyes and an authority in his presence, neither of which were there before, and Dartaun feared it more than he had feared anything in a very long time.

"Hello, Serpent," the boy said.

It took Dartaun a moment to recollect himself before he was able to twist his awe-struck expression into a hideous faux grin.

"I'm sssurprisssed that you recognized me, Nod. Yesss, I am indeed the ssserpent, the sssame which bit you . . . but I am alssso the ssserpent who sssaved you. It wasss I who brought you back, you sssee."

Navah walked calmly to the fire. He opened his hands, and whether it was the flame casting a glow onto the boy or something else, his skin seemed to be glowing a bright red, almost as if he were glowing from within. He had something around his neck and it, too, burned red. Then the boy warmed his hands over the fire and spoke, but it was not the voice of a boy that Dartaun heard. No, this was an immortal voice, one that thundered at him with such authority that Dartaun's spirit shrunk within him, his heart melted inside of him, and his strength fled from him.

"Foolish serpent . . . " the boy uttered. "I see through your deceptions and manipulations. I wasn't supposed to wake up so soon, was I? You just needed me out of the way for a few more hours and they'd be in the palm of your hand! Once you've taught Virion a little magick, led Jeema away from that oppressive orphanage, promised Rho a future, and snatched his little brother from the jaws of death . . . they'd follow you anywhere after that, wouldn't they? Hmmm. There's only one problem. You did not save Nod. You killed him. That boy is gone. I am Navah, and I am sent here on the wings of an Eagle.

"As for you, oh serpent, you liar . . . go and flee! You have never tasted victory, nor will you, in this world or any other. So it is written, so it shall be. Your path is always away from the truth, away from the light, and you are determined to stumble in darkness and deceit for all of your days. You set your course on destruction with a furious cry of, 'Aye, full sail ahead!'

"Now, depart from me you ancient devil, and speak no more."

At this, Dartaun's face nearly combusted of humiliation, frustration, and—most of all—a most pure and sincere hatred. He shot toward Navah and glared at the boy across the fire as he walked closer. He winced at the terrible flames dancing in the boy's awful chestnut eyes. It was as if they were laughing, mocking him. Dartaun the Great gnashed his teeth together like jagged stones, and pools of blood began to well up in his ancient eyes. Navah could feel the hatred radiating out of the serpent's soul and into the world around him, but there was something else there. Fear. It was a fear so strong that it kept the sorcerer from reaching through the flames and grabbing the boy by his throat. He wanted with everything in him to kill the boy, but he was afraid to.

He's afraid of the light, Navah thought. *He dare not lay a hand on me.*

"Go on! Show me your venom, oh Serpent! Show me your sharp fangs! Where are they? Show me!"

The sorcerer spoke not. His teeth were bared in a ferocious snarl and his face grew pallid and contorted itself into a mess of rage. His fingernails pierced his palms, and blood dripped down and out from between jagged white knuckles, falling to the dry, cracked earth below.

"Show me!"

Dartaun seethed and raged against the spirit like a wild animal chained for the first time. He grabbed at his robes and tore them apart with an unnatural shriek. His eyes met Navah's, and although the Serpent could not speak, Navah clearly understood the threats he saw there. Then with the flicker of flame, he was gone.

CHAPTER FIFTY-ONE

Rho sprinted to his little brother's side and wrapped his arms around Nod. He realized as he pulled his brother into a strong embrace that this was perhaps the most joyful and the most whole he had ever felt in his entire life.

Rho felt his brother hug him back, and his tears worked their way down into a head of dusty brown hair. Rho lifted his eyes, and they met . . . Jeema's. He could tell immediately. Virion was gone, and Jeema was back. The darkness he'd noticed in the girl's eyes was gone. There was no question.

She was right, he thought. *Virion disappears whenever Nod's around . . . but why?*

"Where's Dartaun?" Rho finally asked.

"Gone," Nod said.

"Good riddance." Jeema sighed.

Rho grimaced.

"I didn't like him either, but he *was* our ticket out of this dying world."

"I wouldn't trust him for a second," Jeema said. "Not anymore."

Nod turned to look at Jeema and Rho released his embrace, allowing his brother to step away.

"She's right," Nod said. "He is evil incarnate."

"You're being a bit dramatic, don't you think, Nod?" Rho smirked.

"It's Navah, and no—I'm being truthful. Dartaun really is the serpent of old, the devil himself. Don't trust him. Don't follow him. Don't listen to him."

Navah? Rho thought? *What is that supposed to mean?*

"I believed in those things once, when I was young," Jeema said. Her eyes became red and watery as she spoke. "I believed in the Bel Tiev. I believed all of it. Then my parents were killed because they were Tievians. I was young, and weak, and afraid. From that point on, it was against the rules to even speak of the Bel Tiev . . . for our own safety."

Now the tears fell freely. Rho did his best to encourage her with a compassionate smile as he took a step toward her and placed his hand on her cheek, lightly stroking a piece of falling hair with his fingers.

"I was told I was too old to believe in fairy tales. I was told that we were moving forward, that we were growing up, that we were making progress and evolving. I believed it, because I wanted to believe it. I believed it because they killed everything I ever knew to be true. I believed it because I was alone and afraid and so sad that I would have believed anything that made the pain go away. I believed it because I felt so utterly helpless. So alone and so helpless . . . "

Jeema reached down and pulled her deck of cards out of her pack.

"An older student gave me these. She said they held magickal powers. For once, I felt like I didn't have to be helpless. She told me that I could use them to speak to my parents, if I became very in tune with the spirit world. I was so tired of feeling alone. I missed them so much. I started down a dark path. A very dark path. Now I'm a prisoner to that darkness. It's like I'm carrying the slow room around with me everywhere I go. I'm no longer myself. It's like I've been split in half, and I'm afraid I'll never be whole again. I'm just a broken mess."

Jeema began sobbing, and Rho wrapped her up in his arms. She buried her face in his chest and sobbed for a while. Rho ran his fingers through her hair and reassured her. After some time, she grew still.

"The counselor at my school told me to embrace Lady Virion, that it would take time for me to learn who I really was. She said I was making progress, but Elder Dulner knew that it wasn't true. He said that running away from my pain was not a healthy sort of progress. He always said that progress was relative to your destination and that I was progressing down a very dangerous path. He said that if I kept moving away from the light that one day, I would find myself surrounded in darkness. I thought he was ignorant. Well-meaning, but ignorant. I thought he didn't understand me, but now I know he was right. I've been on a dark, dark path, and I've made a terrible amount of progress."

"It's not too late to turn around," Nod said. "You used to walk in the light, didn't you?"

Rho felt it—he could almost see the deep sorrow that swallowed Jeema as she nodded her head, fought new tears, and began to sob once more.

"I . . . I can't . . . see . . . any . . . anything . . . any . . . Not . . . not anymore. Nothing . . . nothing . . . anymore. It's . . . gone. It's . . . it's all . . . just . . . gone."

"It's not gone, Jeema," Nod said.

"It's . . . gone. It's all . . . all gone."

"You know where to find it, Jeema." Nod placed his hand on her shoulder. "It's still there. If you want to find it."

Jeema pulled away from both boys and took several steps back.

"No! It's not . . . It's not there anymore. Not . . . for me . . . not anymore. I'm too . . . I can't . . . see it. I'm too . . . far gone . . . I can't find it. Not . . . not anymore."

"It's not far away, Jeema," Nod spoke gently to her. "It's right where you left it."

Jeema spoke no more. Rho approached her and she buried her muddy face into his drab green cloak once again. He held her there for a long time, bathed in the macabre glow of a red moon rising.

CHAPTER FIFTY-TWO

"I still don't believe he just up and left." Rho shook his head in disbelief.

"He just disappeared," Nod muttered. He sat in front of the fire, sharpening the point of a kimba-limb stick with his knife.

"Didn't he at least say anything before he left?" Rho demanded.

"Not a single word." Nod didn't bother to look up.

Rho was at a loss. He'd finally resigned himself to following the creepy sorcerer, and now, he just up and left? It didn't make sense. Something wasn't right, and while he was elated to have both Nod and Jeema back, they had made it frustratingly clear that neither of them wanted anything to do with Dartaun. While he understood where they were coming from, he viewed the sorcerer as a necessary evil—necessary if they wanted to live.

The last glimmer of twilight had faded and the rising moon appeared larger than ever before. Its ghostly crest continued to rise up over the mountains, covering the Empyrean Valley with an ominous red light.

They had planned to walk for a while, but after only a half-shadow, they came upon a small shun-town and decided it best to make camp for the night. Nod appeared to be completely healthy and was able to walk with no sign of illness or weakness. Rho built a fire just outside the door of a small stone chapel where a large wooden cross still hung all a-tilt on the far wall.

"You don't seem very concerned, Nod," Rho murmured.

Nod glanced up at his brother while his hands kept working. He studied Rho for a moment, apparently deciding the best approach to take. Ultimately, he simply shrugged and focused once again on the task at hand.

"It's Navah," he said with strained patience.

"What is that supposed to *mean?*" Rho shook his head.

"It's my name. Navah."

Rho threw his hands up and looked to Jeema for help on how to respond to that one.

"He's been through a lot today," she shrugged. "Everyone deals with trauma differently. Just let him rest."

Rho let out a long breath of pent-up frustration, relaxed his shoulders, and pulled out a paper and a can of brown leaf. He measured out roughly the right amount and dropped it into the paper. After rolling it up into a grit, he pulled a match out of his pack and stuck it against a rock. The match ignited and he held it up to his grit, using his free hand to protect it from the strong breeze coming out of the east, the direction of Xiara's garden—the direction of the moon.

"Navah . . ." He shook his head in stubborn refusal. "He wants me to call him Navah? I'm not gonna call him that!"

Jeema smiled back with a mixture of amusement and sympathy.

"It doesn't matter if you acknowledge it or not, but either way, he's not the same little boy you left home with. How could he be? He's been through too much."

She was right, and he knew it. He should really cut his little brother some slack, after all he'd been through.

Look out for your brother,
When all you have left is each other.

He threw his grit to the desert floor and stamped it out with his boot. It was funny; he didn't really even want to smoke, it was just a nervous habit—something he'd always done whenever he was stressed. Now he just felt stupid, though he wasn't sure why exactly. He drew a hot breath and looked out at the horizon to that great and terrible time-glass in the sky. He spotted a shooting star just to the left of it, then another, and then another. As his eyes focused, he realized that there were hundreds—maybe thousands—of shooting stars flying all around the blood-red moon. More than that, there was something very wrong with the moon. That is—there was something even more wrong with the moon than usual. As it continued to rise up over the horizon, its lower third burned far brighter than the dim, red glow they were used to seeing. That still emitted from the top two-thirds of the enormous orb. It looked to him as if the moon was suspended over a smithy's furnace, with the lower third as red and fiery as the lava he'd narrowly escaped only shadowmarks prior.

"Are you seeing this?"

"Yeah . . . " Jeema replied absently.

"I've known it for a long time—I felt it in my gut—that the moon was coming down on Noloro," Rho mused, "but it still really shook me to hear Dartaun say it with such certainty. I think a part of me has been in denial this whole time."

"I think I know what you mean," Jeema said.

"Would you recite it for me again? *The Eagle and the Serpent?* The part about the egg?"

They gazed up at the spectacle above them and lost themselves in the dark and deadly hymn of a bleeding heaven as Jeema recited the final two verses of *The Eagle and the Serpent.*

"For though the Eagle fled in fear,

He flew in form of bombardier.

A flaming egg the Eagle hurled,

Which bore down on the dying world,

Once Days To Come did come and go,

The Withering of Noloro,

Delivering a final blow,

A fall to fell all life below."

Nod craned his neck around to look at the moon behind him and immediately found himself hypnotized at the beautiful and terrible sight. As he gazed upon the monstrosity, the desert floor began to rumble, then shake. The increasingly violent tremors shook him to his core, and they soon grew into a roar. A fierce wind kicked up from the direction of the moon, and their faces felt like pincushions being stuck with a thousand needless. Shawls went up over mouths and noses, and cloaks covered faces from a stinging barrage of sand, but the wind only increased until they were forced to run into the chapel for shelter.

They found protection there, huddled beneath the crooked cross inside that little stone chapel, and though the sand no longer stung their faces, they kept their shawls up and their eyes shut.

The wind blasted ruthlessly for a full quarter-shadow before it finally died down to a more manageable state. When they were finally able to open their eyes again to peek out from their refuge, the only thing they could make out was a vague red glow, diffused by the dusty night air before them. Slowly, slowly the dust settled and the moon came back into full view, but as they began to make out its shape, each of them froze in fear at what they saw.

CHAPTER FIFTY-THREE

The moon—that great heavenly body they'd gazed upon their entire lives—was no longer a giant glowing orb in the sky. It was now two horrid halves. Noloro's moon had been ripped apart, vertically down the center. The two halves had pulled away from one another, further away at the bottom than at the top. To Rho, it appeared rather like a great red dragon opening its mouth and bearing its sharp fangs down on its prey. A bit out of breath, he yanked his shawl down to speak.

"What . . . what does this mean?" Rho could barely form the words. He couldn't believe the sight before him.

"The prophecy of the egg . . . " Jeema stared in disbelief.

"The *prophecy?*" Rho shot back. "What prophecy?"

"I understand it now—Dartaun's prophecy. The prophecy of the egg . . . "

Rho looked at Jeema, confused.

"'The egg is cracked!' That's what he said. Except . . . Dartaun wasn't just talking about the moon. He was talking about me . . . and Lady Virion. It's me. I'm the egg. I'm empty and broken. There's nothing left but an empty shell. He was talking about *me!* 'The egg is *cracked!*' It means there's no putting me back together, any more than you can put the moon back together. It means . . . " She looked at Rho with a hopelessness that nearly brought him to tears. "It means that 'nothing will ever be right again.'"

"It means time's running out," Nod blurted coldly. He pointed to the twin reapers which used to be a moon. "That right there is 'the final blow, a fall to fell all life below' . . . and to be honest, I'm not so sure that's a bad thing."

Rho seethed through gritted teeth with fists balled at his sides. He didn't know if his brother was losing it or if he was still recovering from the traumatic snakebite, but he didn't care anymore. He'd had enough of it. Before he had a chance to act on his anger, Jeema spoke again.

"I agree with Navah." She looked up at Rho with worry in her eyes. She clearly feared his reaction. She took a deep breath before she continued. "I don't want to be used for an evil purpose, even if it means . . . even if it costs us everything."

Rho huffed and shook his head, pacing away toward the moon, and then back toward his companions again.

"What is wrong with you?" he shouted. "Both of you! Look at what's happened! The moon just ripped itself apart! The Withering is over. This is the end. We're dead if we stay here! Meanwhile, there's a spaceport right there! Right up on that mountain! That's our *future*! And we are *so* close! I don't know about you, but I plan to get there before the moon crashes down on us."

He paused for a moment to let his thoughts catch up as he stared at his brother. Nod stared back with a submissive expression. Jeema's eyes fixed on the ground, and she didn't dare move. Rho's eyes dropped to the ground, and he let his shoulders relax. Then his eyes peeked back up at them both, and he sighed.

"I'm sorry. I just—I know I lost it. I'm sorry. I get where you're coming from, but I've got to try, you guys. I've just got to . . . and I really hope you'll come with me."

Jeema looked up into Rho's eyes, and he understood her fear.

"I just don't know. It's all too much, you know? Va Eartha? It just doesn't feel right . . . but I also know that . . . "

She closed her eyes and her chin dropped to her chest. She swallowed hard and bit her lip. Then she looked up at Rho with a renewed determination in her eyes.

"I also know that I don't want to live in any world without you."

Rho pulled Jeema close and kissed her forehead. Jeema surrendered herself and melted into his embrace.

Nod stood by the embers of the fire which the winds had snuffed out and wondered if it were actually possible to escape the end of the world. He thought about it and decided there was no way. Even if it were possible, it would be a terrible idea, he thought.

What happens when the world ends and you're not there for it? What happens when God calls you home and you're nowhere to be found? Are you just forgotten? Just floating through space on some rock out there somewhere? Then what? Nothing. Sure, you would go on living . . . until your body finally comes to its end, natural or otherwise . . . but what of your soul then? What of your soul when God has already called you home and you refused to go with Him? What of your soul then? Nothing. No Heaven. No Hell. Just nothing . . . for all eternity, swallowed up in the vacuum of space. You just . . . stop existing.

Then another thought entered his mind, and all at once, he wasn't so sure . . .

If God is the God of all creation, and if He knows me, then He would find me. There is nowhere I could go where He couldn't find me. The entire universe is in the palm of His hand. No point in time or space is beyond His reach. Even on Va Eartha. God is the creator and ruler of all creation.

His thoughts settled on his father's face.

Maybe you were right, Dad. Maybe I will get to see a real rocket ship before this is over, after all. Wouldn't that just be the grand finale of everything?

He chuckled to himself at the absurdity of it all, and then he shrugged.

"I go where you go, brother," he said finally. "Only, I have one condition."

Rho smiled. He was pleasantly surprised by his brother's unexpected cooperation, and he was amused that his little brother was now making demands of him.

"What's your condition?"

"When I was asleep, there was an angel with me. He gave me a gift." Nod grasped the cross medallion on his neck. "He gave me a task—to keep you two from going with Dartaun to Va Eartha. He also gave me a new name, and he told me I am not to answer to my old name any longer. I know you're not used to it, but it *is* my name. That is my condition—that you call me by it. My name is Navah."

"You want me to call you Navah?" Rho shot a playful smile at his brother.

Navah smiled and nodded back. Rho looked up at the stars above and let out a dramatic sigh. Then he looked back at his brother and nodded his head in reluctant agreement.

"Navah. It doesn't sound right . . . Navah."

"It doesn't matter." Navah laughed.

"Navah . . . "

Rho couldn't help but notice how much older and wiser his little brother appeared to him at that moment. His father's song ran through his mind. It was so much more than a song to him. It was a promise to his father—one that he did not intend to break. Truly, all they had left was each other, and he would look after Navah as best as he possibly could.

Jeema was right. This wasn't the kid he'd grown up with in the Darrows. He'd been through so much more than any boy should have to go through, and it *had* changed him. How did that annoying little mickey-monkey grow up to be such a respectable young man?

He suspected Navah may have picked up on the admiration he was currently feeling for him, and he was glad of it. He hoped Navah could see it in his eyes or sense it somehow because he didn't know how to articulate what he was feeling without sounding like a babbling moron.

Navah looked up at Rho with an understanding expression and opened his mouth to speak, but he paused, and his expression became concerned. He turned to his left and squinted his eyes to inspect the darkness before him. There was a faint chorus of clanging metal coming from the darkness beyond the northern edge of the shun-town. It was growing louder, and quickly.

Clang . . . Ching!

Clack . . . Clack . . .

Ching! Clack . . .

Clang . . . Clack . . . Clang . . . Clack . . .

CLANG . . . CLACK . . . CLANG . . . CLACK—CRASH.

PART IV:

YOU SHALL EAT
THE FRUIT OF YOUR LABOR

CREATURES WITHOUT CONSCIENCE

CHAPTER FIFTY-FOUR

They came from out of the darkness. They didn't stop, didn't speak, didn't hesitate. They walked steadily and clunkily, with an awful metallic clamor. As they approached, their shapes looked like people, but there was something terribly off about them, even apart from the metal sounds. They were all different sizes, asymmetrical, jagged, jerky, and most certainly not people. Rho didn't know what they were, but he was certain they weren't friendly.

"Hello?" Rho shouted. "What are you? What do you want?"

Nothing. No response, no change of pace, no indication that they were going to stop and chat. It was hard to tell how many there were, but the tumult was loud enough to suggest that Rho, Nod, and Jeema were vastly outnumbered.

As the creatures emerged from the cloak of night, Rho could see the first few of them with some degree of clarity. They varied greatly in height and build, ranging from waist-height to well above Rho's head. They had the vague shape of people, but he could see now that they were actually machines—and appeared to be constructed haphazardly out of debris. There was no symmetry or even an attempt at realism in the formation of these abominations. The disjointed metal and plastic beings advanced on them with a terrifying indifference.

"Guys?" Jeema probed for a suggestion.

Rho drew Lejin from its sheath and gripped it firmly in his right hand.

"I don't think they want to talk," he yelled as the machines drew closer.

A red light flashed from the mouth of one of the approaching machines, lighting up Rho's entire body. Then another flash of red light hit Jeema. The two exchanged a confused glance. Jeema gripped Spider Guts in both hands and stood at the ready. Seeing as Rho and Jeema had weapons and he didn't, Navah took cover behind them. Rho and Jeema stood their ground as the first machine reached out for Rho, who ducked out of the way. Rho and Jeema struck the android with their weapons simultaneously. Lejin bounced off of its right shoulder, while Spider Guts clanged off of its metal chest. Their blows didn't seem to faze the thing at all. It reached out its mechanical arm toward Rho's head once again and this time, Jeema brought Spider Guts down with all her might on its outstretched arm. It struck right below the shoulder, and the arm fell flaccid, with only a few twisted cables preventing the lower arm from falling clean off.

Navah hollered and guarded his face from the shrapnel with his arms.

"Nice one!" Rho yelled, hacking once again at the machine in front of him. His sword ricocheted off its chest with a clang.

"They're some kind of android," Jeema shouted as she regained her balance.

Rho swung as hard as he could once more. His aim was true and he caught it right at the neck, partially decapitating the android and fully deactivating it. Its iron body dropped straight down to the ground. There was no time to celebrate as Jeema was occupied with a second android, and two more were already upon Rho.

Navah watched as Rho and Jeema hacked away at the approaching machines. He had so many questions. What did they want? Where did they come from? Who would even build such a thing? How were they controlled? He saw Jeema slam her axe-blade into an exposed area on an attacker's stomach and it immediately collapsed. Another one was on top of her instantly. This one had a small, cylindrical head and approached Jeema from behind, but her hatchet was still stuck in the fallen robot.

Navah knew he had to do something, so he looked around for a weapon, anything he could swing. He found nothing but a decent-sized rock for throwing, and he figured that would have to do. He didn't hesitate. He was a pro with dirt clod "grenades," and he felt confident enough to put some heat behind this rock. He let it fly, and it nailed the robot in its cylindrical face. The android's head swirled with a mechanical whir and it fixed its attention on Navah. There was a series of electronic beeping noises and the machine emitted a red light from its mouth, which seemed to quickly scan Navah's face from top to bottom, then back up again. There was another loud beep, and all of the creatures seemed to change direction simultaneously, toward Navah.

Jeema managed to dislodge the hatchet from the hunk of metal at her feet. She spun and lifted Spider Guts overhead, then brought it down ferociously on cylinder-head, splitting his metal excuse for a face.

A few feet away, Rho struggled to pull his sword out of another hunk of metal as a much larger android bared down on him. He was too slow, and the tall android's bulky arm slammed down onto Rho's left shoulder, knocking him to the dirt. He yelled out in pain, clutching his shoulder.

Navah saw Rho at the foot of the giant without a weapon and he looked for another rock. He grabbed the first one he could find and threw it. The rock knocked the giant's arm and skipped off his metal siding. The android was completely unaffected. It grabbed Rho's arm and pinned him to the ground. Seeing his brother overpowered by that hulking metal monster set something off in Navah. He didn't think. He just ran. With all his might, he barreled into the android, hoping to knock it off of Rho. It was no use. His shoulder hit metal, and the metal won. There was intense pain in his shoulder and collarbone, but he didn't let up. He pushed with all his might against the beast, but it didn't budge. The android now had both of Rho's hands pinned down on the dirt, and with that, he remained as still as a statue. Navah caught a glimpse of Jeema, who was now pinned down by two smaller robots who were also still as statues. It made no sense to him. Why pin them down and stop there? What did these things want with them?

One of the smaller robots on wheels zipped up to Jeema's restrained legs and extended its metal arms. A metal band snapped out from its arm and whipped itself around each of Jeema's ankles. She screamed as the metal bands clasped onto her ankles. There was a metallic thrum and the two bands slammed together. The androids released her and headed toward Rho and Navah.

From the North, there was a loud roaring sound approaching fast. Navah had never heard anything like it before, but he knew he needed to do something quickly. He tried to make a break for Rho's sword, but before he could move, he was grabbed from behind by a large android. The thing picked him up off of the ground and began to carry him. Navah flung his body wildly, kicking the metal man as hard as he could, but it was futile. The machine had him around his waist with a firm and unrelenting grip.

"Let me go!" he shouted.

The approaching roar grew louder until he could finally see the source emerging quickly from the darkness. It was a large robot that looked like a boxy motospeeder, except with four giant wheels. On top of the box, there was a crooked robot head, which spun around slowly with asymmetrical eyes and an exaggerated cut-out smile. It roared like a wild beast and sped around the crowd, skidding to a stop right in front of Navah.

Two metal doors opened at the back of the steel motobox and Navah was tossed inside like a mere doll. Before he could get to his feet, the motobox lurched forward and Navah's face smashed hard against the steel floor. He looked up in time to see the doors slam closed, and suddenly everything was black.

CHAPTER FIFTY-FIVE

Rho and Jeema struggled to free themselves, but for all their efforts, there was no escape from the bands around their ankles. Rho had fought his hardest, and the heavy metal bands that held him down wouldn't budge. In the end, he watched helplessly as the motobox sped away into the dark night with Navah on board. The rest of the androids followed, hobbling away with their inhuman gaits and surprising speed. They headed north, back in the direction they had come from.

"Come back!" Rho shouted into the night. "Let him go, you piece of junk! Bring him back!"

Rho scanned the wall of darkness for any sign of his brother. To the south, Mon Uro's volcanic mouth was still emitting smoke and ash up into the glowing night sky. The moon burned brightly in the East. It hung low in two fragments, separated from one another by forces beyond his understanding. Rho's entire world was unravelling at breakneck speed. Would his separation from Nod prove to be as irreversible? He pushed the thought out of his mind and found Jeema on the other side of the fire pit, from which a woeful tendril of smoke drifted up out of the flagging embers like a departing spirit.

"You okay?" Rho yelled over to Jeema.

"Yeah. Just stuck here, that's all."

"Me, too." Rho struggled against the metal bands around his ankles. "What were those things?"

"No idea." Jeema worked at her bands as well. "Some kind of android, like you said. I've never seen anything like it."

"Come back here, you monsters!" There was a harsh rasp in Rho's voice now. "Bring my brother back!"

Rho pulled his feet apart with all his strength, but the bands wouldn't give.

"Please . . ." he said, this time mostly to himself or to no one at all.

Frustrated, he looked up at the stars and began to whisper.

"God, please protect Nod—Navah—from . . . whatever those things are. Please help me and Jeema. Please get these bands off of us so we can find my brother and help him. Please . . ."

A few feet away, Rho heard the callous voice of Lady Virion.

"Do you think He cares? Do you actually think He's listening?"

Rho felt two things simultaneously. The first was a burning shame—a debilitating fear of appearing foolish and naive. That fear carried with it a flagrant pressure to denounce his error.

The second feeling was the stronger and deeper of the two. He hadn't felt in a very long time. It was a profound sense of assurance, an unexpected peace, an awareness, and a self-admission that everything—the Withering, the fate of Noloro, the death of his parents, the fractured and falling moon, the eruption of Mon Uro, the band around his ankles, his brother's abduction . . . all of it—was utterly and perfectly out of his control. It was a feeling that would have caused him a great deal of hopelessness at any other time, but in that moment, he felt a peace that surpassed all understanding. He ignored Virion and the feelings of shame which tried to break their way into his mind. Somehow, he was able to keep them at bay. Maybe this—this peace, this . . . whatever it was . . . was the thing keeping Virion away whenever Nod—Navah—was around.

"God, I know you can hear me, but I'm afraid you won't want to listen to me after the things I've done. There was a long time where I didn't believe in you. If I'm being honest, I think I've always believed you were real, but I didn't always believe you were good. I didn't *want* to believe in you. I think I was *just* angry. I was *so* angry. I told myself that if you could take my parents away from me, that you weren't the loving God that my mother taught me about."

"You were right to be angry, Rho."

Virion's voice sounded desperate, and somehow that made him happy. Her frustration with his prayer only spurred him on. "I was wrong to be angry, and I'm sorry. I'm beginning to understand that you have a plan that is much bigger than me, and much bigger than Navah and Jeema. I'm beginning to see that there is a war being waged on a bigger scale than Va Noloro and Va Eartha, and yet as insignificant as we are, you brought my brother back from a physical death, and it seems you may be bringing me back from a spiritual death.

"I want to say I'm sorry for watching out for myself when I should have been watching after my brother. I've been selfish and stupid, and I've been a coward. I sat and watched as the trapper whipped my brother for something I did. Nod told me to leave that little clay fox alone, and I didn't listen. I knew the law, and I did what I thought was right instead. I thought my way was better, but that baby fox suffered longer, and my brother was whipped for a crime that I committed. I'm done going my own way. I'm done mocking my brother for his faith. I'm done going against you, God. I'm sorry. Please forgive me, God. Please forgive me."

"It's too late for that, Rho."

Virion's words stung. Was it too late? He didn't know for certain. He looked up at the stars and felt he could reach out and touch them. Not with his hands, but with his mind and with his spirit. He felt something that he remembered clearly—it was so familiar—something like being home. It was the unconditional love of his mother. It was the insurmountable strength of his father. It was the unshakable faith of his brother. It was a strange new calling, a command of all things. It was an unquestionable authority, though not his own to wield—it had been entrusted to him, and he was wrapped up in it like a child wrapped up in a father's arms. It was a sudden onset of absolute humility and inexplicable confidence in what was real. It was a recognition of the futility of his own strength and a submission to one much greater than his own. It was a complete reliance upon, and a total surrender to, a truth far greater than himself. It was a flood of regret for having allowed himself to forget all he had once known, and an even greater relief at the comforting arms which seemed to be welcoming him back without any hesitation, without any condemnation, embracing him wholly. It felt like coming home.

Rho wouldn't have known how to describe what he felt, but in that moment, he understood that he held an incredible new authority over Virion. Without so much as thinking, he turned and locked onto her dark and cruel eyes, and spoke with a firm calm.

"Go away. Leave Jeema alone."

He watched as Virion twisted her face into a hateful mess. She grunted, then growled, then shrieked, then convulsed, then slouched with her head bowed down. Jeema breathed heavily and slowly raised a careful hand to her head. Then she raised her eyes to Rho, and he saw new tears forming in Jeema's emerald eyes.

"Thank you." As she spoke, Rho could see questions forming in her eyes, but she couldn't seem to find the words. Her lips remained parted, ready to ask all the questions she could not quite form.

"I don't know how I did that. I just . . . I was praying, and then . . . I just knew that I could . . . so I did. It was like God gave me an authority over her, and I wasn't afraid. I just told her to leave, and she did."

Jeema looked as if the wind had been knocked out of her, as if she might be sick. Her eyes wandered and she doubled over, her left hand in the dirt, her right hand massaging her forehead. Her whole body jolted like he'd seen her do before, just before passing out in Xiara's lobby.

"Are you okay?"

She ignored him and continued scanning the desert floor, trying to catch her breath. She jolted again.

"Jeema?"

At the sound of her name, her frightened eyes met his. Whatever had been going on, he'd managed to snap her out of it. She collected herself, took one slow, deep breath, and began to nod her head.

"Your brother was right."

Rho nodded his head, knowing exactly what she meant.

"The Guidestones . . . it's all real. The eagle, the serpent—only I've been on the wrong side this whole time."

A lump lodged itself in Rho's throat, and he swallowed it painfully. He was well aware of the tears welling up in his eyes, but he couldn't look away from Jeema, who now had tears streaming down both of her cheeks.

"I'm going to die, Rho. I'm going to pay for what I've done."

Rho nearly lost his composure. He wanted so badly to run to her and to hold her, but the heavy metal bands around his ankles rendered him immobile.

"That's not true, Jeema. You're free now. You're free from Virion. She's gone now."

"No, she's not." Jeema was sobbing now. "She's just afraid of you, and she's angry. She's not pretending anymore."

"Pretending?"

"To be nice. She's done pretending. She's done playing nice. She's angry now. She's *so* angry it hurts. She just keeps going, on and on in my head. She won't stop. I can't even think. She means for us to go to Va Eartha, and she'll do anything to make sure it happens."

"Well I'm not going to let that happen."

"She means to get on that shuttle with or without you, and there's nothing you or I can do to stop her."

"Be gone, Virion!" The ferocity of his own roar surprised him, and he conjured up a bit more to drive the point home. "Leave Jeema alone."

A few blinks from the girl and then a soft smile—as fair as the fallen snow—followed by a timid nod of her perfect little head.

"I think she's gone." Jeema's voice was hardly more than a raspy whisper.

"For good?"

"I . . . I don't know."

CHAPTER FIFTY-SIX

A strange voice cried out from the dark of the crimson desert. "Duncan!"

Rho peered out into the northern darkness and saw the vague shape of a man walking quickly toward them. He appeared to be holding something out in front of him. The voice sounded Nolorian, but as it grew closer, he could see that it was another android.

"Duncan, ye piece of junk," the voice cried out again. "Don't think I won't use this! I've got other bodies in the lab, but that's the only one ye've got!"

Rho looked to Jeema. Her wide eyes said everything.

"Don't test me, Duncan," the new robot warned, this time in a darker tone. "Ye git outta here and leave these young'ns alone."

It came to a halt about ten feet away from Rho and looked toward Rho, then swiveled its head in Jeema's direction. The android was an impressive height. It looked like it belonged with the ones from before, except it was clearly bigger and more powerful than the others they'd seen. Two hulking arms extended out in front of it, holding a small, yellow box with a big red button in the center. The button had been covered by a clear, plastic guard, which was now flipped open, giving Rho the impression that this was a dangerous button.

"Is that . . . is it some kind of bomb?" Rho's voice was far quieter than he'd meant it to be, and the android appeared not to have heard him.

"Are ye alone?" One metal finger hovered over the red button. "Did they leave?"

"They went north," Rho answered.

"Ye'll have to excuse Duncan," the new android said. "He's only carrying out commands. That's all he's capable of these days, ye see?"

Rho and Jeema stared blankly, unsure who Duncan was, and still not sure whether this new android was a threat or an ally.

"Well, where are my manners? The name's Archibald, but ye probably know me better as Dr. Wissler."

Rho and Jeema exchanged a brief, questioning glance.

"Ye can call me Archie, though. I'm not much for formalities. I'd be more useful deactivating yer restraining bands now, wouldn't I? Now, let me see here . . . I'll need to get those keys . . . "

A bright red rectangle shone from the android's eyes onto a small numeric code on Rho's restraining band, and then onto Jeema's.

" . . . and I should be able to . . . if I even did this right . . . "

It looked just like the other androids, but it acted and spoke like a human. Rho studied the thing as it rotated its head once again, shining the light back onto Rho's restraining band. With a gentle click, they were released, and Rho was able to remove his ankles from their grip. The robot rotated his head back to Jeema, and there was another click. Rho immediately ran to Jeema's side, who was slower to remove her bands. She looked somewhat absent, or distracted.

The android looked toward the fire and Rho thought that the machine almost seemed to be lost in thought as well. Strange.

"Are you not one of them?" Rho spoke up.

"Them? Them *who* . . . *Them* them?" The machine pointed out into the northern darkness. "Oh, heavens no! No, no, no! Whatever gave ye that idea?"

"You look like they did. I mean, you're a robot . . . just like them."

"Ha! I'm no robot, sonny," Archie spat back. "And I'm certainly nothing like that lot. I'm just a regular, old Nolorian man, same as ye. Them? Them be naught-men."

Rho and Jeema stared back at the metal man blankly, not sure what to make of the absurd claim.

"Let me show ye. Now, just a moment here. Just . . . Wait a tick. Here it is. Okay, it's . . . there we go."

He certainly sounded like an old man.

The robot's eyes lit up once again, and two bright lights projected themselves onto the desert floor. Where the lights met, there was a single image of an old man, sitting in an old armchair.

"Hello there, dear children! I say, hello! Can ye see me? Yoohoo!" The old man waved delicately with both hands.

"We can see you," Rho said. "So you're the real Archie, then?"

"Yes! Well, no. What I mean to say is that *I* am the real Archie." He chuckled in amusement. "Though what ye two are looking at is *not* the real Archie . . . That's just a *hologram* of the real Archie that ye see now. The *real* Archie is up in that laboratory on the hill. I'll blink the house lights so ye can see."

The old man in the hologram shuffled through a collection of remote controls on his side table until he found the one he was after.

"There." The android's left hand went up and pointed into the distance. The rest of its body remained motionless, maintaining the hologram before them. "Do ye see me?"

They followed the android's metal finger to their left and saw nothing but darkness.

"I'm sorry, I don't see anything, Archie," Rho said.

"Nothing? Oh . . . now, wait a tick. Ye're facing west, now aren't ye? So I'm north of ye. Ye'll have to look to yer right, then." The android's left arm retracted itself and its right arm swung upward, pointing off into the distance. "Look up on the mountain to yer right and ye should see the lights blinking. That'll be me."

They looked to their right and saw a set of lights flickering on and off high above them.

"There you are," Jeema said. "We can see it."

"Hello there!" the old man chuckled with amusement. "That's my laboratory up there!"

"So then, you're controlling this robot here?" Rho asked.

"Oh yes, this one here is called Schuff. I'm too old to git 'round anymore, so old Schuff here does the gittin' 'round for me. I control him from right here in my chair. It's quite unusual nowadays, to be sure, but it was quite common before ye were born, back before the Days To Come, ye see."

"And the others"—Rho motioned toward the north—"are controlled by someone as well?"

"Oh . . . no, no. The lot you saw . . . them be a different sort of creature altogether, ye see. Them be naught-men. My brother Duncan is their leader, ye see. Duncan and me—well, we was partners. 'The brothers Wissler' they dubbed us. We worked together for many a year, researching how to map the Nolorian mind and transfer its consciousness into yon machines, effectively achieving immortality. We was successful to a degree, but my brother Duncan and me, we found ourselves on two sides of a mighty vast philosophical divide."

"I don't mean to be rude, Doctor," Rho chimed in, "but I don't have time to talk philosophy. I have to find my brother."

"Call me Archie," the old man said, "and you don't have to find yer brother. I know where they'll take him, to be sure. No, no. Finding yer brother's not the issue at all. The real issue is how do ye figure on getting him back from yon naught-men?"

"Where are they taking him?" Rho demanded.

"He'll be in the labyrinth—of that, I'm sure."

"The labyrinth?"

"Ye heard me right, sonny. I'll take ye there, but ye won't stand a chance against yon naught-men. There'll be more of them in the labyrinth. It's their home, see."

The android shifted its weight suddenly and spun around. It began walking off to the northwest, and the hologram of the old man moved steadily ahead of it. Rho and Jeema followed the metal beast as the old man rambled on.

"Now, just follow Schuff here, and we'll take ye to yon labyrinth. As I was sayin', there be two aspects to every Nolorian. There be the *natural* side—that be yer body and the world around you and how ye interact with the world in a physical sense. There be things like chemistry, physics, mathematics, logic, and so on. Them be *natural* things. Them be *flesh* things.

"Then ye got the other part of ye, the *supernatural* side—that be yer soul. There be things like wisdom, understanding, self-discipline, justice, and love. This be where yer consciousness resides. Them be *supernatural* things. Them be *spirit* things.

"Yer flesh be like a program that responds to external stimuli, just like the yon machines. Yer sleepy, so ye sleep, understand? That's a program."

"You're saying we're just programs?" Rho rubbed his eyes at the thought of sleep. He hadn't slept in two days now, and his lack of sleep was making him impatient with the doctor. All he wanted to do was get to the androids' lair and rescue his brother. The robot seemed to be walking as fast as he was designed to go, so he simply bit his tongue and learned what he could from the doctor's longwinded lecture.

"No, no, no. Not at all. Ye misunderstand me, sonny. Yer not a simple program. As I said, the *flesh* part of ye is like a program. It responds to input and carries out a command. Hungry? Eat. Sleepy? Sleep. Aye, yer flesh be like a program, but ye are made up of more than just flesh alone, aren't ye boy? Aye. We be so much more than that. We be spirit, as well.

"I seen ye rubbin' yer eyes. That's the flesh tellin' ye it be time for sleep. Yer nervous system, yer brain, yer body . . . the flesh receives that information and it wants to sleep because that's what it's programmed to do. But ye won't be sleepin' tonight, will ye, sonny?"

"No." Rho shrugged. "We didn't sleep last night either. We've had more pressing matters to attend to, and still do."

"Ah, more pressing matters! Yes! Ye see? The body says 'sleep!'—but yer spirit says, 'not until I find my brother!' The spirit has the authority to override the program because yer flesh be subject to yer spirit. That's the way it ought to be—the way God designed it. The spirit overrides the flesh.

"Now what do ye suppose would happen if ye reverse it? If ye make the spirit subject to the flesh—to the program? Now the spirit is subject to the program, ye see. That be the curse of yon naught-men. Eternal life spent trapped in a metal cell, a slave to the program."

"And Duncan wrote the program?" Rho asked.

"Not on his own, ye see. He had help. He wanted me to help him, but I told Duncan that mapping minds and transferring them into yon machines would be dangerous—but that's exactly what my brother set out to do.

"I wanted no part of it. I walked out. As it so happened, I was right. When I left, he found help elsewhere. He was a strange feller, a sort of sorcerer, if you will. I have my suspicions that this sorcerer had some sort of influence over Duncan—some kind of dark mind control. They would come up with these screwy ideas together, and Duncan became infatuated with magick and sorcery. They did things that . . . that just didn't make no sense. In the end, you could say Duncan went mad, but I believe it to be something else . . . something the sorcerer did to him."

"Dartaun," Jeema said.

"Aye," the old man replied. "So ye've heard of him."

"Oh, we've heard of him." Rho clenched his teeth.

"With the help of his new partner, Duncan began mapping the minds of wealthy takers and transferred their consciousness into yon machines, the lot ye saw there. Them be the naught-men, as I so dubbed them. They think naught. They believe naught. They love naught. They collect sensory input and respond as programmed. Ye see?"

"Slaves to the program," Rho repeated under his breath.

"Duncan was successful and raised heaps of money to expand his research and experimentation. He took his money and built this laboratory I'm sitting in now. He funded a space program and oversaw many a mission to distant planets, and even lived up in yon space station for a good many years."

"Eventually, the two of them built a great labyrinth in the heart of yon mountain. Duncan was so proud, always asking me to come see his labyrinth. The way he spoke of it, it seemed a dark place filled with black magick and evil things. I didn't want any part of it. I never did go in, even to this day.

"It wasn't long after that Duncan became ill. His time grew short. Dartaun mapped his mind for him and transferred his consciousness to one of them machines. That be without my knowledge, ye understand. If I'd known, I would have stopped him. You'll never know the pain of watching someone you love lose their soul, only to wander this world aimlessly."

Rho's face grew hot and his muscles tightened, his father's soulless eyes in his mind. He felt Jeema's gentle hand on his shoulder, and he pulled away. He didn't want to be calmed. He didn't want her pity. He wanted his dad back.

"The thing about the naught-men is that they *do* think. They be living beings, ye see, but—"

"We get it," Rho snapped. "Dartaun trapped them all in those machines, and he's programmed them to do his will."

Archie scratched his head, then tugged on his beard.

"Ye speak true, sonny. They do the will of their programmer." They be naught but illusions of men."

At this, the old man's gaze once again grew distant and his eyes became sad.

"That's awful, Archie. We've both lost our families, too . . . " Jeema mused, regaining the doctor's attention.

"'I'm sorry, my dear." Archie's voice broke. "But at least ye will see yer loved ones again, in the next life. Not so with Duncan, as long as he remains in that metal cell. Ye see, after their consciousness was transferred, each of yon naught-men attended their own funerals.

They buried their own bodies in a celebration of a supposed 'victory over death.' Very morbid, if I do say so."

"Once we get to the labyrinth, do you know how to find my brother?" Rho asked.

"'Fraid not, sonny. I've never been inside. I can take ye to the entrance, but I dare not enter that 'bom'nable place."

"How did you find us, Archie?" Jeema asked.

"I monitor yon naught-men," Archie said, "and record all their communications. I overheard something very troubling, which is why I came to help ye this night."

"The sorcerer Dartaun still comes to speak with Duncan from time to time. He came to him tonight and he spoke of three children. He was angry as the moon, he was. He said the young'n was causing him a great deal of trouble. He told Duncan to retrieve the boy, but to keep him safe, as he might be needed yet. He also instructed Duncan to make sure that the older two were unharmed. Told him to bind up yer ankles and leave ye stranded. Told him that he would come and rescue ye."

"I knew it!" Jeema cried out. "I'll bet he sent that snake to bite Nod—er, Navah—back in Xiara's Gardens. Lying little serpent . . ."

"What's that, then?" Rho pointed toward the yellow device with the red button.

"Oh, this?" The robot Schuff waved his large metal hand, which held the yellow device. "This be a handheld EMP emitter. Pressing that button will send out an electro-magnetic pulse, which will instantly and permanently disable any electronics within a five-hundred spier radius, including yon naught-men."

Rho looked shocked.

"You mean, you would kill your own brother?"

"Aye, son. I love Duncan very much, and it breaks my heart to see him so. 'Twas not Duncan who bound yer ankles, nor was it Duncan who took yer brother this night. 'Twas the program. Duncan and the others are simply along for the ride, trapped in an eternal nightmare. Aye, sonny, I would end it for him before my days here are through, lest I spend the next life without him."

CHAPTER FIFTY-SEVEN

After powering down the hologram projector, Archie led Rho and Jeema over warm desert sands. Rho had once heard that the desert had been cold at night, once upon a time, but that was long before the Days To Come. It took them no more than three-quarters shadow before they arrived at the entrance of the labyrinth. It was a much shorter journey than Rho had expected, and when they came to the entrance, he felt ill-prepared to face the naught-men who now held his brother captive. He had no plan and no idea how to fight the monstrous beings, but he also had no intention of leaving without his little brother.

He looked up at the enormous mouth of a grand cavern carved into the base of the Neolani foothills. A dim cyanotic light glowed from within. He was afraid but determined not to let his fear stop him, as it had too many times before. He looked to Jeema and reached for her hand.

"Are you sure you want to do this, Jeema?"

"I'm sure." She moved closer and clasped his hand softly. "I know we've only just met, but somehow it seems that you and your brother are the only things in this world I have left."

Rho could feel himself blushing and fought his body's inclination to start tearing up.

"I'm not leaving your side." He squeezed her hand as he spoke. "We'll find him."

Jeema took a deep breath and peered into the eerie blue light ahead.

"Let's go find your brother."

"Take this with ye," Archie's voice called out as Schuff held out the yellow EMP emitter in its metal hand. "If ye can, try and retrieve the boy without a fight, but somehow I doubt it will be that easy. If ye must confront yon naught-men, I don't see any other way. Just make sure they be all within five hundred spier of ye when ye press it. Shouldn't be difficult, as they most always keep tight together."

Rho struggled to find the words to express his gratitude.

"There be no trick to it," the doctor's voice continued to speak through the android. "Ye just press yon red button and fry the suckers."

"I'll free him for you if I can," Rho said. "Your brother, I mean."

"Thank ye, sonny." The android's face was cold and expressionless, but the doctor's voice was somber and remorseful. "Be careful in there. I hear tell of dark magick and wicked creatures, ye see. Keep yer guard up." The robot Schuff gently grasped Rho by the wrist and placed the EMP emitter into his hand. He slipped the yellow device into his inner cloak pocket and looked back up at the android Schuff.

"Thank you, Archie." Rho studied the robot's hollow metal eyes and found nothing behind them.

"Go on, now. Go on and git yer brother back. He needs ye now." What Schuff's eyes had been lacking, Archie's voice more than made up for. Rho could feel the doctor's heart overflowing for the three kids, and he felt grateful for the doctor's help.

"Goodbye, Archie." Jeema smiled and waved her free hand as they turned away. Fingers entwined, Rho and Jeema made their way into the cavern's open mouth. Rho half-expected to find serenity in the alluring blue glow. The other half of him expected to be swallowed up and cast into the ruthless, rotting bowel of mother Noloro.

CHAPTER FIFTY-EIGHT

The cavern was vast and cold. Blue flames danced on evenly spaced bronze sconces, illuminating the innumerable figures sculpted into the cavern walls. They were depictions of Nolorian men, women, and children with expressions of fear and torment across their stone faces. In the center of the cavern stood a giant statue of a woman. The crown on her head and the throne on which she sat told Rho she was a queen. Objectively speaking, she had a beautiful face, though her expression was cold and projected a transcendent malice. The back of the throne on which she sat extended far above her head, and at the top was an emblem of a spider. A giant snake twisted itself around her, beginning at her right arm, with its tail at her right hand. From there, it wrapped its body around hers, then down her left leg and onto the stone floor before the queen. Its fangs were bared and ready to strike, as if to protect the queen from anyone who dared to approach. Inside of the serpent's open mouth, a blue flame burned bright. Beside it was a large ceramic pot with several torches inside, and a few others were scattered about the floor and leaning up against the wall.

"Is that . . . ?" Rho began to ask.

"Lady Xiara," Jeema said coldly.

It seemed so strange to Rho that such an ancient figure—who had been alive since the beginning of time—was now dead. Even more bewildering is that she had met her end not by Nolorian hands, but at the hands of another evil spirit—Lady Virion. He remembered something his mother had said long ago which had always remained with him. She said, "In the war of spirits, our side's greatest weapon is love, seeing as how we will sincerely hope and strive for the betterment of all creatures—even our enemies. Our enemies' most crucial vulnerability is hate, seeing as how they will sincerely plot and strive for the destruction of all creatures—even their own."

It dawned on Rho just how true that statement had proven to be. Lady Xiara and Lady Virion were both set on taking Jeema's place on that shuttle to Va Eartha. They both knew that Dartaun had chosen Jeema for the mission, and yet neither showed any hesitation to elevate their own will above their master's. Likewise, Lady Virion absolutely idolized Lady Xiara, and yet she didn't hesitate to kill Lady Xiara as soon as she threatened to take that spot on the shuttle.

That's what their side does, he thought. *They destroy others in order to save themselves.*

Had he been given the choice, he would have taken his brother's spot in that android motobox. He certainly knew his brother would do the same for him. He already had. Nod had taken Rho's rightful spot at the wrong end of Boss Man's chain. He'd taken the blame and endured the blows that were meant for Rho.

That's what our side does, he thought. *We sacrifice ourselves in order to save others.*

How strange a thing to watch the mother of all civilization die right in front of you, and to watch the moon tear itself in two just above you. Even the ancient things, even the unkillable things were not safe from the Withering. It was simultaneously amusing and terrifying to him that three orphans from nowhere could have somehow survived, just to wander the desolate world until it finally comes to an end. It was as if Death himself came to Noloro, wiped out everything of any importance, and decided that these three wandering orphans weren't even worth the trouble.

Jeema gave his hand a gentle squeeze, and his wandering mind snapped back to the task. He grabbed a torch from the ground and placed it into the snake's mouth, lighting the wrapped end with the blue flame. Jeema followed suit. Rho strained his neck to look up at the image of Lady Xiara once again.

"Good riddance." He sighed, and he continued along past the statue.

Further ahead, the passage opened into a much larger chamber. There were still sconces on the walls marked by blue flames, but the walls were so far apart that much of the chamber was shrouded in darkness.

A wide, rushing stream wound its way in and out, along and across the cavern, and various stone bridges stretched out across the stream at several different points ahead of them. Rho was horrified to see dozens of openings to separate passages, all leading off in different directions.

"Where do we even start?" he asked.

Rho imagined himself following wrong passage after wrong passage, over and over again until he starved or until the moon crashed into Noloro. There was a feeling like a stone in his stomach which told him the next time he saw his brother would be in another world. He realized that it was a very real possibility, but he refused to surrender his little brother to a band of deformed androids. He was somewhere inside this vast labyrinth, and Rho was determined to find him.

"There." Jeema pointed across the river on the far side of the cavern to a stepped tower with a stairway on each side leading to the top. At the very top, there was another throne, and someone or something moving around it, circling the throne with a cat-like prowl. Rho couldn't tell what it was exactly, but it appeared to have a large set of wings.

"It's a sphinx," Jeema said flatly. "An ancient guardian. We'll have to get past her."

"We're supposed to get past *that*, with only *this*?" Rho grasped the hilt of his sword.

"With only *this*." Jeema put one finger up to her temple.

Rho squinted, not understanding her meaning, but he relaxed his grip on the sword.

They crossed three bridges to get to the ziggurat and made their way to the top. As they approached, Rho grew a bit concerned with just how fearless Jeema appeared. After his encounter with Lady Xiara, he was not excited at the thought of meeting yet another mythical creature.

The top of the platform came into view, and the sphinx sat patiently upon its throne, awaiting their arrival. Her head was slightly taller than Rho's, but her wings spread out to a height and span twice as long as himself. She had black fur from the neck down and her wings consisted of black feathers. Her long black hair was worn in braids, and she adorned herself with a large golden headpiece, a golden bodice, and gold jewelry on every extremity. The skin of her face was white as porcelain and painted with intricate designs, which glowed a fierce blue. Her lips glowed blue as well, and her eyes moved to and fro between Rho and Jeema.

"State your purpose," the sphinx demanded.

"We're looking for my brother," Rho answered. "He's been kidnapped by . . ."

"No!" the sphinx bellowed. "That is not your purpose! How is it that I know your purpose, but you do not? Answer my riddle and you may pass. Fail to answer, and I will kill you. Understood?"

A chill pierced Rho's heart. He turned and found Jeema's wide eyes looking back at him, and neither could conjure the courage to respond to the sphinx.

After a moment, the creature continued. "The two of you share a *common* purpose, and therefore you will share a common riddle:

"From something that is living,

You enter, unforgiving.

Though you are not alive,

It's life which you consume.

Then after you arrive,

The living meet their doom.

What are you?"

CHAPTER FIFTY-NINE

Rho looked to Jeema and was relieved to see the wheels cranking in her head, but he himself felt an overwhelming sense of hopelessness.

"I'm not good with riddles," he grimaced.

"Well, I am. The most important thing is to consider every single word in a riddle, and not only that, but the phrasing of it, as well. She asked 'What are *you*?' As in, you and I. So when we answer, we have to make sure that we answer in the form of 'We are . . .' then the answer."

"Okay . . . " Rho tried to hide his irritation. "So, are we going to focus on the phrasing the whole time, or can we start thinking about the actual riddle?"

"I am thinking of the actual riddle, Rho. You won't solve it unless you take your time and consider every word from every angle. You have to unfold the hidden meanings and think outside of the question itself. You have to work around it before you can really get into the meat of it."

Rho shot her a skeptical look.

"Just trust me." She grabbed his shoulders, nodding her head slowly, coaxing him to focus his eyes on hers.

He tossed his head back and sighed in frustration. Then he nodded in resignation.

"I do trust you," he said.

"Remember how she made such a point about our purpose? Our *common* purpose, she said. I think that was a clue. If it was, that will narrow it down for us."

"How so?"

"Because the answer should be something that describes *our* purpose. It's not about me, and it's not about you. It's about the two of us. Get it?"

"To find Navah."

"No," Jeema snapped. "You already said that to the sphinx, remember? She shot that down immediately. Think bigger than that."

"Okay, so it's not alive, right?"

"Not *it*. *We*. *We* are not alive, though it's life which we consume. That means we are something that feeds off of living things, but we are not alive ourselves."

"Like a parasite?"

"Maybe, but that's too general to be the answer. Parasites aren't necessarily deadly. Remember, after we arrive, the living meet their doom. We kill whatever we feed off of. The only thing that comes to mind is a virus . . . Viruses feed off of people and kill them when they enter from another living host."

"Not necessarily, though, right?" Rho asked. "I mean, our bodies fight off most viruses, don't they?"

"True. The other problem is that viruses are alive. The riddle says we are not alive. We'll have to keep thinking, although a virus is our best bet so far."

"You're on the right track," Rho said. "It makes sense with a lot of the clues, but it doesn't make sense for us. How would it make any sense to say that we are a virus?"

Jeema stared back at Rho, and it looked to him as if she meant to say something but thought better of it.

"What?" Rho prodded.

"Nothing, it's just . . . "

"What?"

"It's . . . it *might* make sense," Jeema said shyly.

"That we are a virus? How would that make any sense?"

"Think about it. What did Lady Xiara say? 'When one world ends, another begins,' right? Dartaun has a purpose for us, remember? He wants us to leave this sick and dying world with the sole purpose of corrupting that new world, which is young and healthy. Come to think of it, I don't know that I can think of a better analogy for us than a virus. Viruses are contagious. They spread from a sick and dying host like Va Noloro to a healthy host like Va Eartha. 'After you arrive, the living meet their doom.'"

"That's not going to happen, Jeema. I was wrong before, when I agreed to go with Virion and Dartaun. I just . . . "

"I know." She looked up at him. "It's okay, Rho. I'm scared, too. I don't want to think about . . . the end, but even more than that, I don't want to be a virus. I don't want to corrupt a brand-new, beautiful, and perfect world with our broken and jaded selves. I don't want to be the serpent of the new world."

Rho's eyes widened.

"Serpent," Rho whispered.

"What?"

"A snakebite—venom from a snakebite. It's not alive, and it's deadly."

Jeema's face lit up.

"Snake venom eats away at soft tissue—consumes it—and it's definitely not a living organism, but it comes from something living—a serpent. Once it enters your body, well . . . you know. If it enters the bloodstream and makes its way to your heart, it's fatal."

"Nod—Navah—has lived through plenty of viruses over the years," Rho said, "but that snake venom would have killed him if Dartaun hadn't given him the antivenom."

Jeema recited the riddle aloud once again,

"From something that is living,

You enter, unforgiving—makes sense.

Though you are not alive,

It's life which you consume—yes.

Then after you arrive,

The living meet their doom—it works. All of it."

"We are venom," Rho said again, and this time, the implication set in.

Jeema nodded solemnly. She placed her hand on his cheek and he saw regret in her eyes. "That's Dartaun's purpose for us," she said. "Let's find a new purpose."

Rho nodded.

"We can start by finding Navah and getting out of here."

Rho breathed deeply and smiled. Then he turned back to the sphinx. He stood tall and spoke loudly and clearly.

"We are venom," he said confidently, but not without a tinge of shame.

"That you are, son of Afir," the sphinx replied. "That you are."

The sphinx smiled a wicked smile and motioned with a paw toward her right, where down the steps of the ziggurat, one of the many passageways began to glow the same color as the sphinx.

"I hope you two find what you're looking for."

CHAPTER SIXTY

There were no sconces on these walls, nor was there any source of light aside from their torches. Rho and Jeema crept over the dark floor of the cave with caution, their blue flames lighting their path ahead of them. It was nearly silent, with only a faint trickle coming from the stream back in the great chamber behind them.

Rho stumbled over a rock and reached out to steady himself against the wall of the passageway. In the dark, his hand found nothing he could hold onto, and he crashed to the floor, his knees and one hand slamming onto the rocks. It took a great effort to remain quiet, but he managed, though he knew that his left knee was badly injured. He was glad he had been able to keep his right hand raised, keeping the torch lit during the fall. He brought it near to inspect his left knee. There was a small gash below his kneecap, hardly wider than his thumb, though judging by the sharp and jutting crag he gouged it on, and by the intense pain now beginning to swell, he determined the wound was deep.

Jeema shuffled over to put a hand on his shoulder, and he gave her a reassuring nod in return. With no sound but their footsteps, they needed to remain silent if they were going to have any chance of rescuing Navah. The last thing either of them wanted to do was to give themselves away and be forced to fight a horde of androids again.

Rho stood and shook his head, angry with himself for falling. Even in rising to his feet, his knee screamed out at him and he winced. How could one little misstep result in so much pain?

They continued down the dark and winding passageway, and soon enough, they came around a corner to reveal a dim light up ahead, which grew larger and brighter as the end of the passage grew nearer. Sneaking closer to the opening, they heard a single metallic clang, which startled them. Rho was glad it was dark in the passage, as there was a small hope that Jeema hadn't seen him nearly jump out of his skin at the sound. It took them a moment to catch their breath. Rho slid his hand inside his cloak pocket and retrieved the yellow EMP emitter from within. As he held it, he realized that his palms were sweating now, and he took extra care to hold the device firmly in his uneasy hand.

He looked at Jeema, who looked to him as if asking him to protect her, and that stirred up something rather noble inside of him. He wanted to protect her, and he liked even more that she wanted him to, but a part of him was afraid he would let her down. He hoped when it came to the test, he could be brave enough to do so, as both Navah and Jeema were depending on him now. He knew from the chasm that Jeema was brave enough in her own right, and that she could take care of herself. He had no doubt that she would rise to whatever challenge they found ahead, but he had questions about his own bravery. Sure, he'd been able to run from the Lurkers, and he'd endured being tied to chair by a spider-witch, but when it came time for him to make a courageous choice, to walk out into the light and fight, regardless of the consequences, he'd chosen to hide in the shadows of a cave. He'd let his own brother take a beating on his behalf, as he watched on from the safety of the shadows. He'd been a coward.

As Rho and Jeema carefully made their way out of the passageway, they peered into a new chamber with spiraling ramps ascending and descending all along the walls. The ceiling of the cavern was high above them with many levels of steel platforms and walkways stretching across and around like a vertical maze of some sort.

Rho and Jeema found themselves on a platform two stories off the ground with a ramp to their right, which ascended to the next level, and a ramp to their left, which descended to the cavern floor. Directly in front of them, a narrow metal walkway extended to a platform at the center of the cavern. A spiral walkway ran down from the center platform to the cavern floor, where Rho was both relieved and horrified by what he saw below.

CHAPTER SIXTY-ONE

Navah was alive. Rho made sure to whisper his thanks to God when he saw his little brother. Talking to God felt very strange, but that was beginning to not bother him anymore. It didn't feel natural yet, but it felt right.

Even so, he was horrified to see that around Navah's wrists were thick ropes running up to a large machine equipped with propellers, which hovered and bobbed over a deep pit in the center of the cylindrical cavern, which had no discernible bottom.

Jeema gasped. "Navah!" she whispered. "Is he okay?"

Rho ground his teeth together, and his face became hot with anger. He knew he could do nothing at the moment, as thirteen naught-men stood, knelt, and sat around the floor of the chamber. Each remained eerily motionless. There was silence except for the buzzing drone of propellers whirling.

"What's the plan?" Jeema whispered in Rho's ear, close enough to send a warm shiver through his body. He took a moment to collect himself before he was able to focus.

"I have no idea. I can't use the EMP. He'll fall. I don't think there's any surviving that fall, either."

"Do you think they knew we would try that?" Jeema whispered again, and again Rho's ear melted from her warm, sweet breath on his skin. He shook it off and silently reminded himself that this was not the time for such thoughts.

"Maybe. It *is* almost like they were expecting us. Dartaun must have . . . "

As Rho spoke, the yellow EMP device was snatched from out of his hand. He looked up in shock and found Lady Virion's dark and cruel eyes staring back, a wild and mischievous smile dancing over her pale face. He could see it in that smile that Lady Virion intended to use the EMP to deactivate the naught-men and kill Navah with one swift and cruel push of the button.

She sprang to her feet and sprinted out over the metal walkway into the chamber filled with naught-men, the EMP emitter clutched in her hand.

CHAPTER SIXTY-TWO

Jeema looked out from the shadows of the cave to see Navah hanging from a rope around his wrists, hovering over a pit and suspended by a machine with spinning propellers. She gasped and froze in her tracks. The sight was terrible and she suddenly felt the same sickly sensation she had experienced as she watched Elder Dulner being questioned beneath the murderous blade of Dartaun's death machine.

"Navah!" she whispered. "Is he okay?"

Rho didn't respond. He simply knelt before her, still and solemn. Surely he was feeling as anxious as she was about the situation they found themselves in. She felt close to him. They were something of a family now—all three of them. It was a bond formed by a sorcerer's ambition, strengthened by a witch's schemes and Mother Noloro's wrath, but they were a family, nonetheless. Rho would have made an incredible father. She would have gladly spent the rest of her life with him if a future were in the cards for them. Then she realized that spending the rest of her life with him was something she could still do. That was one thing that the Withering had not been able to take from her. It may not be long, but she could certainly spend the rest of her life by his side, and she intended to. She bent down to whisper in his ear, and fought the urge to kiss his muscular neck. There may be a time for that yet, but this certainly wasn't it.

"What's the plan?" she asked.

"I have no idea. I can't use the EMP. He'll fall. I don't think there's any surviving that fall, either."

Jeema remembered what Archie had said about the naught-man, Duncan, and Dartaun talking to each other. Had Dartaun really given Duncan and the naught-men the task of abducting Navah and leaving Rho and Jeema bound in the desert with steel restraints? Why, though? To get Navah out of his way? So he could come to their rescue once again? To manufacture their trust so they would agree to escape with him on his space shuttle? How strange for them to show up now, only to find Navah suspended over a pit by a naught-man.

"Do you think they knew?" she whispered.

How could they possibly have known they would have an EMP emitter? Then it dawned on her. Archie. Had he set them up? Was he working with Dartaun and Duncan? Of course he was. She had to admit that it was sort of brilliant. Navah was the bait, and Archie's job was to make sure they found it. Dartaun wanted them to arrive here with an EMP emitter and an impossible choice. It was a trap and it put Dartaun in a win-win situation.

It prevented Rho from using the EMP device, leaving them defenseless as they walked straight into his army of naught-men, who would have no problem overpowering them and delivering them to Dartaun as unwilling passengers on an unholy voyage.

If Rho did happen to push the button on the EMP device before fully grasping the situation, Navah would fall to his death and be out of Dartaun's way for good, leaving Rho far more broken, alone, and defeated than he'd ever been before. Surely, he had more naught-men hiding in the case of such an event. Either way, Dartaun would get what he wanted.

"Maybe," he said. "It's almost as if they were expecting us."

It was clear to Jeema. Dartaun and his naught-men were most definitely expecting them. Archie had double-crossed them. She was certain of it now, but would Rho believe her?

"Dartaun must have . . . "

Before Rho finished his sentence, Jeema was overcome by a sudden and intense surge of electrical pain. It took her a second before she really understood what was happening. It was Virion. She'd caught her off her guard and was taking control of her body. Now she was snatching the EMP emitter from Rho's hand and sprinting across the metal platform, over the naught-men below, running toward the center of the chamber, holding the EMP device out in front of her.

No! Virion, don't do it!

The electrical blast Virion sent her nearly knocked Jeema unconscious. Her vision became blurred, her mind was foggy, and she felt an intense pressure inside her head. As she struggled to cling to reality, she heard Virion laughing inside her head.

It's over, Jeema! All the cards have been played, and I'm holding the winning hand!

CHAPTER SIXTY-THREE

Rho jumped to his feet and ran after Virion, who ran toward the center of the cavern where Nod was suspended over the pit. He noticed the naught-men below him stirring their metallic frames into action. He detected more movement overhead in his periphery. He looked up, and there stood two naught-men staring down at him from a precipice one level up.

He continued after Virion, who started to slow as her focus moved to the yellow EMP device in her hand. He was catching up to her, but not fast enough. She popped the plastic guard off from over the red button. He knew he would never make it to her in time; still, he burst forward with everything he had.

His eyes caught more movement from above as one of the naught-men took a slow and deliberate step off of the cliff and came crashing down onto the narrow metal walkway. The flimsy metal structure slammed violently up and down from the impact and knocked Rho and Virion off of their feet. As their bodies slammed against the metal, the EMP device flew from Virion's hand and skipped across the walkway toward Rho. He would have been able to retrieve it had he kept his footing, but the rapid jouncing of the perforated steel bucked him off the edge of the walkway. He grasped and caught hold of the edge, keeping himself from falling off entirely. He landed on his injured knee, and it began to throb with a nearly intolerable intensity.

"Rho!" Navah's voice cried out from below him. Even from that distance, he could see a desperation in his little brother's eyes. All around him, the naught-men were now on the move.

"Hold on, Navah!" he yelled out. "I'm coming!"

The EMP emitter lay on the platform just out of reach of his right hand, and he feared if he reached for it he'd lose his grip. If he could somehow draw the flying naught-man away from over the pit, he could still use the EMP to disable them all at once, but he couldn't reach it in his current predicament. He'd have to work his way back onto the walkway first, and then he'd be able to grab it. To his right, he saw a squad of naught-men ascending the ramp up to their level, and the one who had dropped from above now straddled Virion. It reached down and grabbed her by the neck. He knew he had to act quickly to help her. Virion or not, Jeema was still in there somewhere.

There was no time to waste. Rho pulled up with everything he had and managed to swing his leg back up onto the platform, but at that moment, the platform crashed violently once again. He couldn't see it, but he knew exactly what had happened. The second naught-man had dropped down onto the walkway from above. All at once, the metal walkway slammed up and down just like it had before, flinging his body away from it, knocking him hard in the chin and left forearm. He fell from the platform and finally hit the ground.

CHAPTER SIXTY-FOUR

Jeema wasn't in control of her own body, but she could still feel the pain as the back of her head slammed into the metal walkway. She felt the EMP slip out of Virion's grip, and she heard Virion cursing the naught-man. Virion turned back to find the EMP device, and Jeema could see that it had landed very near to Rho, who was hanging onto the edge of the walkway for dear life. Heavy, clanging footsteps approached quickly, and as Virion swung her head back around, Jeema saw a naught-man leaning over her and reaching its metal hand down toward her. Her instinct was to squirm away, but she was met with electric pains, which reminded her that she still had no control. Virion attempted to move out of the way, but the naught-man caught her by the throat and pinned her down. She knew he could kill her in an instant, but he simply held her there, and she knew why. The naught-men were under orders to detain and deliver, not to kill. Dartaun needed them alive.

Still, the more Virion fought against the metal hand which dug into her neck, the more painful it became. She could tell Virion was having a hard time dealing with it, and it almost felt as if she was starting to panic. Virion was still not used to the pain involved with inhabiting a mortal body. Suddenly, Jeema had an idea.

He's too strong, Virion! He's going to kill us!

Shut up!

A blast of lightning shot through her body and threw her off. It took her a second to collect her thoughts, but she recovered.

You don't understand, Virion! You weren't there when Dr. Wissler told us about the naught-men! They're not just robots—they're real, living people with souls! Very rich and intelligent people, the most powerful people in all of Noloro! They—

Another blast, and this one was much more powerful.

I told you to shut up!

Jeema was dazed. She couldn't see. She couldn't breathe. She didn't even know where she was. Her vision began to clear slowly and she looked into the vacant eyes of a naught-man, who loomed over her and clasped her neck in his hand. She remembered where she was then, and she began to remember what she had been saying only a moment ago. Yes, she had a plan. She had to convince Virion . . .

The elites of Noloro paid a fortune to transfer their consciousness into these powerful immortal bodies so they can live forever, and so they would never have to feel any pain.

What do you mean, "transfer their consciousness?"

There it was. She had her interest. Now, she just needed to keep it.

I mean, there's a real, living Nolorian soul in that thing! It's a person, just like me—except it has supernatural intelligence and supernatural strength, feels no pain, and even has eternal life! We can't defeat them, Virion! It's useless . . . They're too powerful for us . . .

Too powerful for you, maybe. It sounds just powerful enough for me. More powerful than you, more powerful than your little friends, more powerful than Dartaun . . .

No! You can't! Don't leave me here!

Sorry, but I've got a shuttle to catch. Goodbye, Jeema.

Jeema felt a sudden rush of sweetness fill her from head to toe. She thought she could taste honey on her tongue. She reached out her arms and they obeyed. Lady Virion was gone.

She felt the grip around her neck tighten. Virion was no longer inside her, but now she had her powerful hand around Jeema's throat. The pain became too much for her to bear, and her breathing was entirely cut off. She could feel the pressure rising behind her eyes as the Virion-possessed android spoke to her in a deep and grotesquely inhuman voice.

"Goodbye, Jeema."

CHAPTER SIXTY-FIVE

Jeema tried to cry out as Virion squeezed, but there was no sound. What good would it do, anyway? She kicked her legs wildly against the android, but it didn't faze Virion—though it hurt her own legs terribly. A ringing filled her ears, and she hadn't taken a breath in a long time. She didn't have much time left, and she knew that she had made a terrible mistake.

As she looked up into the metal monster's eyes, she saw its body jerk. The hand around her neck released, and the deep, inhuman voice of Virion spoke once again.

"What's this?" Her voice sounded different now. Not as pure and organic. It sounded almost as if it were being filtered through a computer somehow.

Virion pulled her hand away, and Jeema took a deep, gasping breath, just before the metal hand slammed down onto her neck once again.

"You knew!" Virion said. Her voice sounded even more digitized and glitchy now. Jeema's airway was cut off once again, and the robot pressed its face up against hers.

"I'll kill you!" Virion screamed through a mess of randomized beeps and digital tones. Her metal body shook again, and the hand once again pulled away, leaving Jeema gasping and massaging her battered neck.

This time, she took advantage of Virion's lapse in control and scurried back. She climbed to her feet and armed herself with Spider

Guts as the metal Virion jolted back and forth. The android let out a single terrifying shriek, which was quickly swallowed up into a sea of digital noise. Then everything was silent, and the naught-man began lumbering toward Jeema, void of any sign of life. Virion was now a slave to the program. Jeema raised her axe and smiled.

She was finally free.

CHAPTER SIXTY-SIX

Rho was alive. He knew that. He was awake. Sort of. His head felt like it had broken in half. His knee and forearm throbbed. He opened his eyes, relieved that he could see fine. He rolled to his back and looked up at the walkway above him. Was it really only that far? It didn't look like that big of a drop from here, though it felt as if he'd fallen from ten times that height.

"Rho!" Navah shouted again, but this time, his voice was much more distressed. Rho rolled slowly to his stomach and began to lift himself onto all fours. He moved slowly, unsure what to expect from his battered body, but surprisingly, he managed well enough. His knee continued to scream at him, and now his forearm and chin joined in on the chorus in a perfectly succinct pulsing rhythm. He reoriented himself with his surroundings and noticed a loud, rapid clanging, the result of dozens of metal feet stomping on metal plates. At least ten naught-men closed in on him. He pulled Lejin out of its sheath and slowly stepped to the side for a better position where he'd face less of them at once.

Beyond the naught-men, he saw Virion up on the walkway struggling to pull Spider Guts from the chest of one of the naught-men, with three more drawing in on her. She freed her axe, pushed a naught-man over the edge, and jumped down onto the spiral ramp, then down again to the edge of the pit over which Navah was suspended. She held Spider Guts out, trying to reach and hook Navah's feet, which hovered just out of reach. Navah swung his feet, but it was no use.

"I can't reach! Help me!" Navah cried out.

"I'm trying!" Jeema said. "Hang on! Is that thing alive?" She pointed her axe up at the hoverbot which held Navah over the pit.

"I don't know." Navah looked up. "I don't think so!"

"All right, just . . . just hold on!" she said. "I'll figure something out!"

"Hurry! Please!"

CHAPTER SIXTY-SEVEN

The closest of the three naught-men continuing toward Rho was within striking distance now. Rho swung with all his might at its metal neck, and his sword stuck in the side of it, but the creature did not slow. He grabbed Rho by the neck and squeezed with his metal hand. He pulled with all his strength, and the sword was dislodged. He swung once again at its neck and this time, the naught-man released its grip as its metal frame collapsed. The other two were already upon him. He ducked to the side and took a few rapid steps to put some distance between them.

Jeema spun around to study the cavern, and her eyes came to rest on a fallen naught-man. She didn't hesitate. Spider Guts flew up over her head and came down with a clang, severing a long metal right leg. She holstered Spider Guts and grabbed the severed metal leg, then she ran back to the edge of the pit. She held the leg out to Navah. This time, she was able to reach the cords tied around Navah's ankles and hook the jagged foot securely onto the rope. She pulled with everything she had, and the hoverbot drifted toward her, but only just slightly. Jeema collected herself and gave the leg another great tug. This time, she was met with more resistance, and the hoverbot began to pull upward. Jeema stumbled forward toward the edge of the pit.

She tried to gain traction, but the machine was too strong. It pulled upward, and Jeema lost her ground. She realized she had maybe two more steps before the edge, and after that, there was only darkness. The hoverbot was relentless, and she was forced to surrender another precious step, then another. She was right at the edge, pulling with everything she had, but all her weight and all her will were no match for the hoverbot, which dragged her yet another step. This time there was nothing beneath her front foot. She looked down at the endless nothing below her and screamed.

A strong arm wrapped itself around her body and squeezed her tightly, pulling her back from the edge. With one arm around Jeema and the other grasping the metal leg, Rho pulled backward and slowly reversed the momentum. The hoverbot fought hard, but Rho and Jeema worked it downward and toward the edge of the pit.

"Uh, guys . . . !" Navah called. "They're coming! Behind you!"

Rho dug his feet into the perforated metal floor and threw all his weight against it. The machine moved, but still only a little. They were making progress, but not nearly fast enough.

Another slam and the ground shook as another naught-man jumped from the walkway above.

"Right behind you!" Navah shouted.

Jeema screamed as she put everything she had into the fight. Navah was nearly at the edge now.

"Can you grab onto him?" Rho yelled.

"I'm trying!" Jeema yelled back.

"I'll hold it steady! Go on three! One! Two! Three!"

Jeema lunged forward and grabbed a handful of Navah's cloak, pulling him toward her. Rho dropped the leg and reached out for Navah as well, grabbing his foot and pulling hard. Jeema wrapped her arms around Navah's body and pulled him to the edge.

A metal hand slammed into Rho's back and shoved him to the ground. Instantly, the momentum reversed, and as much as she tried, she knew she was no match for the machine. She felt her feet lift off the ground and she reached her hand up, grabbing onto the rope for a better grip. Jeema held on tightly to the rope with one hand and Navah with the other as the hoverbot carried them further off the ground.

CHAPTER SIXTY-EIGHT

Rho managed to get to his feet in time to dodge another metal arm swinging at him. Lejin cut the air swiftly and sweetly, severing the thin neck of the naught-man before him. He buried his shoulder into the metal body, sending it careening over the edge into the dark of the abyss. Two more naught-men were bearing down on him, and he ran to put some distance between them. Looking up, he saw Navah and Jeema dangling from the hoverbot, which was now sputtering and swaying in a wild circular motion.

Rho turned to make sure he was clear of any danger, and then looked back up to see Jeema climbing up the rope, up toward the machine. The thing was steadily ascending, and Rho thought maybe he could help if he made it back up to higher ground. He took the ramp upward and kept his eye on the hoverbot as well as the naught-men following him below.

Jeema had now climbed her way up the rope with her feet on Navah's shoulders, her left hand holding onto the rope and her right hand unholstering Spider Guts. She grabbed hold of the handle, swung it back, and buried it with force into the bottom of the hoverbot. Nothing seemed to happen. The machine continued to rise. Jeema pulled, but the axe was stuck in the twisted metal gash she'd created. She pulled harder, and the machine tilted, carrying them off in that direction. She was steering it by shifting her weight on the axe. She kept the pressure on, and the machine continued toward the cavern wall, moving out from over the bottomless pit.

CHAPTER SIXTY-NINE

Rho made it to the first walkway—the one by which he and Virion had entered the cavern—and ran after the runaway hoverbot. As he ran, he spotted the yellow EMP device lying on the platform before him. It would be of no use to him now. If he pressed the button, Navah and Jeema would fall and possibly get crushed beneath the weight of the hoverbot—that is, if the fall didn't kill them. So much for avoiding a fight, but maybe he'd still have a chance. As he passed by, he scooped it up, closed the plastic guard over the button, and placed the device in the pocket of his cloak. He should have known that just walking in and pushing a button would have been too easy.

Rho readied his sword and came to a stop just in front of the approaching hoverbot. As it passed under the platform, he jumped straight down onto the center of it, between the four extended propellers, and plunged his sword into the center of the its metal body. He heard Jeema scream and realized that the sword must have pierced through underneath. He wanted to ask her if she was okay, but the thing began to sink and spiral out of control under his extra weight, and all he could manage was to hold onto the hilt of his sword for dear life. The hoverbot descended quickly, and soon it was low enough to drop safely. The thing finally leveled out enough for him to get a firm grasp.

"You okay, Jeema?" he shouted.

"I'm good!" she yelled back.

"Can you cut Navah free?"

"I'm trying," she said, "but my axe is stuck!"

"You can't get it out?"

"I said I'm *trying*!"

Rho pulled Lejin out from the metal bot and slid down the side of the bot, careful to avoid the propellers. He dropped to the ground and his knee once again lit up with pain. He got to his feet as quickly as he could and found that Navah's feet were nearly on the ground. He ran toward his brother and raised his sword.

"Jeema! Watch out!"

Jeema looked down and understood. She grabbed onto the axe handle with one hand and the rope with the other, then lifted both feet up out of the way.

Rho jumped up and swung Lejin. The blade sliced through the rope and Navah fell to the ground. As the weight was released, the hoverbot was sent flying in the opposite direction and careened back toward the pit with Jeema still holding on. It was close to the ground now. Several naught-men were headed toward her, and she shifted her weight onto the axe handle to steer the hoverbot toward them. She let go at the last minute and dropped to the ground, then turned to watch the hoverbot's propellers slam into the approaching naught-men. There was a great collision of metal on metal—the most awful sound they'd ever heard—and shrapnel flew in every direction as the naught-men and the hoverbot all went spilling over the edge of the pit together. Jeema hit the ground and shielded her face.

Two more naught-men closed in on Jeema from her left, and she reached for Spider Guts but realized it was gone. The last remaining thing she had from her parents had gone over the edge with the hoverbot. She tried to run back toward the boys, but a metal hand reached out and grabbed at her. She avoided the naught-man's grip, but another naught-man was already standing in front of her, swinging its arm at her. She hit the ground to avoid the impact and rolled out of danger's way, ducking into a small passageway leading out of the larger chamber into a dark passage.

CHAPTER SEVENTY

Rho finished cutting Navah's hands free just in time to block a metal arm with his sword and then bury his blade into the naught-man's body. Sparks erupted and the machine convulsed erratically before falling over backward. Rho dislodged his sword and looked around to get his bearings and assess the situation.

Nothing moved. The chamber was silent and still.

"Is that all of them?" Navah panted.

"I don't know. Where's Jeema?"

He scanned the area but saw no sign of her. Just a lot of disabled naught-men scattered amongst a handful of metal boxes and crates. He jogged across the chamber to an area where crates were stacked up, thinking he might find her hiding, and began peering around and between crates and boxes. Nothing. There were several open crates and he peered inside. Nothing in the first crate, except for packages of dehydrated vegetables and freeze-dried ice cream. It dawned on Rho that this must be part of Duncan Wissler's space port facility. He remembered that these were the sorts of meals that astronauts had taken with them as they journeyed into space on their missions. The thought was so strange to Rho. It was the feeling one had when they discovered that a children's story was actually true.

There was a scream from Jeema. It was short and sharp, and it echoed out from one of the dark passages leading out of the larger chamber. He put his thoughts away and sprinted in the direction it came from, yelling out as he ran.

"Jeema! Jeema, where are you?"

Rho and Navah ran down the passageway from which the scream seemed to have come, calling out Jeema's name and listening.

There was no response.

A FALL TO FELL ALL LIFE BELOW

CHAPTER SEVENTY-ONE

The passageway was illuminated by green flames in gold sconces. They didn't travel far before they came across a series of circular openings in the ground. The boys carefully peered over the edge of one such opening and saw a large, open, white space, with white objects fluttering around in the air, falling from the ceiling.

"What is it?" Nod asked.

"Snow," Rho said. "I've never seen it before, but I'm pretty sure that's snow."

They carefully walked over to a second opening and looked down. This one opened into a separate chamber from the first. They crept to the edge and saw only darkness. They could hear it before their eyes adjusted enough for them to see it, but far below them was a river with a swift current.

They stared for a moment longer in awe and then looked back at each other.

"Do you think she fell?" Navah asked.

"Maybe." Rho nodded. "And if she did, we'd have no way of knowing which one she fell into."

"Let's hope it wasn't that one," Nod look up at Rho with worry written across his face. Rho was suddenly very worried as well. He cupped his hands and yelled down into the opening.

"Jeema! Jeema, are you down there?"

They listened intently, but the only sound they could hear was the rush of water far below.

"Come on." Rho motioned at Navah to follow. "Careful. Stay close. Hold onto me."

They made their way to the next opening. They took each step with caution and Navah held onto one of the straps from Rho's pack. They neared the next opening, but before they could reach it, the floor gave out from below Navah. It was as if he had stepped onto nothing at all. He went straight down and clutched onto Rho's pack tightly. Rho was caught completely off guard and off balance, and Navah's sudden weight pulled him right off his feet and into the new opening in the ground.

The two boys tumbled uncontrollably down a steep and dewy hill of green grass and mud. A moment later, Rho slammed into Navah, who had come to rest at the bottom of the hill.

"Oww!" Navah shrieked. "You're on my leg!"

"Sorry, I'm trying!" Rho scrambled off his brother as quickly as he could manage. "You okay?"

Navah moaned and writhed. "I think so."

"Where are we, anyway?"

Rho traced his way back up the hill they'd fallen down, but there was nothing except a green hill leading up to a dark and threatening sky. There was no sign of a passageway above, or a hole from which they had fallen. Only a deep gray as far as the eye could see. Some labyrinth this was. Before them stood a dark and creepy grove, which Rho immediately perceived as dangerous. A crooked stream cut through the middle of the grove. It was lovely yet eerie.

At the center of the grove stood three trees. These three stood out from the rest. One was tall and sturdy with a large trunk and lush leaves and big, beautiful red fruit hanging ripe and ready to eat. The second was exceedingly thin and ashen white, with small white needles covering its thin branches. The third tree was gnarled, black, and clearly dead. Its withered branches twisted and bowed themselves downward toward the ground. Oddly enough, Rho saw shiny black fruit scattered among its twisted boughs.

Standing in the midst of these three trees sat an old man in faded and torn gray robes, cross-legged and still. He held in his hand the largest gold pocket watch that Rho had ever seen, and from the watch, a gilded cord ran down and attached to his ankle like a golden shackle. At first, Rho wasn't sure if the old man had seen them or not, but his question was quickly answered as the man rose to his feet, holding his watch up in front of him as if to display it to the boys. Then he spoke with a rickety voice.

"Well, now. It's about time."

CHAPTER SEVENTY-TWO

Jeema moved toward the center of an enormous white chamber, slogging her way through the cold, white slush that covered the ground. Her eyes were wide, her mouth gaping with wonder at the magickal white particles swirling around her like fairies in a story. It was cold to the touch and tasted like nothing at all. It hadn't hurt very badly at all when she'd dropped onto it, though her clothes were now soaked through, and she shivered as she walked.

Is this . . . snow?

There was no answer. For the first time in a very long time, there was no other voice inside her head. She was glad to be rid of Virion, but she was surprised at how uneasy and alone she now felt.

The chamber was like an open field, though there was a ceiling high above, studded with glowing blue stalactites of varying length and shape. All around her was open space, though she could see the distant cavern walls in every direction. Unlike the chambers she had been in previously, this chamber appeared to only have one way in or out. She instinctively and slowly made her way across the icy chamber toward the sole passageway.

It was freezing, but it didn't bother Jeema. It made her feel like she could really sense everything around her. It was fresh and new, like walking through a children's story. It was magickal. She trudged through the thick snow until it began to harden. Eventually, there was no snow, only ice. Jeema looked down and squinted. Through the foggy white ice, she thought she could see a fish. She bent to one knee and used her sleeve to wipe in a circle, hoping to make her view more clear, but was only mildly successful.

Did you see that? There's something alive under there!

She closed her eyes and shook her head. She felt like a fool for continuing to talk to no one at all. The silence was absolute, and it made her bones ache. She shivered and reached down to her sides and found nothing to grasp onto. Her beautiful dragonfly teal cloak—the one her mother had given her the morning of the Blood Rain—was gone forever, burned up by the fires of Mon Uro. She rubbed her bare arms and marveled at her breath. She could actually see it escape her mouth.

Let's get out of here, shall we?

No one answered.

CHAPTER SEVENTY-THREE

"Well, now! Dartaun told me you'd get here before the Withering ended, but I was starting to think he was just yanking my chain!"

The old man began playfully yanking at the gilded cord of his pocket watch that attached at his ankle, lifting his leg in the process and laughing all the while.

"He kept telling me, though, you'd be here before the moon came down, and I was really starting to think that ol' Dartaun the Deceiver had pulled the old wool over my eyes! It wouldn't be unlike him to do so, tell it. He's a tricky one, you know!"

Rho and Navah looked on with confusion.

"Well, I suppose it just makes things all the more interesting that you boys decided to wait until now to show up, right down to the final shadowmark! And that's no exaggeration, mind you! I'm counting it down!" He held up his watch. "We've just now come to the final shadowmark! I can't think of a better way to send off ol' Mother Noloro than with one last hurrah! One final battle for the ol' Bromera!"

"Did you say, 'battle'?" Rho asked.

"Oh, yes!" The old man laughed. "To the death, o'course! That's the only fighting ol' Bromera does, mind you. I'm the guardian of the garden. Va Bromera, they call me! "The Fighter" in the old Tebbel tongue. I don't suppose they teach the old tongue in the schools these days. Shame. I 'spect they don't paddle you none either if'n you back talk the teacher, do they? They stopped teaching children to respect their elders and betters, and just look what that got us! Good manners and respecting your betters are things of the past. No respect for the old ways, tell it . . . "

The old man seemed to have lost himself in his own memory and began ogling his watch as if it were a long-lost love. After a pause, he finally looked up, and Rho detected a deep sadness behind his aged eyes.

"I miss the olden days. There wasn't no 'Days To Come' disasters. There wasn't no 'Withering' killing everything dead as rocks. There wasn't no moon fallin' out the sky neither. She just stayed up there in the night sky, all silver and small. Even *she* don't know her place this day and age. It's sad, really. Sad, but inevitable. The time is at hand. I say, my boys, the time is at hand! At least I'll enjoy one last good battle before my times runs out. Unless of course, you want to give up the older one, which I don't 'spect you will?"

He turned the last statement into a question. The brothers exchanged a skeptical look.

"What do you mean?" Rho asked.

"Well, ol' Dartaun says I'm s'posed to take the older one to him and kill the other one. Unless of course you want to give him up willingly. If you did, I wouldn't have to kill you . . . and, well . . . there would be no fight."

Bromera spit on the ground and puckered his mouth in disgust.

"No one is taking my brother anywhere," Navah stated in a calm but firm manner, "but there doesn't have to be a fight."

Bromera peered up with a dangerous smile and a glint in his eye.

"Of course there does!" The man gave an incredulous laugh. "That's my entire purpose. Didn't I tell you I'm the guardian of this grove? My very *name* is Va Bromera. It means 'the Fighter,' for crying out loud. I didn't stand here all these years just to let you go without a fight, mind you!"

Again, the boys looked at one another, entirely unsure what to make of the old man.

"I hope you'll forgive me for saying, sir," Rho chimed in, "but you yourself reminded us only a moment ago of the importance of respecting one's elders. Fighting you would hardly be showing you the respect you deserve."

"On the contrary, my boy! Fighting me is the only respectable thing to do!"

Then the old man's eyes widened and he began to scan his own hands and body.

"Oh, I see." The old man bit down on his lower lip and wrinkled the skin around his mouth, as if working out a puzzle. "On second thought, and given my current appearance, that is a noble consideration, my boy. I fear my reputation has failed me in this case. Not enough people left these days to carry my legend from one place to the next. That must be it.

"In any case, you've somehow come under the impression that you're talking to no more than a weak old man, and I suppose that is understandable. Rather irritating, but understandable, nonetheless. You see, most men who come here to face me in battle have trained their entire lives, but alas, I am no mere man. I am Va Bromera!"

The old man held out his arms in a presentational gesture, and as he did, something strange happened. He seemed to almost vaporize into a mist. In the place of the old man appeared a dark figure, almost like a shadow, only it was not a shadow. It moved like a man, toward them now, and though they could see nothing of him but a deep darkness, they could feel an ebullition of ferocity and aggression.

"There is no time to waste now," the shadow spoke with an inhuman voice. "Three trees. You may each eat of the fruit from one of the three trees. Only one. The fruit you will choose says much about you."

He pointed to one of the trees. It was tall and sturdy, with a large trunk and lush leaves and big, beautiful, red fruit hanging ripe and ready to eat.

"This tree is strong and sturdy. Its fruit will bring you power. You will be stronger and faster, a more worthy opponent for Va Bromera. But the strength does not come from the fruit itself. The fruit works on whatever strength you already have within yourself. Be honest with yourself and only eat from this tree if you have a very strong and courageous heart; otherwise, your strength will not be enough, and I will defeat you easily."

Rho's spine shivered and his hands tingled.

Va Bromera pointed to a second tree, which was exceedingly thin and ashen white with small white needles covering its thin branches.

"This tree is weak and its color has left it completely. Its needle will cause you to disappear entirely so that I will be unable to see you. You may use this advantage in order to fight me, or you may use it to hide from me. It is your choice, but you will not be able to leave the grove until I am defeated. Remember, if you choose to prick yourself with the needle, it is not the needle itself which will hide you from me. You will be cloaked with whatever fear lives in your heart so long as I live. Be honest with yourself and only eat from this tree if you hold much fear in your heart, otherwise you will not remain hidden from me, and I will defeat you easily."

Finally, the shadow creature motioned toward the third tree which was gnarled, black, and dead.

"This tree has surrendered itself to Mother Noloro. The fruit from this tree will take your life painlessly and peacefully so that you do not have to fight me. But remember, it is not the fruit itself that will kill you. You will be killed by whatever hate you hold in your heart. Be honest with yourself and only eat from this tree if you hold much hate in your heart, otherwise you will not be killed, and you will be forced to face me in battle—and I promise, death at my hands will not be painless."

CHAPTER SEVENTY-FOUR

The way he spoke about the fruit reminded Navah of the angel from his vision and the crystal he now wore around his neck. He looked down at it and saw that it had a faint red glow to it. He remembered what the angel had said him, that the crystal would protect him from evil spirits, but only in proportion to his faith. The crystal worked in the same way as the fruit. The thought brought him a sense of peace, and as he felt his anxiety float away, the glow of the crystal intensified. This brought him even more comfort, and he noticed the crystal grow visibly brighter once again.

If he had to fight, and it appeared he did, he knew he would be protected. He had no doubt that he had all the strength he needed already. His God would provide a stronger defense against this dark spirit than any magickal fruit.

CHAPTER SEVENTY-FIVE

Rho stepped toward the Tree of Strength and picked one of the fruit. He'd been a coward, and he had much fear in his heart. He'd watched his brother take a beating in his place, and hid in the shadows. He wouldn't make the same mistake again. This time, he would fight for his brother. He was ready to give his own life to save his brother, like his father had done for his mother.

Rho inspected the fruit. It was red but with a gold shimmer when he rotated it in his hand, and it seemed to almost be kissing the skin of his palm as he held it. He looked up to see Navah picking a small white needle from the Tree of Fear. Rho was surprised at Navah's decision, but it was probably for the best. Va Bromera wanted Navah dead, and Rho alive. Rho would fight the shadow warrior and give Navah time to escape undetected, invisible. The thought emboldened him, and he brought the fruit to his lips to eat, but before he could take a bite, he felt a sharp prick in his arm. He turned to see Navah holding the white needle in his hand. The lower half of the needle was now red with the blood from Rho's arm.

Rho's heart nearly stopped, and he was gripped by a terrible new fear. It wasn't fear for his own safety, but for his brother's. What had Navah just done? Why? This is not the way it was supposed to be.

"What are you doing?" he yelled.

"I was sent back for a reason, Rho," Navah offered up a sympathetic smile. "Trust me."

Rho looked down at his hands and watched as they slowly disappeared into nothing. He had hoped he would be brave enough to give his life for his brother, but it appeared he'd only been fooling himself. "I guess you made the right choice," Rho said. "Turns out, there's enough fear in my heart for me to disappear completely."

"It's okay to be afraid, Rho." Navah smiled. "Fear doesn't make one a coward. Remember the Bel Tiev—'No man has been brave except he had first known fear.' I know you. You are no coward, Rho. Now find a way out of here and go find Jeema."

"Now it is your turn to choose," Va Bromera said, "and choose, you must! Quickly now!"

"I have everything I need," Navah replied. "Do what you will, spirit."

"Very well, boy. It is time."

Navah took a deep breath and grasped the red crystal with both hands. He closed his eyes and took another breath. Rho could see his lips moving in a silent prayer as the shadow creature lunged violently toward him.

CHAPTER SEVENTY-SIX

The passage out of the snow cavern winded downward. Blue flames flickered from sconces sparsely lining the walls. The fact that she was descending deeper into the cavern made Jeema uneasy. She had already fallen from the chamber where she'd last seen Rho and Navah, so she thought she'd better find a way back up if she was going to find them again. There was only one way out of the snow chamber, however, and it seemed to be taking her deeper, down into the heart of the labyrinth.

She walked softly, careful not to make loud noises. She felt uneasy being alone. It was a strange, wonderful, terrible feeling. She felt simultaneously whole and wholly isolated.

She wanted nothing more than to find Rho and Navah, and to find them safe. She hoped they had been able to escape from the naught-men. Part of her was confident that they had, but another part of her still feared for them. The naught-men might have captured them—they had been outnumbered, after all. An image appeared in her head of Rho and Navah chained to the ground in that cold, cylindrical chamber, surrounded by naught-men. If they *had* been captured, she didn't know if she could rescue them all by herself. She tried not to think about it. She wanted to believe they had escaped. They had to have gotten away.

Jeema wound her way through the passage—downward, deeper. She made her way around corner after corner, nowhere to turn, no way to change direction, no way to go upward. She turned another corner and her heart jumped at the silhouette of a figure standing before her in the dark. It was tall and looming, and out of pure reflex, she let out a sharp scream.

Jeema's quick scream gave way to a dark laugh. She knew that voice. Her heart sank. It was Dartaun. His malicious eyes gleamed in the shadows like black venom. His menacing teeth seemed to be decomposing inside that jagged grave of a grin.

"Hello, Little Sun." There was a sinister sort of giddiness in his voice. "Did you miss me?"

CHAPTER SEVENTY-SEVEN

The shadow creature moved like lightning. Its hands clenched down around Navah's neck and made his skin burn. The heat was nearly unbearable, but something told him it was even worse for Va Bromera. The creature pulled back and writhed wildly with an inhuman shriek up at the heavens.

The creature didn't pause for long. After only a second, he was back at Navah's throat, clawing savagely at his flesh and shrieking with each contact. It had all happened so suddenly and he was caught so off guard, but his mind was finally able to catch up with what was happening, and he grabbed at the creature's wrists to stop him from clawing. He found that his muscles were filled with energy like he'd never experienced before. He looked the same, but he felt powerful. He grabbed and found both wrists, holding on with everything he had in him.

Va Bromera pulled away and yanked Navah this way and that, but the boy held firmly to the creature's wrists. His palms began to burn again. The shadow let out a piercing scream, and then Navah heard another sound. A sizzling sound. He looked down at his hands and noticed that black smoke was rising up from Va Bromera's wrists. Navah's hands seemed to be searing into Va Bromera. As much as it burned Navah, the pain seemed to be far more severe for Va Bromera.

"You are no son of Afir," Va Bromera hissed. "Who are you?"

Navah looked down at the crystal around his neck, its red glow now at full intensity, then he raised his eyes back up to his enemy.

"I am a son of the living God."

The creature shrieked again and then lunged at Navah's face with sharp teeth bared. Navah dodged the snapping jaws by ducking away to the side, forcing him to release the creature's hands. He looked back, and Va Bromera was already coming at him again, advancing quickly. Navah found a low center of gravity and lunged toward the creature, wrapping his arms around the middle of the thing and throwing all his weight at it. The entire length of Navah's arms burned, and the creature arched its back and shrieked in pain. He tried, but could not hold onto the creature, and his hold broke as they slammed into the ground.

Navah scrambled to his knees as the creature raised its arms and brought them down with a great and violent slam to Navah's back. The boy felt the impact hardest in his teeth.

The creature kicked Navah squarely in the chest, sending the boy sprawling backward. Navah's head hit the ground hard, but the soil was soft, and he was able to shake it off quickly enough. He looked up in time to see the shadow creature pouncing onto him, and a mouthful of sharp teeth stuck his neck. He swung and landed a solid punch across the creature's face. The blow stunned the creature just long enough for Navah to gain some leverage with his legs and shove the thing off of him. The creature landed on its side and started rising to his feet again. Navah raised himself up as well and collected himself, not taking his eyes off his opponent.

"A worthy foe," Va Bromera said. "The child of God challenges the father of war—a battle fit for the end of the world."

Va Bromera looked up, and Navah's eyes followed. The blood red shards of the shattered moon now pierced through the veil of gray. They were very close now. They seemed nearly close enough to touch.

A violent wind had kicked up in the garden, fierce and hot. It whipped his hair against his face and his cloak flapped and snapped against him in the wind. The creature raised his hands upward toward the sky.

"The Withering is over!" he shouted. "Noloro's time has come to an end!" He lowered his arms and his gaze fell on Navah, "and so has yours, child of God!"

The creature took a step toward Navah, then another, and another, picking up speed until it was rushing toward the boy with its arms outstretched and head down as if to tackle him. Navah braced himself and dug his feet into the ground, hoping to stop his opponent and keep him in the lower, more vulnerable position. It didn't work. The creature plowed into him and Navah was carried backward until his back slammed into the solid trunk of a tree. A tree knot drove itself into the back of his ribs on his left side, and he screamed out.

As bad as the pain was, he knew he couldn't spare a second to focus on it. He was able to work his arm around the creature's neck from the top, maneuvering it into a headlock, and he squeezed as hard as he could. The shadow creature snarled and shrieked and snapped, but Navah held tight as the burning increased and the creature's neck began to sizzle. Its piercing cry hurt Navah's ears, and Va Bromera lunged backward, then forward again, knocking Navah's ribs against the knot once more. He winced and sidestepped away from the knot. The creature caught him mid-step and knocked him back against the tree. Va Bromera managed to get one hand on Navah's face, shoving his head against the tree trunk, his neck exposed. His claws dug into Navah's skull. The creature reached out with his other hand and grasped the chain of Navah's necklace, then ripped it away from his neck with another shriek, breaking the chain. Navah heard more sizzling as Va Bromera threw the necklace aside and brought his free hand around Navah's neck.

The weight of the creature's hand on his face left him unable to move, and now he couldn't breathe as the thing began to crush his neck. The power which he'd felt moving through and energizing his muscles was now gone. He tried to yell, but it came out as a whimper. He heard a deep and evil laugh that seemed at the same time to be mocking him and declaring victory over him. He squirmed and tried to bite at the creature's hand, but couldn't manage to open his mouth. He was suffocating. He couldn't see the shadow creature at all. He felt a stream of blood run down from his hairline into his eye and he was forced to shut it. His face was pushed upward against the tree and stuck so that all he could see out of his good eye was the shattered moon hurtling toward him, all ablaze with its wrath and fury. The red sky swirled above him and he became light-headed. He was going to pass out now. He made one final attempt to break himself free, but it was useless. It was over.

CHAPTER SEVENTY-EIGHT

Jeema ran toward the light as Dartaun's sinister song echoed through the dark of the tunnels.

"I found me a broken boy! I found me a broken girl!

I found an old spaaace shuttle,

I figured I'd give it a whirl!

Don't you want to come with me?

Don't you want to live today?

Then hop in my spaaace shuttle,

Together we'll fly away!"

As she came out of the dark tunnel and into the enormous snowy cavern, Jeema slipped and smacked her forehead on the ice. She pushed herself up on all fours and saw blood on the ice. She scrambled to her feet and ran as quickly as she could away from her pursuer, being careful not to slip again.

There was nowhere to run. She spun around and scanned the distant walls, but they were solid in all directions. As far as she could tell, there was only one way in or out. She scanned the ceiling, hoping to find the hole she fell through when stumbling into the cavern, but she saw nothing aside from endless stalactites bearing down on her like a mouth full of sharp fangs.

Dartaun emerged from the passageway with a wide grin.

"Oh, Little Sun," Dartaun said. "When I first met you in that cold, dark, metal box, I took you for someone who craved freedom! You looked like a girl who was ready to start a new life! What happened? Where did you and I go wrong?"

Jeema panted and tried to catch her breath. Her wounded head hurt with each heartbeat. She reached up and touched her forehead. It was tender, and when she lowered her hand again, it was red.

"You've got blood on your hands, my dear." Dartaun snickered.

"I'll bet there's more blood on yours," Jeema said through heavy breaths. She thought of the volcano that destroyed Qaro, her home. "You killed everyone I ever loved."

"The Blood Rain?" Dartaun feigned surprise. "Surely I can't be blamed for that! I may have whispered in Jim Jasser's ear from time to time, but it was he who held the blade, now wasn't it? No, I prefer to keep my hands nice and clean if I can help it."

"So you manipulate others to do your dirty work for you," Jeema realized she was seething. That was fine with her. She wanted him to see how angry she was. She had never thought about it, but it all made sense now. Of course Dartaun was behind the Blood Rain. Of course he had stirred up Jim Jasser and the Brood against the Tievians in Qaro. She was certain now that Dartaun had been the one person truly responsible for all of the death she had endured in her life.

Her hand gripped Spider Guts. She didn't know why. She began walking toward him. She wasn't thinking at all. The pace of her steps increased, and she began to run. Rage filled her mind as she raised her axe up over her right shoulder. She was sprinting toward him now. There were no thoughts in her mind, only blind fury. She was ready to kill him. He had taken everything from her, and now she was going to kill him for it. Somehow, it didn't feel wrong. It didn't feel like anything.

As she ran toward the sorcerer, a great shadow surrounded him until he was entirely cloaked in darkness. She stopped short of the dark, swirling storm in front of her and began to back away slowly as the storm grew. The darkness swelled outward, and she was pushed backward onto the ice.

Out of the dark storm came a burning red light, as if there were a flaming furnace inside of the storm. High above her, a shape began to emerge from the storm. The fearsome face of a black horned dragon appeared from out of the swirling darkness and let out a bone-shattering roar that shook the entire cavern. Stalactites fell all around her. Jeema got to her feet and began to run.

There was a great crack like an explosion, then another, and more followed as the weight of the dragon shattered the ice beneath its feet. Jeema turned to look in time to see a flame gathering in the dragon's raised mouth. Its belly glowed like a smelter's furnace. It whipped its neck and aimed, shooting a stream of red fire out of its mouth. The fire shot off to her right and melted the ice in an instant. Steam hissed up, and the heat was fierce. The dragon moved its enormous head, and the stream of fire made its way around behind her, then to her left until there was nowhere for her to run.

The dragon stomped forward toward Jeema, crashing through solid ice and generating great waves, which broke against the cavern walls. It lifted one of its foreclaws and reached straight for Jeema. She quickly found herself enveloped by its closing grasp. She lifted Spider Guts and struck with all her might, but her axe simply bounced off of the dragon's scales with a metallic clang that left her arms weak. Before she could recover, she was being squeezed firmly within the dragon's firm grip. She dropped her axe and the dragon lifted her upward, high into the air, until she came face to face with the beast.

"Go ahead and kill me!" she screamed. "Just like you killed my parents! Just like you killed Dari and his parents!"

The dragon's expression softened, and the heat emitting from his breath began to fade. His black scales began to glow with a blue, electric light.

"Now why would I kill you, Little Sun?" The dragon's deep voice somehow tittered with the same repulsive glee she'd heard from Dartaun. "No. I've got a cold, dark, metal box with your name on it."

With that, the dragon opened his mouth and a bright blue light spilled out. Jeema's eyes grew heavy. Her thoughts fled from her until she was blissfully wrapped up in the glow of that beautiful blue light.

Then Jeema closed her eyes and fell asleep.

CHAPTER SEVENTY-NINE

The pressure on Navah's neck let up, and his face was free from Va Bromera's heavy hand. He tried to inhale, but it hurt and he coughed. His vision was blurred, but the creature had let him free. He blinked and tried to focus. Before him, he could now see the shadow creature on its knees, and there was Rho. Rho had Va Bromera in a headlock. His left arm was wrapped around the creature's neck and in his left hand was the crystal cross which was burning as red as the falling moon.

Navah saw that Rho had something in his right hand as well. He tried hard to focus his eyes in on it, and he was finally able to make it out. It was a black fruit, picked from the Tree of Death.

The skin around the shadow creature's neck began to sizzle and smoke, and it let out a blood-chilling shriek, its sharp teeth wide and terrifying. Rho didn't hesitate. He reached out his hand and shoved the dripping black fruit into the creature's mouth. Va Bromera's shriek stopped abruptly as it began to choke on the fruit. It wrapped its own hands around its neck and heaved. Rho stepped away and looked on at the writhing monster with horror.

It was clear to Navah the shadow creature was an evil thing that had described itself as a "father of war," but this didn't change the fact it was a living creature, and it felt wrong. He knew that it was going to kill him if his brother hadn't intervened. He knew it was either Va Bromera or them. None of it made Navah feel any better about watching the creature struggle to breathe. There was a law above all reason, which weighed heavy on his soul. Navah began to cry as he watched Va Bromera's movements slow until the creature finally collapsed to the ground. His motions grew sluggish, and he rolled to his stomach, completely silent. The shadow creature slowly gave way to the form of a pitiful, weak old man. All the color had been drained from his skin, and veins protruded from his neck and forehead as his gaping mouth gasped to no avail.

A moment later, all motion ceased.

Va Bromera was dead.

"Thank you," Navah choked out with a heavy rasp.

"I tried to sneak up on him a couple times before that," Rho said. "I saw how he screamed whenever you touched him and it gave me an idea. I was too slow, though, and to be honest, I think I was too afraid. Then he had you up against the tree and I just lost it. I didn't think after that, I just . . . did."

"I could see you," Navah said.

"Huh?"

"I could see you. Remember what Va Bromera said about the white needle? The Tree of Fear? It would only hide you in proportion to the fear already living in your heart. When you attacked him, I could see you the whole time. There was no fear in your heart, Rho. That crystal was burning red. It only lights up like that if your faith is strong."

Rho smiled modestly and shrugged.

"I'm just glad you're okay. I love you." He wrapped his arms around his little brother and hugged him tightly.

"I love you, too." Navah hugged him back. He thought about the angel from his vision. He'd tasked Navah with saving Rho, but somehow, Rho ended up saving him. His mission was to act as a guiding light to Rho, but the crystal burned brighter for Rho than it had even for himself. He didn't really know what that meant, but he didn't think it really mattered anymore. What mattered now was that Rho had become something very different from what he had been only days ago, a long shot from what Dartaun first saw in him.

The sorcerer had tried to take Navah out of the picture repeatedly, and every time, Rho came back for him. When he was snakebitten, his brother had watched over him. When he was kidnapped, his brother had found and rescued him. When he was defeated in battle, his brother had fought for him. Without even realizing it, Navah began to weep into Rho's chest. He didn't think he deserved a brother like Rho. He never could understand why God took his parents from him, but right now, for the first time in his life, he felt like the only thing he would ever really need was his big brother. Rho was all the family he'd ever need.

Rho hugged him tightly, and Navah looked over to the dead guardian of the grove. He dried his eyes and cleared his throat. His voice was coming back to him.

"Now what?" Navah asked.

"We've got to find Jeema," Rho said.

"How do we get out of here?"

"Over there," Rho motioned toward one end of the garden. "Past those trees, there's a door, but it's locked."

Both of their eyes moved to the fallen guardian, then back up again. There was an unspoken understanding of what they had to do, but neither of them wanted to do it. Finally, Rho sighed and nodded, then walked over to Va Bromera's body. He knelt down and carefully reached out to grab hold of the guardian's cloak. He swept it aside to reveal a ring of keys, and he wrestled them free from the ring on the fallen warrior's thick leather belt.

A few moments later, the boys exited the garden through the unlocked door and stepped out onto a rocky bluff. The wind was even more fierce than it had been in the grove, and they had to fight strong gusts with each step in order to walk out of the door onto the rocky bluffs before them. Directly in front of them was . . . water. As far as the eyes could see, nothing but churning, red water, which reflected the color of the falling sky.

"Is this . . . ?" Navah began.

"The Sea of Antiquity . . . " Rho whispered.

"Beautiful, isn't it?" Dartaun said.

The boys spun to their right at the same time, and it took them each a moment to even process what they were looking at.

Before them, the rocks rose to a summit, where Dartaun stood, and directly behind him . . . what was happening? It was a towering and enormously complex structure, and on the side of it stood . . .

"The space shuttle," Navah shouted over the howling wind.

"He was actually serious . . . " Rho shouted back.

"Dead serious," Dartaun smirked.

"Can it really fly?" Navah asked.

"It can." Dartaun beamed. "And it will. That is, as soon as your brother is safely aboard. We're going to take a trip to a little place called Va Eartha."

"I won't be going with you," Rho said flatly. "I've already seen what damage a little venom can do."

"Very good!" Dartaun's eyes brightened. "Well said, my boy! And a noble thought, to be sure. Though I think you'll change your mind once you've seen the shuttle's . . . amenities. Follow me, boys!"

Rho and Navah stood still as the sorcerer began walking toward the launch platform.

"This baby's got technology like you've never seen in your primitive lives. It's got a climate-controlled cabin, which means you'll never be hot or cold! It's stocked with first-rate cuisine! Every single day of our journey, you'll be eating *by far* the finest foods you've ever tasted in your short life! We've also got—and I think you're really going to like this one—a local white-haired nut case with the prettiest face you've ever seen and a whole lot of personality!"

Dartaun gestured with his arms, and a steel door flew open at his command. Inside was Jeema with her hands tied behind her back her feet tied together as well. She began to hop toward the door and shout out to them.

"Don't listen to him, Rho! Run away! Don't . . . "

With a gesture from Dartaun, the door slammed shut again, and Jeema's voice was cut off.

CHAPTER EIGHTY

"Now you have a choice to make, Rho." Dartaun was shouting to be heard over the violent winds. "You could have the whole rest of your life ahead of you, a wife, children, a long life on a thriving new world, or you could stay here . . ." His voice trailed off as his eyes migrated upward toward the fractured moon, which was crumbling further as he spoke. "If you stay here, you'll be made into ash before this shadowmark ends."

He lifted his hands up toward the fragmented moon that blocked out the heavens, enormous hunks of rock burning brightly. "There's nothing to think about, Rho! Would you rather stick around here for the end? No! Va Eartha is perfect! It's filled with the greenest grass, the most luscious vegetation, clear blue streams, and most of all, a young lady to share it with! You can claim whatever lands your heart desires, build a proper home, and fill it with little Rhos and Jeemas. You'll live a long, full life and die of a good, old age, the way you've always wanted. The way it's meant to be!"

Rho clenched his teeth, and then he looked over to Navah.

Navah's eyes turned from disdain to shock.

"You're not thinking of going with him, are you, Rho? You can't!"

"Seems like a pretty simple choice to me." Dartaun snickered. "But then again, it's not my choice to make. It's yours, Rho. What'll it be?"

"We can fight him, Rho!" Nod grabbed the crystal cross from Rho's hand and held it up. It emitted a very dim light, barely discernible from the red light all around them. "Just like we fought Va Bromera. We can do it together. We can save Jeema!"

Dartaun's wicked smirk made Navah want to charge the sorcerer and put an end to the whole matter right then and there. Rho put his hand on Navah's shoulder and met his eyes with a knowing look.

"I need you to put some faith in me now, Navah."

Navah squinted, searching for the meaning of his brother's words. His face scrunched up in frustrated confusion.

"You said it yourself. My faith has grown a lot stronger. I know it doesn't make sense to you yet, so I need you to have some faith in *me* right now. I have to do this. I have to go with him. There's no other way. Trust me."

Navah's desperate eyes protested, and he took in a deep breath to calm himself. He looked up and saw that Dartaun was right. The moon would be slamming into the planet's surface any moment now. The enormous shards of the fractured moon grew larger and closer by the second. He shrugged and fell against his brother's chest one last time, wrapping his arms around him tightly. He tried to speak, but there were no words. Rho squeezed him and whispered in his ear.

"I'm just taking the wagon out riding, that's all. Do you remember what Xiara told me? That one day I'd get to swim in the Sea of Antiquity, you remember?"

Navah was puzzled by the last part, but he said nothing.

"I'm done running, Navah. I think I'm ready to go for a swim."

Navah buried himself further into his brother's chest.

"I don't want you to go. I'm going to miss you so much," he sobbed.

Rho began to cry as well.

"Me too, buddy. I'm gonna miss you so much, too."

Rho kissed him on the top of the head. He squeezed his brother tightly one last time and then let go. Navah stepped back and wiped his tears away. He looked up at his brother with eyes that were red and wet and his throat burned with the pain of loss that he already knew too well. Rho nodded at him with an encouraging smile that told him to be strong. It was almost like looking at his dad. Rho really was the spitting image of their father.

"I'll see you again, brother." Rho's eyes motioned upward. "Real soon."

Navah looked back at him with all the resolve he could muster and nodded. Then Rho turned and walked toward the launch pad.

Dartaun curled his lips into a sneer and put his skeletal arm around Rho's shoulder as he approached, as if he were claiming Rho for himself. As the sorcerer turned away, he shot Navah one last look that—subtle as it was—could not be mistaken for anything but a silent declaration of victory. Dartaun said nothing, but Navah received the message exceedingly clear:

It's over, boy. I've won.

CHAPTER EIGHTY-ONE

The door opened and Jeema squinted as the bright light poured into the elevator. The silhouettes of two figures stepped in, and the door closed again. Jeema watched Rho pass through the door, and she surrendered herself to defeat. Tears began to form in her eyes.

"Why?" She shook her head in disbelief.

"I love you," he said. And he kissed her.

The tears rolled down Jeema's cheeks and she resigned herself to the welcome warmth of his touch and the solace of his embrace. In that moment, she knew she wanted more than just this single kiss. She wanted a life with him. She knew it was selfish and wrong, but for that brief moment, she finally allowed herself believe she *could* have it—that Rho *would* be her husband. That she *would* have babies, and raise them in a land of green hills and clear streams. That they would grow old together and that one day, when they were good and ready, they would be buried in the fertile soil of a young and healthy world that would be home to her children, and their children, for generations to come.

Dartaun rolled his eyes and resisted the urge to stop them. This was exactly what he wanted, after all, he just couldn't stand to watch it.

The two kids looked into each other's eyes and smiled. Rho ran his fingers through Jeema's white hair, loosely held the nape of her neck, and studied her red lips. Then his eyes met hers and she was swimming again in his steel blue eyes. She had found what she was looking for.

The door swung open and Dartaun cleared his throat in order to get the lovers' attention. On the other side of the door was a steel walkway high above the ground. To their left were a set of tall metal cabinets. To the right, there was nothing but railing between them and the murderous sky. Dartaun waved his arm and the metal cabinets opened up. Inside each of the cabinets was a yellow space suit, a large helmet, a pair of gloves, and a pair of boots.

"You'll have to put those on," the sorcerer instructed.

Rho and Dartaun stepped out of the elevator and onto a walkway. Jeema didn't.

"And how am I supposed to do that, exactly?" she asked, clearly a bit annoyed.

"Oh. Right." Dartaun nodded.

CHAPTER EIGHTY-TWO

While the sorcerer was busy untying Jeema, Rho browsed through the boots until he found a pair that looked like they would fit. He pulled the suit on over his clothes and then strapped on the boots. The other two were on their way now. He donned the gloves and decided to wait on the helmet. Jeema started sorting through the suits as Rho peered over the railing up at what was left of the moon. For the first time in a long time, Rho looked up and did not feel fear. In his mind, that great and terrible time-glass in the sky had been counting down to the moment of his death. Now the moon no longer had any power over him.

But Navah . . . His eyes shot down to the doomed planet below. It only took him a moment to find his little brother, just standing there looking back at him. He looked so small. He remembered what Navah had said that day they had first left the Darrows.

Imagine how small we must look from God's perspective.

He held his hand up and waved to Navah. Navah returned the gesture.

Something moved behind Navah and caught Rho's eye. A clay fox—not a baby, but a fully matured clay fox—emerged from a grove of tall pinleaf trees and walked across the clearing. The red sky reflected off its regal coat like fire. The creature seemed completely at peace as it moved across the clearing, like a king of old on a stroll through his palace gardens. It walked right up to the very edge of the bluff and sat down right there to watch heaven fall into the sea of antiquity without any hint of fear. It was as if he was daring the moon to fall on him.

Rho thought back to the baby clay fox with the mangled leg, sentenced to die before its life had really even begun. He could still hear that shrill yelp as it fought against an already sealed fate. He winced as he pictured its nearly amputated leg dangling as it hobbled away. It made him sick thinking of the poor thing thrashing against the steel jaws of death, fighting so hard against an inevitable end. There was never any chance of survival, and he could see that now.

Off in the distance, beyond the trees, flaming pieces of rock shot out of the sky and slammed into Noloro, shaking the planet as well as the walkway he now stood on. He held on tightly to the railing as metal clanged above him and the planet rumbled down below.

On the edge of the bluffs, the clay fox remained unmoved as it gazed out at its own approaching demise. Rho wondered if it somehow knew—if it could somehow sense that this was the end, and that there was nothing to be done about it except to face it with dignity.

Rho's eyes landed on his brother one last time. He wished he'd told him that he was proud of him. He wished he had told him how much he admired him. He wished he'd been a better older brother to him. He wished a lot of things in that moment, but there was nothing left that he could say or do except to wave back, so he tried to fit everything that was left—all of it—into one last wave of his hand.

Jeema finished donning her space suit, and the three of them made their way to the shuttle door.

It opened.

Inside the cockpit were three seats—one at the controls, and two behind it. Dartaun motioned toward the rear seats. Everything was vertical, making it difficult to seat themselves, but they managed, and they strapped themselves in.

Dartaun closed the door and crawled into his seat, strapping himself in as well. He turned to look back and paused for a second. He had no helmet and no suit. Rho wondered at this, but it hardly surprised him.

"I'm really glad we could all do this together." Dartaun smiled.

Rho wasn't sure if it was sarcasm or sincerity, but it bothered him either way. The sorcerer turned back to the control board and began flipping switches to prepare for takeoff.

CHAPTER EIGHTY-THREE

Navah looked on from the rocky bluffs below. He didn't understand why Rho felt he had to go with Dartaun, but after all they'd been through over the last few days, he had faith in his brother. He knew he could trust Rho to make the right decision. Had he failed his mission? Maybe. Yes, he suspected that he had. He looked up at the foreboding fragments of flaming rock hurtling toward him, and the fear of failure floated away. There was no time left for fear or regret. He closed his eyes and folded his hands tightly. He asked God to accept him, despite his failure. He asked God to watch over Rho and Jeema, and to give him courage so that he might now face his death with honor.

There was a great explosion and the shuttle roared loudly. Navah opened his eyes to white smoke rising up from the base of the craft. Some sort of mechanical arm removed itself slowly from the nose of the shuttle. The platform where he'd seen Rho standing moments ago retracted. There was a second, even louder explosion that drowned out everything else, and sparks began to fly across the launch pad beneath the shuttle. The sparks quickly became a raging fire and the shuttle jolted upward and lifted off into the air.

Navah gaped at the rocket ship blasting off, a sight he had dreamed of seeing his entire life. His dad was right, after all. He could almost see his dad smiling down at him.

I bet you will, buddy. I bet you will see a rocket ship someday.

Navah smiled and watched the rocket rise into the air. It looked like it had a clear path through the moon fragments, but it still made him nervous.

CHAPTER EIGHTY-FOUR

The seat rumbled beneath Jeema. They were in the air now. A sudden wave of panic shot through her entire body. This wasn't right. She saw Dartaun's gnarled white fingers flipping switches and pushing all the right buttons. There was nothing right about this. She felt used. She felt dirty. She felt manipulated and defeated.

She reached out a gloved hand to Rho. He reached out for hers and they held each other with fingers squeezing gently. She wanted to be with Rho, but not like this. She'd known better, but what could she have done differently? She had fought and failed. She looked up and feigned a smile at him, and he smiled back at her. His smile seemed so genuine, so clever, so out of place. There was something in his eyes, too. It wasn't what she would have expected to see from him. Whatever he was feeling right now, it certainly wasn't what she was feeling. It wasn't defeat, it was something more like . . . hope? Determination? Victory? She thought perhaps that's what she saw in his eyes.

Those beautiful, steel-blue eyes—eyes the color of truth—were absolutely brimming with purpose. This intrigued her to no end. She cocked her head slightly and made a question with her eyes. He smiled wider, and through the glass of his helmet he answered with a reassuring nod and a long, deep breath. Then his gloved hand emerged from his pocket holding Dr. Wissler's yellow EMP device. He popped the plastic guard up, and his thumb hovered threateningly over the red button.

Jeema's eyes widened, and she swallowed hard as she understood his intentions.

Yes.

They had not been defeated. They had won. This was checkmate, the winning move. There would be no virus, no venom, no curse of corruption on that perfect new world. She and Rho would stay here on Noloro after all, together, right where they belonged.

Jeema smiled and squeezed his hand, unable to control her tears. Rho squeezed her hand in return. They stared into each other's eyes, and they knew that they were in love, and they hoped they would see each other again very, very soon.

CHAPTER EIGHTY-FIVE

Navah watched the shuttle, still trying to come to grips with the fact that he would never again see his brother, the only family he had left. He knew it as a fact in his head, but he was having trouble letting that fact sink into his heart. It didn't feel real. He felt the same way he felt the day he stood at the entrance to their cave in the Darrows, scanning the horizon, waiting in vain for his father's return long after everyone else had given up.

As his eyes followed the space shuttle's ascent, he noticed that the stream of fire propelling the engine disappeared. It just stopped. Was that supposed to happen? He'd never seen a rocket launch before, but it didn't seem right. Then the shuttle began to arc, and then it fell out of the sky. A moment later, the roaring noise ceased completely, and all that remained was the howling of the vicious winds.

For a second, Navah nearly panicked, but then he remembered his brother's parting words. This was his doing. This was his plan. This was how they won.

He could hear Rho's voice in his head, reciting his father's song.

A greater love no one has other
Than giving your life for another.

He didn't know how Rho did it, but he understood now, and he smiled a weak and lonely smile. The mission was complete. Rho and Jeema had made the right decision. Had he been a guiding light to them? Maybe. Yes, he suspected that he had. He looked up and watched the shuttle continue to fall out of the sky, his only family trapped inside. It turned end over end and finally plummeted into the Sea of Antiquity with an enormous splash and a deafening roar. Navah winced as his heart took the brunt of the impact. The tears were hot on his cheeks. He couldn't breathe.

The roar only grew louder as something else slammed into the ocean just after the shuttle and steam rose up along with a horrible hiss. He couldn't see what the object was, but then a third object hit. This time he saw it. It was a piece of the moon. It was finally time.

He remembered the words of the angel in his vision of Va Eartha:

Navah. It means "dwelling." The Lord will make His dwelling within you for as long as you remain on Va Noloro, and once your days on Va Noloro have come to an end, then you will make your dwelling in the House of the Lord forever.

He looked up to heaven and instead saw a million pieces of red rock burning across the sky above him. There was another impact behind him, and then another to his right. The rate of impact only increased, and he felt the heat from the burning sky beginning to envelop him.

Navah stared out at the bleak scene before him with a somber reverence, trying to imagine what exactly he was headed toward, and what he would see once he arrived. He closed his eyes and prayed one last time as the moon rained down around him.

EPILOGUE

A WANDERER ON THE EARTH

Blood-caked hands shattered the crystal-clear surface of the stream. He was too young to rightly be called a man, but his eyes were so burdened that you couldn't rightly call him a boy. A dark and heavy mark besmirched his forehead, and his cheeks were smudged with a mixture of dirt, blood, and tears.

He scrubbed his hands furiously. The dried blood was stubborn, and it took him a good while. When he had finally managed to wash it all off, he reached down and cupped his trembling hands together to splash water onto his face. He did this until he felt clean again—clean enough, anyway. The smudges below his eyes disappeared. The mark on his forehead did not.

He was startled by his own reflection. He didn't recognize the face looking back. What had he become? A wanderer. An exile. Cursed above any man to walk the face of the earth.

His feet sunk into the soft mud. There was a thicket upstream with trees that bore plump fruit in a variety of colors. Unknown to the boy, hiding near the edge of that thicket stood a man in a black hooded cloak who watched him silently.

The wanderer's hands moved down his face to cover his panting mouth. He allowed himself to catch his breath, and he gazed out at the green hillside beyond the lush and vibrant valley. There were sheep grazing and cattle lowing, a world brimming with promise and life. He resolved to find a spotless male lamb for sacrifice as a show of repentance. He deserved death, and he knew it. Yet, he was allowed to live. How could it be? An innocent lamb to take his place? Washed clean by the shedding of innocent blood? It didn't make sense, but it didn't matter. He would listen this time. He would listen and obey, and just maybe, by some miracle, he could make things right. He buried his face in his hands and began to weep again.

Something bumped up against his bare ankle, and he jumped back. He wasn't himself today. Not by a long shot. Something told him he would never be himself again.

He looked down and was relieved to see that it was just a piece of bark bobbing its way downstream with the gentle current. There was something else, though. Something written on the bark. How could that be? No human had yet been to this new land to the east of Eden, of that he was certain. Yet, there it was, carved deeply into a piece of tree bark.

Three distinct letters.

One solitary word.

Nod.

ABOUT THE AUTHOR

My real name is Patrick, and I am a speculative fiction author and songwriter based on the Central Coast of California.

I'm a husband and father who spent my early years reading superhero comics, writing and illustrating comics of my own, learning the secrets of the ooze, the balance of the force, the deeper magic from before the dawn of time, awakening the wind fish, shooting marbles and slamming pogs, collecting and trading Pokémon cards, rescuing the Tribals from Mizar and his drones, restoring Hyrule and becoming the Hero of Time, searching the Scriptures, studying eschatology, and feeling just as—if not more—fascinated with the worlds created by Shakespeare, Dickens, Salinger, and Steinbeck as with those of Rowling, King, Lewis, and Tolkien.

On occasion, I'll use a run-on sentence for effect.

I currently reside in a small town on the Central Coast of California with my wife and best friend Andrea, my children Sophia and Phin, and a rambunctious Boston Terrier by the name of Rocket.

Ten percent of all my proceeds from book sales will go to feeding local families in need through Loaves & Fishes in my hometown of Paso Robles, California.

LOAVES & FISHES
Feeding the Hungry with God's Love

LETTER FROM THE AUTHOR

Dear Reader,

Thank you for reading *The Withering*!

I'd love to know what you loved (or didn't love) about this story! Reading genuine reviews—yes, even the not-so-generous ones— helps me connect with you, my reader! It helps me to improve my craft, and to understand what is working for you as well as what you could do without. Turn the page to find out how you can best contact me.

I hope you'll consider leaving an honest review of *The Withering* on Amazon or your favorite retailer. I will do my best to read every review. An added bonus is that reviews make it easier for new readers to discover my stories!

Finally, I want to thank you from the bottom of my heart for taking a chance on this story. I am thrilled that you decided to come on this journey with me. Now that we've escaped Noloro, it's off to other exciting worlds! I'll be posting updates in my newsletter and on my social media channels as I make progress on my new projects. I hope to connect with you there!

Sincerely,
P.S. Patton

CONNECT WITH P.S. PATTON

Website: www.pspatton.com
Instagram: @P.S.Patton
Twitter: @PSPattonWrites
Facebook: /PSPattonWrites
TikTok: @PSPatton
Goodreads: /PSPatton
Bookbub: @PSPattonWrites

I would love to see *The Withering* out in the wild! Where are you reading? Where has this book traveled to? What are your thoughts on this story? If you post on social media, don't forget to use the hashtag #thewithering and/or tag/mention me so that I can be sure to see your post! Thank you.

Ambassador International's mission is to magnify the Lord Jesus Christ and promote His Gospel through the written word.

We believe through the publication of Christian literature, Jesus Christ and His Word will be exalted, believers will be strengthened in their walk with Him, and the lost will be directed to Jesus Christ as the only way of salvation.

For more information about
AMBASSADOR INTERNATIONAL
please visit:

www.ambassador-international.com
@AmbassadorIntl
www.facebook.com/AmbassadorIntl

Thank you for reading this book. Please consider leaving us a review on your social media, favorite retailer's website, Goodreads or Bookbub, or our website.

www.ingramcontent.com/pod-product-compliance
Lightning Source LLC
Chambersburg PA
CBHW050025030726
47506CB00001B/118